COUNTERPARTS

COUNTERPARTS

GONZALO LIRA

G. P. PUTNAM'S SONS NEW YORK

G. P. Putnam's Sons
Publishers Since 1838
a member of
Penguin Putnam Inc.
200 Madison Avenue
New York, NY 10016

Library of Congress Cataloging-in-Publication Data

Lira, Gonzalo.
Counterparts / Gonzalo Lira.
p.   cm.
ISBN 0-399-14312-2
PS3562.I68C6   1998
813'.54—dc21   97-27210 CIP

Printed in the United States of America

1   3   5   7   9   10   8   6   4   2

This book is printed on acid-free paper.♾

BOOK DESIGN BY AMANDA DEWEY

Because of their
gift for myths the
Natives can also do
things to you
against which you
cannot guard
yourself and from
which you cannot
escape. They can
turn you into a
symbol.

ISAK DINESEN,
Out of Africa

Perhaps philosophers
need arguments so
powerful they set up
reverberations in the
brain: If the person
refuses to accept the
conclusion, he *dies*.
How's that for a
powerful argument?

ROBERT NOZICK,
Philosophical Explanations

for Amalia Nitu

Part 1

More Than Just Some New Sensation

Margaret Chisholm was an FBI special agent. She didn't look the part. Driving like a demon to RFK Stadium, slipping in and out of the slower traffic, the red magnetic siren light on the roof of her silver minivan was what gave her away. Without it, she would have looked like just another harried and hassled suburban Maryland housewife on some Sunday-afternoon errand: to pick up some groceries maybe, or maybe on her way to a neighborhood block-party barbecue. But this wasn't a chore or a picnic. This was troubleshooting.

Rivera's insistent, slightly desperate call had dragged her away from Robby's soccer game. Robby (Robert Everett on the rare times she was upset with him) was the right midfielder on his school's team, the Tigers. Margaret was still wearing her "Go Tigers, GO!" sweatshirt, featuring a little striped tiger with a cheerfully arrogant smile kicking a soccer ball on a sky-blue background. The eleven- and twelve-year-olds on the team, Robby included, hated that cutesy sweatshirt, but their parents wore them to games religiously.

Margaret drove off the beltway, taking the freeway exit twice as fast as the speed limit allowed. By her watch, she figured the first period was finishing up. No way she'd make it back before the beginning of the second half. If she was lucky, she might barely make the tail end of the game.

She tried hard to think about the Tigers and their game, hoping they'd win. But as she neared the stadium, Robby, the Tigers, even Rivera—everything just slid off her mind, the priority at hand pulling at her like a bad undertow. And as she turned a corner and came within sight of the stadium, all she kept hoping for was that she wouldn't get the chance to kill anyone today.

Even with the windows rolled up, even a half-mile from the stadium, she could hear the roar of the crowd. Their approaching presence sucked out the oxygen and added weight to the atmosphere in the minivan's cab, making Chisholm feel the air around her like a comfortable glove, wrapping around her whole body seamlessly, like water. Maybe it was the crowd or the anticipation of something exciting, but as the stadium grew big on her horizon, she felt it, the old feeling like a best friend, coming on and washing her mind clean. God, she hated that fucking feeling. Inside the stadium gates, by the rear, she stopped the minivan and got out.

An FBI SWAT officer, Sherylynn Price, was the first to spot the silver minivan with the fake wooden sidings. Like the other SWAT officers here on crowd control duty, Price didn't have all that much to do, she and the other half-dozen officers milling about in barely controlled desperation. So when she saw the minivan stop and a woman with long curly red hair jump out of it and duck under the yellow-and-black-striped perimeter barrier tape, it was Price who went to pounce on this new arrival. The redhead's scowling face put her off a bit, but the desperation of the situation made her bold.

"Hey! You can't go here, get out of here!" Price had her assault rifle at the ready. She assumed the scowling redhead to be one of the first of the slew of reporters the FBI was expecting to show up; Price didn't notice the flashing light on the minivan's roof. "Get behind the tape!"

The redhead whipped out her badge and gave Price one mean look. "Chisholm, FBI; I'm in charge now. Where's the officer on site?"

"By whose authority?"

"Deputy Director Rivera's."

"Oh. Oh, uh, okay, sorry ma'am. Officer Dexter's in charge of the site—right through there."

"Is that rifle on safety?" Chisholm asked as she walked toward the shadows under the stadium's seats.

"Yes ma'am," Price lied, aiming her assault rifle up into the air as she followed Chisholm.

"Liar," she said before turning away. Weapons safety—Chisholm made a mental note to be sure to write a memo to the head of the Bureau's SWAT section. It wouldn't do for someone to get accidentally shot by a SWAT officer giving directions. Wouldn't do at all.

The other SWAT team members watched as Chisholm made her way to the underside of the stadium with Price in tow, the outlines of a huge revolver clearly visible underneath the back of her "Go Tigers, GO!" sweatshirt.

Inside, light made its thready way through the columns of the stadium.

Dexter, the officer on site, was a tall, thin man with a small gray mustache. He was carefully interrogating a man on his knees, squatting to be at eye level with him.

The kneeling man, handcuffed behind his back, with matted, mouse-colored hair and wearing glasses, smiled stupidly and serenely. At least he had some poise. Shuffling around, surrounding the geek, were seven clearly anxious SWAT officers, three women and four men, all of them dressed in those one-piece black jumpsuits, bulked up by their bulletproof vests.

The tableau gave the impression that the Heavies were putting the hammer down on the perp. But for all their equipment, for all their dark style and silkily crafted surface, one look at the SWAT officers' headless-chicken shuffle and Chisholm knew how out of control the situation really was.

"I won, don't you see?" the nutcase said casually, smiling dreamily. "I won. And nothing you do can change that."

Dexter tried to keep cool. "Mister, I don't know what your beef is, but all those innocent people are gonna die."

"No one is innocent. It'll be nice when it's all over, when all the bodies start flying through the air. I wonder if it'll make the network news . . ."

Chisholm stepped forward and introduced herself to Dexter. "Chisholm, from Rivera's office. I'm in charge here."

Dexter had been waiting for the promised FBI special agent like a life raft, but he was underwhelmed by the woman before him. Where was the mean, revved-up carnivore Rivera had called "big bad Maggie"? Not here. Here, there was just a tired, in-shape but middle-aged woman in a stupid sweatshirt. She looked like the president of the local PTA, which made Dexter figure that the stories he'd heard about Deputy Director Rivera's infamous attack dog were just that—stories.

"What do you have?"

"We got ourselves a disgruntled chemical engineer, no priors, nothing above a parking ticket, then he gets fired a couple of days ago, so since the coworkers are big Redskins fans, he decides to rig RFK Stadium to blow up. We have teams searching, but this is a big big stadium and I can't—"

"How many minutes?"

"He says it'll blow at the end of the half. Eight and a half minutes, and we don't have time to find the bombs *or* evacuate the place, I mean, this is a *big* stadium . . ."

Since the Oklahoma City mess, the FBI had fallen into the habit of overreacting to every bomb threat that came its way, running its agents ragged. Chisholm had had to deal with more than her fair share of false alarms, so a little casually, a little tiredly, unconvinced that this was for real, she asked, "How do you know he's serious?"

"He's a chemical engineer!" Dexter nearly shouted. "He's got all *kinds* of access to that kind of material," he went on, as if she were some kind of idiot.

"Stadium security."

"Asleep at the wheel."

Interrupting them, making both Chisholm and Dexter glance his way, the nutcase said, "I've won," in a final punctuation to his ramblings, much as if he were bidding them all goodbye. Then he looked away and was completely silent. Dexter decided to have one more go at him. "Blowing up a stadium's a serious charge. Just threatening to blow one up *is* a crime. So why don't you start to cooperate and maybe we could work something out . . ."

Chisholm took a good look at the suspect while Dexter blathered on. She had to size him up. Was he legit or not? She stared at his right eye. It jittered ever so slightly from side to side. *Nerves,* thought Chisholm. The nutcase just smiled, like there was nothing more to be said, but he was nervous. Not about the attention of Dexter and his men, though. If he'd been nervous about them, he'd be responding to Dexter's babble. The only reason Chisholm could think of for this guy to be nervous would be if he was worried that something might go wrong with his bombs. His own uncertainty and doubt would make his eye jitter.

And that's how she knew the nutcase was serious. No one's ever nervous if they're bullshitting.

"Hey!" she said. "This guy is serious. *You* get serious."

Dexter's composure broke for a second as he glanced at Chisholm. "What more do you expect me to *do,* goddammit!"

All eyes were on her. Dexter and his platoon of SWAT officers glared at her with that "show me" look she hated. But the panicky gleam in their eyes told her that for all their disdain, they hoped she'd take the initiative.

Ignoring Dexter and his people, Chisholm directed her attention to the nutcase.

"Okay," she said, "tell me where you put the bombs."

"I'm sorry, I can't do that."

Chisholm bowed her head. She was tired and she'd run out of patience years ago. She was tempted to just shoot the guy and they could all take their chances.

"A bunch of innocent people will die," she said calmly, as she felt the desperation of the SWAT officers around her pick up some more, pushing to turn the tide within her. "Why don't you just tell me where the bombs are, mmm? *Are* there any bombs?"

"Oh yes," the man said, smiling happily, again with that hint of nervousness.

"*Do* something, goddammit!" Dexter blurted out, forgetting for a moment that Chisholm was way above him on the FBI food chain. He was furious, and he took it out on the nutcase with more desperate pleas, not laying a finger on him. The word around the Hoover Building and in Quantico was that Chisholm was one mean bitch, no one you wanna fuck with, the troubleshooter who could shoot any trouble down. And yet here she was, employing the same tactics she'd just chewed him out for using. Dirty Harriet my ass, she was just another one of those pencil pushers with an unearned rep.

Chisholm ignored Dexter and everyone else. Her gaze wandered around the room as she decided what to do next. That's when she noticed the ax.

God knew what the ax was for, since the entire structure was built of concrete. Ax the concrete in case of fire? Chisholm didn't think so, but like a surfer paddling on the swell of what was going to be a big, nasty wave, she slowly, steadily approached the fire ax, careful at first, then knowing damn well what she wanted and what she was going for.

The SWAT team was focused. Now that Chisholm had pronounced him legit, their desperation had intensified. They peppered the nutcase with questions and taunts in an effort to get him to talk.

"Now mister, if you're really serious about having some bombs here, why don't you tell us where they are, huh?"

"Come on mother*fuck*er, where'd you put 'em!"

"Shut up, Kelly! Or did you call in your bomb threat 'cause you just wanted to get your picture in the evening news? C'mon, we can work something out."

"If you don't start talking I'm gonna plug you right *now!*" shouted one of the SWAT officers, sliding a round into her assault rifle with a scary finality.

But neither she nor Dexter nor any of the others were gonna plug anyone. That was the thing—none of them dared, and the nutcase knew this. He continued to smile happily, his right eye still twitching.

Chisholm stood staring at the ax as the wave inside her started to build. Rivera was gonna eat her alive for this one. Oh yes. A good boss, he let her have her rope, and occasionally hung her for her troubles. But he had said explicitly on the car phone that he wanted this taken care of. "Clean it up, fix it up, just get this problem off our hands. You're the troubleshooter, Maggie. Go shoot this trouble down."

Chisholm carried a very large revolver, a .45 with an extra-long barrel. She liked the heft. Weapons safety had been a worry of Chisholm's since the start of her career with the FBI, right after law school. Whenever she handled lighter weapons, she worried that she'd forget that she was handling a firearm, the idiot worry breaking her concentration. But with her thick, heavy revolver, just shy of a foot long from end to end, she never forgot that it was a gun she was holding. So now, she grabbed her revolver by the pipe and firmly cracked the glass guarding the fire ax with the butt of the handle.

No one saw Chisholm break the glass, but they all heard it, turning her way as she struck the glass once to break it and three times to clear it.

It was thin, designed to shatter into small, harmless, dull little cubes that couldn't cut. Some in the Bureau called her Rivera's hatchet lady. Today she literally was. For four years, she had gone where Rivera told her to go, done what he told her to do, and that was fine by her. Her job was the end of the line as far as her career was concerned, everyone knew that. Beyond this, in the not so distant future, there might be teaching at Quantico, if that; she'd never go any higher. But *now* . . . The things she got to do on a daily basis. She replaced her gun and pulled the fire ax off the wall mounts.

"Uncuff him," she said as she turned back to face them all. "Uncuff him and hold his hand to the ground."

Dexter and the seven other SWAT officers all gawked at Chisholm. The nutcase frowned, the wisest among them, his eyes finally locking steady on the approaching Chisholm. She didn't notice any of them. All she saw was the nutcase's now steady eye. And all she thought of was fingers.

"Uncuff him, I said," she repeated, mildly peeved.

"Agent Chisholm, what do you think you're doing?" said Dexter, none too pleased now that the genie he'd summoned was finally out of the bottle.

"Officer Dexter, I have the authority of Deputy Director Rivera. Uncuff him."

He didn't at first. He just kept silent, hoping to cow this desk agent with his size and his stare. But it failed, because she wasn't looking at him. She was looking at the steady eye. Dexter knelt and uncuffed the nutcase.

"What now?"

"Spread the fingers of his right hand on the ground."

"What do you think—"

"If you question my authority one more time, I'm going to have you for breakfast Monday morning. How would you like to be in South Dakota investigating cattle mutilations till pension time. Spread his fingers on the ground."

Dexter relented. He did as he was told. Whatever she was up to, this would be on Chisholm's head.

Chisholm only had eyes for the nutcase as she hefted the fire ax with both hands. It felt good. It was heavy, but not too heavy. She swung it around with both arms, feeling her muscles pleasingly stretch with its weight. Chisholm had chopped her fair share of wood on Maryland winter weekends before Robby was old enough to do it; by touch alone she could tell that this ax handle wouldn't snap on a bad swing. She took a couple of steps to her left and stood to the nutcase's right as Dexter held down his wrist.

When he had the nutcase's hand firmly in place, palm flat on the ground, Dexter looked up. *My God, she's going to do it,* he thought idiotically, realizing that what Chisholm had been implicitly threatening since the moment she cracked the glass was no idle threat. *This woman is crazy!*

The nutcase, aware now of what was about to happen, tried hard to stare back at Chisholm through his horn-rims. But this redhead with the brown eyes stared back at him vacantly. It wasn't that there was fear, or worry, or hesitation. The scary thing was, there was nothing—just massive pupils, pools of black, completely indifferent. There was nothing there to connect with.

"You can't do that, that's violating my rights!" he squeaked, his composure breaking for the first time.

Caught between the exhilaration of his soon-to-be-released desperation and some total fear, Dexter said, "Ma'am, I think he's right."

"Oh, really?"

The secret to chopping wood isn't to aim for the log—you have to aim for the base of the chopping block. Automatically, as Chisholm dragged her eyes off the nutcase, she aimed for a point a foot and a half below the surface of the concrete, beyond the fingers she was about to crop off. The nails, curiously enough, were manicured and spotless. Pianist fingers. And as she pulled her arms back and raised the ax up above her head, she reminded herself to be careful to keep her arms straight, like when driving on a golf course—the straighter the arms, the fuller the swing, the more power was released. The muscles on the backs of her shoulder blades clicked in as she pulled back, bunching up under her "Go Tigers, GO!" sweatshirt. The nutcase looked helplessly into the eyes of the soccer-playing tiger.

She brought the ax down.

The sound was awful. It was like when the flat of a knee bumps hard against the edge of a desk. A scream came out of the nutcase's mouth, a sound all from his head, and it rose so swiftly and sharply that it turned nearly supersonic, drowning out the grunt that came from Chisholm's chest and the gasps from Dexter and his squad.

All these sounds were masked by the roar of the oblivious crowd above, the roar at a fever pitch—some play that must have brought delight to the spectators at the stadium and multiple instant replays for the folks back home.

Dexter and the other SWAT officers couldn't take their eyes off the severed fingers. They *moved* for a fraction of a second before they were finally, completely still; Dexter thought he'd never seen anything quite like that before. *Worms,* he thought.

Chisholm meanwhile leaned on the handle of the ax, the edge of which was still on the concrete, separating the fingers. She brought her smiling face directly into the sound of the man's screaming.

"You wanna tell me now where they are, or do I go for your shriveled little pecker? Where are the bombs, what are the switchers like? Tell me right this second or you're really gonna be singing soprano from now on."

For the first time since he'd lost his fingers, the nutcase—still screaming in agony and surprise—looked at the woman who was speaking to him. She was peaceful. She was *happy.* She was enjoying this. Her skin was smooth, silky and freckleless, with only minimal crow's feet, even when she smiled. A single drop of blood—his blood—had splattered her left cheek, the only flaw that broke the smoothness of her skin. At first glance, the drop looked to be a beauty mark.

"Do we do the other hand now or do we do your little pecker? All the same to me, I'm enjoying this."

"No please please *pleeeeeaaaaaaase—*"

"Dexter, get his other hand."

Dexter did no such thing, staring, frightened, frozen at the sight of the severed fingers.

"Dexter. Wake up, I need you conscious."

"Hi-hi-his left hand?" he hiccuped.

"Yes, his left hand. Look alive, Dexter, will you?" she said as she smiled some more. God, she was enjoying this! On the wave, hanging alone in midair—decisions already made, consequences so far in the future they might as well not exist, only an ever-present, unending Now. If only she could live all her life like this, now, in midair, forever.

Speaking through the guy's screams, ignoring them, Chisholm said, "I was just kidding about cutting off his pecker—I'd need a knife for that. Let's do his left hand and see if maybe we can't get something out of him that way. If the left-hand fingers don't work, I think we should try for the toes. What do you think, Dexter? Isn't this what you wanted to see?"

Dexter wasn't thinking anything. This indeed had been what he wanted to see, but now that it was happening, he couldn't believe it. Even as the ax came down, he hadn't really thought she would do it— he'd thought she would "accidentally" miss and just scare this loon. He'd thought he'd see pretty sparks when the ax blade struck the empty concrete. He hadn't. There were no sparks, as there should have been, because the blood from the fingers drowned out any friction. All Dexter had seen was blood—lots of it, leaping out of the nutcase's fingers, splashing mostly onto the guy's shirt, some drops spattering on him, some on this crazy woman. He was scared, which was why he wasn't thinking. He looked at Chisholm.

"What?" he said.

"I said— fuck it, just do his left hand, got that? Put his left hand flat on the concrete and get out of my way, I'm gonna chop him again." With that, Chisholm dragged the ax blade back across the concrete, the sound like . . . like an ax-blade edge being dragged across concrete. It ended when Chisholm raised the ax one more time. The ax head, painted red up to the blade, polished, unpainted steel on the blade itself, was now a uniform shade of red, covered with blood. At eye level, almost unconsciously, Chisholm shook off the excess blood. It wouldn't do to have drops of blood fall into her hair when she raised the ax over her head again. She looked around.

She wasn't impatient. Now, completely in the flow, she was only mildly interested to know where the stadium bombs were. Only the sight of Dexter and his seven twerps kept her in context. But with them or no, Chisholm knew who she was and what she was doing. And she liked it pretty damn fine.

Dexter held the nutcase's left hand at the ready.

"No no no, I'll tell you, I'll tell you, they're on the backs of the twelfth, thirteenth, seventh, eighth, and-uh-uh-uh—first columns, seven feet up, yes yes hidden in the shadows of the columns."

Hearing this, Dexter released the nutcase's hand so he could radio his units. The nutcase, crazy but no fool, yanked his left hand back before Chisholm could chop off some more fingers. And that's when it came—all of it: a rage so fine and hot it made her sick.

"Units four, five, seven, and eight, check the back sides of the support columns about seven feet up, columns are twelve, thirteen, seven, eight, and one, do it *now!*" Dexter turned and looked straight at Chisholm, and what he saw scared him worse than the finger chopping.

It was rage, all rage. The little suburban housewife with the stupid sweatshirt was so furious she literally couldn't speak, staring at the empty spot where the nutcase's left hand was supposed to be, seeing nothing but blank concrete and blood and fingertips. There were no more fingers to chop. And as she looked up at Dexter, the lone thought that crossed his mind was: *She really would have preferred chopping this guy's other hand to finding the bombs.*

"I may not be done with him yet," she said. "He's probably lying. I'll need you to hold his hand out again."

"Agent Chisholm, I can't do that," Dexter said, frightened, *really* frightened—the possibility of RFK going up in a fireball seemed better than having to report to this woman. Dexter's right arm swung discreetly behind him, to make sure that he still had his assault rifle, still looking at Chisholm straight in the eye.

"Chief," the open transmitter squawked tinnily. "We found them all. We're cool."

Keeping his eyes on Chisholm, Dexter grabbed the transmitter and spoke.

"All the charges?"

"Every damn one, right where you said. We're checking the other columns but we haven't found any others."

"Good, keep on doing that. Dexter out." He looked at Chisholm.

There was just a suburban housewife there, looking at nothing in particular. She dropped the ax as if she had been casually examining it just now.

"That's nice. No more mess," she said. She examined herself from chest level to feet, then dabbed at her face, spreading the single drop of blood around her cheek like morning Nivea. It added color to her cheek. She looked about.

Chisholm would never be able to speak to any of these SWAT officers again. If she saw them again somewhere, around the Hoover Building say, or at Quantico, they would murmur polite greetings and get out of her way as quickly as frightened mice.

"Four missing fingers, or a bunch of dead mushrooms," she said to no one in particular. But she wasn't desperate to justify her actions. Once, she would have tried to justify what she had done, but that was a long time ago. It was something she didn't bother with anymore. After all, wasn't it precisely for her ability to make the tough, hard decisions that Rivera chose her for such jobs? They could disdain her all they wanted. They could take a step back. But every SWAT team needed a Chisholm now and then.

Chisholm turned away from the still-crying nutcase and made her way back to her minivan, everyone staring after her. Then she stopped and turned. Looking around, she realized how much she wanted to smash their faces—all their faces. The faces all said the same thing—the initiative was still on Chisholm's side. So she took it, raising her voice to be unambiguously clear, her face a leering sneer.

"Don't forget his fingertips. Can't fingerprint him without 'em."

Their faces now smashed like eggshells, she left the dark underside of the stadium.

The drive back home was uneventful, for the most part. Margaret knew that there was no way she'd make the end of Robby's game.

She liked watching Robby play with his friends. That was the important thing. She loved watching them play in their sky-blue-and-white uniforms, then driving them all to some fast-food place for an after-game meal. There were mothers who tried to be part of the gang, but Margaret was far wiser. She let Robby and his friends pretend they didn't know her. She kept a furtive eye on them from a distance, making sure that they never left her sight.

They had secret, odd handshakes. They listened with rapt attention to cacophonous, mind-numbing music. Margaret noticed every detail, every nuance of their ever-changing alliances: who was closest to whom.

Robby, with war paint of blood streaked on his face, his limbs ampu-
tated, dying on a green soccer field, her son's blood turning the grass red
and his brains shining and glimmering yellow and gray in the afternoon
sunlight.

The vision caught her so by surprise she stopped the minivan, got out, and vomited by the side of the road. She hadn't eaten much today, so all that came up from her heaves was sickly yellow and brown bile, splattering on the side of the road as she held on to the right-side mirror of her minivan for support, the oblivious cars rushing past, the gusts of wind they threw her way cooling.

A car pulled up ahead of her parked minivan, a white convertible two-seater runabout. A middle-aged man got out and approached Margaret.

"Are you okay?" he asked, genuinely concerned.

Margaret looked up. What was she going to tell this stranger? That she felt good about having chopped off some poor bastard's fingers? Or that she felt sick about it? "Yeah, just a little ill."

"You want me to call someone or something? I have a phone in my car."

"No, but thanks a lot. I have a cell phone too."

"Oh, well okay then. You sure you're okay?"

"Yeah. Thanks a lot though."

The man went back to his convertible, waved as he got in, then drove off. Margaret bowed her head at the disappearing car, trying to calm herself down. Soon, she was calm enough to drive on.

Both Margaret and Robby were fairly fastidious about how they lived, so their home in Silver Springs, Maryland, was always neatly arrayed. But Margaret spent the afternoon fixing it up some more anyway: washing clothes, cleaning dusty dishes from the cupboards, even trimming some hedges in the fading light, though that was technically Robby's responsibility. She liked losing herself in the simplicity of everyday chores.

The house was two-storied. On the second floor, there were three rooms, Margaret's, Robby's, and a guest room which neither of them ever really went into but which they were forever talking about turning into a TV room. As it was, Margaret and her son watched television in the kitchen when they had dinner together.

Robby was a good, smart little kid, so their relationship wasn't so much that of a parent and child but more like that of two roommates. With no prodding, he did his schoolwork and his house chores. He made sure to always tell her where he was. He never seemed to have any problems, and it made Margaret nervous sometimes, this burgeoning self-possession of her twelve-year-old.

Robby had left a message on the answering machine, saying he had gone to the mall with his friends after the soccer game, that he would see her tonight when he got back. He would be back by seven.

It was ten after seven. Margaret was already frightened. She had arrived a little after four in the afternoon, badly needing to talk to someone, anyone. Not just talk but have a Talk. A Talk about . . . well, *things*. But with no one home, all she could do was do the chores, a likely soporific that was really just postponing her need to air out what had happened and what was going through her mind. Now though, what with the chores done, there was nothing to do but wait and think about her Sunday afternoon.

She very badly wanted Robby to be around, so she could hold him tight.

Impulsively, she turned on the kitchen television set in time for a news item about a madman in Oregon who had sodomized and strangled three teenaged boys; then turned the set off, realizing that news censoring ought to be implemented for the peace of mind of *parents*. She had already dried all the dishes she had washed, and it was too dark to go outside and see if something else needed to get done, so Margaret opened a can of Coca-Cola as her imagination ran through the possible pedophiles in the Maryland area.

Images cruel and sickening tried hard to make a beachhead on her mind, but she kept them at bay. But then there were the images that weren't so unreal, images of this afternoon. Airing them out would have stopped them. But there was no one to air them out to, at least not until Robby came home. So she prowled around the house, patrolling it as if the images might turn animate and deadly, keeping a sharp eye on the darkness outside, watching as it bore down on the house's windows, a night pressure evil and fetid. It was 7:15, and Robby still wasn't home.

Robby came in alone, slamming the front door behind him, carrying a paper bag with CDs and fantasy paperback books, where all his money went.

"Hiya Mom," he said pleasantly. Margaret was on him like a shot.

"Robert Everett, where have you been!" she shouted as she dashed from the kitchen into the living room, staring at Robby wildly as he stood there, looking back at his crazy mother.

Robby rolled his eyes. "I was at the mall! Mitch's dad drove us over and he was a little late picking us up."

He still hadn't had his growth spurt, standing at about four feet nine, which worried Margaret a bit though it proved advantageous now as she grabbed him by the shoulders and bent down to talk to him.

"Do you know how worried I was? You could have called! There was a story in the news about a—a—a *bad man* out in Oregon—"

"Oh yeah," Robby interrupted, fascinated, "the guy who raped and strangled little kids—gross, huh?"

Margaret pulled Robby to her, then pushed him away. "Next time *call* that you're gonna be a little late."

He rolled his eyes again and for an instant she wanted to smack him right then and there. "Oh Mom," he said, then stopped suddenly in midshrug and looked up, surprised that he wasn't smelling anything. "What's for dinner?"

She had completely forgotten dinner. They went to the kitchen, where Robby attacked the refrigerator, spreading thick dollops of cream cheese on some celery sticks for the two of them while Margaret made pork chops and brown rice.

While dinner was cooking, they ate their celery sticks. Robby sat on the kitchen table, going through his bag of CDs and fantasy books, a little mesmerized by them, talking about them in soothing rhythms, his body slim and small and . . . weak. Weak, narrow shoulders, a weak, scrawny neck, a tiny, dimpled chest that Margaret was sure she could still cover with a single span of her hand. A small boy too weak to support . . . anyone.

Not weak, she thought. *Just small, tiny. Just a boy—still. Thank God. God help me.*

Very cautiously, Margaret took all the images of the past afternoon and carefully, daintily stowed them away, out of sight of her son, ashamed of what she had wanted from him.

They talked a little talk about their respective days. Margaret gave Rob a severely edited version of what she had done, telling him in such a way and with such lack of detail that he didn't pay her story any mind. For his part, Rob gave her an equally edited version of what *he'd* been doing. At the mall, he and his friends had supposedly gone to see a comedy about a fat man and his weaselly sidekick. In fact, once inside the Cineplex, they'd snuck in to see a different movie altogether, a movie about a gorgeous psychotic woman who had graphic sex with her pursuers and business associates before killing them in fairly gruesome scenarios. It had been really neat.

"So how did you make out against the Buffaloes?" she asked, referring to the team that had played the Tigers, blowing the image of the sexy psycho clear out of Robby's mind and bringing him back to a reality he didn't much enjoy, the reality of being on a consistently losing team.

"We lost," he said curtly, looking at the floor between his dangling feet. Margaret put an arm around his shoulders, not daring to ask the score or say anything he might interpret as "mothering." She just waited . . . and waited . . . and waited. And for her pains, he let her see him be sad.

And she? She let him need her, neither asking nor demanding anything in return.

TWO

The Man with the Shark Smile

It was some dinner party, and Denton was having a wonderful time.

There were nine people sitting at the table, including Denton, the only one who had come alone and probably the youngest man in attendance. Under the conversation, he could hear selections from *Idomeneo*, specifically the "Ballet Music"; slightly tacky music, but it went well enough with the conversation, which was bright and lively.

At one end sat Keith Lehrer, Denton's boss. On the other end, to Denton's immediate left, sat Mrs. Lehrer, well kept and sixtyish. She was talking to Denton about his newest novel, indulging the teeniest crush she had on him.

"I loved it, especially all the double-dealings and double crossings. Is it really like that, Nicky?"

Denton smiled. He was slim, with blondish brown hair, mild blue eyes, and pale skin, yet what that dark smile hid was really impossible to know, a smile like a shark's smile, the teeth even and, somehow, sharp. People who casually met that smile would remember Denton as being several shades darker than he really was; willing to swear to it that he had deep brown eyes and dark brown hair, yes he did, yes he did, no he didn't—it was all in the smile. Nicholas Denton turned to Mrs. Lehrer with that smile and said, "I'm just a lowly Langley bureaucrat, Mrs. Lehrer. If *only* my life were as exciting as what I write."

"You're teasing me again," she flirted outrageously.

"Are you flirting with my wife again?" Lehrer called out down the table, smiling at Denton, who answered him without missing a beat.

"Sir, she said she wants to run away with me, but I've been telling her for months now—I'm unworthy of her."

Everyone laughed at the stupid, boring joke. There was something about Denton, a wild sense of humor masked under an icicle facade, that made even a trivial comment funny, as if the world itself were some monstrous joke. It made Denton a welcome and popular member of the Georgetown cocktail circuit, which he played endlessly.

Amalia, an aide of Denton's, walked into the closed-off dining room. A small, mousy girl, dressed conservatively and inconspicuously, she was fairly invisible as she walked in and whispered in Denton's ear. Denton smiled all around, excusing himself as he left the dining room for a distant foyer, Amalia right behind him.

Denton knew Lehrer's house intimately; after all, he'd been the man's deputy for close to two years. Amalia escorted him through the house not as a guide but to make sure no one would be in earshot when he picked up the phone. As he got to the foyer where the phone lay, Amalia faded into the scenery, leaving her boss alone.

"This is Denton. . . . Yes. Yes, I see. I see. Too bad. All right, this is what I want: As regards issue A, give her a fifteen percent raise and a bonus while you're at it, say fifteen thousand. Give her lots of praise, she lives for it—be lavish. As regards issue B, Bluebird him. . . . Yes, not so much as an obituary in the *Winnetka Sentinel*. . . . I don't care, either do it or I'll inflict Amalia on your squad. I am unimpressed. . . . I see. Yes, I'm sure. . . . Of *course* this phone is safe—I'm the one who's tapping it. . . . Very well. Goodbye."

He hung up the phone and whipped out a little black book from his inside jacket pocket. The black book was Denton's most valued possession. It was where he wrote down all the interesting phrases he heard or came up with during the day, phrases and sentences he used in his novels. He opened the book and wrote as he mouthed the words: "Not so much as an obituary in the *Winnetka Sentinel*." It had a ring.

He turned and walked back to the dining room, Amalia falling in step behind him and to his right, staying outside the door as Denton reentered the room.

As he sat down again, all smiles to the others, he wondered how he was going to handle the assassination he'd just ordered. It didn't affect him directly, but Denton believed in being prepared, so he started thinking up a plausible response to the assassination as Mrs. Lehrer turned to him and resumed her little flirtation.

"Planning secret missions?" she teased.

"Hardly," Denton laughed. "Just taking care of a little personnel problem."

Then he gave a shark smile all around. Life was good.

Denton was an alumnus of a group of CIA men and women known from the mid-eighties to the early nineties as Tiggermann's pups, and not because they were cute and cuddly.

Roman "Tiggy" Tiggermann, now out of the picture, had been an agency hack and occasional ombudsman. Potbellied, a little too voluble for polite company, with prize-winningly bad taste in clothes, he had sort of a monkey face behind unfashionable square-framed glasses, the eyes bugging out just a wee bit. To top it off, he had this sickening habit of brushing what few hairs he had across the top of his bald head, as if this would fool anybody. During his first seventeen years at Central Intelligence, he had gained the reputation of being very intelligent but dumb as they come, which was why he was ignored as a nobody, fobbed off to the ombudsman's desk to wait out the time to his retirement.

But suddenly in 1985, at age forty-eight, Tiggermann woke up.

The first indication that Tiggy Tiggermann had awakened came in the form of an operation that soon became known in legend as the Spring Cleaning. The Spring Cleaning resulted in a slew of arrests, total chaos in Mossad and the GRU, a bunch of markers from the Senate Intelligence Committee, and a new man where Tiggy Tiggermann used to park his car.

After the Israeli coup, Tiggermann used the office of CIA ombudsman to set up his own little shop within the Agency. One of the people who begged to be in that particular Brownie troop in early '85 was a young analyst just two years out of Dartmouth: Nicholas Andrew Denton III.

At their first meeting, Tiggy gave Denton his monkey smile, leaning forward in his chair as if he were the one asking for something from the calm and composed young Denton. But what Tiggy said didn't sound like a supplication: "For three weeks, ten times a day, every damned day, I've had to put up with your miserable badgering. Now here's your chance. Deliver and show me what you can do, or stop wasting my time."

Denton, then twenty-four, for once in his life shat bricks like other mortals, the last time he ever did. But even while shitting bricks, he still had nerve. He leaned back in his chair and lit a cigarette, even though Tiggermann had specifically told him not to smoke in his office.

"Either you take me on your team or there's no point in having someone like me working in the Agency."

"Quit away, what do I care," Tiggy laughed, moving and gesturing too fast, making him seem so insecure, his great weapon in his new incarnation. "I'm just the lonely ombudsman looking for some company."

"I can analyze—"

"I got analysts," Tiggy laughingly interrupted.

"I can plan—"

"I got planners. Surprise me, kid. What can you do that I really *need?* What makes you worth hiring?"

Denton paused, thinking, coming up blank. But then his mouth, seemingly of its own volition, smiled and opened and came up with the one thing Tiggy really wanted to hear: "I can fuck people over so they'll never come around to fuck with me again."

"You're hired."

And fuck 'em he did, getting neck deep in the Spring Cleaning and living to tell the tale. After that, Tiggy and his pups ran their own private agency within the Agency, answering solely to Tiggermann, running operations so far beyond the pale that no one except people with X-ray eyes could spot what was going on. But at its core, Tiggy's little shop was really rather simple. All that had to happen was for funds to appear in the correct columns. Since Tiggy was the ombudsman, the funds always did.

"Tiggy, am I out of a job?" Paula Baker asked one day in '88, at twenty-three the youngest and absolutely sexiest kid on the team, a corn-fed accountant from Wisconsin, the only one who could vaguely follow all the financial machinations of their boss. "I just got a severance package with my last paycheck."

"No!" Tiggy laughed, kissing Paula on the forehead, clucking over her like a mother-goose. "In three months you'll be rehired. Just necessary to square up the figures."

"Oh!" Paula said brightly, reassured. Three months later, there she was, employed on paper once again, technically working for a man by the name of Ron McDonald. Along with waking up, Tiggy had developed a weird sense of humor all his pups tried hard to emulate.

Tiggermann might look like an old beat-up hack, and he still might keep the unchic basement offices with the same cheap furniture he'd had before his awakening (he was quite the sentimentalist), but from the moment he woke up, Tiggermann was where the action was, where all the bright young agents of that generation wanted to be, and screw the Russia desk. After all, in '87 Tiggy told them that the Eastern Bloc was going to collapse in a financial bonfire, and for two years all the pups operated on the assumption that that was exactly what was going to happen. When '89 rolled around, Tiggy and the pups looked fairly clairvoyant, gaining direct access to that old CIA hand, George Bush, who knew a good thing when he saw it.

The press would remark how a vacillating president such as Bush had shown such uncharacteristic firmness when dealing with Saddam Hussein's invasion of Kuwait in August of '90. The upper floors of Langley knew better, rolling their eyes down to the basement of the building and the smiling Buddha figure of Tiggy, surrounded by his pups. When Tiggy "suggested" that one of his kids, Kenneth Whipple, would be the ideal choice to take over the Middle East desk, making him the youngest section head in CIA history, no one argued with him. No one could afford to, because Tiggy took care of his pups and the pups stuck together. Fuck with one, you were fucking with them all.

The Director of CIA found out about this in 1991.

"Tiggermann," he told the old man in the summer of that year, "I think it's time you thought about retiring from the ombudsman's job." *And incidentally stop exerting all that power,* was the underlying worry. It made everyone nervous that Tiggy not only had the President's ear but also had surrounded himself with a bunch of greenhorns who were doing who knew what. So the Director started leaning on Tiggy.

Tiggy didn't do anything. Instead, he let his pups handle it.

"They realize that you're still relatively young, that you might be around for another ten, fifteen years," said Denton. "Your fault, Tiggy—you should have seen this coming before it came out into the open. Now we'll have to be messy about it." Only Denton could have said something like that to Tiggermann's face.

"Maybe so, Nick. But I want you guys to handle this one," he told them at the Wednesday morning meeting. "I don't want to hear about your solution, just solve it."

Tiggy left the office early. He was frankly curious to see how the pups would play this one out, so this way he'd find out what they were capable of, left on their own.

The pups toyed with ideas, banking on their strengths. Ken Whipple was all for playing psyche games. Arthur Atmajian was hot to bug the Director's office, but everyone else thought that was stupid. Paula Baker suggested doing some major financial manipulations which sounded way too snowy to everyone else. It was a closed meeting, so after the first ten minutes, the ideas started turning insane, to everyone's delight.

"Let's just take ol' Fart Face [*id est*, the Director] down to Adams Morgan and get pictures of him being butt-fucked!"

"Hell with that, let's forge a letter canceling his golf club membership."

"Booooo!!!!"

"I say we threaten to send his brats to public schools!"

"*Yeah!!*"

They were kids. They were having a wonderful time. But after an hour of this bullshitting they grew tired of it and decided to play ball with ol' Fart Face for real.

Denton was the one who came up with something good. He came up with the idea to blackmail the Director of the Central Intelligence Agency.

Nothing unusual about that. Denton had become the resident blackmail specialist of Tiggermann's unit. But *how* Denton was going to blackmail the Director of the Central Intelligence Agency was probably something only Denton could have dreamed of pulling off. It was crazy and it was absolutely foolproof.

They had to wait for a slow news day. That Wednesday evening would be bad, a minor plane crash in Minnesota dominating coverage. Thursday and Friday it was Bosnia. Saturday some actor died. But Sunday morning there was nothing coming down the pipeline. So they decided that Sunday was the day, all of them praying that nothing too newsworthy took place before seven P.M. Eastern Standard, the news-cycle cut-off time for print.

Denton contacted a *Washington Post* reporter in a manner that was pure cloak-and-dagger. He used a voice scrambler to call the guy up around noon. A meeting in the Georgetown Gallery? Can do, said the reporter.

At the shopping mall, wearing shades and an earpiece transmitter, Denton was the epitome of the secret agent; the transmitter didn't work, but it added totally to the effect, Denton knew. He feigned nervousness so well that the *reporter* dropped his tape recorder not once but twice. Walking around the crowded mall, they looked so conspicuous that Denton was sure they would have been blown if it had been a real intelligence operation. As it was, most of the pups were anonymously hanging around Denton and the reporter in the shopping center, hugely amused by the performance.

First, Denton authenticated his CIA credentials by producing his marine-green parking pass, only given to senior officers with indoor parking slots. Then he told the *Post* reporter how the Director was trying to ease out the ombudsman because of alleged irregularities Tiggermann had discovered in the accounts of the Director's office.

Denton flashed but did not hand over to the reporter some fabricated documents that looked authentic as all get out. As he did so, Denton kept looking around the mall like a frightened rabbit. Denton told the reporter that he was positive he was being followed and that lives might be at stake. Denton was *sure* his family was threatened; there'd been calls, a dark car idling by the curb whenever he went to pick up his kids . . .

Then, suddenly, without warning, Paula Baker, in shades too, jumped out from behind a bush and snapped off a couple of pictures of Denton and the reporter.

"Why didn't you just scream 'Boo!' while you were at it?" Denton later complained.

"It was close, it was oh so close," she said, casually leaning back in her chair, her perfect breasts shifting ever so slightly underneath her blouse. God, Paula Baker was sexy!

When she jumped out from behind the bushes, Denton ran off as if the hounds of hell were after him, but not before mentioning something about "offshore accounts." The reporter ran too, and Arthur Atmajian and a couple of his gnomes had quite a time following him back to the *Post* offices.

"The shit-for-brains kept taking these detours, trying to shake coverage. I mean, the longer he took to get to his office, the more opportunities he gave me to snatch him, if I'd had a mind to. What a dumb fuck."

Within two hours, most of the pups still nominally working under Tiggermann were contacted at home by this *Post* reporter. All the pups claimed to be unavailable for comment, but all of them shaded their "no comments" to make it sound as if the reporter had gotten his facts straight. And as luck would have it, there was nothing very important on the news cycle that day.

The next morning, a Monday, Langley felt if not looked as if a neutron bomb had been casually lobbed down a ventilation shaft and into the building, all work grinding to a halt, everyone glued to CNN while compulsively rereading the front-page stories in the *Post* and the *New York Times*.

"The *Post and* the *Times*? Why don't you set up a media circus right outside by the gate?" said Tiggy the next day, trying to be upset with Denton but really unable to.

"What can I say?" said Denton casually, smoking a cigarette and tossing burned microwave popcorn into Wenger's and Caruthers's mouths across the room. "The *Post* story was expected. The *Times* story and the CNN coverage? Well, we just got lucky, is all."

It took the Director three weeks of appearances before the Senate Intelligence Committee to dispel the notion that there was any pressure on the ombudsman's office. The Director repeated over and over again how hunky-dory everything was going with Ombudsman Tiggermann. Replace him? You've *got* to be joking. And Tiggermann, for his part, swore up and down that he, the ombudsman, had found nothing irregular in the Director's accounts—with a very smooth and subtle but audible "yet" to that statement.

"Kids," Tiggy told them at the next Wednesday morning meeting, "you've been very, very naughty." They all celebrated with a bottle of Apple-Zapple someone had been saving for a special day.

It was Denton, though, who lent the perfect touch to the operation he had concocted, a little "fuck you" to the Director's office.

During his meeting with the *Post* reporter, Denton had mentioned something about "Gravity payoffs," which all the fallout press reports ignored, but which were included in the twelfth and thirteenth paragraphs of the *Post* story that Monday. To outsiders, it sounded all very confusing. But to the Director's office, it was a clear signal—Gravity payoffs was the name given to off-the-accounts work, work that was technically illegal since it was not audited by the Senate Intelligence Committee. Gravity payoffs was work directly supervised by the Director. Very few in the Agency had even *heard* about Gravity payoffs. Mentioning them was the clear signal that someone with very good information had spilled the beans to the *Post*. It said to anyone in the know, "We've got teeth, so don't fuck with us no more, not unless you wanna go all the way." And the Director, wisely, decided to back the fuck off, the pups in the basement happy as they tossed burned popcorn at each other across the room.

They had some great times during the Big Eighties, toying with the big money and the grand designs. But it was time itself which finally did in the basement office. In late '92, Tiggermann suffered a massive stroke, forcing his retirement, but not before he had managed to place most of his pups in some very good shelters. The rest of the Agency feared Tiggy by then, not really understanding him, and they gave a huge collective sigh of relief masked by concern when Tiggy had his stroke and left the Agency.

Like all bureaucracies, CIA depended on consistency—either you were an asshole or a saint or smooth or rough or fucking *something*. It never did—never could—understand how one of its own had suddenly and for no apparent reason walked in a changed man, as Tiggy had in '85.

"I don't understand it myself," Tiggy told Paula Baker and Phyllis Strathmore when they went to visit their now dying mentor. "I walked into Langley one day in early '85 and it was suddenly as if I could see everything more clearly than I ever had before."

"Mmm," said Phyllis, one of the few pups who had left the Agency. She was dressed to the hilt in Wall Street banker gray, made up, sporting a two-hundred-dollar hairdo, looking on her way to becoming a multimillionaire already as she gently and inconspicuously wiped the drool falling out of the paralyzed side of Tiggy's mouth. She could have called Tiggy; a trip from New York to Tiggy's apartment in Maryland was a whole-day affair. But she came, as they all did except for Arthur Atmajian. Atta-boy, the pup who was now an all-purpose wet-boy, much to everyone's chagrin, couldn't bring himself to visit Tig-germann, which Tiggy and everyone else understood; assassins are weird that way sometimes.

"We did have some fine times there," Phyllis told Tiggy, for no rea-son, thinking.

"Not with me you didn't," Tiggermann teased lecherously, surpris-ing Phyllis into tears.

Tiggy was buried that dead week between Christmas of '93 and New Year's of '94, not even fifty-seven years old. But Tiggy changed the Agency, even though the Agency itself didn't know it.

The very existence of the pups was the thing—an agency within the Agency, made up of the most talented young agents. In the basement, there had been shouting matches, little alliances and enmities, just like in the rest of the Agency. Strathmore and Denton, for instance, had spent most of '87 trying to one-up the other. But once in the presence of outsiders, the pups were solid, sticking together in a bizarre rela-tionship, as much brotherhood and marriage as demonic pact. After all, they'd been *chosen* by Tiggy, that was the thing; chosen by Tiggy when they were all young and not too bright. Now, when Denton talked to Phyllis or Whipple, he didn't see a Wall Street investment-bank part-ner or the head of the Middle East section—he saw a couple of eager-beaver geeks, which is how *they* saw *him*, and which was why they were all friends: they didn't fear each other.

As the Big Eighties became the Timid Nineties and all the pups started to move out on their own, all but Denton took heavy-duty line jobs. Strathmore left the Agency altogether; Jayne Caruthers took over the Western Europe stations; Wenger, perversely, took a field position, posing as an AP stringer but running most everyone out of Eastern Eu-rope; Paula Baker, amazingly, made head of Covert Finance; Atmajian controlled most of the wet-boys of the Special Directorate. In short, all the pups made big splashes outside the basement. Except Denton.

"Me? Well, I've decided to take the shadow road," he said at a bar, and everyone gave a start. The blackmail specialist smiled that smile of his and gave a pass on all the line jobs tossed his way, going straight for the shadow road instead, and no one could understand why.

The shadow road was the realm of staff—men and women without the talent or drive or initiative or inclination to make it in the kind of line jobs that all the other pups had taken. Staff work was advising people, analyzing data, dealing with the monumental paper mounds generated by line jobs, staying in the background, in the shadows of the real agency work. No one who'd tasted the raw power of a line job took the shadow road voluntarily—except Nicholas Denton, Tiggy's heir apparent, the only pup to gravitate to that peculiar world built of paper.

"He knows what he's doing," Tiggy told Paula Baker, who along with every other woman in the basement had the hugest crush on Denton. "No offense, but Nicky's the smartest one of the bunch," he told her the fall before he died.

Baker, never one to argue with her daddy, as she mentally regarded Tiggermann, took what he said on faith. But as months and then years went by, she and the other pups started wondering what Denton was doing.

The pay was bad, the abuse never-ending, and to top it off there was no real power to be had. And of course, since it was known that Denton had been one of the pups, everyone wondered why such a supposedly talented agent was working the shadow road. As time passed, it seemed as if Denton was becoming more and more foppish, more concerned about looks rather than results, the antithesis of the pup mentality. Strains began showing, other pups concerned and frustrated with Denton as he gained the reputation within the Agency as a lightweight and no one to worry about. After a while, people started forgetting he had once been Tiggermann's golden boy.

"All you're doing is fucking around," Arthur Atmajian told him one day, "accidentally" running into him in a Langley hallway. Everything involving Atta-boy was *always* "accidental."

Denton's non sequitur to this—"Did you read my newest novel?"—made Atmajian furious. Atta-boy, along with the rest of the pups, had been frankly shocked that Denton was wasting his time writing novels as a hobby. The fact that he wrote novels was no big deal; Kenny Whipple at the Middle East desk had published a well-received collection of poems, a source of facetious derision but secret pride among the pups. But Kenny was also whipping the Middle East like a chef casually making an omelet. Denton was dressing expensively and wasting his time at cocktail and dinner parties.

"Fuck your fucking novel! Your career is going down the tubes! You're turning into a zero, for Chrissake!"

Denton maneuvered the conversation back to his publishing problems, oblivious of Atmajian's fury. When they finished, Atta-boy figured that Denton was one of the also-rans, a fop who wasn't what he had advertised when working for Tiggy. He and the rest of the pups didn't freeze out Denton, exactly, but they didn't pay him that much attention during the first few years of the nineties.

Then one day Carl Roper showed up and Denton's new incarnation became perfectly clear.

Carl Roper was made head of North American Counter Intelligence, in charge of exposing and if possible controlling foreign assets in American and Canadian territory.

"I shut 'em up and then I shut 'em down!" he'd told Denton early on in his tenure at NACI, Roper being one of those men who naively think intelligence work is something closer to a straightforward good guy–bad guy deal. "I'm a man who won't put up with any foreign assets on *my* turf."

He was also a prick with the deserved reputation of being sloppy. When Denton started pursuing Roper, hoping to land a job with him, the pups all but wrote him off.

"The Peter Principle," Makepeace Oates told Paula Baker over lunch. "Denton just can't cut it. Work for somebody as dumb and bloody-minded as Roper, he wants to be a pencil pusher with no responsibilities and therefore no power"—which became the general consensus. Atta-boy, the wet-boy of the pups and Nicholas Denton's best friend, was the only one who could not stand on pretense. Much as he loved him, he made it clear that he did not want to deal with Denton anymore, not even socially. Everyone else wrote Denton off as an also-ran, a failure in the race.

But Denton . . . well, Denton was amused by all this.

Carl Roper of course hired Denton and proceeded to make a mess of NACI, drawing attention to himself. But with every mess Roper made for himself, it seemed as if Denton wound up with a new contact, or picking up some stray dirt here and there. Paula Baker was the first to get a glimpse of what was going on, when Denton showed up at her office one day, unannounced.

"I have a finance review-board meeting," Paula told him coolly, willing to be sociable with Denton on the off hours but unwilling to cut him slack during office time.

"This is something you want to hear," said Denton, closing Paula's office door and telling her how Roper's counterpart unit for Latin America—a unit way outside the scope of Denton's responsibilities—was being used to siphon off monies for an independent covert unit operating out of Estonia, a unit which Baker herself should have known about but hadn't heard a whisper of.

This was the summer of '95, almost three years since Denton had started on the shadow road, and now the payoff started trickling in. He went on a little spiel about the Latin America unit and her own finance group that was so casually detailed and well informed that for a brief moment Paula felt she was in some particularly surreal episode of *The Twilight Zone*—Nicky Denton, foppish king of the Georgetown cocktail circuit, seemed to know more about her own unit's workings than she herself did.

"How did you manage to come up with this poop?" she asked, more than a little scared.

"Papers papers papers, Paula. The shadow road is built on papers."

Papers. It was all about papers, since everything in CIA is written down and date-stamped. The shadow road is called that because the paper makes a shadow that simply cannot be denied. Only problem is, the shadow road is built on so *much* paper that it's virtually impossible to extract anything useful out of it. It had taken him three years, but Denton had finally managed to tame the beast, using Roper's sloppiness as the perfect cover, his lack of supervision making it possible for Denton to drive down the shadow road without worrying about cops pulling him over.

"What if you get caught?" asked the stunned Paula Baker, beginning to see the real power of the shadow road.

"Traceable to Roper, for the time being. And if I *do* get caught, so what? After all, I'm not in a line job—I'm in staff. I'm *supposed* to be cruising the shadow road. It's not *my* fault if I come across something juicy."

At Langley, there are so many sensitive documents that there is a strict procedure for disposing of them. They are taken to a central collection point under guard, where they are first shredded en masse, then turned into pulp, which is recycled (the CIA is, after all, a green bureaucracy). In November of '95 Denton called the estranged Atta-boy and persuaded him to do something that was as close to sacrilege as was possible in CIA—create a pipeline which would divert the papers heading for disposal to create a shadow file cabinet, an office building in Alexandria where Denton deposited literally tons of paper, all carefully organized and catalogued.

"You're *back*!" Atta-boy shouted gleefully, when the document pipeline was operational and some serious information started to flow.

"I was never *gone!*" laughed Denton.

"You are God," Atta-boy insisted, as was his way. Paula Baker suspected that Arthur was more excited by Denton's return than by the cool operation he had engineered.

The scheme to divert the paper was the first covert unit Denton had concocted since being a part of Tiggy's unit four years earlier. But Denton never thought of it as a covert operation. At its core, Denton considered the shadow file cabinet a giant research project. But it was the most ambitious research project anyone anywhere had ever pulled off, with all the secrets of Langley making their way to Denton's Alexandria office and eventually to microfilm.

The shadow file cabinet boiled down to information, the holy mud that could bestow vision on the blind. Information gave views and glimpses of what was out there in the greater world beyond, but they were always unstable little peepholes that were always being slammed shut. But the shadow file cabinet was no solitary, unstable window, or even a collection of windows—it was a power window, which showed not just some of the sights but *all* of them, together, at once. The power of the shadow file cabinet was that it could give a window on real, complete knowledge. And knowledge, as they say, is the only power around.

The money to run the operation came from funds Paula Baker blocked from being siphoned off the Latin America unit; that's why Denton brought up the problem to begin with—he needed underground money to finance his research project. As a side deal, Denton got a cut of those monies for use in staffing the shadow file cabinet, which became a major pillar of Denton's power base, especially since only Baker and Atmajian knew of its existence. Atta-boy and Paula of course got first dibs on all this accumulating information, in exchange for protecting the shadow file cabinet.

"Can they trace the men working on the shadow file cabinet?" Paula Baker asked Atmajian when they were first talking about the logistics of Denton's research project.

"Can they trace the money you're siphoning off?"

"Please, a little credit here."

"Exactly."

A double-blind covert unit—that is, a unit that does not know either what it is doing or for whom it is acting—was set up in early '96 to systematically analyze all the documents originating in central files in Langley and create copies for the shadow file cabinet. By mid-1996, there were twenty-seven individuals involved in running the shadow file cabinet, organized along a trapdoor system of interconnection, no two people in this unit knowing what any other two people were doing.

But the shadow file cabinet, while major, was only one of Denton's pillars. The other was sheer nerve.

By the mid-nineties, Roper had antagonized so many people that his days were numbered, not that he could appreciate this fact. Nor did he notice that one of his subordinates was making a very subtle sort of name for himself.

One of the people who did notice Denton was Roper's boss, the Deputy Director of CIA for Counter Intelligence, Keith Lehrer.

Lehrer was of Tiggermann's generation, and like most everybody else, he had dismissed Tiggy as a hack; after all, Tiggermann had worked the shadow road. Fortunately—for Lehrer—he'd been in England when Tiggy woke up, so he hadn't antagonized any of the pups when Tiggy started tightening the screws around Langley, cementing his position under cover of the ombudsman cleaning up the "rampant corruption" around CIA. By the time Lehrer showed up back in Virginia, Tiggy was running his own little shop, already far more powerful than the traditional ladder-climbing Lehrer.

But Lehrer was steady, so when Lehrer gave Denton a call, Denton knew how it was.

"With Roper out, they might well give you someone else to answer to," Lehrer astutely opened, dangling the one asset Denton had that might change—namely, his freedom.

"I don't mind answering to anyone," said Denton, the two of them sitting in their respective offices, only secure phone lines between them.

"What about having a little more leeway of your own?" Lehrer pushed when they met for a second interview, this time in an anonymous steak house in Potomac, not too far from where Denton lived.

"Leeway?" asked Denton, the picture of innocence. "I've got plenty of leeway, why would I need more?" In fact, he looked so innocent that Lehrer briefly thought that maybe Denton really *didn't* need any more leeway. The talks broke off.

Meanwhile, the shadow file cabinet was humming along like a finely tuned engine, delivering information every week. Denton decided that the time had come to lose Roper and cement the position he wanted. Lehrer was Denton's ticket, but he had to do the job smoothly, or the effect would be lost on him. Denton decided to turn to the safety deposit box.

The safety deposit box was at a bank just off Dupont Circle. Inside the box, there was an Apple Macintosh PowerBook inside a magnetically sealed protective pouch, capable of storing literally millions of pages of information. Three people knew of the box's existence—Denton, Atmajian, and Paula Baker—and they were all wary of it, because it contained the distilled information the shadow file cabinet had accumulated, positively radioactive stuff.

Paula and Atta-boy got first crack at the raw intelligence coming out of the shadow-file-cabinet office in Alexandria, as did Denton. But information that was useful and/or important but not obviously necessary was put inside the Mac, a Pandora's box of secrets of the most varied sort. Some of the secrets were trivial in the larger scheme of things, others earth-shattering, sure to bring down governments. But the common element to all the information stored was that it was perfect blackmail material, Denton's stock-in-trade.

Denton turned to the Macintosh computer, "Moonshine," to get some ideas for getting rid of Roper, and what he came across was perfect. Perfect because there was only one person who would be splattered, and perfect because the information was untraceable. Not even a sidewise glance would fall Denton's way. It would be a slow process, but it would work to a T.

Denton called up Lehrer from the bank. "You know, Roper is still my boss, so I think our conversations were interesting but academic."

"I see," answered Lehrer.

"But even if Roper resigned, I wouldn't want his job. I like my job. I wouldn't mind having a job like the one I have, similar to the one I have, analogous if you will, for the rest of my career."

"I see . . ."

"I must be going now."

Lehrer thought Denton a little weird when he hung up, but paid him no attention. Obviously, he'd been wrong about Denton—he *was* a lightweight, always whipping out that stupid black book of his to note down interesting phrases and sentences he heard, always talking about his novels. Good dinner party guest, but no one to take seriously. His novels weren't even very good, in Lehrer's opinion. He forgot all about Denton.

Six weeks later, on a Friday evening, Lehrer was finishing up at his office, getting ready to go home, when he opened a package that had arrived through the interoffice mail. It was a videocassette with no markings. Lehrer popped it into his office VCR, hit play, and saw something on the television screen that sent chills up his spine.

It was a gray-bearded black man sitting in a suit and tie—Ed Bradley, the nemesis of the Agency PR department. *Oh shit*, thought Lehrer, *another* 60 Minutes *exposé*. And that was exactly what it was, complete with interviews with "CIA operatives," who were in actuality just a cut above office boys in the outside world.

The piece detailed how the French, of all people, had some assets in Seattle, working at Boeing on some silly radar equipment. But the *60 Minutes* piece treated this trivia as if it were right up there with nuclear secrets, managing to neatly smear Roper by name and face while alleging that the head of North American Counter Intelligence had ignored repeated warnings that the radar people in Seattle were security risks. Lehrer braced for the whack *he* would take. After all, Roper worked for *him*.

But then, there was music in the air.

"The remarkable thing," Bradley droned on in a reasonable facsimile of evenhandedness, "is that Carl Roper's superiors at Langley did not know about his willful ignorance of the evidence against these French spies."

Lehrer felt giddy. He watched the rest of the tape, rapt, the piece unfolding like a Shakespearean drama and all the shit falling squarely on Roper. Lehrer was so enraptured he played the tape again, not even noticing that the phone had been ringing a half-dozen times. He picked it up.

"What!"

A voice bright and full of a smile said, "Like the tape?"

It was Denton. It would be lucky if Roper managed to get through the Langley gates at all, come Monday morning. When the piece aired on national TV Sunday night, the fallout scandal would end Roper's career as abruptly as the fall of a guillotine. And here Denton was calling—

Denton, who had somehow managed to manufacture the end of Roper. The *nerve*, to manipulate the national press that way and expect to get away with it. And the frightening thing about it was, Lehrer knew that Denton *was* going to get away with it. But he didn't let on.

With a voice steady and a little bored, he said, "I'm finishing up here, but I have a minute, if you really want to talk."

"Thank you, but I can't tonight. But how about Monday evening?"

"Fine, fine."

"I'll see you then. Goodbye. Oh, by the way, do you know something amusing? Your name."

"I beg your pardon?"

" 'Keith Lehrer.' You have the same name as a famous philosopher. He wrote a very influential book about epistemology, called *Knowledge*. Keith Lehrer-the-philosopher is a very well-known skeptic. Isn't that amusing?"

"I suppose so . . ."

"I'll see you on Monday. Goodbye."

Denton hung up before Lehrer could say anything to that. A week later, Denton took the job of chief assistant to Keith Lehrer, the same position Denton had held under Roper, only two rungs higher. Denton was now Assistant to the Deputy Director of the Central Intelligence Agency—the head of the agency but twice removed. The position he had wanted all along.

That had been two years ago. Now, Lehrer and Denton sat alone in Lehrer's study, smoking and thinking over the evening just passed. The study was small and cozy, with a massive desk counterpointed by an equally massive fireplace, the only source of light in the room. Two wing chairs faced the fire, and the two men sat there, staring as they let time pass.

"Interesting people, tonight," said Denton. He had already written down their names on some index cards he always carried, along with a brief synopsis of what they had been like and what they did.

"Yes . . ." said Lehrer dreamily, thinking openly. "Sepsis . . . ?"

"What about him?"

"Where are you?"

Denton didn't press to know why Lehrer was asking, knowing by now that Lehrer asked first, explained later. "He's in the country. For sure. Came across the Canadian border three days ago. Something's up. I think we can come up with something in the short to medium range. But we don't know exactly what's going on at this point."

"Find out."

"I'm working on it."

Denton rose to change the music playing in the background. The music was the von Karajan version of Grieg's *Peer Gynt*, a piece Denton loved but considered inappropriate for this meeting. Lehrer had no taste for classical music, so Denton found himself giving his boss classical compact discs for birthdays and Christmases so that he, Denton, would have something decent to listen to when he visited. Now it paid off as he chose Solti conducting Debussy's *Nocturnes*; such a wonderful conductor, delicate without ever being too deferential.

"Do you want simple elimination or turning?"

"I'm not sure," Lehrer finally answered, opening the door for Denton's suggestions.

"Turning would be costly but possible. He *is* simply a gun for hire."

"A bomb for hire," Lehrer said dreamily, a phrase that instantly captured Denton's imagination. He whipped out his little black book and noted it down.

"Yes . . . yes, interesting phrase that, 'a bomb for hire.' I like it." He replaced the notebook in his Huntsman suit and stared at the fire once again. "If he's in the United States he's here for a reason, nothing that will be beneficial to us. I think it would be best to eliminate Sepsis from the picture."

"Let's not be too hasty. Find out first, then we decide. . . . The Director has been hassling me again about 'jet-set terrorists,' someone like Carlos," Lehrer said, turning to Denton.

"Ah yes, the Kaiser Söze of professional assassins. I heard that the guy they captured a few years back wasn't the real Carlos, that the real Carlos got away," Denton said.

"Carlos? Yes, that man they picked up was just a patsy. The real Car-

los is retired. But Sepsis is active. The Director wants something flashy
to show the Senate Intelligence Committee."

"Sepsis would be ideal," Denton said, meaning it. Sepsis was a
flashy—if decidedly shadowy—assassin for hire.

"Yes. . . . But Sepsis is useful. He's not a washup. Find out first, then
we decide whether to turn him or expunge him."

"Very well."

The first movement of the Débussy piece gave way to the more stri-
dent "Fêtes," and Denton for one considered that something.

THREE

A Life of Ease and Pleasure

She lived because she was late.

Sister Marianne belonged to Opus Dei, a strict Roman Catholic order with carefully delineated limits as to what any one of its nuns could do. It wasn't for everyone. It was a difficult life based on order and structure, totalitarian in the demands it made on its nuns. Certain books were proscribed, actions that other Catholics wouldn't raise an eyebrow over were out and out forbidden.

But like certain other professional women her age (she was thirty-six), Sister Marianne didn't bother with the limits of her life—her satisfactions came from doing all the things the freedom of this life allowed her. Because she *was* free: Though the restrictions of her religious life might be impossible to most, all her pleasures and thrills were safely within its borders. The things she would be doing this morning were no exception.

Chronic insomnia had gotten her out of bed early, again. Making the most of it, she'd jogged four miles, keeping an easy pace so as not to tire herself out before first light. Afterwards, while she showered and got dressed, she turned her considerable attention to mapping out her morning. It was barely five and Mass was at seven, so in the two hours she had, she would write notes for her students, answer personal letters, prepare a couple of points in her lecture notes, and if she had the time—if and *only* if she had the time—she might indulge in preparing for her project.

Dressed and ready for the day, she walked to her office in the main building of the convent. The stillness was inviting. Walking down the hallway in the dark morning, Sister Marianne looked a pious version of a commuter, her habit starched and ironed, a discreet cross hanging from her neck, her left hand tightly gripping a battered leather briefcase as her right hand held her morning tea and a bagel precariously balanced on the lip of the mug. No Communion for her this morning; she hadn't confessed in two days.

Lately, her confessions seemed to fall into the same rhythm, the same texture to her pleas for absolution.

"Forgive me, Father, for I have sinned, it's been three days since my last confession."

"What sins have you to confess?"

"I thought cruel thoughts about Sister Elizabeth and Sister Danielle. I was too harsh on a student. My temper slipped. This last term has been grueling. Thank goodness it's almost over."

"And . . . ?"

"And I also took the Lord's name in vain." Marianne cringed. "Twice."

"Marianne, we've discussed this several times now. This is a dreadful habit you simply *must* break. It's not just a bad habit, it's a sin."

"I know, Father, I know. But old habits die hard. I'm not smoking."

"Should we be thankful for small miracles? *Think*, Marianne. . . . Your prayers?"

"I've prayed for my child. For those poor people in that Atlanta building that burned down. For those soldiers in that helicopter, so sad for their families . . ."

It would go like that, but that would be all. Her confessions, or her celibacy or poverty or obedience or modesty—they all seemed a paltry price to pay for the serenity and sense of place that was hers here, in her New Hampshire convent, as safe and snug as a bug in a rug. None of the sacrifices of her life seemed like sacrifices at all. Sometimes, after confession, more often as of late, she did not feel absolved but uneasy; ashamed that so much was hers for so very little.

She got to her office and opened the door, which was of course unlocked.

Maintaining two offices was difficult. She had one in Carpenter Hall, where she tried to keep only her students' materials. Her convent office was supposed to be strictly for her research. But nothing was ever like it was supposed to be, her college office overflowing with research material, her convent office desk groaning under the weight of student blue books and their delicately deep thoughts. And when she was in one office, she was always missing things that were in the other.

She set her briefcase on her desk and started reviewing the new day: Mass to 7:30, drive to Hanover by 8:00, catch up on her blitz mail and snail mail by 8:45. Class would be through 9:50, so she would talk to students until 10:00, take a break through 10:15, and then the rest of the morning would be spent preparing her Freshman Seminar. Then, a bright spot in her day: Marlene Heck over in the history department was supposed to pick her up at her office and the two of them would have lunch with Marlene's husband at EBA's, or maybe the Sweet Tomato in Lebanon. As she opened her briefcase and arranged the morning's work, she decided to splurge and allow herself a full-hour lunch today with Marlene and Kevin.

At 1:40, no later, she had to be back in her Carpenter Hall office. She had to finish up her student notes before giving her senior seminar at 2:50. Come 4:15, she would begin today's office hour, which would probably run through 6:00 if that poor Dugan boy showed up, as she was sure he would. But Dugan boy or no Dugan boy, Marianne would be driving back to the convent at 6:15, no matter what. Her favorite niece—actually her only niece, little Marianne—would be five tomorrow, and big Marianne had every intention of calling her up in Kyoto and being the first to wish her a happy birthday. She'd already sent her present in the mail, a Malibu Dream-Girl Barbie little Marianne had none too subtly hinted at.

Sister Marianne sat down, her papers arranged in front of her. She took a yellow legal pad from one of the bottom drawers, flipped over the two front pages without writing in them, and then began on her student notes, taking up one sheet of paper per student. She had been thinking about her seniors all night, and now she tried hard to get her small conclusions on paper. If she was lucky, she would give them some clues that might help them along. She prayed she would.

She started slowly, but then her hand took over, writing effortlessly. Overnight, it was as if all her thoughts had arranged themselves along logical lines. But then she got to the poor Dugan boy.

The Dugan boy worried her so much. He was too lonely, Marianne decided, and too willing to spend all his time doing work for her class. She wished he would take some time to enjoy his last year and not push so hard. Whenever he came to her office hours, she had the odd sensation she was talking to a colleague rather than to a student. Marianne found it decidedly unsettling. What kind of a life could such a boy be leading? And making her more nervous still, the Dugan boy was a brilliant student—he could afford to take the time to do other things. But he wasn't, sacrificing those other things that might be more important, for the sake of his studies. Marianne didn't think he was old enough to be narrowing the scope of his life so drastically, specializing in art history and ignoring everything else. It worried her, and she didn't know what to do.

Before she could stop herself, Sister Marianne thought that what the Dugan boy *really* needed was to get laid. She scrapped the idea, but was tempted to write it down in her notes: "Dugan—get laid." Sister Marianne laughed out loud.

Another worry was a young woman in that same senior seminar by the name of Packair, Jenny Packair. She wasn't . . . applying herself.

"You mean she's been cheating?" Marlene had asked when Marianne first brought up the problem.

"No! She's not cheating. It's only that her papers contain ideas very similar to Edmund Gettier's . . ."

"Is the language also 'very similar' to Edmund's?"

"Well, to an extent, maybe, I'm not sure . . ."

Edmund Gettier, her doctoral thesis adviser and an eminence in the field, read one of the papers Marianne sent him, calling her back the evening he received it. "The girl is cheating! She stole some of my best stuff! This is just like when I was teaching in Hamburg in '71," he moaned, going on about his days teaching in Europe, back when he'd been an itinerant lecturing professor before he finally settled down to a tenured chair at Harvard in the early eighties. "She'll keep cheating if you don't stop her now! Do something about her!"

But Marianne couldn't. For the past two weeks, since she'd noticed the . . . misappropriation, for lack of a better word, she had tried to solve the problem as it ought to be solved. But it seemed that the more she prayed, the less will she had. It left her feeling miserable.

Like a junkie eyeing her next fix, Marianne started glancing at her computer as she came no closer to any solution to the Packair problem. The machine hummed softly, little toasters with wings flying across the screen. Finally, unable to resist, she set aside her student notes and turned to the project, soon to start.

She had tons of notes, meticulously arranged. Here were the research notes on previous restoration efforts, here were the field calculations Edmund had made last February. On a separate file, she had mapped out a work schedule for the eighteen months she would be working on the project. Every week had been carefully planned out, with little arrows pointing to what she and her team would be doing if they fell behind or beat the schedule. She knew she ought to be writing her letters instead of working on her project—she shouldn't be doing a Dugan. But the spirit is willing, the flesh weak. Sister Marianne started working on her notes.

It was not quite six when she started thinking about the project once again. But it was ten minutes after seven when Sister Rose suddenly came into her office.

"Marianne!"

"Huh?" she asked, looking as guilty as if she'd been caught with a needle in her hand and a rubber cord wrapped around her arm. She blushed a deep crimson.

"You're gonna be late *again!*" Sister Rose said before dashing off, already late herself for morning Mass.

I'm late because I'm absentminded. You're *late because you* sleep *late,* she said to herself, instantly feeling guilty over such a cruel thought. More to confess about this evening, she thought, quickly saving what she was doing on the computer's memory. She began printing up her notes for her morning class.

As the printer gave off that vague ozone smell and slowly began printing up her lecture, Sister Marianne packed her briefcase. She walked to the printer by the window and stood over it, willing it to print faster. It didn't. She sighed and looked up.

Outside, through the window, she could see Sister Rose running into the convent's chapel, fifty yards away. Sister Rose went in the front door just as a man in a Roto-Rooter jumpsuit came out the back, from the service entrance. He was a thin, dark-haired young man with a casually anonymous face—a bizarre sight at seven in the morning. Sister Marianne thought nothing of him as the printer coughed up her notes: last winter, Roto-Rooter men were coming out of that service entrance almost every day, walking right past Marianne's window, trying to "unscrew the unscrewtable," as one of the men working on the water heater had so memorably put it. Marianne waved at the young man, who was not ten yards from her office window by now, but he didn't see her. The sunlight reflecting off the window made Marianne invisible to anyone outside.

She was about to open the window and call out to the young man when the printer finished up with her notes, beeping to let her know it was done. She picked up the printed sheets and tamped their edges, forming a neat little pile as she looked around for a manila folder. When she glanced up, the young man in the Roto-Rooter jumpsuit was gone. She put her briefcase on the window ledge and began stowing her notes away, hurrying, aware she was late for Mass, not liking that it would be the second time this week. She snapped her briefcase shut, and then the chapel exploded.

It exploded outward, then inward. No fire, but gray-black debris spewed out of the chapel's windows, the stained glass shattering with the force of the explosion. The roof, a shingle roof, rose up in the air and seemed to stay there, as if levitating, as if deciding what to do next.

The chapel had been built of stone and mortar, sturdy stuff, only the roof and windows rickety. So when the explosion came and the roof rose, bodies—nuns' bodies, black-dressed and blood-soaked—came out of the windows and the roof, as if the whole chapel were a pot which had suddenly come to a boil and then overflowed. But none of the walls so much as cracked.

Bodies landed on the surrounding grass, on fire, mutilated, ruptured, broken, dead. Sister Marianne, uncomprehending, her conscious mind emptied of everything, watched as the roof collapsed back in on itself, crashing into the chapel. Then her mind snapped back.

She ran out of her office, leaving everything behind. Through the convent halls she ran, bursting through the front door and across to the wreckage of the chapel, pulling off her black habit and black over-clothes as she got to her burning sisters. With her overclothes, as big as blankets, she tried to smother the flames that burned some of the nuns around the chapel, not recognizing which nuns were which.

Oddly, there was no sound. No screaming, no crashing, no grating sounds. There had only been the sound of a great balloon popping, and then the sound of a giant sheet of paper being crumpled up be-tween two great hands as the roof collapsed. No unusual sound at all.

And the look of the explosion was, curiously, ordinary, even expected. Some clumps of grass were burning, the neat lawn around the chapel now blackened for ten yards all about. The chapel itself, its sturdy walls still standing but otherwise destroyed, was an ordinary sight, so remi-niscent of buildings seen in a war or a terrible riot. And even the sight of bodies, too, was expected. Marianne had seen them all before, count-less times, on television, films, passing photographs. The sight was clichéd enough to be normal.

But the feel was the shock. Walking on the ground, Marianne felt her feet being singed, even through the thick soles of her shoes. The air was humid but cold, a strong breeze blowing in toward the chapel as if it were a black hole that was sucking out the air of the world. And the bodies of the nuns Sister Marianne touched . . . they had the consistency of warm wax.

Beating the flames out of the burning nuns, her hands seemed to sink into the bodies, as if they would first suck in her arms and then rip them from her shoulders. The ruined bodies of her sisters were black hulking masses of Play-Doh, the kind of plasticene Sister Marianne had given to her little niece on her birthday last year, the kind she was touching now.

Marianne beat the flames out of one nun and then went to the next, trying to stop them all from burning, and if it had been just the warmth and softness of wax, that would have been enough—bad enough, but enough. But there was more.

Some of the bodies didn't give like warm wax. Some of the bodies were hard and stiff and unyielding. And *these* bodies . . . they flaked. They flaked splinters of flesh.

Sister Marianne looked away from the body whose flames she was trying to beat out, the body of Sister Danielle, which was smoldering evilly, ready to catch fire again. Marianne had closed her eyes when she looked away, and when she opened them, she saw not two yards away the waist, genitalia, and legs of a nun, naked, her clothes blown clean off. There was no body attached to these limbs.

The last shreds of Sister Marianne's mind mercifully faded away. She functioned, but God was good and no longer allowed her to perceive.

Roto-Rooter man with a gun. Sirens. There were sirens sounding. And steaks. Steaks there were a-cooking. And then there were men and women in dirty yellow coats and helmets and they were stopping and they were covering and they were pushing them over away and then there were bright burning flat lights and then there was sound and then there was darkness and then there was silence and then there was nothing, nothing, nothing at all.

Chisholm was at her desk the morning the convent chapel exploded. As luck would have it, she was working on a project known as Archangel.

No significance to the name. FBI investigations are always assigned arbitrary names, as much to mask the scope of the investigation as to keep them straight in the minds of the agents. Since Rivera had made her his troubleshooter, Chisholm's unit had begun twenty-seven investigations, from Amiability (illegal immigrants paying off border patrols in New Mexico) to Zoolook (improper use of the photocopying machines at the Hoover Building—ooooh). But the twenty-seventh case, Archangel, was a doozy.

"Sanders," Chisholm called, looking through some interview files spread out on the glass desk. "Get me the interrogation report on Robert Hughes." No Sanders materialized, so Chisholm looked up.

"Sanders? Sanders!"

Howie Sanders was standing amid a bunch of Chisholm's agents, all of them looking at the wall-mounted television set. The little shit—or rather, the monstrously hulking shit dressed in cheap suit pants and white shirt, his service revolver in his shoulder holster—hadn't heard her, engrossed as they all were in what the television was showing.

"Sanders, goddammit, will you get over here?"

Sanders turned around, catching his boss's eye and feeling a little nervous. He ambled over to Margaret Chisholm as he talked. "Maggie, you won't believe what just happened—they blew up a nun's convent in New Hampshire."

"Who did?" she asked, uninterested.

"*They* did, who knows. Why would anyone kill some nuns?"

"I don't know why they'd off some penguins, but I *do* know why I'm going to off one of my deputies—Archangel. You know that little case we've been working on for two months? The one that isn't producing results because my agents are too busy watching TV?" she said, raising her voice slightly and looking at the knot of agents staring at the television. They pretended to ignore her but broke up anyway, going back to what they were doing. Morale, Margaret thought. No good when a big case brings in no results.

"But Maggie—"

"Archangel, Sanders. *Archangel.* Today."

Howie Sanders lumbered off to look for the Hughes interrogation report. Archangel had ground to a halt in the past three weeks, and the strain was showing. With no leads, Chisholm was falling into the habit of avoiding Rivera, who was not happy with what he was getting, which was nothing. *Any day now, any day the ax is gonna come down.* The imagery reminded her of last weekend, so she shunted it aside, plugging away at the files and field reports, but not before catching a glimpse of the television screen.

It was on CNN, a live shot. The cameraman was panning around, then focusing distantly on a woman with short auburn hair, dressed in what looked like a slip or nightgown, sitting on the running board of a fire engine. Over this footage, an off-camera reporter droned on and on. The firemen tried shooing away the cameraman, but he pushed through anyway. The woman in the white nightgown looked completely lost. Then there was some more footage, shot earlier.

". . . was first on the scene, the images as you can see shocking and . . ."

In the background of this footage, the wrecked, exploded chapel was clearly visible. In the foreground, there were blackened masses, burned bodies scattered about, and the same woman in the white nightgown running around with a big black cape, looking, bizarrely, like a matador. But the woman wasn't egging on some animal—she was using the black cape to smother out the charred bodies, some of which were out and out on fire, others only smoldering.

Sister Marianne was unaware that she was doing any of this, at the time. From the footage, it was clear too that she was unaware of the camera filming her. But the cameraman from the network, up in New Hampshire for some tomato festival, was thrilled to be getting this footage, as was his producer. Neither of them thought to help the nun. The producer was thinking about the "human drama" angle the story would generate. The cameraman was hoping he had enough tape to catch it all.

". . . cannot imagine the human tragedy of what has happened. The bodies of nuns are lying all about this peaceful New Hampshire convent . . ."

As the footage rolled on, the first of the firemen arrived in a big truck, two more trucks racing behind on a road that curved around the back of the convent. A couple of the firefighters from the first truck, a man and a woman, grabbed Sister Marianne and led her away from the bodies as the other firemen set to putting out the remaining fires and helping the burned nuns. But there was really no need, and the firemen knew it, all of them looking shocked and resigned as the camera rolled on and on.

The footage cut to a live shot of a reporter, the bombed-out chapel just over his shoulder. Then the camera panned to Marianne once again as three people, a higher-up from the New Hampshire police and a couple of plainclothesmen, approached the nun and blocked the camera's view.

Marianne was lost. Bit by bit her perceptions were coming back, her conscious mind seeping in, a tub slowly filling up with sense data, sensations, and then awful, certain knowledge. She looked up and saw a man and a woman, Colby and McKenna, both of whom knelt by Sister Marianne, while the New Hampshire policeman stood behind them.

"Sister?" asked the woman. "I'm Agent Georgina Colby, of the FBI. We have to ask you some questions?"

"What?" asked Marianne. She had heard the words clearly, but they made absolutely no sense to her at all.

McKenna glanced at Colby, then away. The nun had reminded him too much of his mother, Clara, and her Alzheimer's.

Colby pressed on. "We have to ask you some questions. Maybe it would be a good idea to get you some clothes. Do you have any clothes?"

"In my cell," Marianne said absently—making Colby think, *Is she a nun or a felon?*—realizing then what the Sister meant.

"Sure, we'll get them. Why don't you show us where they are? Where's your cell?"

Sister Marianne stood up, glancing at the chapel. Then she started getting the shakes, bad. The cameras, though, didn't see this. The New Hampshire policeman for once was glad he was overweight. He was so big and so fat he blocked the cameras' view.

Edmund Gettier was the first on the scene. He had been on his morning walk to his office in Cambridge, his headphone radio tuned to the news, like always, when a special report came in that an Opus Dei convent had been blown to smithereens in New Hampshire. He knew it was Marianne's convent; there weren't any other Opus Dei convents in all of New England north of the Massachusetts line. So he rushed to the closest automated teller machine, withdrew as much money as it would give him, hailed a cab, jumped in, and told the cabbie in his peculiar, clipped accent, "A wager—fifty dollars against you getting to Logan Airport in less than ten minutes."

"You're on, buddy."

He scarcely noticed losing the bet, he was so wrapped up in the news he heard. The flight up to Lebanon, the closest airport to the convent, took all of thirty-five minutes—ten minutes off par, a seeming record—but all during the flight he kept changing the stations on his headphone radio set, searching for more news, paying more attention to what he heard than to the flight or to the crazy driving of the cabbie who took him from the Lebanon airport to the Lyme police station.

So by eight-thirty, exactly an hour after he first heard the news, he finally took off and pocketed his headphone radio as he walked into the Lyme police station. The place was crawling with press.

The Lyme police station wasn't used to all the attention. After all, it was just a small-town cop house. By the front counter in the lobby, reporters—both local and network—kept pestering the desk sergeant in hopes of getting something quotable, *anything* quotable. The desk sergeant had tried being polite and helpful at first, but already he was sick of the reporters. They didn't seem to want niceness—they wanted quotes, stories, something to go on. To Edmund Gettier's relief there weren't any cameras here, only reporters with tape recorders swarming around, lighting on the desk sergeant (who had better things to do) and then buzzing around the lobby, all of them knowing that the *real* feeding was going on at the site of the explosion.

The bombing was going to make the national news, for sure . . . if it *was* a bombing. If it wasn't, the news producers were already thinking of playing up the irony of God's wrath descending on a chapel full of nuns, a morbid kind of raillery that they thought so witty so long as it was at someone else's expense. So if it was the "wrath of God" angle, the producers were going to need as many "human interest" stories as possible to milk the story over at least a couple of news cycles—hence the reporters here at the Lyme police station.

The professor made his way to the desk sergeant through the hive of press, who ignored him. "I am Edmund Gettier," he told the sergeant, clipped and polished.

"You don't look like the Pope to me, and even if you did, you're still not getting in," he said, much ruder than he ever thought he could be.

"I am the father of one of the Sisters," he said, a huge mistake on his part. The desk sergeant suddenly paid him some serious attention, but then so did all the reporters, zeroing in on him like fresh meat.

"Which one?"

"Fuck, where's a goddamn *camera!*"

"What are you feeling now, not knowing if your daughter's dead?"

"Do you think it was a bomb that killed your daughter?"

"Do you have any comment about the bombings?"

"Do you think any abortion rights group is responsible for bombing your daughter's convent?"

"Do you think this is an anti-Catholic reactionary action?"

As the desk sergeant shepherded him into the back of the station while simultaneously swatting away the reporters, that last phrase spun around in Gettier's mind: "reactionary action." *What kind of a phrase is* that? he thought trivially, too surprised to think logically about what he had just witnessed.

The door leading away from the lobby was buzzed open and Gettier and the desk sergeant walked inside down a long white corridor, the sight of the two reminding one of the reporters of Abbott and Costello—the European-sounding character a tall, elegant man wearing a bow tie, the armed police sergeant a short, fat, waddling Emmet. They disappeared from sight as the door closed.

"Betcha this whole thing is tied into those church burnings down South."

The reporters fed on that, and on each other.

Gettier was led down the hallway to an interrogation room door, where he was asked to wait. Presently, Colby came out and introduced herself.

"You're the father of one of the nuns?"

"A white lie," he said. "I am a colleague of one of the nun's, Sister Marianne. We're very close, we've written books together. Is she all right? The news didn't say anything about survivors."

"And your name is . . . ?"

"Edmund Gettier. Is she all right?" he said, a bit more forceful and desperate.

"Can I see some identification please?"

"Of course." Gettier produced his Harvard faculty library card, the only photo identification he had this morning, since he didn't drive. Colby gave it a careful scrutiny before reluctantly handing it back.

"I'm sorry about that—a lot of reporters have been trying to get in," she said, and Gettier let out a long breath, relieved.

He took another breath and said, "Can I see Marianne?"

"How did you know she was all right?"

Gettier frowned and looked down on Agent Colby. "You don't look as if something bad has happened to her."

"Quite an observation. She's fine," she said. "She was late for morning Mass at the chapel, where the explosion took place."

"The water heater, eh?"

"Beg pardon?"

"I said, the water heater. There were troubles with the water heater all last winter, never quite solved."

"Yes, yes. The water heater," she said . . . and now she knew how she was going to handle the press. "Would you like to see the Sister?"

"Very much."

Colby opened the door for Gettier and watched as the nun instantly recognized him. So Colby closed the door and let them be, walking to the reporters to give them the preliminary lowdown: Apparently a faulty water heater, not a bomb.

Gettier, in the room alone with Sister Marianne, hugged her. Supported her, he realized—her legs had given out on her.

By eleven, she was all talked out. The privilege and curse of an educated mind—words seemed like a box of tools, tools that were supposed to be used to put back together every moment, every feeling, every sensation and emotion until the machine was up and running once again, ready to go out on its mission of torture and repetition. That's what her words did for her, at first—they repeated and replayed the explosion over and over. But, like with a ticking clock and a set of screwdrivers, or like with a working engine and a torque wrench, language and words could take the machine apart and make it stop, leaving it useless, or harmless. And so that's what she did: she kept at it with all the words in her toolbox, working on the evil machine compulsively, not stopping until all the discrete parts were spread out on her workbench, the words running dry only when the machine was finally and completely still. For now.

Through all this, Edmund Gettier listened. He didn't know what else to do. He sat and listened and rubbed her shoulders, old enough not to feel guilty that he did nothing else, old enough to realize there was nothing else he *could* do. He just let her talk through his relief that she was all right. Marianne talked until there was nothing left to say.

Around eleven, Colby came in again briefly and asked to speak to Gettier for a moment. Gettier left Marianne after patting her hand and giving her a sad smile.

"I'll be right back," he said. Marianne nodded, too tired to say anything. A uniformed policewoman, Trish, came into the interrogation room and sat in a chair a little distance from Marianne on the sofa. With a small part of her, Marianne realized that the policewoman was there to make sure she didn't hurt herself somehow. She couldn't work up the energy to find this amusing. Instead, she looked out the window, staring at a small ridge in the distance, green and lightly populated with trees but no people.

Gettier and Colby walked down the hallway and into another interrogation room, this one colder, an interrogation room for suspects and criminals. They sat at a small table across from each other, Colby taking out a stenographer's pad and a small portable tape recorder.

"Thank you. This is for the record," she began, flipping the tape recorder on and setting it on the table. "I want to ask you some background information about Sister Marianne and her convent. Rules say that I have to tell you that you can have a lawyer present."

"That won't be necessary."

"Thank goodness. Some people think because you ask them questions you're charging them with something," she said, smiling, trying to break the ice. But Gettier didn't react, so Colby got serious.

"All right then, this interview is on the record. Please state your name and relationship to the witness."

"My name is Edmund Gettier. I am a professor of art history at Harvard University, where Sister Marianne was my student. She now teaches at Dartmouth," he said in a somewhat haughty, somewhat cool voice. But heck, Colby wasn't supposed to like the guy, just pump him.

"But you keep in touch."

"Of course we do," he said as McKenna, Colby's partner, walked into the interrogation room and stood by the door.

"Sister Marianne's real name is Faith Crenshaw, is that correct?"

"Yes."

"So you're close to her?"

"Merely knowing her name does not make me 'close to her.' But yes."

Gettier said nothing more, Colby having to lean forward and motion with her hand. "Yes you . . . ?"

"Yes I what?" said Gettier, looking at her seriously.

Colby frowned. "You're not from this country, are you," she stated, hoping the miscommunication was a language thing. It wasn't.

"Correct," he said distantly. Colby sighed. She'd thought this would be easy. But now that she wanted something from Gettier instead of the other way around, she realized he wouldn't give her anything unless she asked for it specifically. She hated these kinds of witnesses.

"Since when and under what circumstances have you known Sister Marianne?" she asked without inflection.

"I have known her for fifteen years, since shortly after she took her vows and became a nun, shortly after I started teaching at Harvard. I supervised her doctoral thesis in Renaissance architecture."

McKenna walked toward one of the empty chairs facing Gettier and sat down as he spoke. "Do you know anything about her background?"

"Some," he said, leaving it at that.

"And?" he asked.

Gettier sighed condescendingly. "Her family lives in New York, very prominent bankers as I understand. She has an older brother, who is married and lives in Japan."

"What about her work?" asked Colby.

"Professionally she is very much respected. In fact, last year she caused quite a stir."

A clue maybe. "Oh?"

Gettier smiled at McKenna's interest, looking at him casually, as if from far away. "Professionally speaking. She published a very controversial book on Renaissance construction."

"Oh."

Colby suppressed a smile and continued writing in her notepad, not looking at Gettier as she spoke. "What do you know about her order? She is a member of Opus Dei, correct?"

"Obviously," he said, with the naturally condescending voice of a born lecturer, "since the convent was an Opus Dei convent."

Colby lost the smile. One unnice guy, this Gettier. "Do you know anything about them?"

"Very little, actually. Come to think of it, Marianne and I have never spoken of her order."

"We've heard they're pretty controversial," McKenna butted in again. "You wouldn't have any idea why anyone would want to harm them, would you?"

"I thought it was the water heater," said Gettier, looking at McKenna carefully. Colby could have strangled her partner. She cringed when he pressed on.

"But if this was deliberate, do you know of anyone who might be behind it?"

Gettier leveled that haughty, distance gaze on McKenna, pausing for effect. "No, no idea at all. For all I know, the wrath of God descended on them for no reason."

In the pleasantly furnished interrogation room, Marianne stood up and walked around. Trish, the female police officer, watched her narrowly but surreptitiously. She was a big, hefty woman, and if this nun tried anything . . . She wouldn't try anything.

Marianne walked around the room, lost, touching things casually and then turning her attention to the window, placing her hand flat on the glass as she looked out at the distant ridge.

She saw something, distantly, indistinct. But she had sharp eyes, 20/5. At about a hundred, a hundred and ten yards, peeking above the ridge, Sister Marianne saw that anonymous young man's face again, the man in the Roto-Rooter jumpsuit of this morning, looking straight back at her. He was looking at her through a telescopic sight.

The bullets ripped the glass of the window, tiny little slivery shards leaping away, pelting Sister Marianne as the hefty Trish jumped up from her chair and tackled the nun, sending her to the ground; she was so forceful that she nearly cracked one of Marianne's ribs.

The room was showered with more pieces of glass, but Trish knew they were safe, below the angle of the bullets' trajectory. She whipped out her walkie-talkie as she called for help, instinctively checking Marianne for bullets. Trish knew glass sharded. She didn't know bulletproof glass did too.

Part 2

FOUR

Matter C
(Building Bridges)

They watched it on videotape, the times' new witness with the untouchable reputation.

Rivera and Chisholm were alone in a medium-sized conference room, sitting at an oval table big enough for twelve people.

Tall, fat, living in the dominion of cheap cotton-blend suits and still cheaper patterned ties, Mario Rivera sat at the head of the table, looking a lot more like some small-time Boston pol than a Bureau deputy director. In his pudgy, doughy hands he restlessly rolled a black remote control, staring at the television set in the wall cabinet as the videotape scrolled by.

"This is Matter C," he rumbled without looking at Chisholm. "We're handling it."

Chisholm didn't react to this. Dressed in an understated business suit, she sat to Rivera's right, leaning back in her chair and watching only snatches of the tape before looking away at the thick tan carpeting. The videotape made her queasy.

Neither Rivera nor Chisholm trusted videotape much. Everything outside the frame of the viewfinder, the motives, the explanations, the truth that expressed its end result in the videotape—that was all hidden, and therefore unknown. But they watched it anyway, looking out that window and trying to figure out what was just beyond its scope.

This footage would never make the evening news. It was more than a little disturbing. It showed the remains of the nuns' chapel.

Blackened, dismembered bodies lay on green grass. Some patches of the manicured lawn were soot-stained and smoking; other spots had obviously needed to be doused by fire extinguishers. All of the bodies smoldered. There was a blackened clump lying on untouched grass, trailing a black something or other. The cameraman, curious, approached it steadily, then jittered suddenly before turning steady once again. The basketball-sized clump was a nun's head, her habit still covering her hair and trailing away across the green grass; she had had black hair turning to gray at the temples. No way this would ever make the network news.

"Twenty-two dead nuns, damn near a twenty-third," said Rivera, staring mesmerized at the screen. "The sole survivor is one Sister Marianne, and she nearly got nailed at the local police station. If it hadn't been for some bulletproof glass, she'd be dead too."

"Can you turn it off?"

Rivera glanced at Chisholm, then snapped off the television instead of the videotape player by mistake, which was just as well. With the screen suddenly black, Chisholm could pretend that she'd imagined what she'd just seen.

"We've got a couple of agents on site, Colby and McKenna. This Sister Marianne says she saw a man dressed in a Roto-Rooter outfit make it out of the chapel just before it blew. She said it was the same man who took those potshots at her. We got a sketch artist up in Burlington. He's talking to her right now. Lab reports came in yesterday afternoon and get this—plain old mercury switches and an el cheapo wireless trigger, but cellulose casing."

Chisholm whistled, her eyes vacant, on automatic. She knew she was going to have vivid nightmares about her son tonight.

"Yeah, I hear you," said Rivera. "Real bad guys. Real well-funded bad guys. From matches we got through Interpol we traced the stuff to Sepsis."

It was enough to break her away from what she'd seen. Chisholm looked at Rivera for the first time since the tape had begun rolling, remembering what she knew about Sepsis.

He was the new Carlos, one very nasty assassin for hire. He'd hit the scene six or seven years ago, and he was no one to mess with, not when there were no pictures of him, no leads on him, and especially when there were no informants to weasel him out.

On cop shows and news programs, the piggies are always bright and clever. But that's just TV. Ordinary police work, whatever the level, whatever the situation, depends on snitching a lot more than on any kind of fancy sleuthing, because for whatever reasons—moral, practical, psychological—there are simply very few people on this earth who can plan and pull off a murder all on their own and get away with it. Someone aside from the killer knows who did it, and this someone always winds up talking too much.

But a man who *could* commit murder without confederates, by definition, had no one who could finger him. That's the problem with serial killers: They kill solo, the crazier ones not even aware that they're doing it. The police take years to catch them not because the cops are stupid but because there's no one around to snitch them out.

So take a man who can murder for hire without confederates and without any motive except money—that man is priceless and nearly impossible to catch. No one can snitch on him, and since he's doing it for money he has no motive and therefore no connection to the target. Unless he gets woefully sloppy or unlucky, no evidence will surface to pin the blame on him.

Such a man was Sepsis, aka Gaston Fremont, aka Guillermo Covarubillas, aka Helmut Vollmann, aka a half-dozen other aliases. The times' new Carlos, Sepsis murdered cleanly, nearly surgically, usually with no collateral damage, or at least not much anyway. And unlike

Carlos, Sepsis didn't even leave a whiff of political motivation—he killed strictly for money.

He'd gotten his name at the start of his career with a series of car bombs that had killed off a half-dozen Swiss bank officers for a Bolivian drug kingpin, the cars "bursting like popped blood cells," as a Zurich police captain had described it.

For the first three years of his career, Sepsis was strictly a bomber, blasting everything away. But then, suddenly, Sepsis had gotten uppity and started using much more refined modes of assassination—a hit on an IRA informant made to look as if the Brits had done it, the garroting of a former East German Stasi official while in his own jail cell, a spectacular one-shot kill of a Canadian politician in broad daylight, and the killing over a six-day period of the entire family of a CIA informant in Egypt, up to and including the strangulation of the man's three-month-old child—all done while carefully not laying a finger on the informant himself.

Sepsis was one assassin on a roll. And the craziest thing about him was, he was supposed to be all of twenty-four years old, which if true (and that was a big if) would make him way too young to have left any but the most superficial, innocuous paper trail. It also left open the obvious question: Where the hell had he gotten all this training?

"Sepsis ring a bell?"

"Enough of a bell that I know I ought to take a pass on this one, Mario."

"Sorry, I want you to take care of him."

Chisholm rolled her eyes. "I'm on Archangel," she said.

"Screw Archangel," Rivera shot right back. "You've been working on that for two months and so far you have jack. I see you avoiding me lately, I know you aren't producing results. Archangel is a moot point. This is important, Maggie. This Sepsis fuck made all these nuns very very dead. I want you to put a lid on him."

"Mario, I have my hands full. I can't start another major investigation. Use Willis. Use Jakobson."

"You're my troubleshooter, Maggie. Put Archangel on hold and go and shoot this Sepsis trouble down."

She sighed, knowing she would give in to what Rivera wanted. "How bad do you want this, Mario? I mean, how far can I go?"

He smiled and leaned back on his chair. "If you get this fuck, you can chop his fingers off and I'll kiss your sweet little ass instead of chewing it out. Good enough?"

"Good enough," she said, resigned to losing Archangel.

"But you're not gonna be alone," Rivera added, none too happy-camperish, getting ready for Margaret Chisholm's tantrum.

"Huh?"

"CIA's gonna be coming along for the ride," he said as he snatched up the phone and spoke into it.

"CIA? CIA! This is on American soil! CIA's only foreign, this is my ball game!" she spouted as Rivera hung up the phone, got up, and went to the door of the conference room, pretending piss-poorly that he wasn't hearing what he was hearing. And Rivera knew Margaret was only getting warmed up. Which was why he'd scheduled his next appointment for right after this briefing.

"Uhn-uh, no way," she went on as Rivera got to the door and opened it. "I *refuse* to run this with some CIA sleaze buckets hanging around my neck."

Rivera turned to Chisholm as his two guests, his next appointment, walked in.

"Margaret, this is Keith Lehrer and Nicholas Denton, CIA," he said.

Always nice to be appreciated," Denton said as he walked in, flashing his shark smile, thoroughly amused.

Rivera motioned for Lehrer and Denton to sit across the table from Chisholm, to Rivera's left, as he made his way back to the head of the conference table, introductions going all around. "Agent Margaret Chisholm, this is Deputy Director Keith Lehrer and Assistant Deputy Director Nicholas Denton."

Chisholm didn't bother to offer her hand, leaving Denton's dangling in midair. "Charmed," she said, Denton smiling as he held his tie to his stomach and sat down. Lehrer ignored Chisholm altogether.

"Agent Chisholm is going to be handling this investigation for the Bureau," Rivera said to Lehrer and Denton, before glancing quickly at Chisholm and smiling a quirky little smile, unable to resist. "She is our hatchet lady, and she reports to me and to the Director only. She has our full and total confidence in this investigation," he finished seriously, and he meant it, which was why Chisholm didn't walk out of the room right then and there over the "hatchet lady" crack.

Lehrer already didn't like this Chisholm woman, so he spoke to Denton though what he said was for Chisholm's benefit. "Deputy Director Rivera and I were discussing the Sepsis matter and we realized that we were working on the same case from opposite ends."

"Really," Margaret Chisholm drawled, in such a tone that Rivera couldn't tell if she was being sarcastic or not. Only Chisholm could say it that way. Denton and Lehrer, though, caught it clear. Denton jumped in.

"We've been trying to locate Sepsis for about a year. No luck. We knew he was in the country, but we didn't know why. Now we know."

Chisholm glanced at Rivera, then leaned forward on the table. "You think he came all the way from wherever he came from—"

"From Rome," said Denton helpfully. "He's been sitting out in Rome for the last four months, very inactive as far as we know."

"From Rome then. You think he came all this way to kill some nuns?"

"Not just any nuns," he said in his best diplomatic voice and tone. "Very important nuns. They belonged to Opus Dei, a conservative Catholic order with awesome political connections. Opus Dei is based in Spain. This bombing might be merely political, but then why did Sepsis come all the way to the United States when there are more than enough Opus Dei in Europe?"

"Good point," said Chisholm, again in that tone that wasn't straight and wasn't quite bent . . . but still bent enough to be insulting. Denton instantly liked her, though Lehrer and Rivera wished Chisholm would just indulge that tone a nick more, to have an excuse to fry her. Lehrer finally turned to face Chisholm dead on.

"Anyway, that's really unimportant. Who he shoots, why he shoots, we could care less. We just want to lay the Sepsis file to rest, as it were. Permanently. And as a way of building bridges between our two agencies, I thought it would be a good idea for a joint investigation into this matter."

Chisholm stared at the two CIA men like at some ugly trash that had piled up. "How 'joint' are we talking about? I worked with some CIA three years ago and 'joint' meant a marijuana cigarette that they didn't want to share with me."

"Mr. Denton will act as liaison with the FBI."

"Oh. So *we* get to grunt and sweat and drag ourselves through the mud while Denton here gets to watch. Peachy," she said.

Denton could feel Lehrer was about to lose it, being roughed up by a paltry FBI special agent, so he jumped in again. "Agent Chisholm, this isn't some turf war we want. We want Sepsis over with. If you put him to rest, that will be fine by us. If a truck runs him over and puts him to rest, that too will be fine by us."

Lehrer didn't lose it, but an Ivy League superciliousness poured out of his mouth like slow-moving lava, as insulting as Chisholm's clipped little jabs. "Just as you are Deputy Director Rivera's closest associate, Mr. Denton is my right-hand man. He has the full authority and all the resources of the CIA at his disposal. Mario?"

"Cool lima beans," said Chisholm, dancing oh so close to the edge of insubordination. Denton, his diplomatic smile frozen in place, mentally did cartwheels, thrilled to be working with someone as crazy as Chisholm. It was Roper *vu* all over again; she was bound to be sloppy enough to leave him alone.

Rivera and Lehrer were staring at Chisholm, both wondering what to say. Denton, though, pulled out his little black book and thumbed through it like nothing was wrong.

"A very nasty assassin trying to kill a nun, of all people. That's got to be a first," he said to himself as he flipped the neatly written pages of his notebook. "What are you calling this investigation?" he asked.

"We've just assigned it a letter, we're calling it Matter C," said Rivera.

" 'Matter C'? Hmm! I think a good name for this operation would be, mmm . . . Counterparts?" he said to the other three. "What do you think?"

Chisholm snorted and gave Rivera a look, but Rivera ignored her. "I like it," he said.

"Good," was all Denton would allow himself; he was frightened he'd crack a smile so wide that the top of his head would fall off. "I'll go to Langley and assemble the material we have on Sepsis so you can go through it. But what I would most like at this time is to acquire the nun and see where she takes us."

"She'll be flying in from Burlington the day after tomorrow," Rivera said. "We'll bring her here, and we can run this investigation, Counterparts, from here. Agreed?" he said to Lehrer.

"Agreed."

They all rose, Lehrer shaking Mario Rivera's hand but not bothering to so much as look Chisholm's way. "I'll be in touch, Mario."

Rivera ushered the two CIA men out, then turned to Chisholm, wanting to chew her out but knowing too well that CIA had earned Maggie's loathing.

" 'Counterparts'?" said Chisholm dubiously. "If CIA's all gung ho about helping us on this thing, you should have called it 'Counterproductive.' Or how about 'Count-your-silverware-before-they-arrive-and-after-they-leave'?"

He spread his hands helplessly. "Maggie . . ."

Margaret Chisholm plopped down in her chair. "I *hate* those fuckers."

Rivera sighed and walked over to where she was sitting, rubbed her shoulders as he talked. "Okay, go down to your office and shut down—"

"Wha—?"

"*Temporarily* shut down Archangel. Set up that office to run Counterparts."

"Give me a skeleton crew. I have a bunch of interviews I have to run. Sanders could run them while I work on this Counterparts 'building bridges' stuff."

Rivera sighed and stopped rubbing her shoulders. "Margaret . . .

Maggie, understand my position. CIA wants this guy badly. He's shown them up one too many times, and people like Lehrer and Denton don't like being shown up. I've been getting some serious pressure to put my best people on this Sepsis mess. Y'know, sooner or later the press is going to find out that this wasn't some water heater foul-up. When they find out and we have no results, we're going to look like fools. Find this Sepsis character and stop him. Then you can run Archangel to your heart's content."

"Have you thought about what'll happen when this Sepsis guy leaves the country? I mean, for sure he's gone already."

"When we know that he's split for sure, then it's CIA's problem, if they want to pursue it. We file our report with Interpol and let the Europeans or CIA or whoever else wants to dig through to Sepsis. But for now, until we know for a fact Sepsis is out of the country, we assume he's still here and therefore under our jurisdiction."

Chisholm crossed her arms and gave Rivera a stony silence, letting him squirm until she figured she could get her way. "So if I work on Counterparts, will you let Archangel continue?"

Rivera let out a bear growl and walked away to the door as he said over his shoulder, "I swear you're like a dog with a bone."

"Well?" she said as she got out of her chair and turned to face him.

"Okay okay okay, do whatever you want so far as Archangel is concerned, but you *personally* handle Counterparts *exclusively*. You have till tomorrow noon—from then on, only Counterparts." He left the conference room.

"What a stupid name for an operation," Chisholm mumbled as she gathered her things and walked out after Rivera.

Lehrer and Denton drove back to Langley in an agency car, Denton at the wheel as they talked about the meeting. But Denton's mind was far away. He was wondering what was on *Lehrer's* mind.

As head of CI, Lehrer decided what operations and/or plans took place under the official (and unofficial) control of the Counter Intelligence branch of CIA. Denton then took the list of approved and assigned them to the section heads—North America (Roper's former job), Central and South America, Middle East, Europe, and so on. Denton wasn't supposed to run a case. Yet here he was, personally involved in an investigation with a possibly deranged FBI agent.

He talked about it with Arthur Atmajian, Atta-boy being one man who would know what to make of it. Atta-boy didn't like it one bit.

"This is bad," he told Denton the following night, after the first day Counterparts had been up and running, on the eve before Chisholm and Denton acquired the nun.

"How do you mean 'bad'?" Denton asked, the two of them in the basement of Atmajian's house, surrounded by plumbing tools and equipment as, up above, Atmajian's eight children and dozens of their friends ran riot through the house. Atmajian thoughtfully ran his fingers through his beard.

"Bad as opposed to being good. The Deputy Director of CIA for Counter Intelligence assigns a specific case to his assistant and expects him to devote all his time to it. If I didn't know better, I'd say you were on your way down, if not out," said Arthur, giving Denton a hard glance before gulping half his drink.

Denton thought it over. "Yes, sure. But he backed me up solid at the meeting with the FBI people."

"That's what's so weird!" Atta-boy exploded. "He backs you up, so it can't be that you're going down or out. It can't be a test either. An operation as open-ended as this could presumably take months, maybe years. Lehrer's up to something, and whatever it is it's not good. . . . By the way, I really like your new novel. But why did you make that Armenian operative so fat?"

"Because you *are* fat, Atta-boy," Denton laughed, slapping him on the back.

"I am not," he said defensively, pissed as he started fooling with some plumbing gear Denton didn't understand or want to understand. Denton was sure that if things had been slightly different, if Atta-boy hadn't been so smart, he would have been happy fixing people's toilets for a living. Certainly would have made more money than at Langley. Which reminded him—

"Buy Zenith and Motorola stock before the end of the week," he said.

Atmajian nodded. "From the . . ." he said vaguely, unwilling to even whisper the name of the shadow file cabinet out in Alexandria.

"No, Phyllis Strathmore and I shot the breeze this morning—she gave me the tip."

"Legal?"

"Of course."

"Good, 'cause the IRS is set to audit me. I swear, those guys are worse than my unit."

"So what do you think I should do?"

"About this 'building bridges' bullshit?"

"Yes."

"I think you should watch your ass, my good man."

They talked some more, reaching no more intelligent conclusion than that.

That first day of Counterparts had gone well enough. Chisholm definitely did not like Denton, which he could live with, especially since Chisholm spent so much time wrapping up her other cases, probably as an excuse not to deal with him, Denton assumed. But he didn't have things his way as far as the running of the operation was concerned. Earlier in the afternoon, Chisholm had made that clear.

"Who are these two?" Chisholm asked.

"They are Amalia and Matthew Wilson, two of my assistants," Denton said.

Chisholm eyed Wilson especially, a huge kid of twenty-six with the face of a mass murderer; he looked like he killed people for a living, which he thoroughly enjoyed. Then Chisholm looked straight at Denton, unintimidated: "Get rid of this wet-boy," she said, hooking her thumb in Wilson and Amalia's general direction. "And get rid of the spacey kid too."

Amalia and Wilson looked at Denton, surprised.

"This is an FBI investigation, not a CIA project. We run it with Bureau people only. You, Agent Denton, are only on for the ride."

"I'm not an agent, I'm just a bureaucrat."

"Whatever. Get rid of them."

So Denton sent Amalia and Wilson on their way; they had other Agency things to do anyway, so it was no great loss. He was secretly amused by Chisholm's demand.

But then he wasn't so amused a couple of hours later.

"So what does that mass murderer do for you, anyway?" she asked Denton while they were organizing reports and getting Chisholm's Bureau people to hunt down information.

"Wilson? This and that," Denton said amiably.

"Wilson?" said Chisholm absently, not even bothering to look at him. "That gorilla probably doesn't know which is the business end of a gun. It's the Amalia woman I'm talking about."

Denton didn't freeze, thankfully, going about what he was doing as if nothing, reeling from this insight. Amalia was one of Denton's best-kept secrets, the girl everyone at Central Intelligence assumed was his lover—an impression Denton had worked hard to create, to mask what she *really* did for him. Now, he chuckled at Chisholm and said, "What makes you think *Amalia* of all people is a wet-boy, or wet-girl as the case may be?"

Chisholm stopped and just looked at Denton hard and a little condescendingly. "Don't kid a kidder. What are you doing with your own personal wet-boy? Or 'wet-girl' if you're so hell-bent on being PC about it. I don't know much about how you people work, but I *do* know that wet-boys are kept in their own little kennel. Someone like you, a staff man, isn't supposed to have one working curbside detail, no matter what."

Denton faked a good disinterested look and let the subject drop.

"So how's the FBI woman you're working with?" Paula Baker asked the morning after his talk with Atta-boy, Paula and Denton sharing a pear-and-coffee breakfast in her office.

"She's crazy."

"Okaaay," she said, smiling at this.

"And she's a lot smarter than I thought. She spotted Amalia for what she was."

"My my. You *think* so, or you know so?"

"I know so. This Chisholm woman just flat out up and asked me what I was doing with a wet-girl on my staff." Denton finished off his pear and casually walked around Paula's desk, dropping the core in the trash can beside her and sitting on her desk, putting on the charm. "Can you do me a favor?"

"What, you wanna go for it right here and now, cowboy? I'm married, y'know," she teased outrageously.

"Paula!" he whined prudishly, and she laughed.

"Okay, don't worry, I'm on it," she said, smiling as she made a note. "C-H-I-S-H-O-L-M is it? I can get you a superficial briefing by the morning, an in-depth one by the day after tomorrow."

"No twigs broken?"

"That'll be tough, but I'll try. Financial or personal or both?"

"As much as you can on everything, but don't make it a big deal—anything will be good enough. Thanks," he said, pretending he didn't notice Paula drumming her fingers on her desk, giving him an expectant smile as she leaned back in her chair and looked up at him.

"Hmm?" he asked innocently, smiling.

"In exchange for . . . ?"

"In exchange for what?" he said, capitulating good-naturedly.

Paula Baker rummaged through her desk as she said, "Get me the lowdown on . . . something caaalled . . . ah, here it is! Lamplight—something they're running out of North American Counter Intelligence."

Denton wrote it down in his day-pad as he thought randomly. "Margaret Chisholm. I think Tiggy would have loved having her in the basement."

Sister Marianne prayed.

She was in an airplane hangar, alone, surrounded by the coffins of her sisters waiting to be shipped to their respective homes. All the lights of the hangar were turned on, but even with the doors closed to keep it out, the night seeped in anyway.

Fifteen hours ago, they had all gone to Mass. Now, all the nuns were going home. There were so many coffins that there was no room in the hangar for the airplanes, so they loitered outside on the tarmac, looking like friendly whales and dolphins waiting to take the nuns on their separate ways.

All of the nuns had been teachers. They taught at Dartmouth, at a couple of the Seven Sisters, at both of the Phillips schools; one of the nuns, Sister Danielle, had even taught at the nearby prisons. So perhaps, as invisibly as they had educated, they might have preferred this departure—at night, alone, waiting for airplanes to take them away without remark. It might have been unsatisfying for the living, this lack of ceremony, but then only Sister Marianne was alive to mourn, and she didn't mind.

Sister Marianne prayed. She did not know what else to do. But it wasn't sadness she was praying against. It was bitterness.

Edmund Gettier came up behind her, stopping a ways from Sister Marianne, watching her and loving her in his peculiar, distant way. He was tired.

After the shooting, Gettier had held back all the people who'd wanted something from Marianne, and it had taken a lot more out of him than he had expected it would.

"We don't want to *interrogate* her," the fat, slatternly Agent McKenna had told Gettier, trying to use his bulk to impress him as they stood outside the windowless interrogation room where Marianne had been resting. "All we want to do is ask her some questions, that's all."

"I really don't see how Sister Marianne can help you," Gettier told him and Colby stiffly, despising Agent McKenna; Edmund Gettier objected to even mild obesity on general principle. "First she watched as all her sisters were killed. Then she herself was almost killed. I suspect it is *you* who needs to answer some questions, not her."

"Professor Gettier, sir, we understand—"

"Oh *dooo* you," Gettier said, arching his brows in that way of his that unnerved even the most conceited of his graduate students in Cambridge: arrogant and pedantic and so superior it could only make you feel stupid, or pissed. "You *understand* oh so *many* things, do you? You understand everything so well that now you want to browbeat a nun, is that it?"

"Professor Gettier," said Colby finally, feeling stupid and pissed off about it. "If you don't step aside and let me talk to Sister Marianne, I'll have you physically removed and charged with obstruction of justice."

"Fine," he said, stepping aside and presenting them the door with a sarcastic flourish. "And then I'll go outside to all those waiting reporters and tell them all that the police here *weren't* chasing after some photographer that was trying to take pictures. I'll tell them the truth: how a hit man of some sort nearly succeeded in killing a nun here in the police station. And even though the police station was full of policemen and FBI agents, this hit man somehow managed to elude them."

Colby and McKenna glanced at each other. McKenna sighed and turned his back on Gettier, but Colby was more patient. "Do you want to start a panic in this little New England town?" she asked reasonably. " 'A hit man on the loose'—do you want every New Hampshirite to break out his rifle and accidentally shoot every passing stranger or shadow, thinking it's a hit man on the loose?"

"Leave her alone, she's told you all she knows," said Gettier. "At least let her sleep."

So they left her alone for an hour or so, only to come back again, the three of them going through the same routine with only minor variations.

The thing was, the locals and Colby and McKenna were in way over their heads, and they knew it. Car thefts, a little amateur gunrunning, minor drug busts—that's what they knew. On any other day or case, Gettier would have been mincemeat. But what with bomb squads flying up from Quantico, high-powered rifle shots, and dealing with the national press, it was all just a bit too much for Colby and McKenna as they waited around for orders from On High. So they let Gettier guard the nun, too worried about not fucking things up to be concerned about a pedantic old fart upset that they weren't letting the nun sleep.

Sister Marianne, though, didn't sleep at all. Even in her happiest, most relaxed days, Sister Marianne suffered from insomnia. She had trouble falling asleep and she woke early, unable to sleep again. Now, with everything, she paced like a soldier, walking back and forth across the windowless interrogation room where they'd put her, chosen because it was nearly at the center of the Lyme police station but was still large enough for a cot. She paced so much she got dizzy.

"How about some lunch?" asked Edmund Gettier as he walked in with a tray of food for the two of them. They set it on the interrogation table and sat across from each other as he lectured.

"Last night I was watching *Hudson Hawk*. Simply brilliant. The first movie ever made that is truly, genuinely Pynchonesque in its sensibility," he said, flapping his hands around and describing the intricate details of his analysis as they ate.

Sister Marianne smiled at Edmund. She didn't understand a thing he said, the words sliding off her mind like curlers across ice, but she loved him for what he was doing: Edmund Gettier didn't know how to comfort; instead, he lectured, going on and on about his pet peeves and secret hobbies.

"Do you know what films like *Six Degrees of Separation* and *The Usual Suspects means* to film?"

Sister Marianne shook her head, smiling, debating and deciding against correcting his grammar.

"It means that films are finally abandoning that silly linear structure. I tell you, we are in a golden age of film. Take *Twelve Monkeys*, for instance . . ." And off he went.

But after they finished eating, Sister Marianne was alone again in the interrogation room, trying to sleep but assaulted by the bitterness, and the guilt. Mostly guilt. After all, she was alive. But bitterness too.

Now, in the hangar, surrounded by coffins, Edmund Gettier coughed politely to let her know he was there. She turned and smiled.

"Come," he said. "Let's go."

Marianne silently nodded but made no move to leave. Edmund offered his elbow and Marianne slipped her arm in his, the two of them standing there.

"It's finally quiet," she said, looking up to meet his eyes, then looking around at the coffins.

"Oh?"

"All day, it's been so . . . noisy. The explosion. And then the reporters. And then talking to you. And then the rifle shots. And then all the FBI agents, talking, moving. Only now it's finally quiet."

Gettier didn't know what to say, or even if he *should* say anything, if something occurred to him. Then, horrified, he remembered his lunchtime lecture.

"Sorry about—"

"Don't be," she interrupted, reading his mind.

So they stood there until he remembered why he had come here.

"Your parents called, they want to come. I think they *are* coming, in the morning."

"I'll call them. There's no point in their coming. You should go back to Cambridge."

"I'll stay," Gettier said simply, and Marianne rewarded him by squeezing his arm. Then she remembered her work.

"What am I going to do about my students? I have to—"

"Don't worry about them, I took care of it. I also spoke to Cardinal Barberi. He wants you to call him tonight. And Archbishop Neri called," he said. "He wants you to call him too."

"How is Cardinal Barberi?" she asked.

"He sounded good. He said they'd just given him a transfusion." Gettier remembered, then smiled. "He called himself 'the first vampiric cardinal in church history.' "

They laughed quietly at this. Dominic Cardinal Barberi, an old man of seventy-eight, suffered from chronic leukemia. Every few weeks, he received massive blood transfusions to keep him alive.

Cardinal Barberi was the head of the project, making him, nominally, Sister Marianne's boss. But now that he was so sick, Marianne would really be running things.

If he had had nothing left, Cardinal Barberi was sure he would have skipped treatment; he was an old man, he had lived a full life. But the project kept him alive as much as the blood did. When the Pope had ordered him to go ahead five years ago, Cardinal Barberi couldn't re-member when he had been happier, feeling like a young priest off to minister to his first parish. Lately, as he counted the days until his favorite pupil arrived in Rome and started things up—a question of mere *days*—he seemed to have even more life in him.

But when Archbishop Neri came to the Vatican hospital to tell him the news of the bombing in the United States, for the first time in years Cardinal Barberi felt genuine, unadulterated fear.

"We have a problem," the Opus Dei bishop told him without preamble. "Sister Marianne's convent was bombed. All the nuns save Sister Marianne perished." Then Archbishop Neri looked away, straightening his jacket and wishing for a cigarette.

"Which Sister Marianne?" Barberi asked, confused as the blood was pumped through his veins.

"*Our* Sister Marianne," Alberto Neri said impatiently. "She's not dead," he repeated, then walked away like a man who had been clobbered with a sledgehammer, leaving Barberi to stare after him, wondering in fear. The old Cardinal, sitting up in his hospital bed, with his arm immobilized as tubes came in and out of it, watched the younger bishop walk away, the old man realizing he had just received another piece for his collection of moments, a menagerie of moments that formed the shape of his life.

If the bombing frightened Cardinal Barberi, it sent Archbishop Neri and the Opus Dei contingent in Rome into a tailspin. In one stroke, the death of the nuns destroyed close to twenty years of patient, agonizing labor on the part of Opus Dei. Archbishop Neri wondered how they could repair the damage. But even as he wondered about this, another part of him, a part acting against his Christian nature and thinking things over from a purely political perspective, realized that the bombing was one of the best things to ever happen to Opus Dei—Opus Dei as helpless victim. He hated himself for thinking this way, even as he thought of ways to exploit this advantage.

If you want to be slightly right of Attila the Hun in the panoply of Catholic positions, Opus Dei is where you want to pitch your tent. Opus Dei, the Work of God, founded by the Spanish Monsignor Escrivá de Balaguer in 1928—he'll soon be canonized for having created what in all likelihood is the most conservative, educated, and wealthy clique within the Catholic Church. They're a small, independent little band, but they are in the United States in a big way.

What Opus is doing in the United States is one of those devious, conspiratorially practical agendas American paranoids would have a field day with: Opus Dei is out to convert American Catholics into Conservative Catholics—and they are succeeding.

American Catholicism is, so far as Rome is concerned, one of the most troubling problems around, a potentially heretical group which has to be handled with kid gloves. Truth be told, few Catholics outside the United States like American Catholics, for the plain fact that they *are* becoming heretical, and there seems little the Church can do to prevent the eventual schism. Take Catholics for Choice.

Catholics for Choice are American Catholics who are in favor of abortion. But in terms of Catholic doctrine and Catholic teachings, Catholics for Choice as a group and as a name is as oxymoronic as Jews for Jesus. Catholics for Choice are espousing an idea—abortion—which flies smack-dab in the face of what the Church believes and espouses, as heretical as Catholics for Rooster Worship.

So with such a country as heretically inclined as the United States, what is the Church to do? That's where Opus Dei comes in, the new Soldiers of Christ, the shock troops of the conservative wave.

Opus is small certainly, but it is organized, and it knows what it can and can't do. There was no way Opus could convert the so-called baby boom generation of Americans, that demographic blip born between 1946 and 1959, a generation characterized by a general cynicism, rampant hysteria, and pure arrogance founded on true ignorance. But the generations *after* them . . . well, that's a whole new ball game. So Opus set up small convents and ministries around the United States to preach the Way, but not in major cities. They set them up near college towns.

Hence Sister Marianne's convent. Opus convents like hers were first set up in New Jersey, close to Princeton University, and of course in Washington, D.C., close to Georgetown and the Catholic University;

that Washington is a Jesuit town was only a minor inconvenience. the aim of these ministries was—and is—to convert young, intelligent Catholics to traditionally conservative doctrines, specifically to the Way—the achievement of grace through work. After all, one day, the college kids at these elite schools would be running the show.

Opus wisely did not send many *priests* to America. In the last two decades or so, the United States has been experiencing another of the periodic Great Awakenings that wash across that great land. Since the seventeenth century, roughly every seventy years, a period of intense religious fervor grips the country, creating an enormous religious impetus that inevitably leads to extremism. The tragedy of the Salem witch-hunts is one example; the foolish temperance movement is another. In the Great Awakening of the end of the twentieth century, the extremism has fallen, paradoxically, on men in general and priests in particular.

Accusations of sexual abuse have reached nearly cataclysmic proportions, a hysteria which has gone so far as to include Satanic worship as one of its principal aspects. Some reputable psychologists and therapists have actually claimed that one out of every four cases of abuse involves Satanic worship.

But hysterical or not, the current Pope, John Paul II, is unwilling to let the American Catholics drift so far that they have to be declared a heretical church, as many cardinals have very privately and very cautiously suggested. So John Paul ordered Opus Dei to bring the American Catholics back into the fold.

This is where Archbishop Alberto Neri came in.

"Don't send priests," the then-rising young priest told his superiors back in 1979, when his orders came down. "Send nuns—*only* nuns. Who'll ever accuse them of raping college-age boys?"

So they sent nuns, nuns like Sister Marianne. Before she was ordered to go to America, she had been working in Torino, teaching university students there, fully expecting to live out her days in Italy. She didn't expect to even visit the United States again.

"How would you like to go back to the United States?" Archbishop

Neri asked her at their first interview in 1993; he had already made up his mind that he wanted her to go, the interview a formality.

"I don't think I would like it very much," she said. "I haven't been there since my graduate school days. I didn't even finish my thesis there; I finished it here in Rome. The United States . . . it's just too painful to be there again."

"I understand. So you wouldn't go if it were up to you."

"No," she said.

"But if you were needed there, would you go?"

"Yes," she said without hesitation, preparing for the sacrifice, the cost her life demanded.

"You are needed there."

So she went, fearfully at first, prepared for a difficult, guilty return to America. But it wasn't like that, not at all. She hadn't been in the United States in five years, but living and working in New Hampshire was like being in another country altogether, teaching students as naive and unsophisticated as her students in Torino. It was nothing like her New York days or her own college-age years. It hadn't been a sacrifice at all, to teach in America.

Until now. Now the coffins in the hangar seemed like sharks swimming around her, mute accusations. This, she thought, was the sacrifice for the life she had led and the peace she owned. And it was . . . vaguely . . . inadequate—insufficient. No sacrifice at all. Guilt, and bitterness, and a sadness she could not express. But no sacrifice. After all, she was alive.

"Let's go," she said to Edmund Gettier, squeezing his arm to get them on their way.

"Some new FBI agents are here," he said, switching to Italian. "No more dealing with Agent McKenna's fat belly. These new agents, they're taking us to a hotel of some sort. Or a *mo*tel, I think. After that they're taking us to Burlington."

"You don't have to come. Go back to Cambridge."

Edmund Gettier ignored the suggestion. "They want us to fly to Washington soon after."

"Why?"

"I don't know. But Archbishop Neri told me to tell you to do whatever they ask."

"All right," she said.

The Georgetown Four Seasons Hotel had seen the type a thousand times before: the highly educated, highly successful young businessman on a business trip. The look to the man was so casually expensive—such a cliché, really—that no one noticed him as he approached the front desk amid the hushed bustle of the lobby. But the way he spoke was what drew attention. He didn't have that arrogant hard edge of the young hotshot. Instead, he spoke softly, lightly, politely, the words as evanescent as smoke.

"Messages for room twelve-oh-three, please."

The desk clerk couldn't remember if he had seen him before, but the man was so assured and patient that the clerk didn't hesitate, merely snapping his hands a fraction as he began typing in the computer to check for messages, coming up with nothing for 1203. When he looked up from the terminal, it was as if he'd never seen the face before, a face that could never be remembered.

"No messages, Mr. Schlemel."

The man in the casual clothes, called Sepsis by intelligence services around the world, smiled a delicate smile as he walked away toward the elevators, the desk clerk forgetting his face almost as soon as he was gone, as he ought to have—Sepsis had paid $78,000 for a Swiss surgeon to make his face as forgettable as was medically possible.

The money for the operation had come from his best hit, the Canadian federalist politician, four years ago. For $250,000, Quebec separatists had contracted him to take out a Quebec politician. The man thought it was a good idea for the province to remain a part of Canada. Quite dangerously, the man had the charisma to make a difference. So the man had to go. It had been a tough shot, but one Sepsis was always proud of, taking out the politician at a thousand yards from an office rooftop.

The target was going to be exposed for approximately four and a half seconds, Sepsis had written in his diary, writing, as always, in Italian, the language of confession. *There would be no other opportunities, as his cavalcade would be passing between two other buildings when my shot would take him. These two other buildings would give him cover if I failed. But they would give me cover if I succeeded.*

Up until that point, Sepsis had been a hired gun—or rather, a hired bomb, as Keith Lehrer had so rightly put it. Sepsis had been simply following his connection's steps, bombing things left and right, almost casually, not really thinking about what he was doing. His connection, his main contact and the man who taught him how to be a killer, would tell him what jobs were available and would "suggest" a way of doing them. And they were always bombs, just bombs, blowing everything apart, as inelegant as a sledgehammer.

At the time, however, Sepsis didn't really care about how he went about doing his job. All he cared about, then, was the who, and the how much.

But one morning, walking down a street in Montreal on his way to plant the bomb that would kill the Canadian politician, he had suddenly stopped in the middle of the sidewalk as the oblivious pedestrians passed him by. With a pound of plastic explosives literally under his arm, Sepsis had realized two things.

One, he didn't need his connection anymore—after three years of bombing targets, he had networked all of the man's contacts, making his connection, his main go-between, completely superfluous.

And two, Sepsis realized he was tired of just blowing things up. There had to be more to it than just putting a pound of Symtec underneath someone's car.

As soon as Sepsis realized these two things, he dropped his connection as casually as he dropped that pound of plastic into a wastebasket on that Montreal sidewalk.

He began to seriously rethink his career, starting with the Canadian politician.

The method was the key, now that he had reached this plateau as an assassin. Since he was no longer interested in just *doing* the job, but rather, interested in *how* the job was done, he started to seriously consider the different options, thinking fully awake, in control for the first time.

There were many ways to do the job. A car bomb, of course, was the no-brainer, foolproof way to go. But Sepsis rejected the method almost out of hand. A rifle shot, the toughest mode of assassination, was what he chose instead. He chose it very carefully, thinking about the obstacles. It's very difficult for a man with a rifle to get away, let alone actually kill someone. So rifle shot it was, the method settled.

Then came the place. Montreal wasn't Riyadh or St. Petersburg or Bangkok; Montreal was an open city, free and easy. There would be an overabundance of opportunities. But small, cramped Ottawa wasn't like that at all. In Ottawa it would be tough—tough to find the right opportunity, tough to shoot, tough to get away. So Ottawa it was.

Then the only question to settle would be the range. In a secluded field in Ontario, Sepsis practiced until he could hit a moving target half the time at a thousand yards. So a thousand yards it would be.

The day in Ottawa started out rainy and foggy, but became clear and lovely, fast winds shearing the low clouds so that the afternoon rally against secession proceeded on schedule. At noon, Sepsis left his hotel room, dressed in a suit and tie, carrying a thin leather attaché case where he had his rifle and his lunch. He strolled to the building he had selected, easily getting to the rooftop and carefully making his preparations. When he was done, he ate some mushroom soup out of a thermos bottle while reading Proust's *The Past Recaptured* in the original; French was his native language, and Proust always calmed him down.

By three in the afternoon, perched twenty stories up above, Sepsis was in position, scope and rifle at the ready. The man's caravan came, amid the other marchers, a happy time in Canadian politics, a popular federalist politician from Quebec, a new era of Canadian unity . . .

Watching through the telescopic sight, Sepsis waited patiently, thinking things out. His window of opportunity—barely four and a half seconds long—would mean that he would have to fire almost at the instant he saw the politician's car, since the bullet would take 2.34 seconds to cover the distance. In the few seconds before he fired, Sepsis suddenly realized, surprised and pleased, that there were maybe five men on this earth who could make the shot he had designed for himself.

The politician appeared between the two buildings a thousand yards away, the wind high, the distance awesome. And then the man was dead, his open car still driving along as if nothing were the matter, disappearing behind the other buildings.

Sepsis lay there on the rooftop, unmoving, his mind completely blank. He waited to hear something, but it was too far away. He couldn't see anything, the buildings blocking his view, obscuring what was happening beyond his field of vision. And yet he knew.

As he'd let the bullet fly and watched it disappear through his telescopic sight, Sepsis had felt a small, black hole puncture the fabric of reality, a feeling of a small vacuum hole sucking up a life in the distance. The feeling was what made him know that he'd done it. A thousand yards in high wind, between two buildings, firing on a moving target: five men on earth who could have made such a shot, maybe. *He* had. No way Carlos could have managed such a shot. *I did.* Sepsis dismantled the rifle and stowed it in the attaché case. Then he put on his tie again, replaced the cuff links on his shirt, slipped on his suit jacket, and walked back down the building.

On the street, walking back to his hotel, Sepsis was so amazed at his success he didn't pay attention to where he was going, getting lost. The pedestrians around him, having heard the news of the dead politician, bobbed and weaved down the street, shocked, but Sepsis only smiled shyly, savoring the moment.

The sensation of succeeding at an impossible task, Sepsis wrote that night after the assassination, *is difficult to put into words. It is all a matter of proximity. The closer you are to the event, the more you know about it and its difficulties, the more you can feel it. There is no feeling without knowledge.*

He stopped writing and picked up his drink. Alone in the hotel room, with all the lights blazing, even the bathroom lights on, he prowled around, constantly looking at himself in the mirror and at the television news programs that were endlessly repeating the assassination of the politician. Of course, the footage didn't show Sepsis on his rooftop, though a part of him—a vain, foolish part of him, he knew—wished that he too was on screen.

Carlos never could have made such a shot. Sepsis checked his face in the mirror, turning his jawline from side to side, examining his face with the detachment he brought to bear on targets. Carlos never would have put those obstacles in his path. Only he could have—Sepsis.

It wasn't that Carlos hadn't had the equipment. True, the rifle Sepsis used was something technologically impossible in the sixties and seventies, but that wasn't the issue. The issue was difficulty. Any fool could shoot an approaching target from two hundred feet, the way Carlos had done in Dallas from the grassy knoll. Any fool could stage commando raids using suicidal politicals, the way Carlos had in the past. But Carlos had never had the nerve, the raw *nerve* to kill with impossible difficulty—to add counterweights like stones to a saddle and still manage to cross the tape the winner. Carlos had had things easy, and then when age and enemies grew tough, Carlos had cowardly slipped away.

Sepsis knew Carlos's story well, and he despised him. Carlos was the granddaddy of all professional assassins, an almost apocryphal figure. But he was quite real. Everyone thought he was one Ilych Ramírez Sánchez, but Sepsis knew for a fact that that wasn't his name, only his alias. The real Carlos wasn't even fully South American—Carlos's father was German, from Alsace-Lorraine. He had been trained by the Russians, yes, but then he had gone off on his own in 1960 after he lost faith in his Marxism and became a kind of . . . well, Sepsis wasn't sure. From all he had heard, he deduced that Carlos had become a sort of apolitical anarchist revolutionary with a soft spot for leftists. That's why he had done so many jobs for the Red Brigade, the Japanese Red Army, and all those other little leftist terrorist groups. But his politics hadn't kept him from doing the Kennedy job for the American Teamsters Union and then using Jack Ruby—Jimmy Hoffa's friend—as the man to kill Carlos's patsy, Oswald.

When Carlos made up his mind to retire, back in the early eighties, he had quite cleverly allowed a foolish Venezuelan lowlife to pass himself off as the real Carlos, the Syrians taking care of this impostor until they sold him out to the French. The real Carlos was living very happily now in obscurity, thinking himself so wise for having retired at the peak of his profession.

But Sepsis despised him. Assassination was like golf—you lost your edge only in your own mind. Carlos had walked back to the clubhouse while still a relatively young man because he had lost the stomach for the risk. Sepsis wouldn't.

Denton might have appreciated Sepsis's job. Right around the time the Canadian politician was getting his head blown off, Carl Roper was having *his* head served up on a platter by *60 Minutes*. Different methods, but there are many ways to destroy people. Murder was, in Sepsis's opinion, the messiest. Which was why now, at twenty-four, after six years as a professional assassin, what he was beginning to look for was the elimination of people without their elimination—meta-murder.

George Wallace was the textbook case. In 1972, while running for President of the United States, the racist politician had been crippled by a would-be assassin. Wallace was not killed; he lived to be an old man. But George Wallace ceased to be a factor once he was crippled, good as dead after he was shot. *That* was what Sepsis considered meta-murder, inadvertent as it might have been. The man was killed, though he lived.

Now, on his way to the next plateau, Sepsis was trying to duplicate the same effect, though consciously, awake.

He had done something similar already, killing the entire family of an Egyptian CIA informant. But that had been specifically ordered by his contractors, as an example to other would-be turncoats, which was why Sepsis had killed one family member per day, a logistically very difficult assignment.

The nun, however, was different: she was the first rung on this ladder to the next plateau.

He had planned on killing the nun outright at the chapel, regardless of the deal he had made. After all, he *needed* to kill her, and he had thought at the time that he had to kill her in such a way that it wasn't obvious that she had been the intended target. So he had destroyed the entire chapel, hoping to simultaneously kill the nun and send a good clear message to his old connection. But luck being what it is, she hadn't been inside when he detonated the bomb.

When he saw her rush out of the convent building, alive and untouched, Sepsis had shaken his head, stepped out of his RotoRooter van, and pulled out his gun, ready to just shoot her. Approaching her from behind and to her left, her blind spot, Sepsis casually watched as she tried to suffocate a flaming corpse, fully prepared to kill her. He had been barely five yards away, actually in the process of raising his gun to shoot her, when suddenly the nun turned to face him, her eyes shut tight. When she opened them, Sepsis was sure, she would stare straight at him and his raised gun.

But instead, her eyes locked on the naked lower torso of a dismembered nun, her eyes going suddenly blank, as if whatever it was that made her human had drained away.

Sepsis had stopped himself from killing her then, watching her, fascinated. She ran around the waste of the chapel, completely oblivious of his presence as she tried to save her sisters, but her eyes looked like those of a dead woman. After a few minutes he heard approaching sirens, so he walked back to the RotoRooter van and drove away.

In his room at the Hanover Inn, he thought things over. He realized then that it didn't really matter if people knew she was the intended target; it wouldn't hurt or change his plan one way or another. That was when the idea first occurred to him—use her to get to the next plateau. Kill the nun without killing her.

So when he had her in his sights at the Lyme police station, Sepsis had been careful not to actually aim for her head when he shot the window she was looking out of. After all, if he had really wanted to kill her then, he could have used armor-piercing bullets to drill their way through the window and through her brains.

After the potshots in Lyme, there was so much security around the nun that anyone else might have thought it impossible to get close to her. But Sepsis had gotten very close indeed, following her around in his $78,000 face and his perfect American accent (he had been a boarder at St. George's, after all). He was there when she went into a sealed hangar and bid goodbye to the Sisters of her convent, all lined up in coffins, so many they seemed never-ending. And he was there when she was put up in the Burlington FBI station with agents covering her around the clock. And he would be there when she arrived in Washington, D. C., the day after tomorrow.

A car bomb would have been enough, which was what his connection would have done, the conservative dolt. Carlos would have used a telescopic rifle, at a range of maybe two hundred to five hundred feet, the wimp.

But Sepsis wasn't either of those two men. He was reaching for the new plane, the third plateau, the new ideal. Meta-murder was on his mind. Already he had some ideas.

FIVE | Horse Play

"I want Phil Carter and his men on the penguin's guard detail," Chisholm told Rivera after the first meeting with Denton and Lehrer. "I want them to be the ones to bring her down from Burlington."

"Why Phil Carter?" Rivera asked, a little nonplussed.

"We won't get any blowback."

An escorting agent says something about the events a witness was involved in—some half-assed theory or assumption or plain scuttlebutt that very well might be on the dark side of the moon so far as the truth is concerned. The witness hears it. Then when the witness gets interrogated for real, the witness winds up telling the interrogating officer the first dummy's fucked-up idea about what might have happened as if it were Holy Writ. That's blowback. Young agents, especially bored guard-detail agents, always create it, like farts after a kidney bean dinner. So the escort from Burlington was made up of older, more disciplined, tight-lipped agents, agents like Phil Carter.

He was perfect for the job. He was unmarried, middle-aged, a mere single generation away from border-state white trash, with no children of his own—and most important, the Bureau was his life. Men like Carter are common in bureaucracies like the FBI, or the armed forces or CIA or the Secret Service for that matter—men who at some point consciously decided to sacrifice their lives for the good of the bureaucracy.

Little is said about such men. They are gray and anonymous, hard and unattractive, none too bright, with no discernible ambitions of their own. They look and sound and feel interchangeable. But they are good men. They are decent men. Yet they are so often swept away and ignored in the frantic race to the top that they become as invisible as the asphalt on a wide, open highway—essential, but unnoticed. Someone as self-absorbed as Margaret Chisholm would never notice them. Someone as bright and shiny as Nicholas Denton would notice them as an object for a witty remark or a slightly contemptuous snicker.

But Sister Marianne noticed Agent Carter and the other men on his team. It was hardly possible for her *not* to notice them—they surrounded her night and day, Carter himself handling the first night shift, standing just outside her door as she tried to sleep. But she noticed Carter and his men in a human way that Denton wouldn't have understood and Chisholm wouldn't have bothered about.

"Would you like a chair?" Sister Marianne asked, that first night at the Washington hotel where she was being kept until Counterparts didn't need her anymore, looking up at the giant gray hulk of Carter. "You can't stand here guarding my door all night," she said, smiling, then frowning quizzically. "Can you?"

"No ma'am," Carter rumbled ambiguously.

Marianne blinked, a little perturbed by his demeanor. That might have been the end of it, but she scrunched up her courage and asked, "You don't need a chair, or you're not going to stay here all night?"

"I don't need a chair, ma'am."

She looked up at him doubtfully, wondering how he would stay awake all night. To her, an insomniac, it seemed a cruel way to spend a night. So she went into her hotel room and dragged out the desk chair anyway.

"At least you can sit while you stay here," she said. "Good night."

A few minutes later, she came out to pace the hallway.

"Why aren't you sitting?"

So Carter sat. Marianne paced silently, thinking, then went back to her room to try to sleep. So Carter stood. Around two in the morning, Marianne came out again to pace some more. But quicker than she could catch him, Carter sat down before Marianne noticed he'd been standing.

"Isn't it better than standing all night?" she said, smiling happily for Carter.

"Yes ma'am," Carter answered brightly.

All the gray men in Carter's squad liked her very much. Even though she was upper-class and even though she was a nun, they recognized her as being one of them. So when they finally had to leave the relative security of the hotel to go to the Hoover Building for the first interview with Chisholm and Denton, all the men on Carter's squad were armed to the teeth, surrounding the nun as possessively as if she were a great jewel, or a much loved child.

In the Hoover offices where Chisholm and Denton were running Counterparts, things were a little different.

"Is *that* all?" Denton had said facetiously as Bureau clerks brought in four banker's boxes of documents on the first day of the operation. "I thought you had some information, not just scraps."

"Ho ho, so funny," said Chisholm. Denton laughed.

Once they'd assembled all the material, the two of them spent two days going over every scrap of paper relating to the attempts on Sister Marianne and what was officially known about Sepsis.

"Those two boxes on Sepsis are yours, this one on the attacks and this one here on Sepsis are mine. Tomorrow, we trade boxes."

"*Ja wohl, mein* Agent Chisholm," said Denton as he smartly clicked the heels of his shoes.

Maggie Chisholm gave him a withering look and then got to work, not saying a thing to him during all the time they spent together, making it crystal-clear how much she despised CIA.

Sitting very straight in her chair, dressed in a white blouse and a Prince of Wales plaid skirt, her ankles crossed under her seat, elbows planted on the table on either side of an open file, the plane of her face parallel to the surface of the table, her hands bunched at her ears—this was Chisholm reading. She rarely moved, for hours on end.

Denton moved. He moved a lot. He'd have one foot on the table, the other hanging from the armrest of his chair, tracing lazy circles, his entire body leaning back on the chair while his hands constantly shuffled the papers and file folders like playing cards. Sometimes he sat on the sofa at the far end of the room, his feet up on the small, tasteful coffee table. He read nothing through all the way, instead seeming to read a sentence in one document, a sentence in another, pausing to think and smoke a cigarette.

Chisholm read on and on. Sometimes, she flipped a page. That was how Denton knew she wasn't comatose. He went back to the file that had been put together on Sister Marianne.

"Ah!" he said, delighted. "Garthwaite—Gene-Garthwaite-Gene-Garthwaite-Gene-Garthwaite." He looked happy, then he turned to another piece of paper. Chisholm ignored him.

The day after that, Sister Marianne arrived for her first interrogation with Chisholm and Denton.

"Faith Crenshaw?" Chisholm said, rising from the conference table as Richard Greene and Howie Sanders, Chisholm's underlings who were doing the spadework on Counterparts, finished setting up the tape recorders for this first round.

"Please. Sister Marianne," she said, smiling and reaching out to Margaret. They daintily shook each other's hand, for vastly different reasons.

"Sister Marianne then. I am Special Agent Chisholm, FBI. This is Mr. Denton, CIA. We are handling this case—"

And then Denton took over. Sitting on the sofa, his tie carefully

loosened, his jacket off, his shirtsleeves haphazardly rolled up to the elbows, he stood up and started putting on the charm, wearing a soft but
confident voice that cut Chisholm off. "Would you like to sit down,
Sister? You must be exhausted from the flight."

Like a magician, he was next to Marianne, shaking her hand and taking her by the elbow, guiding her to an armchair by the sofa as he said,
"The last time I had a long conversation with a nun, I was fourteen
years old, and Sister Alice was *swearing* I'd burn in hell for all the things
I'd done. And to give me a taste of hell, she gave me a week's detention
plus weekend detention," he said, laughing at his own story as he willed
the nun to find the story as funny as he did. She did. "I'm Nicholas
Denton."

"How do you do, Mr. Denton," she said, aware that Greene and
Sanders were scrambling to get the recording gear to the coffee table,
but unable to look away from Denton's smile.

"Be careful what you say around me," Denton whispered conspiratorially as he deposited the nun in the armchair. "I work for the CIA!"
he hissed, then guffawed.

The nun laughed, and everyone else in the room—Chisholm,
Sanders and Greene, Carter and his men—was left far far behind.
Pissed off, Chisholm turned a look on Carter and his squad, and they
disappeared.

"This is my FBI counterpart, Margaret Chisholm," Denton said, sitting on the sofa, leaning toward Marianne. "We are in charge of the investigation into the events of last Tuesday," he went on, easily slipping
into serious mode. "Now, I know these events have affected you deeply,
but please understand that it is vital that you help us with our investigation. Would you like some water? Tea? Coffee?"

Marianne hesitated and Denton mock-scowled. "Ah! come on now.
Sanders," he said, nearly snapping his fingers as if at a waiter, "why
don't you bring us some tea?" He turned solicitously toward Marianne.
"And maybe something to eat?"

"Just tea, if it's no trouble," she said.

"No trouble at all! Cream? Lemon?"

Marianne hesitated. "Cream," she said finally.

"Two teas, Mr. Sanders," he said, then leaned back in the sofa. Feeling foolish, Margaret stood there, unsure whether to sit or stand or what, watching as Denton smoothly steamrollered the interview.

"I understand you are a professor?" he asked the nun casually, as if they were at a cocktail party.

"Yes, I teach art history at Dartmouth. I specialize in architecture."

Denton sat up straight. "Really? *I* went to Dartmouth, class of '83."

"Really?"

"Yes! But I majored in economics. Never did take a course in art history— Wait a second," he said suddenly. Even Chisholm looked his way. "I *did* take an art history course, with a professor . . . Garth . . . Garthput? No, that doesn't sound right . . ." Denton looked and sounded as if he were on the brink of discovering the unified field equations.

"Garthwaite?" Marianne interjected helpfully.

He snapped his fingers like a thunderclap. "Garthwaite, yes! Gene Garthwaite, that was his name. Great prof, great prof."

"He's the chair of the art history department now," she said, then added almost girlishly, "He's my boss."

"Really? Outstanding, outstanding. But he's not really your boss, is he?"

"Well, no. But I don't have tenure, so in a way he is my boss. I'm just an associate professor."

"But I bet it won't be long before you have tenure, eh?" he said, eyeing her shrewdly, as if she were a cardsharp he had to keep his eye on.

"Well," she said modestly, "God willing, maybe . . . who knows."

Chisholm had had enough. "Could we—"

"Gene Garthwaite," said Denton, leaning back again, looking as if he didn't even realize Chisholm was in the room. "I liked him a lot."

Marianne was no fool. She could feel Denton manipulating her, but it was as if he had a secret control box wired directly into her heart. She tried to get a grip, but Denton robbed her of control once again as he pressed exactly the right button.

"How do you like teaching?" he said casually. "I mean, really. It must be boring, grading all those papers, writing up lectures, no time for your own research . . ."

"I adore it," she said with undisguised emotion. "I teach four courses a year, but I still have time for research. A lot of professors dislike teaching, but what would be the point of being a teacher if you don't *teach*?—uh, but, eh, yes, I think teaching is a very important part of being an art historian," she finished tinily, feeling foolish, fifteen once again, embarrassed by the excitement her work provoked in her.

Denton, though, saw right through her, and used her weakness to cement his position. "Oh I agree!" he said vehemently, saving her from her self-consciousness and simultaneously—more importantly—winning her over. "What's the point of knowing so much and not passing it on!"

Sister Marianne smiled wide and nodded excitedly, captivated by the attention of someone who understood. And Denton thought, *He shoots, he scores.*

"What's your area?"

"Italian Renaissance architecture,"

Just then, Howie Sanders arrived with a couple of cardboard cups of tea. He handed them to Sister Marianne and Nicholas Denton as, suddenly, the air was charged.

Magnetic fields seemed to come out of Denton as he stirred his tea with the plastic stirrer. He wasn't *doing* anything: he wasn't looking tough or squinting his eyes or anything foolish like that. All he was doing was stirring his tea and watching it swirl in his cup. But by sheer force of personality, he had everyone's eyes riveted on him.

In a soft, light voice, but somehow hard underneath, Denton began: "Sister Marianne, this attack was . . . despicable. No other word to describe it. Your order seems to have become a target for some very unsavory characters. We don't know why. So until we do, we'd like you to stay here in Washington for the next few days. It would help us very much in our investigation."

"Of course. Anything I can do to help."

Denton smiled a very sweet smile, so sweet it seemed to melt Marianne's fading resistance to his manipulations. "Thank you. Now—"

Chisholm had had enough.

Standing, with a brittle, hard voice, she began. "You saw a man dressed in a RotoRooter uniform come out of the chapel just before it exploded, the same man who you say fired at you when you were in the Lyme police station, correct?"

"Yes," said Sister Marianne, almost leaping to attention.

"Could you identify this man if you saw him?"

"Yes."

"Are you sure?" Chisholm said, boring in on the nun. "Don't say that just because it would help. Are you sure you could identify him?"

"Yes, I'm sure," she said, almost desperately.

"What did he look like?" she asked. Then like an order she added, "Take your time, think clearly. Tell us what you *saw*, not what you *think* you saw."

"He was young, early twenties, thin, clean-cut, black hair—brown hair. Dark brown hair."

Now they were finally getting somewhere. "Any particular nationality?"

"No, he didn't look like anything. He was average-looking."

"Marks, scars, anything distinguishing?"

"Nothing. He was . . . anonymous-looking."

"So what makes you say you could identify him?"

"I have a photographic memory," Sister Marianne snapped in reflexive defense from this onslaught, and Chisholm pounced.

"I'll see it when I believe it," she snapped right back.

Denton rolled his eyes as Chisholm went right on cowing the nun.

Women eluded Denton to an extent. He liked women, and he understood them most of the time, but the dynamics between them was something that was just a little bit beyond his ken, like listening to foreigners speaking their own peculiar language.

But that wasn't on his mind as he followed Chisholm out of the conference room after she announced a five-minute break. What was on his mind was what Chisholm knew.

"That was a slightly severe Q and A, wouldn't you agree?" he said over her shoulder as they walked down the hallway, Denton trying to figure out a way to finesse what she knew out of her.

But Maggie Chisholm didn't play ball, ignoring him the way she had for the last three days as she walked into the ladies' room. Denton followed right behind.

Inside the bathroom, Chisholm turned on him.

"What are you doing here?" she asked, but Denton ignored the question as he checked the stalls to make sure no one else was around.

"I know why you don't like me, that's no great leap of the imagination," he said checking the last of the stalls. "I *don't* know why you dislike the nun so much, but frankly I don't really care."

He turned to face Chisholm across the empty, white bathroom, nothing but air between them. Chisholm stared at him straight in the eye, Denton unwilling to back off but feeling her reach into his very skull. They stood there looking at each other for a beat, until Chisholm finally relented; she had to pee, after all. "I don't dislike the penguin," she said, then turned and walked into a stall, closing the door behind her.

Denton sat on the edge of the row of sinks facing the row of stalls, lighting a cigarette as he said, "I see. Then why the little interrogation back there? But like I said, I don't really care. She is a major asset. In her pretty little head, she has the face of Sepsis locked away. And for whatever reason, our friendly neighborhood assassin wants that pretty little head blown clean off. Your job, as well as mine, is to protect her and get information out of her, regardless. Don't blow this, Chisholm. Don't antagonize her. I am aware that you have a reputation for, shall we say, ham-fisted solutions to problems, if not *pig*-fisted—"

"What are you talking about?" she interrupted, unable to see Denton through the stall door but staring at the point where his voice came from. Instinctively, she knew. "You pulled my file, didn't you, you son of a bitch. That's confidential and private."

Like a DJ taking requests, it rolled off his lips: "Ohio State '79, Stanford Law '82. Married '84, divorced '87, one son, Robert Everett, you've been the hatchet lady for Mario Rivera for the last four years—nice job at the stadium, by the way."

"Bastard."

And the bastard had the nerve to tsk. "Don't act so offended, Margaret, you've been sniffing around my hydrants ever since you heard we were going to be working together, isn't that right? You're not pissed off that I know so much. You're pissed off that you know so little." He sucked down some nicotine and felt pleased with himself. There was something to be said about laying your cards out on the table.

Chisholm didn't back off so easily. "At least I don't lie whenever I open my mouth. 'Sister Alice' my ass—you're not even Catholic. And I bet you didn't even go to Dartmouth."

"The funny thing is, I did, but that's not important." He glanced at his nails, thinking, then decided he didn't want to mess around with this woman anymore. "I'm not going to appeal to the better devils of your nature, Margaret. Instead, I'll appeal to your practical sense—the sooner this investigation is over, the sooner I'll be out of here."

"Good riddance to bad rubbish," she said as she pulled up her panties and flushed the toilet.

"Funny," Denton said as Chisholm came out of the toilet stall and walked to a sink to wash her hands.

"I thought so."

"Margaret: The way to finish this investigation quickly is to share our information and not piss all over each other." Denton looked hard at Chisholm as smoke clouded his face. "You know something. I want to know what."

Chisholm smiled as she lathered her hands over and over. "What makes you think I know something?"

"Because you didn't *care* about the background information. You asked the nun questions about herself—not about her order, not about what the other people around the convent were up to, not about anything, only questions about her. What do you know?"

Chisholm rinsed her hands and pulled some paper towels out of the dispenser, letting the silence hang there, for eons if necessary. It was so simple it was amazing it hadn't occurred to Denton yet.

"Well?" he finally asked.

Her hands dry, she threw the towels away and gave Denton her full, amused attention. "This is a cut down for you, isn't it? You're Lehrer's lead homeboy. You usually assign cases, you never run a case. Why are you here? Why is CIA so interested in Sepsis?"

"Maybe I'm on my way down in the Agency," he said casually.

"You're not," came her lapidary reply. "Lehrer wouldn't have backed you up the way he did unless you were still his top mutt."

Denton looked impressed, whipping out his little black book and jotting the phrase down. " 'Top mutt,' I like that." He finished writing, put out the cigarette in the sink, and turned all his force on her, for the first time losing his smile.

"What do you know, Margaret?"

Chisholm could feel herself being pushed by Denton, but she held on to her amused look and smile. "You're not trying to catch Sepsis, are you. You're trying to turn him. That's it, isn't it? You want him all for yourselves, your brand-new toy."

"No, that's not it," he said, relenting a bit but still keeping the pressure at the ready. Chisholm could *feel* him debating how tight to put the screws on her, and it was . . . exciting actually, in a bizarre kind of way.

"It would be nice to have someone like Sepsis inside our tent pissing out rather than outside pissing in. But we're not interested in turning him. We want him out of the picture, and that's the truth. Now, what do you know?"

It started slow this time, but it was building to a terrific steam. "Let's cut a deal," she said, still leering at him in an amused way.

The leer was what ended his patience. He suddenly pushed, hard. "You are no longer entertaining me, Agent Chisholm. What do you know. I want to know *now.*"

"We cut a deal, then I tell you what I know. Maybe. *If* I know something, I don't really have to tell you now do I."

She was right. This was FBI turf; he was only on for the ride. Denton considered this as he eyed Chisholm, wondering what it would take, what kind of information he would need to break her. He relented—for now. "I see. Very well. What's your deal."

"I run this investigation and you do what CIA is supposed to do—

provide intelligence. I have final say-so on all field decisions and you just stay out of my hair. You keep me informed about everything. And I mean *everything*. No holding back, no playing games."

"Concerning Sepsis."

"Concerning Sepsis and whatever is related to Counterparts. Agreed?"

Denton lit another cigarette, pretending to consider her offer, though both of them knew he didn't have much of a choice. "Agreed," he said finally. "What do you know about the nun's order, this Opus Dei?"

Chisholm laughed outright. "You CIA guys aren't that clever. I know Langley's been combing the files on Opus Dei. You're thinking terrorists, you're thinking politics, you're thinking religion, you're thinking about the combinations, you're thinking all these elaborate permutations, but you're not looking at the problem in the right way. It's not the *order* that's important. It's the *penguin* that counts."

I will be heading the Vatican restoration project in three weeks, along with Professor Gettier," she told them.

The three of them were alone, without the tape recorders, facing each other across the conference table. "Our job will be to renovate the interior structure of St. Peter's Basilica. There have been no major renovations in over two centuries. The structure has been weakened considerably due to the natural wear and tear, the tourists, and the acid rain in Rome."

Denton was the first to ask the obvious question: "Why you?"

Marianne looked at him as if it were the simplest question in the world. "Because I am the foremost expert on the Basilica."

"False modesty aside, please," said Chisholm, eyeing the nun.

Sister Marianne eyed her right back.

"False modesty is a sin of pride, Agent Chisholm. My doctoral thesis was on the internal architecture of the Basilica. I designed the renovation process by which the arches and main support columns could be strengthened without damaging the structure as it stands or compromising its future integrity. I've devoted a large part of my life to this project. . . . This project *is* my life."

Denton leaned back in his chair and looked at Chisholm. He couldn't say what he wanted to say, but a couple of hours later, as Chisholm took the elevator down to the basement garage at the Hoover Building, he allowed himself to go.

"That's it? Some stupid project to renovate the Vatican? *That's* what this is all about?"

"Exactly," Margaret Chisholm said, tying her sneakers as the elevator took them to the bottom together. She had changed into athletic gear, a gray sweatshirt and black baggy sweatpants, her purse and a big duffel bag slung over her shoulder. "This renovation project is what counts."

Denton sighed, combed his hair with his hand, then lit a cigarette in the elevator, giving a mental fuck-you to the No Smoking sign. "You are so off, Chisholm, it isn't even funny."

She stood up and kept her eyes on the floor lights above the elevator doors. "Sepsis has been working out of Rome for the last four months, you told me so yourself. The penguin—"

"Would you please stop calling her 'penguin'? It seems so cruel to call her that."

She glanced at him, amused, as she continued. "The *nun* then is going to be in Rome in three weeks. Sepsis tries popping her a couple of times. Why? Because Sepsis doesn't want her in Rome. Why doesn't he want her in Rome? Because she's going to do something he doesn't want her to do."

"What, restore the Vatican? That's silly."

"Maybe he likes it the way it is. Or maybe he wants to try his hand at some renovations of his own."

As if on cue, the elevator doors opened and Chisholm walked out, Denton trailing after her.

"Sepsis wants to blow up the Vatican? Why kill the nun? How does that fit?"

"I don't know, do I look psychic?"

"No, but you do sound silly," he said as they got to her minivan. Chisholm tossed the duffel bag into the back seat and then climbed into the front, rolling down the driver-side window to finish off the conversation. She looked right at Denton.

"Denton."

"Yes, Margaret," he said condescendingly.

"He tried to kill her not once but twice. The first time, maybe he was trying to kill some other nun. Or maybe he was making some kind of big political statement. But the second attempt? Sepsis wanted her *specifically*—it was about her. Not about Opus Dei, not about anti-Catholic sentiment. The only thing about her that is of any importance is the work she does, or in this case the work she *will* do. He's trying to kill her because of this project of hers. How this fits into the Vatican, I don't know. But our boy does love to blow things up. The Vatican's the target."

"That's absurd. He doesn't need to expunge the nun to do that."

She made a mockingly amazed face as she started the minivan's engine. " 'Expunge,' ooooh, I like that word, Denton—is it from your little black book? Or is it the in word they use at Langley these days? Have *you* ever 'expunged' someone?"

Denton couldn't help but smile, somehow liking this difficult, crazy woman. "I don't expunge people, Margaret—I have my people expunge them for me."

She laughed as she pulled out of her parking slot, leaving Denton behind. He stared after her, a smile playing on his lips. He hadn't made up his mind if she was an enemy or not, but he was beginning to like her against his better judgment. But then again, he'd liked Roper, and that hadn't stopped him from doing him in. He turned and went back into the building.

Like any other multilevel parking structure, the basement of the Hoover Building curved and sloped at subtly crazy angles, as if it had been designed by sloppy kids a thousand feet tall. It always unnerved Margaret a bit—she felt like she would slide off if she wasn't extra careful in her driving. So when she got out of the basement and onto the pleasing flatness of Seventeenth Street, she was relieved, casually waving at the armed guards at the exit. She turned south and motorvated on down to M Street West, on her way to the gym.

Truth be told, and though Margaret hated to admit it, she was growing more vain as she aged. Up to her early thirties, she had rarely worn makeup aside from some mascara (her eyelashes were such a light red they were almost invisible). Now, pushing forty, she was wearing more than she ever had before—very little compared to other women her age, or even younger, but a lot for her. So as she drove to the gym, she hunted for something to wipe off the makeup with.

The gym, though, wasn't out of vanity. Rowing, swimming, running, bicycling—the routine she did was so boring and repetitive that it shut down her mind, leaving her free to not think for a couple of hours three times a week. The routine was *so* numbing in fact that her mind now seemed to live for it, burning bright and hard in the hour or so before she went to the gym, before shutting down for good.

"Hello?" she called on her cellular phone.

"Hi Mom," said Robby, normal and bored-sounding, which was a relief—nothing was the matter and he hadn't done anything.

"Listen, put the meat loaf in the oven . . . No no no, if you nuke it, it's gonna taste all soggy and yucky. In the oven, at two seventy-five. . . . What *kind* of a 'study date'? Doesn't that girl have a home of her own? . . . Okay, but no Nintendo and no making out. . . . Oh yeah, right, sure. With all these study dates, it's a wonder you haven't graduated from high school yet. . . . Yeah yeah yeah, I've heard it all before. I'll be home in an hour," she lied (it would be closer to three), "and you'd both better be dressed. Love you," she said, absently blowing kisses into the cell phone before hanging up. An hour was far too little time for twelve-year-old hormones to do any serious damage, she thought, idling on M Street at Twenty-first, the cross traffic thick. At thirteen though, it was gonna be a completely different story.

She finally found an old Kleenex in her purse and turned her attention to her makeup. To look at her, Margaret seemed vacant-eyed and fairly mongoloid as she went through her high-gear phase, ticking off everything in her mind as she started to wipe off her makeup. Things to do tomorrow, the day after, people to call, groceries, get stamps . . . she went down the list as she wiped off most of her base. But she could still feel little splotches of makeup on her face, so she grabbed the rearview mirror and swiveled it her way.

That's when she saw them.

As she turned the mirror, for a brief moment, she could have sworn she had caught a glimpse of something that was not supposed to be there, before she saw her face staring back at her in the mirror. She moved the mirror around, retracing the arc of movement, and then she saw them good and clear.

They were behind her and to her left, patrolling her blind spot in a delivery truck. Not actually a *truck* truck, but not quite a van either: It was sort of like those UPS delivery trucks, only this one was gray and unpainted, fairly anonymous-looking. The windows were tinted, the inside of the truck invisible. But out the passenger-side window she could see the barrel of a machine gun. Not much, only about four inches or so. But that was enough. She was being set up for a drive-by shooting.

No way she would have seen them if she hadn't moved her mirror around to see herself. Even now, she wasn't observing them through the rearview mirror directly, but rather through a caroming reflection, going from her eyes to the rearview mirror to the outside driver's mirror and ending in the machine gun. The truck with the drive-by itch was behind the car next to her. Casually, Margaret glanced left, to see if she had some more company.

The car to the left was a commuter talking on a cell phone, innocent. His black-and-yellow-striped tie was loose but not undone. She could tell by his posture that he was unaware of her; he seemed pissed about something someone was telling him over the phone. She glanced to her right. Another car, also with an innocent mushroom, a college-age kid, also unaware of her: he was softly singing along to the tune on the radio. She looked at the right-hand outside mirror of the minivan. Behind her there was no one, the light on the cross street behind still red, holding up the traffic a good two hundred yards back. The cross traffic was so tight back there, nobody had managed to turn into her street. Which was just as well.

So the gray truck was gonna come up on her blind spot, blow her away, then turn left at the first available street. Sounded to Chisholm like a good plan. Probably the commuter in the bee tie was a fast driver; it was a Lexus two-door he was driving. So Mr. Bee Tie would hit it, the truck edging up behind, passing Chisholm and spraying her good, killing her before she knew it. Nifty.

Chisholm saw her light was still red, the cross-traffic light still green. She replaced her Kleenex in her big purse, keeping her eyes glued to the rearview mirror. Then she glanced to her left, at the cross-traffic light.

It was still green, but the pedestrian walkway sign started flashing.

The gray truck inched ever so slightly closer.

"Keep it slow, babe," she mumbled. "Keep it slow, but keep it coming."

As if on demand, the gray truck moved forward just a bit more. The bee tie in the Lexus also started rolling as pedestrians were scared off by the blinking walkway sign. The college kid to her right turned up the volume of his radio, the quiet, dark music drifting through his open window.

Chisholm put the minivan in gear with her right hand, searching through her purse with her left, glancing at the shifting traffic lights around her. The cross-traffic light on the intersection snapped to yellow, the WALK/DON'T WALK sign now a steady, silent red-negative.

"Yes honey, it's gonna be so sweet when I fuck you over . . ."

Her right hand was gripping the wheel so tight her knuckles seemed ready to tear through her skin, but Chisholm didn't notice that or the beating of her heart. All she saw was that up ahead, beyond the trickling flow of cross traffic, the street—her street—was wide open and empty. God, it was gonna be messy.

". . . so sweet and yummy . . . you'll never want another . . ."

The cross-traffic light was yellow, and then it went red.

Her light turned green.

The Lexus took off like a shot, but the squeal of tires didn't come from Mr. Bee Tie—it came from Chisholm's minivan, which didn't go forward but *backward* as her left hand came out of the window holding her gun, and then it was *BLAM! BLAM! BLAM!* right into the passen-

ger side of the gray truck, the shooter's brains and blood neatly spraying the driver as Chisholm continued to drive backward and fire her revolver out the window at the receding gray truck—

The truck: the truck just hit the gas, screaming forward and away as
Chisholm slammed the brakes and switched gears, the minivan spinning rubber and losing ground on the surefooted gray truck, twenty
yards ahead already and putting space between itself and Chisholm
when her minivan finally bit down on the road and roared tractor-loud
out away toward the truck, and minivan or not, it had the *oomph* to eat
the distance between itself and the truck like sugar cubes and hungry
horses.

Suddenly, halfway up to the next street, the truck hit the brakes,
hard.

Chisholm had finally picked up some speed, the minivan really
cranking, when the truck ahead of her suddenly slammed to a stop. She
hit the brakes and downshifted to first simultaneously, the minivan's
engine venting an angry machine neigh as its nose end seemed to want
to plow itself right into the concrete of the road.

Dead stop at four feet from the rear of the shooter truck, those rear
doors flew open and three men, looking sort of like Aryan Nation pro-
totypes, were right in Chisholm's *face*—and all of them had machine
guns.

Kalis, Chisholm thought randomly, close enough to see the make of
the guns as she dove into the passenger seat of her minivan as the cab
was sprayed, bits of upholstery and glass and tan leather and press-
board flying about, the smell of cordite thick and cutting.

Miraculously the minivan's engine hadn't stalled out, so now, lying
prone on her side, she did the only thing she could think of—she hit
the gas and slammed the rear of the truck—*WHAAASH!!!*

She hit the back once, the truck bounced forward, then she hit it—
cruuuAUSH!—again and sat up, the truck getting the message and
ending this bumper-car bullshit, picking up speed and taking off—but
not before one of the Aryan Nation good buddies lost his footing and
fell off the back of the truck and onto the ground mere *yards* ahead of
Chisholm. And like a roughshod rider, Chisholm's minivan drove right

over the man who fell, squashing his head and knees, leaving a huge stain across the pale gray concrete of M Street.

The minivan's windshield was gone, blown, streaked and punctured and shattered to shit, but the factory plastic mixed in with the glass to turn it into "safety glass" held it together, making it impossible to see. So Chisholm kicked out with her right foot up over the dashboard as she floored it with her left, and fuck the transmission, which was making sounds like a maddened horse. The windshield popped off and there she was, twenty yards behind the truck, its two rear passengers holding on for dear life. Chisholm shifted to second and then to third, easing up on the engine, which responded with a great leap forward and an evened-out band, riding hard on the truck that she knew she was going to catch for sure.

Chisholm hit the speed-dial function on her cell phone, holding the receiver to her ear with her right shoulder, not thinking to use the speaker phone as she screamed into the mouthpiece, the wind or her blood so loud she could barely hear a thing.

"Center, this is Chisholm five-five-seven-six-Alpha-Tango-Zulu, request emergency backup and I mean right now, high-speed chase westbound on M Street at Twenty-second in North West— Hold on!" she shouted, dropping the phone as the boys on the back of the truck got their bearings and raised their weapons again. She didn't swerve but went for them with her gun—*BLAM! BLAM! BLAM!* Out of bullets but *boy* did it feel good when one of them took it right in the throat and the red red blood flew out, caught by the wind, the fucker going down in her path as she drove right over his stinking corpse, out of bullets now, the speedloader at the bottom of her purse as she picked up the phone, speaking again as she hunted for the speedloader and drove like a demon down M Street saying—

"Center, are you still there? A delivery truck, nominal five targets, two are splattered all over M Street, get some cleaning people, there's the driver and there's one more in the back, also a guy riding shotgun, but he's dead. Two live targets, I say again two live targets, one driver, one in the back, the rear guy has a machine gun so assume the driver does too."

—and whatever Center said or was saying was gone as she whipped the minivan's engine on third till it was screaming in machine head pain for fourth and she gave it to it, for her torture getting a huge surge forward that tore up the pavement, Chisholm positive she was leaving huge divots of concrete in her wake, positive but too wrapped up to look back, only seeing as the truck came closer—

And then it fooled her, suddenly turning hard left at a corner, going south against traffic at Twenty-fourth, passing the red light that shone on M Street. Chisholm slammed the brakes and turned with all her strength while still holding on to her gun and the speedloader as the minivan lost lateral traction and skidded across the intersection, amazingly not hitting any car or pedestrian but to her right she could see she was skidding sideways right toward a parked ambulance—

—*SLAM!* went the minivan against the ambulance, leaving the whole right fake-wooden siding and snatches of silver paint and red red blood from the two she'd run over splattered and smeared across the ruined ambulance—and all the while Chisholm only accelerated, shaving the ambulance and another car parked behind it as she raced after the truck.

The truck was getting away, driving right down the middle of the street as the oncoming cars, few but enough, turned away onto the sidewalk to avoid it, the minivan's engine screaming, frothing steam from the front hood from a bullet hole wound, chasing hard and as oblivious as the truck of anything and anyone else.

The bitch can drive—Sepsis, the driver, slamming his truck forward, lighter now that two were off it, but knowing that the weight made no real difference, it was just a delivery truck, slow and steady, he wasn't gonna be able to get away.

Ahead of Sepsis was a rotunda and he drove right through it; miracle of miracles, the truck didn't get clipped as it seemed to leap into the rotunda and gallop right across it, steadying out as he made it halfway through, glancing back in the rearview mirror.

Chisholm came right after Sepsis, but not so lucky as she got clipped in the rear by a car racing around the rotunda that wasn't quick enough to avoid the minivan completely. But still the minivan rode on, straightening out as it hit the rotunda and went right after Sepsis, who stared, amazed, and didn't see as he came off the rotunda on the other side and got hit, hard, on the nose, the truck spinning ninety degrees, perpendicular to Chisholm's onrushing van.

She saw it and slammed the brakes, the tires tearing the rotunda grass, the tail end swerving, turning her around till she was parallel to the stopped delivery truck, six yards to the minivan's right.

The truck stalled out, Sepsis furious as he banged the wheel and tried to turn the engine, flooded—no way he'd have the time to wait out the truck, so he reached behind the driver's seat for the Uzi he was carrying in case of an emergency just like this one as he screamed in French to Gaston, the lone survivor of his team, *"Get out and kill the fucking bitch!"*

The minivan wasn't stalled out, Chisholm in the cab, speed-loading her gun as she watched the delivery truck try to start up again, then stop, nothing happening as she realized, *They're coming out, they're gonna spray me in the minivan,* out out, *fucking gotta get* OUT RIGHT NOW!

Blindly reaching into her purse—another speedloader fell right into her palm as she burst out of the driver's side and crouched by the engine block, hoping it would give her cover as Gaston, tall, tan, brown hair, came out from the back of the truck crazed with fear and bloodlust and just sprayed the minivan with his Kalashnikov, not knowing where the fucking bitch was, spraying the whole thing as Sepsis too got out with a full clip in the Uzi, desperate but not panicked, watching the minivan without shooting as Gaston let go of all his bullets, which pinged and ricocheted off the engine block.

And behind the engine block, Chisholm crouched, unmoving, unscreaming, unbreathing, unshaken, as Gaston fired on full automatic, the sound of his grunting in an animal cry fierce and hateful; she knew what she was going to do come the lull in the firing, and then it came—Gaston was out of bullets.

Maggie raced to the tail end of the minivan and when she popped out from behind it they were right there, right in front of her, aiming at the minivan's cab, Gaston reloading, never expecting her to pop out from behind the back of the minivan as she ran for the back of the truck and let go, firing left-handed as she ran, *BLA-BLAM* quick succession, controlled, and one of the bullets hit Gaston in the head, sweeping him off his feet as three quarters of his brains vacated his skull, the bullet flying off with better than two pounds of gray matter before Sepsis even saw what had happened, instinctively racing for the *front* of the truck, keeping the vehicle between himself and Chisholm.

They stopped. Between them was the delivery truck, Chisholm behind the tail end, Sepsis by the front. The cars in the rotunda had stopped, people were racing from the street, ditching their cars, in a panic at the sound of the gunfire. Chisholm and Sepsis, though, were sitting tight, thinking things out as they kept the truck between them.

Time was on Chisholm's side, they both knew, so sooner or later Sepsis would have to make a run for it. Either that or wait to deal with Chisholm's reinforcements, be they cops or FBI.

Sepsis had been through this before, and he wasn't panicked. Two years back, just before he turned twenty-two, he'd been in a Mexican standoff with a couple of South African blacks, Communist terrorists. A Mexican standoff, easy: Be quick, casual, and aim straight for the head, which was how he'd gotten out of that one. But this would be tough, since aside from the delivery truck and the hulking remains of the minivan, there wasn't any cover for a good twenty yards around.

Abruptly, Sepsis raised his Uzi over his head and fired through the windshield of the delivery truck, the bullets coming out the back side, Chisholm already crouched but crouching lower still as the bullets whizzed by above her head.

That was when he ran. He ran in the direction he had been going in the delivery truck—south, running onto the continuation of Twenty-fourth Street, racing down the sidewalk before Chisholm knew what was going on, and then she saw him: a man racing with the other pedestrians but so far behind the others that it had to be him. And so she ran, ran right after him, and she knew there was no way he was going to get away from her.

Sepsis ran, glancing behind him, racing down the sidewalk and weaving between the telephone and electrical poles and trees, spraying random cover fire behind him as Chisholm ran after him.

Up ahead, a street cop, alone, appeared out of fucking nowhere, holding a gun in a two-handed, wide-legged stance, and screamed "*Stop!*"—Sepsis whipped the Uzi forward close to his body, his left hand steadying his aim, and just sprayed the stupid cop dead where he stood before running right over his corpse.

"*Get out of my way get out of my fucking way!*" Chisholm screamed senselessly as she chased, seeing Sepsis suddenly turn right and disappear behind some bushes, making her slow down in caution before she realized what it was—Foggy Bottom station.

The metro station entrance was recessed a good ten yards from the edge of the sidewalk, and when Chisholm passed the bushes that partially hid it from view, all she could see was a huge maw, descending endlessly, the impossibly long and steep electric escalators taking pedestrians down, seemingly straight into hell. Sepsis was already halfway down one of the escalators, pushing and shoving people out of his way as he ran down, Chisholm racing too, but to a different escalator, emptier than the one Sepsis had taken, rushing down as she screamed, "*Get down get down get the fuck* down!*" and so he turned on her, standing steady on the moving escalator and fired good and calm right at her—

She dove forward onto the hard edges of the escalator steps, slithering down just as she had at Quantico, a million centuries ago when she was at the Academy. *So that's why they force you to slither through the mud on your belly under a mesh of barbed wire,* she thought idiotically as she crawled down the moving escalator, feeling the bullets of this Sepsis fuck punk puncture the escalator's metal sheathing, but behind her, behind her—up ahead she was just four yards from the bottom of the escalator, she was going to make it there. *And then I'm gonna—*

Sepsis stopped shooting but kept running down the escalator, unwilling to lose slugs when he couldn't see Chisholm anymore, jumping down the last few steps of the escalator and hitting the ground just as Chisholm started shooting from a crouch on the ground at the bottom of the escalator she was on, one of her bullets nicking the collar of his polo shirt.

My throat—! he thought as he returned fire—*Ra-ta-ta-ta-TA!*—full stop.

Sepsis was out of bullets.

In anger as black as Chisholm's was red, Sepsis grabbed the Uzi with both hands and slammed it to the ground at his feet before turning and running into the metro station.

Seeing him drop his machine gun from behind the cover of the escalator, Chisholm picked herself up off the ground and ran too, running after Sepsis into the dark metro station as she screamed at the pedestrians that seemed to flood the dark cavernous station and get in her way, "*Out of my way, federal officer, GET OUT OF MY WAY!*"

Sepsis was barely fifteen feet ahead of her, grabbing mushrooms and throwing them in her path as Chisholm ran after him. He jumped over the ticket machine and disappeared down an escalator to the track level, Chisholm right behind him, with five bullets in her gun, she was going to get him yes she was.

She hit the top of the escalator to the track level below, right behind him, and there he was, sprawled out on his back at the bottom of the escalator, tripped up by mushrooms that were fucking *everywhere*— but Sepsis was holding a gun, aiming it right for Chisholm's face.

She dove just as he fired his gun—*PLÄT-PLÄT-PLÄT!*—landing on her left side, safely below his line of sight.

On the track level below Chisholm, Sepsis got up and looked around, literally unable to believe his eyes—a silver metro train was just sitting there, its doors wide open, as if it were *waiting* for him, just as a voice over the station public address system, a monstrous voice like some bored and decrepit third-rate god, said, "This is the orange line to . . . Vienna. All passengers please get on board."

And that's what Sepsis did—he dove into the train.

Chisholm was already on her way down to the track level of the station, unhurt and unscared and unwilling to let go, rushing down two steps at a time to the track level as she saw a man—Sepsis—dive into the metro train five yards away just as the doors of the train slammed shut, and then the metro train was moving, he was getting away, and then the metro train picked up speed and it was gone.

Did she see him? Did she see his *face*? No way, fuck, no way, she hadn't seen his face and he had gotten away, as around her on the station platform people screamed and shouted, in pain and panic, Chisholm all of a sudden remembering to call, call Center, and there was a phone right there on the track level and she picked up the receiver and dialed automatically the toll-free number that was Center and then it was all in her mouth—

"Center, this is Chisholm, I'm at Foggy Bottom station, I lost him, I fucking *lost* him, I'm not hit but get some ambulances, mushrooms shot up all over the goddamned place, fuck fuck fuck *fuck!* and my car's got no insurance!" she screamed.

In a red red rage, she slammed the receiver against the silvery silent telephone, slamming it over and over and over before dropping it and stepping away, raising her left arm, her gun arm, the gun aimed straight at that fucking phone fucker—*BLAM! BLAM! BLAM! BLAM! BLAM!*

It was over. She was out of bullets. People ran from her. Her tailbone hurt, but not too much. Both her shins were bruised, she could feel them. The nail of her right-hand ring finger had cracked to the quick. Her boobs felt mushed up, her sports bra painfully bunched up beneath them. She looked down at herself, expecting blood somewhere. There was none. With nowhere to go, all that adrenaline made her feel weak and light. She was going to levitate any second now, she was sure. Then it came down, sucking up her body, squeezing her innards until she thought she would faint. But she didn't.

She took a last look at the black tunnel down which Sepsis had disappeared on the metro train. In her pocket, she could feel the bulk of her remaining speedloader. It was patient, but it was demanding, like a bottle of booze or a syringe full of smack. But she held back and didn't feed it to her gun. She didn't because Margaret Chisholm didn't know who she would have shot.

SIX

Blowback and the Intel Source

Chisholm didn't even bother to tell Denton what had happened. That was left to Amalia, who caught him at home watching a Mexican League soccer game, the better part of a whole avocado spooned away. He was scraping the last of the meat of the fruit off the skin when he got her call, eating and listening as she told him all about the chase, the shoot-out, and some other interesting little tidbits.

"So she's at the Hoover Building?"

"No sir, she just left. She's filing her report tomorrow in the morning."

"Where'd she go?"

"Home."

Denton drove a black convertible Mercedes Benz. It was a great car. The advance on his third novel had paid for it, and though the book never earned back his advance, Denton got to keep the Mercedes anyway. That night he put it to good use, driving all the way to Silver Springs on the other side of town in twenty-five minutes flat. When he got to her place, Chisholm herself opened the door.

"Oh, it's you," she said in a flat, weird voice. She let him in as she retreated to a small table by the door.

"Why didn't you call me?"

"I had other things on my mind, Denton," she said offhandedly. That was when he saw her discreetly replace her gun in the drawer of the foyer table. Without a look back, she walked into the living room, Denton following.

The living room was empty, but Denton could feel someone else in the house. "Anyone around?"

"They'll be here in a minute," she said cryptically. An open suitcase and a pile of clothing fresh from a laundry dryer lay on the sofa; a pink antistatic dryer sheet slipped out from between the clothes as Chisholm picked up a T-shirt and began folding it. But the pile was of boys' clothing, Chisholm packing it in the suitcase neatly, almost done now.

"Who'll be here?" asked Denton.

"Sanders."

"Oh."

Presently, a boy of not much more than twelve bounded down the stairs in a baseball cap and red T-shirt and jeans, with a knapsack stuffed to near overflowing.

"Hiya, I'm Robby," he said to Denton winningly, sticking out his hand just like a grown-up.

"Hi, I'm Nicholas Denton," he said, instantly liking the kid as he shook his hand and glanced at Chisholm.

Chisholm was frozen, staring at her son. Denton looked back at Robby, feeling waves coming off of Chisholm that he could recognize. They were mothering waves. Oddly, he was moved.

"You work for the CIA, huh?" the kid said, wild about the mystery of the place.

"Yes, I work for CIA," he said.

"Do you like, run secret missions and stuff?"

"Oh no, I just hang back, just little stuff, y'know. It used to be more fun when the Russians were around, but now it's pretty boring."

"I can imagine," he said in a remarkably accurate mimicry of adult thoughtfulness. "I'm all packed, Mom," he said to Margaret, who snapped out of her reverie and turned an all-business look on Robby.

"You're not taking your Nintendo to San Diego, are you?"

"Why not?"

"Because it makes you stupid."

"It does not," he said, rolling his eyes in a way that Denton found startling; it was Margaret Chisholm's eye roll all the way.

Chisholm just stared at him with a doubtful look, willing him to leave the video game behind. But the look had no edge to it—those red red tendrils were absent. Robby turned to Denton and kept talking as if his mother weren't doing anything.

"So what do you do now that the Russians are gone?"

"Oh, this and that, mostly make sure that we know what's happening in other places. The world's pretty big—lots of trouble in places besides Russia."

"I bet," he said, growing uncomfortable under his mother's stare. "Mom!" he said finally, exasperated and embarrassed.

"Okay," she said, "your father will have to deal with this stupid addiction." The doorbell rang and Margaret went to answer it as she said over her shoulder, "But this isn't a vacation. You're starting school as soon as you get there."

From where they stood, neither Robby nor Denton could see the front door, or the foyer table. Denton was positive Chisholm had her gun ready to blow away anyone she wasn't happy to see.

"So you're going to San Diego, huh?" he said, turning his attention to the kid. "Why's that?"

"I don't know, my mom thinks it's a good idea I see more of my dad. But I'm gonna be there in June anyway, that's just a couple of months away. Mom is so weird."

"She sure is," he let slip, then added quickly but casually, "All moms are. I'm thirty-seven, and my mom's *still* bugging me. She's always telling me to dress warm," he said, looking confused. Robby nodded sagely, recognizing an equal—another scarred and bloodied veteran of the Apron String Wars.

Chisholm came back with Sanders and his partner, Richard Greene, in tow. Agent Sanders knew Robby well, and they gave each other the smooth five. "How's my little brother, all set to go?"

"Ready Freddy," he said. Chisholm finished packing and zipped up the suitcase, which Richard Greene picked up.

"I'll go put this in the car," he said, darting his eyes at Sanders, who got the message, the two of them going outside to give Robby and Margaret a minute alone. Denton faded back, but he didn't leave as Chisholm turned her attention on Robby.

"Now, this isn't your vacation yet. You still have to finish up school."

"I know, Mom."

"Your dad's going to pick you up at the airport, but if he's not there, you wait by the gate."

"I know, Mom."

"Don't talk to any strangers."

"I know."

"Where's your ticket?"

"In my knapsack."

"You sure?"

"Yes I'm sure."

"Let me see it."

Robby looked up at her condescendingly, but Margaret didn't care; she looked right back at him. Sighing, Robby dropped his knapsack and opened the outside pocket, pulling out his plane ticket. "See?"

"Okay. You have money?"

"No," he said brightly.

"How much you got?"

"Just a twenty."

"Twenty dollars? That's plenty," she said, Robby bowing his head in resignation, more than a little aware that Denton was watching them. He knew what was gonna come next.

Unable to resist, Margaret hugged her son tight tight, giving him a kiss on the cheek. "Mmm, I love you so much. Take care, and I'll call you as soon as you get there."

Robby, humiliated, gave Denton a desultory little wave as he walked out the front door, Margaret following him with her eyes as he got in the car with Sanders and Greene and drove off. She closed the door and turned to Denton, noticing him for the first time.

"The trials of parenthood."

"I can imagine," he said.

"So what are you doing here, anyway?" she asked, looking at him quizzically.

"One of my people told me about your adventure."

"It did make the evening news, you know," she said, amused he needed an aide to tell him what was going on. Denton caught on and ignored her.

"Amalia dug up some stuff on the shooters I think you might like to know."

"What did you get?" she said, all business as she walked to the kitchen, Denton following her.

"I think you're going to be happy," he said as she opened the fridge. "The four shooters were all Québecois Libre—"

"There were five," she said as she offered a can of Coke to Denton.

"No thanks. I meant the four you killed. All came over with false papers, all papers that are traceable to guess where—Rome."

"They were carrying their papers on them? Dummies."

"No no, they were clean, not a scrap of paper on any of them. But one of them *was* carrying a motel room key. Amalia—"

"Ah, your favorite wet-girl," she said, smiling at Denton as she popped the can. "I thought we agreed we'd run this with Bureau people only."

"Well, it was just easier—"

"Forget it," she said, holding up her hand and bowing her head. "I'm too tired to argue with you. Go ahead, what did your people find?"

Denton smiled. "Amalia traced the key and she and her squad searched the place. Bingo. There were four sets of docs. Now get this:

The documents *weren't* actual forgeries—they were official, Canadian-issued passports. But Amalia did a little digging. All of the documents turned out to be hollow."

Chisholm raised an eyebrow, drinking this in. Hollow documents were identity cards, passports, whatever, that did not have birth certificates to back them up. Only bad forgeries were hollow, and they were usually easy to spot—the document itself had been tampered with. An officially issued hollow document, however, was rare. Unheard of, actually.

"This is weird," she said, thinking. She snapped out of it. "What about the fifth guy?"

"Well, pity you didn't get a good look at him, but I think it was Sepsis."

Chisholm paused, the can at her lips. "I think so too," she said before taking a swig. "And I'll tell you something else—you know all that talk that this guy is like twenty-five or something absurd like that? Well, he is."

"He's what?"

"He's a *baby*. I thought it was all bullshit when all these source reports kept saying he was just a kid. But the fifth guy—he was young, but he had the moves. The moves, the coolness, he knew *exactly* what he was about. There's no question about it—the fifth guy was Sepsis, and that fifth guy was just a kid. And that's a big problem for us."

"What do you mean?"

"Where did he get this training?" she asked him, unconsciously dinging her Coke can with the nail of her index finger. "He's been operating, what, for the last six, seven years? Who taught him those moves? Not in the Soviet Union, that's for sure. Patrice Lumumba U was shut down back in '88 or '89, long before this guy started in on the scene. If we can't figure out who trained him, tracing him's just about out of the question. Who'll snitch on him if we don't know who to squeeze?"

"Do you think you could recognize him if you saw him again?"

She shook her head casually. "No way, everything was happening way too fast. Skinny, dark hair, that's it. Could run into him right now and wouldn't place him."

Denton looked right through Chisholm, thinking. Then he refocused and said, "Okay, let's leave that alone for now. About the Québecois Libre types. Remember that Canadian politician that got shot a couple of years back?"

"Yeah, I remember. Rifle shot in downtown Ottawa, right in front of the Prime Minister in broad daylight. The little birdie tells me Sepsis did that guy."

"A little birdie told *me* something else: Sepsis didn't do that guy for some drug dealers like everyone was saying. He did him for Québecois Libre. He did the Canadian politico for them, so now they help him do you. Quid pro quo. Very fashionable these days. Also great for security. If we'd picked up one of these guys, he wouldn't know why he was doing the job. Come to think of it, I think I will have a Coke."

Chisholm opened the fridge and pulled out a can as Denton mulled things over. He absently used his handkerchief to pop the tab on the Coke as he stared thoughtfully at Chisholm.

"Now, question: Did he try to take you out because of Counterparts? Or are you working on some other case where they might hire Sepsis to take you out?"

"No no. My other cases are paper-pushing stuff. I might get sued, but I won't get shot. Sepsis must have figured I had the nun with me. That's an assumption, but it's the only assumption that makes sense."

"So why are you sending your son to stay with his father?"

"Call it parental paranoia." She drank some more Coke, thinking, then said dreamily, "He must have some amazing intelligence source, an intel source that's doing us no good."

Halfway in the middle of a drink of his soda, Denton's eyes locked on Chisholm. He swallowed and then asked, "How do you mean?"

"Sepsis knew the nun was in her convent. Okay, fine, no problem with that. Anybody could have known that. I mean, she lives there, right?"

"Ye-es," he said, following her but not quite seeing where she was going.

"Then he tries to nail her at the police station, on the same day. Again, fine. Maybe some local told him where she was, maybe he followed her to the police station. Whatever," she said dismissively as she hopped onto the kitchen table.

"*But*," she continued, "we brought her from New Hampshire down here with incredibly tight security. Maybe twenty people, total, knew she would be here in Rivercity under Bureau protection. A grand total of *five* people knew I would be handling this case: you, me, my boss Rivera, and your boss Lehrer. And the penguin of course. Not even Phil Carter knew I was running Counterparts until this morning. Sepsis has an intel source."

She finished her Coke, then aimed to throw it in the trash can. Denton raised the lid and Chisholm made the toss.

"Three points," she said.

"That was an easy shot, you were almost on the paint."

"You try it then."

Denton smiled casually at Chisholm. "A source that's tipping off Sepsis. I see your point. You think one of us five is his intel source," he said deadpan, testing her, but Margaret laughed out loud.

"I'd be getting a little too paranoid for my own good if I seriously thought that."

"That's a relief to hear," he said mock-facetiously, but the idea started flitting about in Denton's brain. "So this intel source, if it exists, tipped off Sepsis that you were handling the nun. Sepsis figured you were taking her from the Hoover Building to the hotel."

"I was driving in the direction of the hotel when we ran across each other. Sure, he figured I had the nun. I bet he figured I was just in his way, that he'd have to take me out in order to get at the nun."

Denton stood there, thinking. "It seems iffy," he finally said.

"What do you mean?"

"What about putting a bomb in your car, or Phil Carter's car for that matter? He's the one driving her around, after all."

"The parking lot at the Hoover Building has armed guards. Carter's men watch over things at the hotel."

"Oh," he said, but Denton was still not convinced. "Why would he waste his time following you unless he was sure you had the nun?"

"Maybe he wanted to check me out first. You know, first see if I had her with me, and if I did, blow us both away."

"That doesn't make that much sense. What if he was following you just as Carter and his men moved the nun to the hotel. He'd miss her altogether."

"If he wasn't going for the nun, then why would he shoot up my car? What, you think Sepsis is trying to kill *me* now? What for?"

Denton pondered that one. "Good point."

But it was something to think about.

They stood there in the kitchen, mulling things over, neither of them happy. There was too much in the air that was incomplete and just a little strange. A lot strange, actually. Denton lit a cigarette.

Chisholm gave a start, looking around the kitchen. It was vast and cold, empty now that Robby was gone. She turned to Denton and said, "I'm going to camp out at my office till this all blows over. You mind giving me a ride?" She smiled sardonically. "My car's in the shop."

He took a drag on his smoke. "Sure," he said, and smiled.

Tirso Gaglio?" asked the immigration officer at Leonardo da Vinci Airport. "Welcome home." He handed the passport back to the young man standing across from him, who smiled shyly and a touch nervously, the way people with nothing to hide do.

"Thanks," he said in perfect Milanese Italian, keeping up his pretense of nerves.

Replacing his documents in the inside pocket of his sports jacket, Sepsis picked up his valise and passed through the gates, lighting a cigarette as he walked.

Rome was lovely as he stepped out into the morning sunshine. From the air, he could tell how beautiful the day was going to be, and Sepsis for one was grateful.

He hadn't felt fine in Washington. The chase might have ended for Chisholm at the metro station, but once away on the train, it had only begun for Sepsis. There he was, covered in blood and bits of brain from the shotgun shooter, trying to turn invisible once again. At the next metro station, he had gotten out and stolen a taxi at gunpoint from a Salvadoran cabbie, driving around on a forty-five-minute nightmare until he finally found a hose in an empty alleyway in a black ghetto on the South East side of town. Washed up but shirtless, he'd ditched the car and taken the metro to the Mall, buying a "Support Our MIA's" T-shirt at one of the kiosks there and killing time by walking from the Lincoln Memorial to the Washington Monument and back again, trying to calm himself down. It took all his discipline not to make a break for it right then and there—just get on a plane and *go*. Instead, that night, he'd gone to the Kennedy Center, to watch a performance of Beckett's *Endgame*.

In the cab in Rome, sitting back as he rode to his hotel, the chase in Washington all in the past, Sepsis gently slipped into his well-rehearsed thoughts on Beckett, pleased at his own equanimity. Beckett's plays were beautiful, he thought, but his prose was trivial. It always surprised him how no one had ever seemed to notice the similarities between Beckett's novels and Dostoevsky's *Notes from Underground*. Dostoevsky's little novel, Sepsis was convinced, encompassed all Beckett had ever tried to achieve in his prose. *Notes* was in two chapters, and the first was equal to if not better than any of Beckett's later novels, such as *The Unnamable* or *Malone Dies*. Actually, Chapter 1 of *Notes* achieved the same effect as those novels with far more elegance and dexterity. And Chapter 2 was written in the same style as Beckett's early novels, only more interestingly and revealingly. Sepsis's conclusion was that Beckett-as-novelist was just a cheap Dostoevsky knock-off. Beckett-as-dramatist, however, was a wonderful thing to see.

How the hell did she catch on? The thought completely derailed his little train, pissing him off. They had been in her blind spot, sure that she wouldn't notice them, Sepsis himself driving extra carefully, wanting to be sure that she wouldn't know they were there until it was too late. And then out of nowhere, as if she had always known that they were there, she had shot the shooter. A miracle *he* hadn't been hit; any one of the bullets that hit the shooter could have drilled right through his body and killed him. Too tight, too tight, the schedule was too damned tight. He never should have taken multiple jobs. And with his opportunity blown, Sepsis didn't have time to mount another effort—he had to be back in Rome to start with the preparations for the basilica.

The back of the cabbie's head was just an arm's length away. With every second that he thought of that fucking woman, the angrier he became, the more he wanted to kill the taxi driver. The cabbie hadn't said a word during the entire drive, but Sepsis abruptly decided that if the cabbie tried any mindless banter, he was going to kill him. He would put his right hand flat on the cabbie's forehead, his left hand would grab his left ear, and then he would just twist.

Sepsis stared at the base of the cabbie's head, daring him to say something, anything—any excuse to snap his neck. But the cabbie—miraculously, for an Italian—said nothing, which was about as insulting as if he had. With an effort, Sepsis tore his eyes off the cabbie's head and looked out the window, trying to think about Dostoevsky and Beckett, but unable to.

Outside, in the distance, he could see the basilica, waiting for him, and finally the memory of the slippery bitch slid out of his mind, the excitement coming back again, the excitement of being so near his target, and the raw fear of failure, now that the nun would no longer be near the basilica. If the target had been a library, he would have balked. But Sepsis was not one who appreciated architecture. For him, old buildings were nothing more than monolithic bric-a-brac.

Chisholm stood behind her, patiently drinking some coffee as Sister Marianne went through the pictures.

The day after the shoot-out had been a zero-progress day for Counterparts. Chisholm spent most of it talking with the Bureau's Tactical Supervisory Board, a kind of clearinghouse for shootings, going over every detail she could recall of the chase and shoot-out, and always stumbling on the one detail.

". . . and so after you called Center, you shot the phone," they said in that patronizing way of theirs. They were all senior agents, experienced men and women, but Chisholm thought of them as an amorphous, pathetically ponderous blob.

"Yes, I shot the phone," she said firmly, with a "so what?" look to her eye. Screw it, if they wanted her skin over the mantelpiece, they'd have it. No need to humiliate herself in the process.

"Why?"

"I was—angry. I was furious actually. The bastard got away."

"You could have accidentally shot somebody. You could have killed somebody."

"No, nobody was around. I qualify as a master marksman. There was no danger."

"There was no need either," an older woman interjected.

Margaret hesitated. "No," she allowed.

"But you shot it anyway."

"Yes." *So what?*

"Let me get something clear: You were in your car when you happened to swivel your rearview mirror. Why did you do this?"

And then it went on, until again it came around to the phone-shooting incident. Margaret would have happily *paid* for the stupid phone if it would have saved her from this interrogation. They didn't seem to understand at all what it had been like, the excitement, the *thrill* of it like gangbusters, the flip side of course being this interrogation and the underlying fear: If they canned her, where would she go?

But they let her be—for now. The next day, she went back to Counterparts and dealing with the penguin.

"Good morning," Marianne said to Chisholm, smiling up at Phil Carter and his squad as they left her for the day.

"Let's go," Chisholm answered, leading the way through the guts of the Hoover Building, going for the basement terminals.

Downstairs, in the big white room filled with nothing but computers and equipment, random accessing of all that the FBI knew about everything, Chisholm sat the nun down in front of a terminal. It was loaded with the faces of every man between twenty and thirty who both matched the description the nun had provided, and had applied for and received an Italian passport during the last six months—five hundred and twelve matches.

"Sit here," Chisholm said, keeping her distance from the nun as she pointed to the joystick by the terminal's keyboard. "Go through these pictures with the joystick, right to advance, left to go back. If you recognize the man you saw, stop. Don't worry if you come to the end of the run of pictures—we have more you need to go through," she lied. Witnesses tended to get sloppy when they thought they were running out of mug shots, missing the possible suspect if he happened to be at the end of the run.

"I'll be around," she said as she turned to go find herself a cup of coffee, Sister Marianne looking after her with hollow eyes.

"Where are you going?" she heard herself asking after her.

"Get some coffee. Start looking at the pictures," she said over her shoulder.

"Could I have some tea please?" asked the nun. Chisholm didn't answer, but something about her walk and posture made Marianne think she'd been heard. So she started looking through the pictures.

Marianne didn't understand why she wanted to be liked by this strange, violent woman. Unlike her, it seemed that Agent Chisholm didn't need to be liked or likable, a secret Marianne could not understand. Agent Chisholm did not fear being liked, the way misanthropes did; Marianne could sense this. Yet she did not want to be liked either. At the core, a fundamental indifference.

Marianne flipped through the photographs, looking at them quickly but carefully. After a dozen pictures or so, Agent Chisholm came up behind her and left a cup of tea by the terminal before withdrawing. But though she didn't see her, Marianne was sure Agent Chisholm was standing right behind her.

She did not know why she wanted to be liked by her, but she did. She wished she could discuss this with Edmund, but he had already left for Rome, to start his phase of the renovations.

"Call me, for anything at all, even if it's just to talk," he told her just before he left for the airport.

"I will," she said as she hugged him.

"Promise me," he insisted.

"I promise," she laughed, touched by how much he loved her, as much as she loved him. But as she flipped through the photographs, Marianne knew she wouldn't ask Edmund's advice. He was her best friend, her father figure in many ways, but there were some things he would not understand, like her need to be liked by Agent Chisholm. Edmund, she knew, was afraid of liking people and being liked by them in turn. Marianne suspected it was because he had been an itinerant lecturer for so long—sooner or later, either his students graduated and left him behind, or he moved on to another university, his past students all gone and forgotten. It might be easier not to like and grow to love people than to be hurt by them when they moved on with their lives. It never occurred to Sister Marianne to wonder why he liked and had grown to love her.

Marianne paused at the terminal as her thoughts got her wool-gathering, the pictures forgotten for the moment.

"Yes?" Agent Chisholm asked, making Marianne turn around. As she'd suspected, Agent Chisholm was right behind her, a mere three or four yards away, leaning on a desk, watching her with flat, brown eyes. And those eyes held only a flat, empty indifference.

No idle chitchat would do, nor a politeness, something Agent Denton would have responded to and expanded on. Agent Denton would have smiled and laughed, telling a joke to pass the monotony.

But he would have been insincere, something Agent Chisholm would never be. That was the thing, the key to her indifference: Agent Chisholm could not lie. She would not like Marianne, only respect her or despise her. And as it stood, Agent Chisholm did not respect her. The flat indifference in her eyes said so. She had judged her and found her lacking, and it burned like a sulfurous wound. It burned because Marianne suspected she was right.

"Nothing," said the nun as she turned back to the photographs.

As she watched the screen over the nun's shoulder, all the pictures looked the same to Chisholm by now—dark-brown-haired anonymous men of a youngish indeterminate age. She doubted they would come up with anything useful, but there was no sense in being sloppy; by the very act of being tidy, sometimes leads came up. So she decided to have the nun look through all the pictures at least twice more, maybe three times more before calling it off.

Denton arrived and stood beside Chisholm, watching the nun go through the passport pictures. "Hey there," he said softly. "So what did prints get?"

"Nothing. Sepsis must've been wearing gloves. I didn't notice that."

"No prints at all?" Denton whispered, surprised.

"Not even on the spent shell casings."

"The Québecois Libre?"

"The Canadian Mounties are looking into them, but if they didn't have anything on file they could send us immediately, I doubt they'll get anything useful at all."

"What about the surveillance cameras in the metro station?"

"A blur."

"Great." Denton looked around, frustrated, unaccustomed to the lack of breaks. "What's she doing?"

"You told me the Québecois Libre men had hollow documents, right? But that they were officially issued?"

"Yeah, so?"

"So if they had officially issued documents, I bet Sepsis did too."

"I see. You're a clever girl, Margaret," he whispered brightly. Chisholm couldn't help smiling at him.

"Interpol got us the pictures of every Italian who's been issued a passport in the last six months. The Canadians are sending us their pictures this afternoon, tomorrow morning at the latest."

"There must be *thou*sands," he hissed.

"Yes, thousands who *applied*, but only five hundred and twelve Italians who match the age and physical description. The Canadians are sending us about two hundred more."

Keeping his distance, Denton looked over Marianne's shoulder as she went through the pictures, Chisholm patient and calm. After the nun had gone through a dozen or so, Denton turned to Chisholm and said, "They might as well be twins, all of those. This is a waste of time."

"We'll see," she said. "No sense in being sloppy."

Denton wanted to say something clever to that like, "You should talk," and then make a gun with his index finger and thumb, mock-shooting at her. It would've been exciting to see her reaction, but a little too unpredictable, so he stopped himself—barely. Instead, he asked her, "What if she doesn't identify any of them?"

"Then we'll get another sketch artist to get another drawing. But if it gets to that point, we can forget about her usefulness as a witness."

Marianne didn't hear them. Instead, she had forced herself to stop thinking and just stare at the pictures, flipping and staring, flipping and staring. She stared at one of the pictures. And then she stared again. And then she stared some more at an anonymous young man—an anonymous young man with a name: Tirso Gaglio.

"Agent Chisholm?"

Interpol confirmed that a man named Tirso Gaglio left Rome two weeks ago for Montreal," Chisholm started off without so much as a how-do. "There's no record of Gaglio entering the U.S., but he arrived back in Rome two days ago, on a direct flight from Washington. Our man. Ten bucks gets you even money he went back to try to figure out a way to blow up the Vatican," she finished, looking around Rivera's conference table.

The four of them were alone. Mario Rivera was looking at her intently with his thick arms crossed over his massive chest; Keith Lehrer was leaning back in his chair as he stared at his leather folder on the tabletop; and Denton beside him took notes.

"Why do you think this involves blowing up the Vatican?" Lehrer asked without looking at Chisholm.

"The penguin is not exactly running drugs," she said tightly, looking at Lehrer with an arched brow. "She is a college professor in hicksville with no ties to the mob, no ties to Colombians, or Arabs, or anyone carrying anything more deadly than *Roget's Thesaurus*. Sepsis on the other hand has an established reputation for blowing things up. If *you* can come up with a better hunch as to why he wants this nun so bad, do feel free to be so kind as to tell me."

"It's a stupid assumption," he casually shot right back, though he was looking at Rivera. "Sepsis kills people. I've never heard him try to kill a building. You shouldn't be running this investigation based on an—"

"You mean, *we* shouldn't be running this investigation," she said.

Lehrer didn't even blink. "Running this investigation on an unsupported hunch could blind us to other, more likely motives."

Rivera sighed thoughtfully. "Maggie, I agree. Interesting possibility, but don't bet the ranch on it. Look at this Opus Dei, look at the other nuns in the convent. Look at things she's doing back in New Hampshire."

"You're the boss," she said, noting it down. "But the fact remains, she's given us a major scoop. No one has Sepsis's face on file, but now we do. I say we put it on the Interpol wire."

Lehrer, though, was unsatisfied with this break. "How confident are you the nun made the right identification? Maybe in your eagerness to produce results . . ." He trailed off, still not looking at Chisholm but at Rivera.

Chisholm snorted; she was ready for that one. "We had her go through all the pictures twice more, in different order, without the names. She picked him all three times. With the bizarre flight pattern of Tirso Gaglio, I'd say it's him."

"Agreed," said Mario Rivera. "A confirmed picture of Sepsis, no question. Put it on the Interpol wire. About the nun now—what's your bottom line on her?"

She leaned back in her chair and looked at Rivera, giving him her formal recommendation. "I say we send her back to New Hampshire where she belongs and allow this investigation to continue in Rome." *Without us*, was her unspoken but audible conclusion, since FBI deals only with domestic matters, and foreign situations only when an American citizen is directly, physically involved.

"What's to say they don't make another attempt on her life up in

New Hampshire?" Lehrer said, unwilling to give up the ghost. If it were a CIA project now that it was moving to Rome, then even though he was head of Counter Intelligence and the matter wasn't technically under his jurisdiction, it would still be his responsibility if things got fucked up; after all, Lehrer got the Sepsis ball rolling here in the U.S., "I want to hold on to her until this is all over. She'll be safer here."

Chisholm blinked at Lehrer. "I'm surprised you're so concerned about her safety. I thought you CIA types only worried about producing results."

"Maggie, quit it," Rivera said, with no real conviction; she was going at this the way he wished he could. He turned to Lehrer, ganging up on him if only silently.

Lehrer still didn't look at Chisholm, picking up and glancing at his closed leather folder. "Your people can give the nun better protection if she stays in Washington."

"There's no point in holding on to the penguin," Chisholm kept insisting, holding the pressure. "She pinned the guy, Gaglio or whatever his real name is, so as far as I'm concerned she's now useless. Anyway, if Gaglio *is* Sepsis, he's in Rome right now—the nun's safe. So let's ship her back to New Hampshire with some baby-sitters. Get some of the locals to keep an eye on her."

"Sounds good," Rivera finally said. "Now about going to Rome, I don't think the Italians are going to like you heading out there in force," he said, tacitly throwing the ball into the CIA's lap.

Lehrer opened his leather folder and glanced at the notes he'd written, without really looking at them. "I've spoken with the head of the Italian terrorist unit, a man named Frederico Lorca, and he will allow us to send Agents Chisholm and Denton as observers and advisers. They, the Italians that is, will handle the actual apprehension."

Rivera frowned at this, not liking it, as he glanced at Chisholm. She caught the glance, her signal, and so she leaned back in her chair as she idly twirled a pen in her fingers, giving Lehrer a detached look. "If the Italians are going to handle this, then there's no point in my going. The nun is going to be in New Hampshire, Sepsis is going to be in Rome—

since no American citizen is going to be in the middle of this, this is now *your* problem, Mr. Lehrer, not the FBI's."

For the first time, Lehrer looked right back at Chisholm, but flashing not-so-subtle glances at Rivera as he spoke. "That's where you're wrong. In two weeks' time, the nun is going to be in Rome for that restoration project of hers. That would make her *your* problem, *Miss* Chisholm. I've spoken with Detective Lorca. If the nun goes to Rome, you would function as liaison between us and the Italians, specifically with his office."

"Liaison? We don't have any information to liaison with. The guy came here, took three shots at us, then left—aside from his picture, that's all the liaison the Italians are gonna get."

"You would be acting in an advisory capacity," Lehrer pushed.

"An advisory capacity." Chisholm nodded, underwhelmed. "Then why send Denton along?"

Lehrer smiled. "You advise the Italians and Denton will advise you."

"You're funny."

"Maggie," said Rivera in reflex, trying to get his bearings as he saw that the FBI wouldn't be able to fob off this problem on the CIA. But Lehrer went on unfazed, seeming to dare Chisholm to say something.

"Anyway, once the nun goes to Rome, who's going to watch over her then?"

"The Italians," Chisholm said.

"Please," said Lehrer.

Chisholm paused and stared, getting everyone's attention. "So actually, what it is is, I'm going to Rome to baby-sit the penguin, and Denton here is the one who's going to be the actual liaison with the Italians. All the while, this is still going to be an FBI operation, 'cause CIA isn't providing any more manpower or support than it already has. So if things go haywire, the Bureau gets covered in shit while you guys get to stand around pointing the finger at us." No one said anything to the truth of that, Rivera counting his stars that at least *someone* was calling a spade a fucking shovel in this little dig. But then, of course, Maggie went a little too far, trying to egg Lehrer on.

"The FBI gets screwed, no matter what happens. Isn't that right, Lehrer? Excuse me—Deputy Director Lehrer. Why didn't you just say this from the beginning? Why do you have to play these games with us all the time? Why do you CIA people have to be so goddamned *sneaky* about every goddamned thing?"

"We are not trying to be *sneaky*, Agent Chisholm. We are trying to expedite matters," said Lehrer, meeting Chisholm's stare and more than a match for it.

"Expedite matters? With Denton? No offense but Denton is a bureaucrat, he told me so himself. I doubt if he's ever fired a weapon in his life, let alone run a *real* investigation. What is he going to do besides cozy up to the Italians while I'm stuck with the penguin?"

Lehrer finally lost his temper. "If the damned nun stayed here in Washington, *you* wouldn't have this problem, now would you."

"What does that have to do with the price of guano in Palooka?" Chisholm shouted right back. "I don't know how you people work, but I have no reason to hold on to her. She's committed no crime, she's not under investigation, and as a witness she's now a dry well. We don't need her anymore!"

"With her in Washington, she's not going to go to Rome and bring us all these headaches! The Italians would get to deal with this bullshit entire! It would be out of our hands—*all* our hands—if the nun stays here! By letting her go to Rome, you make it necessary to send someone to coordinate this whole mess, you—"

"Now I get it. You're hiding behind the nun's skirts because you don't have the balls to assume the responsibility for this situation."

"Who do you think you are, you—"

"You try dragging us with you to Rome, thereby making it an FBI investigation. And if you can't have *that*, you want us to hold on to the nun illegally while *you* drop the CIA's role in this investigation and let the Italians deal with the whole Sepsis mess, ready or not."

"I don't have to take this from you, you piddling little zero—"

"I swear you people are the lowest scum of the earth, I swear to God—"

"We're getting nowhere here," Rivera interrupted finally, mercifully, stunned at how quickly Lehrer and Maggie were at each other's throats. Maggie he could understand, but he didn't dare look at Lehrer, embarrassed for him, as if he'd peed his pants in a parade and didn't know it. To cover himself, Rivera spoke to Maggie. "This is how it is: Both you and Denton watch the nun *and* act as liaison with the Italians."

"Under whose aegis?" she asked, turning to Lehrer with a "show me" look, the whole crux of the matter finally out on the table.

Rivera too stared hard at Lehrer. Rivera was a big guy, a good six feet three, and Chisholm was as mean as they come, but Lehrer just looked around the table with all the poise in the world. He might have been watching a game of lawn tennis. The silence yawned, and Rivera knew he wouldn't get anything from Lehrer.

"The FBI's," Rivera finally said.

Chisholm slammed her pen hard on the table. Rivera knew exactly how she felt. God, he hated these fucking Certifiably Idiotic Assholes.

He went on, turning to Chisholm and Denton. "Use the Tirso Gaglio lead to find Sepsis. You provide information to the Italians on a need-to-know basis only, but I don't want any screwing around. Don't hold on to information just to be clever. That goes for the both of you. Understood? . . . This meeting is over."

They all rose to leave, the CIA men leading off, but as he passed her, Chisholm realized that Denton hadn't said a word throughout the entire meeting. That wasn't what was troubling. What was troubling was how smug he looked, an ate-the-canary smile that was just a shade on the creepy side.

But before she had a chance to think about this, Rivera touched her elbow.

"My office," he said with a look.

Why? Why?! *Why?!*" she shouted, the two of them alone in his office, Rivera keeping his desk between them, if only for protection.

"Enough of this already!" he shouted back. "I don't want to hear about it. That finger-chopping thing was way out there—"

"It was either his fingers or the stadium—"

"Oh, and that chase you had the other day? No problem with the chase, mind you, but then you shot the *phone*? The way you've treated the nun has been deplorable—"

"I haven't treated the nun any different from—"

"The way you treated Lehrer—he's an asshole, yes, but Lehrer is a deputy director of the CIA, the *CIA*, and you just *slammed* him back there—"

"He deserved it," she snarled right back.

"Okay, yes, he deserved it, but Maggie, you need a break—"

"I'm fine!"

"No!" he said, killing the rhythm of the fight. They looked at each other but it was Chisholm who broke away first. She started prowling around his office like a caged panther, unwilling to look at Rivera.

He decided to try one more time to bring her back into the fold, and if it didn't work, he'd let the shit land where it may. He put his palms flat on his desk and looked at her as she paced around. "Maggie, listen to me. You're a great agent. You have the best instincts of any agent I've ever known. You're loyal up and down, you're patient, you land convictions, everyone respects you, everyone likes you—"

"No one likes me, Mario," she said calmly. "They're afraid of me, which is a whole lot different."

"Well, you're a scary bitch, what can I say. But Maggie, you're burned out. You need to take a breather. This Rome business—it's perfect for you. You're going to baby-sit the nun and let Denton handle the Italians. You're going to be bored out of your skull, but believe me, you need the time to pull your shit together."

"What about Archangel?" she said cautiously. "I'm so close, just give me a couple of weeks." But Rivera was wise enough not to pounce at this show of weakness.

"Archangel's your big white whale," he said softly. "You're obsessed with it, but you've got nothing. You're angry all the time—"

"Do you want my resignation?" she asked frankly, straight, no pussy-footing around, truly surprising Rivera.

He looked her right in the eye. "If I wanted it, we wouldn't be talking. The Tactical Supervisory Board wanted your ass, and they wanted it now. You're still here because *I* want you here. And what I want is for you to take some time off."

They stared at each other until Margaret sighed and her shoulders sagged. It reminded Rivera of when he was a teenager in Wyoming, watching a bear fight to get out of a trap. The bear sighed and slumped, only to try to break away again and again, literally exhausting itself to death. He walked around the desk and faced Margaret, rubbing her shoulders as he looked down at her.

"Look, Maggie, this Rome business—it's perfect for you. Go to Rome, nail some Italian stud—relax. Let Denton worry about Sepsis. You just take it easy. Just calm down, okay? There's nothing wrong with taking a breather. There's no shame to it."

Chisholm looked up at her boss. He had missed it, missed it entirely. It had nothing to do with shame. She could care less about that. It was far different, far simpler than that. But even though he was wrong, Chisholm knew she was trapped good.

"Fuck me," she finally muttered, then looked away.

Rivera smiled sadly. "That's my girl."

Denton and Lehrer drove back to Langley in silence, Denton at the wheel of his Mercedes. But, one cool customer, Lehrer seemed to be ignoring the tension in the car, seemingly oblivious of the scene he'd just made. Definitely a point-scoring attitude, in Denton's mind.

"So you want me to go to Rome," Denton finally said.

"Yes," said Lehrer, offering no more.

"It's going to be tough running my other projects, being on another continent," Denton wondered aloud.

"You'll manage," said Lehrer, and Denton went into a tailspin. *What is on this guy's mind?*

But he said nothing. Instead, he drove on. Oh, he had scenarios in mind all right, questions and hints and phrases he could use to try figuring out what Lehrer was really thinking. He could even be frank; the experiment with laying his cards out on the table with Chisholm had been quite the educational experience for Denton. The only problem was, Chisholm would be up-front about things, while Lehrer wouldn't. So Denton decided to let the Rome thing slide under the table and fake Lehrer out.

"Look, Keith," Denton started, "if I'm on my way out, tell me. Don't play these bullshit games with me," he said, sounding hurt.

Lehrer turned to Denton, surprised. "You're not on the way—"

"If you're thinking of getting someone else to take over my job, the least you could do is be up-front about it," Denton went on, carefully letting a slight hint of desperation creep into his voice. "Don't send me on some wild-goose chase to Rome, specially not with a bitch like that Chisholm woman."

Denton was staring straight ahead at the road, but out of the corner of his eye he could see Lehrer thinking, unprepared for this exchange. Finally, Lehrer said, "You're not going on some wild-goose chase. I've made up my mind—I want you to turn Sepsis. Bring him into the fold."

"How the hell am I gonna do that?" Denton said, glancing at Lehrer morosely.

"I don't know, that's your problem. But since this *is* counterintelligence, I want you to recruit him. Money is no problem, let me worry about that. Recruit him, that's what I want you to do."

"All right," said Denton, faking relief. "What do I do about Chisholm?"

"Use her to get to Sepsis. But don't be dumb—don't get in Sepsis's way," he finished.

"Oh, I won't," Denton assured Lehrer as they drove on.

But it wasn't that Sepsis's way was leading to Sister Marianne—it was really turning out to be the other way around. For now, though, big old gray Phil Carter was watching out for her, the nun and Carter and his squad holed up in a Maryland safe house the FBI used for witnesses. Once she identified Tirso Gaglio, Chisholm moved her there as the tug-of-war over what to do with her started up. But it wasn't only between the FBI and CIA. Opus Dei was also smack-dab in the middle of it.

"What do *you* want to do?" asked Archbishop Neri over the phone as he talked to Sister Marianne that night. "Do you want to go back to New Hampshire?"

"No," Sister Marianne said. "Too many—"

"I know," Neri said quietly.

"I want to go home," she finally said.

"New York?"

"Rome," she corrected, obscurely touching him. "I want to work on the project," she went on. "I want to do something that . . . frees me from my own mind."

"That might not be possible," Archbishop Neri finally said, but he knew she would be coming to Rome. He needed her in Rome, despite Cardinal Barberi's objections.

"What if something happens to her?" the cardinal had wheezed, sucking down oxygen between sentences as he and Neri spoke in the cardinal's apartment off the Piazza Colomo. "What if this monster tries to harm her here?"

"We can protect her here better than the Americans can," said Neri.

"The American CIA wants to keep her until they find the assassin. Their man, Lehrer, spoke to me for an hour. He told me that the assassin is here in Rome, that it would be stupid for her to come here. Edmund Gettier could lead the renovations instead of the child Marianne."

Neri was familiar enough with what was going on to use what he knew against the cardinal. "Gettier is a fine man, but you yourself told me he doesn't have the drive anymore, the fire to lead the renovations."

"Yes, I suppose . . ." said the old cardinal doubtfully, unable to go back on what he had said even though the situation had changed.

"And anyway, do we really want a Communist radical leading the renovations of the Basilica?" said Neri unwisely.

Cardinal Barberi scowled, perking up now that he had some ammunition. "Alberto, Edmund was a student radical over thirty years ago. And he wasn't a *Communist* radical, for your information—he was an *anarchist*. Please, be a little more forgiving."

"Yes of course, of course," he said, backpedaling furiously. "Of course his politics aren't important—"

"Heh, thirty-year-old politics, at that," said the cardinal.

"Yes of course, but the problem remains—he is too old, without the drive, while Marianne is still young enough to really lead the renovations."

"I suppose," said the cardinal again, again unsurely.

"Yes," he said firmly.

"Are you *sure* this is a good idea?" asked the old man again, fearfully.

"Yes," said Neri, not at all sure. "We can protect her here better than they can there," he repeated. "And she needs us."

The old cardinal's misgivings turned into physical tics, the way they will with the old. He started shaking his head spasmodically as he frowned at the floor of his apartment, staring at a point next to Neri's feet. "I will agree to her coming if you can give me proof that this will be good for the child Marianne," he said finally. "If there is a *spiritual* reason for her to come, I will agree."

"I can't sleep anymore," Marianne told Neri now over the phone. "I can't sleep, I can't think. Please don't send me back to New Hampshire. If I can't go to Rome because of this . . . situation, send me somewhere else—anywhere but New Hampshire."

"All your work must have been destroyed in the explosion," Archbishop Neri commented offhandedly, knowing full well that that hadn't happened.

"Oh no," Sister Marianne said, surprised. "I have all my notes with me. In fact, I've been going through them and I've realized that Edmund and I have been basing our estimates on incorrect stress-tension figures."

"Oh?" Neri asked, completely uninterested as the nun went on for the better part of an hour on stress-tension data and other building problems Archbishop Neri didn't understand at all. He wasn't listening to what she said but to the way she said it, hearing her gather strength and equanimity from the boring and really tedious minutiae she described. She became so excited Neri could *hear* her forgetting the bombing tragedy, overcoming it.

But that's not what convinced Neri to have Sister Marianne come to Rome. As he listened to her without paying much attention, what convinced him was the simple choice before him: have an agnostic, perhaps even atheist professor lead a major renovation, or have Sister Marianne—a mere nun—garner an enormous amount of prestige for Opus Dei.

"Come to Rome then," he finally interrupted. "I'll talk to Cardinal Barberi and convince him to let you come. Don't worry about anything, just work on your project. Work will see you through."

Monsignor Escrivá de Balaguer would have been proud.

Denton, Chisholm, and Sister Marianne took off from Andrews Air Force Base on a Wednesday afternoon. They flew in a little jet plane that belonged to the army, a Gulfstream that was used to shuttle VIP's around Europe. It was based in Wiesbaden, but it had been sent back to the States to get an electronics upgrade. Flying back to Germany, it was no trouble at all to get it to make a pit stop in Rome before going on to its home base, so the three of them had the plane to themselves.

Roughly around the time the Gulfstream was rounding Nova Scotia, Paula Baker, the head and most of the brains of Covert Finance, got into her car and drove home.

She lived far, actually in a suburb of Baltimore, but she didn't mind her endless daily commute. In fact it relaxed her very much, the monotony of the driving. Usually she would deal with the administrative trivia of her job over the car phone, getting the small stuff out of the way before she even arrived for work in the mornings, mapping out her next day on the drive home at night.

She made her home in Baltimore because her husband worked there, running a small advertising firm that was always on the very edge of going broke. He could have made three or four times more money working at a big firm. Paula Baker could have made ten times more money following Phyllis Strathmore into the money piles of Wall Street banking. But neither of them even thought about moving on to greener pastures, the very fact that they were always strapped for cash making their marriage stronger—an odd kind of aphrodisiac, perhaps compensating for the bitter reality that they could not have children of their own, a reality which money and the time to think about it that money could afford would have brought to front and center stage, to their regret.

Out of Washington and into Maryland, Paula Baker drove on. Even at night, roughed up by her workday as she was, she looked as sexy and beautiful as a model, which she had once been in college. The road was almost empty, Paula catching the fast lane and passing the slower cars.

When it happened, it was fast. A half-ton pickup truck, jacked up and looking monstrous, came up behind Paula's five-year-old Audi, beginning to pass her on the right lane. Suddenly, it swerved into her, smashing the nose of her car against the center divider. The Audi, a front-wheel-drive car, didn't stand a chance. Going as fast as it was, its front left tire found some purchase on the concrete divider, flipping up over it and twirling in midair, landing upside down onto the oncoming traffic on the other side of the divider. The roof collapsed with the force of the impact, Paula Baker's skull getting crushed, her neck snapping instantly, a second before a car barreling south crashed head-on into the wreck, both that car and the Audi bursting into flames.

The jacked-up half-ton drove on into the darkness, the driver, Beckwith, feeling very very pleased.

The Eternal City

L ike Washington, Rome is two cities: the town of monuments and the city of the living.

The monuments stand around sort of like pushers in a big park made of gray and brown mortar and stone, waiting sluggish and restless for the next marks to show up, giving them a nasty sneer when they finally do. But the cast of the city of the living is altogether different—even in the mornings, it's like late-afternoon light: slow and old and more than just a little tired. Maybe the light of the living city is a sort of reminder of how far Rome is from Empire, the daily sun beating away the little that's left of it.

When she woke up and looked out the window of the plane, it struck Chisholm as odd, this shade of the morning—dappling mercury sunlight of a lazy late afternoon. In Washington, it might be sunny or it might be snowy or foggy or dark, but always there was the same saturation: steel of the dawn. A sort of reminder as to what kind of city Washington is, the Empire of Democracy still a few decades from apogee.

Denton and the penguin were already awake and looking fresh, the three of them alone in the little jet plane. The penguin was reading a book, Denton talking on a cellular phone, both of them looking to Margaret to be in their own little worlds. She got out of her seat to go wash up.

"Good morning," the penguin said to her, folding her book on her lap. "You slept well," she stated. Margaret didn't say anything, just staring, the nun faltering a bit but pressing on. "We're going to be there in twenty minutes," she finished, picking up her book but not looking at it yet.

"Good," Margaret said.

Sister Marianne nodded as Agent Chisholm walked away to the bathroom, returning to her book. It was Marcus Aurelius's *Meditations*, and she read: *You will not easily find a man coming to grief through indifference to the workings of another's soul; but for those who pay no heed to the motions of their own, unhappiness is their sure reward.* Words to live by. Marianne tried reading on but kept returning to the same passage, finally closing the book and trying to think of the project. She couldn't.

Denton was still on the phone, listening mostly, looking kind of bored. Absently, he lit a cigarette, even though he hadn't during the entire flight out of deference to Marianne. She thought about asking him to put it out, but they were so close to landing that it would have been rude of her. Instead, she forced herself to go back to the *Meditations*.

"A profound man, that Marcus Aurelius," Denton said as he put away his cellular phone. "I should get a copy."

"I try reading him every two or three years or so," Marianne replied, the two of them starting a casual little conversation about the dead emperor and his ideas.

Sister Marianne couldn't tell, but Denton was on full autopilot. He'd been on the phone with Kenny Whipple and Arthur Atmajian, learning about the worst thing that had happened to him since Tiggy died.

"Something bad happened, Nicky," Ken Whipple began. "Get ready: Paula Baker's dead."

"Really," was all Denton would allow himself. Across his belly, the muscles stretched and cinched like too-tight seat belts, acid bile erupting right from the pit of his stomach, shooting all the way up to the back of his mouth where he could taste it. He thought he was going to have a heart attack. "That's too bad," he said in a voice that was all boredom and half-listening attention.

"You can't talk."

"Not really," Denton drawled lazily, glancing at Sister Marianne beside him and the still-sleeping figure of Chisholm across the aisle. "What was it exactly again?"

"She was murdered, Nicky," Atmajian croaked, hoarse but in-control.

"It was a bad accident on the beltway," Whipple interjected. "She was driving home, lost control of her car, smashed into the center divider."

"She was killed," Atta-boy croaked again.

"Don't know that," Whipple insisted, then relented. "Don't know for sure."

"I seem to be having a hard time understanding this," Denton said, cool and bored-sounding, almost as if he were about to yawn. He felt his heart beating too fast and too hard, his head pounding with its rhythm as his body started to sweat all over even though it was cool in the plane's cabin. With a steady hand, he reached for and turned on the overhead air conditioner. Then, with the same hand, without a hesitation, he reached for and drank some of his morning coffee as the pilot announced they were approaching Rome, and look out the window, you can see some of the lovely ruins . . .

"I'm gonna put the hit on the motherfucker who did Paula," Atta-boy threatened aimlessly. "I'm gonna put the hit on him myself, with my bare hands."

"What makes you think it happened that way?" Denton asked.

"Skid marks, paint scrapings, little clues that *might* point to a hit."

"Might my ass, it was a hit and you—"

"Arthur," said Denton softly, quieting him. "So the question is who."

Kenny sighed loudly. "No ideas. It might've been a real accident."

"There are no accidents, Kenny. Nothing is *ever* an accident." Denton couldn't disagree with Atmajian's logic.

Ken Whipple pressed on. "No accidents, then fine. Question: Why put the hit on Paula Baker? A hit on Atmajian, head of the wet-boys, okay. A hit on Denton, assistant to the Deputy Director for Counter Intelligence, okay. A hit on Whipple, head of the Middle East desk, okay. A hit on Baker—no sense to it."

Denton suddenly realized that Ken Whipple couldn't handle Paula Baker's death, so he was pretending it had never happened, pretending it was just another contingency that was being game-played.

"So who gets to replace Baker?" Denton asked.

"No firm candidate, Covert Finance is in chaos right now."

"I say we hit them and hit them good," said Atmajian in a beaten, almost whimpering voice that frightened Denton and Whipple. "Blow them all away."

"Put the hit on who?" was all Whipple had the heart to say.

The three of them were silent, lost as Denton drank his too-sweet coffee, thinking. And then it came to him—they needed someone they could trust, someone who knew plenty about money.

"Call Phyllis Strathmore," he said as he finished off his coffee, Whipple and Atmajian realizing what Denton was getting at: If it was a hit—*if* it was a hit—then it was over something Paula Baker knew about or had heard about in Covert Finance, something to do with money. The only people who could possibly care about covert finances—the only people who might worry about what Paula Baker might have found out—all worked and played within the Langley compound. *If* it was a hit, it was over money, and it was from the inside. And Phyllis Strathmore was the only one with the money smarts to follow whatever Paula Baker had been uncovering.

Whipple grabbed the receiver, cutting off the speakerphone. "You fucking serious?" he whispered to Denton, really shaken as he looked up at Arthur and then looked away. Atta-boy was listening on the other extension in Whipple's office, all the while yanking curly black hairs out of his beard to keep himself together, absently wincing with each tug.

"No one else would have a reason to do a Silkwood on her," Denton said. "Strathmore can figure out what Baker knew or found out."

"And if she doesn't?" Whipple asked. "If whoever it was tries pushing Strathmore aside?"

"I do believe Strathmore is going to need an executive assistant who used to work in Atmajian's unit," Denton drawled.

"I'm gonna put a whole goddamned *squad* on Phyllis, anyone even *thinks* about touching her and I'm gonna—"

"If you say so," Denton interrupted, using all his powers to keep up the bored facade as he watched Chisholm out of the corner of his eye wake up and go to the bathroom.

Whipple, Denton, and Atmajian started working out the logistics for getting Strathmore hired; who to push, who to cajole, office-politicking stuff, the three of them putting off the inevitable until there was nothing left to talk about except what none of them could handle—the funeral that would make Paula Baker's death real.

"I can't go," Arthur said outright, ashamed at his cowardice but more willing to admit to it than either Denton or Whipple. Denton did a little song and dance about his Rome commitment, Whipple something about some Saudi dignitaries he was going to meet. So Paula Baker would be buried alone, with no one from her days in Tiggy's basement offices. But she wouldn't mind, Denton justified. After all, he thought, she was dead; past caring.

Once he was done with Whipple and Atmajian, he turned to Sister Marianne and started talking about Marcus Aurelius, keeping up a liquid surface. He felt his innards squeezing inside, turning his feces mushy and hot.

A year ago at Langley, Denton had run into Paula Baker accompanied by an elderly couple with "hick" written all over them—her parents, out in Washington for a visit to see their daughter. She had introduced them to Denton and on cue he had sung her praises to the old people, flirting so outrageously with her it had been facetious. And she had preened like a little kid, smiling and blushing, looking not sexy at all but merely—impossibly—lovely.

Talking to the nun, he pretended he didn't remember much of Marcus Aurelius as he reflected on a passage he thought apropos to Paula Baker's death. Not, *All things fade into the storied past*, nor the endlessly quoted, *In the life of a man his time is but a moment, his being an incessant flux*. Instead, he thought of an obscure passage in the fifth book: *Shame on the soul, to falter on the road of life while the body still perseveres*. He didn't know why he thought of that passage, but it seemed fitting. He yawned, as always politely covering his mouth.

"Excuse me," he said, smiling with a slightly sleepy look, thinking of the dead Paula Baker while his face grinned for the nun's benefit. "I didn't sleep as much as I should have."

Waiting for them at the end of the long, vast, empty corridor of the airport terminal were Edmund Gettier, Cardinal Barberi, and Detective Lieutenant Frederico Lorca of the Italian police, Anti-Terrorism Branch. They were mere yards from the opening of the sleeve. The cardinal, sitting in his wheelchair, was talking to Edmund Gettier. From what Lorca overheard, they seemed to be talking about someone suffering from a nervous breakdown, the two of them wondering about "stress tension" and "frailty." The detective was about to assume they were talking about this American nun, until he heard a little bit more.

"What were they thinking, eh?"

"I don't know, Cardinal. But if the stress tension is too high, we're going to have to replace the catacomb pillars instead of just reinforcing them."

Architecture. Lorca drifted off, uninterested, smoothing his suit and tie, waiting. He was a tall man, six feet one inch, looking very much like a darker, slightly crueler version of Denton. Like Denton he always smiled, but unlike most Italians, he was understated and cool, rarely motioning with his hands, keeping his distance from everyone. An intimidating policeman in a country full of touchers and feelers.

Outside, by the secure entrance, a platoon of his plainclothesmen were waiting to take the party to the safe house he had arranged, but Frederico Lorca had wanted to be alone when he met the Americans.

He had worked with some before, mostly CIA people attached to their embassy, never with FBI, at least not in person, so this would be a first for him. He lit a cigarette and watched through the window as the Gulfstream jet taxied to the terminal sleeve, connecting smoothly, all three of them falling silent as they waited.

Sister Marianne was the first one out of the plane, rushing to Edmund and Cardinal Barberi, smiling hugely.

"Ahhh!" she said, dropping her suitcase and awkwardly hugging Cardinal Barberi in his chair.

"Ah Marianne, it's so good to see you," he said in Italian as Marianne hugged Gettier, the cardinal eyeing Frederico Lorca so that the nun was aware of him. Lorca offered his hand.

"I am Frederico Lorca, Italian police. Please," he said, motioning down the long empty hallway. "We can speak later. Leave your suitcase, my men will take care of it."

"Thank you," she said.

Marianne, Gettier, and Barberi started walking away, Gettier pushing the wheelchair as the three of them chattered on and on. Shortly, Denton and Chisholm emerged and Lorca introduced himself.

"Frederico Lorca, Anti-Terrorist Brigade," he said in slightly accented English. "Welcome to Italy."

The three of them shook hands, introducing themselves. Lorca was surprised. Denton's handshake was firm and to the point, but Chisholm's was dainty, almost shy. "Please," Lorca said, "leave your baggage on the plane; my men will take them through customs."

"I have a firearm in my suitcase," Chisholm warned him.

"Not a problem," said Lorca casually, motioning them after the others. "Please."

They walked on at a leisurely pace, keeping their distance from the others as they talked.

"I have arranged for everyone to stay at a secure location. My men will guard it until the Sepsis threat is neutralized."

"Perfect," said Denton.

"Now about your coming here to Italy . . ."

As the three law enforcement people got up to speed, the other three did pretty much the same.

"No no no no!" Cardinal Barberi was insisting to Marianne in Italian. "Of *course* Edmund hasn't *touched* the catacombs! That is your territory!"

"I wanted to," Gettier teased, "but Cardinal Vampire wouldn't hear of it," he said, and Marianne laughed.

"You have more than enough food on your plate," said the cardinal with an ornery huff, pleased Marianne looked so happy. "So: Edmund works on the first level, and you on the catacombs."

"I can't wait to get started," she said.

Behind them, at a safe distance, Lorca was talking to Chisholm about her theory about Sepsis's real target. "My superiors do not agree, but I think you are correct in assuming that the Vatican is the target of this man Sepsis. My people are trying to find his current hideaway as we speak."

"How?"

"Using the forger lead. We haven't contacted the forger yet, but we have his shop under a—how do you say?—a passive surveillance."

"What's the security arrangement like at your safe house?" Chisholm asked.

"Strict," Lorca assured her. "We have not had any problems there."

"Good. What about when she goes to the Vatican?"

Lorca sighed as he took a drag on his cigarette. "That will present a problem. Church authorities will not allow an escort into the Vatican City, but they will provide Swiss Guards to guarantee the Sister's safety within their borders."

"I did a little research," Chisholm said. "The Vatican City borders are some white lines painted on the street. Insist."

"I will try, but this is not the terrible problem it seems to be. The area the Sister Marianne will be working in is secured. It is closed from the rest of the Vatican."

"But she will be alone when she's working?" asked Denton.

"Yes," Lorca admitted.

"No offense, but I don't trust the Swiss Guards to keep a close eye on the pen—on the nun," said Chisholm. "Can't you get some of your men in there?"

"I will try, but I doubt they will allow Italian security to enter the Vatican City—they have not allowed us in for several centuries."

"What about Americans?" asked Denton, making Lorca roll his eyes. "Thought so," Denton finished lamely, not thinking clearly as he struggled with Paula Baker.

"What about a friend of the Sister's?" Chisholm thought out loud.

Denton did a double take. " 'A friend of the Sister's'? You?"

"Yes."

Denton laughed outright, but Lorca got the idea.

"They will not allow you to carry a weapon inside," he said elliptically.

Chisholm smiled at Lorca, the two of them maneuvering each other into sync. "Will they search me?"

"No, they will not search your person," he said, waiting for her to find the limit.

"Then I will—"

He interrupted her. "Threatening to carry a weapon into the Vatican City is an international offense, since the Vatican *is* a foreign power. I would have to detain you if you say such a thing."

Chisholm retreated. "I will accompany Sister Marianne on her daily routine."

"That is acceptable," said Lorca, satisfied. "You will, of course, carry the usual tools of your profession?" he asked, giving her the rope.

"Yes?" asked Chisholm, testing it.

"Very good," said Lorca, their arrangements set. "Now concerning transportation . . ."

The six of them walked on down the long empty hallway.

It was amazing he was a forger, considering he didn't have the use of his right arm. It wasn't shriveled exactly, merely stunted, as if it had never outgrown infancy. The fingers were there, the elbow joint, everything. But from the normal-sized shoulder joint, the arm was suddenly miniaturized, no bigger than an eighteen-month-old baby's, the tips of the fingers reaching barely as far as the elbow of the forger's normal left arm.

"Andolini," the forger called out to the back of the shop, his tone hard and clear as he dusted the counters. "Sweep the sidewalk." Andolini, a huge man with a light mental retardation, lumbered out from the backroom of the shop carrying a broom that looked like a twig in his hands.

The lack of a right arm hadn't really hurt the forger much. Lorenzo could easily manufacture documents using just a single arm, just as he easily forged stamps, which was his real business. Lorenzo Aquardiente ran a stamp and coin shop that had precious few coins but all the best forged stamps the skill of his left arm could create. No customer had ever realized his stamps were forged, just as no one had ever realized by touch and look that the documents Aquardiente made were fakes. Only machines could detect the deception, and even they could be fooled.

There are two parts to forged documents: the actual physical document, and the computer entry that guarantees the document is legal. Paradoxically, even though every scrap of official paper has an entry in some computer, the tough part of making valid forged documents remains the actual physical papers and cards. Breaking into a computer and forging a valid code is the simple part.

Aquardiente didn't worry about that side of the equation. He devoted himself to making documents only, assigning them random numbers and letting his customers break into the computers. His specialty was creating birth certificates and soon-to-expire identity cards, the backbone of any fake identity; with those two, passports, driver's licenses, credit cards, even new identity cards—all legitimate and proper—could be easily gotten. A photograph wasn't even needed. All that a customer had to do was provide a rough age and rough physical description of the individual who needed papers. The rest came easily.

On this morning, without a customer around to distract him, Aquardiente wandered about the shop restlessly, dusting the stamp cases as he waited for the new order to come in. The order wasn't what was making him nervous and fidgety; not at all. The expectation of seeing the dummy boy, however, was.

The dummy boy was a courier for a buyer of documents who never showed his face in the shop. Aquardiente's only contact with the buyer was an occasional telephone call and the arrival shortly thereafter of Tonio, the dummy boy, who brought the money and the orders. The buyer never requested the same kind of documents, always asking for a slew of papers from the oddest places, without apparent rhyme or reason, which was why, when he bothered to think about it, Aquardiente had the suspicion that the unnamed, unknown buyer was actually a middleman. It would have upset him a bit, being cut out of the extra money, if it hadn't been for Tonio.

Aquardiente lusted after the dummy boy, truth be told. Whenever the mystery buyer contacted him, he never thought about the job at hand. Instead, he thought of Tonio. He wanted to worship and ravage the boy—kiss the boy's neck, squeeze his ass, fondle his sweet young balls and rub the boy's cock all over his face before taking it into his mouth. You could say he lusted after him to distraction.

The boy wasn't so much beautiful as helpless and stupid, needing a strong man to guide him, to open his ripe cheeks and take him like a man. In fact, Aquardiente could hardly recall what Tonio looked like, having one of those anonymous faces that blend in and are quickly forgotten. But the *idea* of him remained with Aquardiente. For the past six years, he had watched as Tonio grew from an eighteen-year-old stripling into a twenty-four-year-old fresh bloom of a man. And he liked it that the dummy boy was a fool. Smart boys could become too independent.

Aquardiente began losing his concentration thinking of the dummy boy, wanting him so bad his lower belly hurt. The forger suddenly realized he had an erection. Embarrassed, he went to the backroom and put on an apron, leaving it loose around his belly so that it hung slack over his uncontrollable hard-on, hiding it, the desire for the boy overwhelming.

As if on call by the gods, the doorbells chimed and in walked the dummy boy, calling out in that reedy young voice of his: "Sir? Sir?"

He rushed out of the backroom and into the shop. "Tonio!" Aquardiente called to the fresh, delectable young man who he knew didn't have a working brain cell in his entire skull. "How are you, eh?" he said, rushing to meet him at the threshold and throwing his good arm around the youth, stroking his shoulder.

Sepsis knew how much Aquardiente lusted after him. There is a difference between backslapping touchiness and out-and-out fondling, subtle but telling. Aquardiente wasn't into subtleties. The second time Sepsis came into the shop, the crippled old forger had cupped his crotch almost without realizing he was doing it. Now, he maneuvered himself behind Sepsis and rubbed his erection into his backside, using it almost like a prod to guide Sepsis into the rear of the shop. "It's been so long, so long. How are you?" he asked lecherously, leaning his face into his ear.

"Good, Mr. Aquardiente, good, he-he," he said, keeping up with the charade as he mentally sighed. *What a sick fuck,* he thought in English.

"My boss says I have to give you something," Sepsis went on in Italian, letting the lids of his eyes relax and his smile go slack, accentuating the impression of idiocy.

"Yes but don't *you* have something for me?" Aquardiente preened, guiding Sepsis into the backroom, still behind him and still trying to rub his erect cock against Sepsis's ass.

"I brought the money, I brought the money," he said, playacting to hide his revulsion, knowing Aquardiente would try to cop a feel off him and would probably succeed. Aquardiente closed the curtain dividing the backroom from the short hallway that led to the front of the shop, his good arm dropping and squeezing Sepsis's ass in passing. Sepsis stifled a wince. One day he was going to tear the good arm off the fucking cripple and ram it up *his* ass. But for now, he needed him.

"I brought the money, but I have to count it," he said, sitting at a worktable, keeping it between himself and the forger. "Let me count it first." Sepsis took out a scrap of paper, pretended to examine it with care, then began counting the money laboriously, wetting his fingers with his tongue, the sight of which sent Aquardiente into paroxysms of imagination.

Sepsis and the forger went way back, since his earliest days as a killer. The forger could provide papers, that was the thing—all sorts of obscure but useful documents. In Italy alone, Sepsis had four computer software designers who could break into the computers and give the documents a history. But Sepsis had never been able to find another forger as skilled as Aquardiente, which infuriated him, this dependence on one source. It had happened to Carlos before him, so he was resigned. But unlike Carlos, who had identified himself as the buyer, Sepsis had gone one step farther—he had created a "boss" who was supposedly the real buyer of the papers. Much cleverer than Carlos, who had exposed himself when he bought from Aquardiente.

This time, Sepsis was paying out fourteen thousand dollars for seven sets of papers. He had already counted the money before coming here, but he carefully kept up the pretense of his mental decrepitude for the crippled old forger. Andolini, the man's bodyguard, had given him the idea the first time he walked into the shop, Sepsis realizing at a dazzlingly young age that it was far better to seem stupid than too bright to sellers like Aquardiente. He counted the money, took out another slip of paper, then handed the bundle to Aquardiente.

"This is from my boss," he said smiling, catching Aquardiente in mid tongue roll. The forger took the money and examined the slip of paper. It called for seven sets of EC papers, all for men roughly the same age, mid-twenties, all looking the same, Mediterranean. An easy job. Aquardiente smiled at Sepsis, the idea not even occurring to him that one of the sets of papers would be for the dummy boy.

"Tonio, tell your boss I will have these ready a week from today, in the afternoon."

"Okay," said Sepsis, using the American word with a thick Italian accent, the way everyone did.

"A week from today, at five, when I am closing, come to my shop, we can talk, eh?" he said, helping Sepsis out of the chair, casually brushing (and squeezing) his thigh.

"Okay," said Sepsis, resigned to having Aquardiente make a serious pass at him once the shop was closed. He was meeting the men from Valladolid at seven anyway, so it would have to do.

Aquardiente held open the curtain, standing there to allow him to go out to the hallway first, smiling at Sepsis as he put his hand on the small of his back, leading him out. A couple of early-morning customers had drifted into the shop already, looking through the cases of stamps as Andolini stood at a discreet distance, watching them. Too many people to cup Tonio's buttocks—Aquardiente pinched it anyway, winking at him as he jumped in surprise and looked his way. There was a flash to his eye, something hard and cruel, something that made Aquardiente's heart flutter—a shade of wildness. Tonio quickly walked out the door, smiling and waving stupidly at Andolini, who smiled and waved equally stupidly at his fellow retard. Aquardiente hated retards. They were just so easy to use.

On the street, Sepsis continued as before, playacting Tonio as he thought about what he had to do. The job had paid $400,000, and what with the transportation, the paying of the men from Québecois Libre and their documents, the bomb in New Hampshire, and now the men from Valladolid, Sepsis had spent close to $170,000, which he was not pleased about. Abruptly, with his eyelids still drooping and his mouth hanging a little slack, Sepsis decided that if the men from Valladolid weren't enough, he would quit screwing around with meta-murder and just kill the nun outright. Dealing with Aquardiente was just getting on his nerves. Still having to think about the job was killing his peace of mind.

As he walked down the street, the passive surveillance Frederico Lorca had put on the forger got to work. They were across the street, looking out on the shop from a third-floor apartment, and they managed to snap three photographs of Sepsis—one from the back as he walked in, one when he walked out, and the last shot, a full frontal shot, as he was walking down the sidewalk with his slack-jawed look.

"When are we getting relieved?" Buttazoni asked as he checked the camera's exposure, keeping an eye out on the forger's shop for any more customers coming in or out.

"How the fuck should I know," said his partner, Cabrillo, who was sitting in an armchair with his fist supporting his head. They had been there all night, waiting for the morning team, snapping pictures with an infrared lens of the people who passed the shop, lovers and potential, indecisive thieves. "I hate these fucking assignments," Cabrillo spat out.

Buttazoni shrugged, noticing he was a frame away from ending the roll. He took a quick snapshot of the morose Cabrillo before rewinding the film and slipping it out of the camera. He put in a fresh roll of film just as another person approached the store and proceeded to walk in. Buttazoni got a nice shot of him too. At least they wouldn't be stuck having to go through all those pictures.

The safe house the Italian police had arranged wasn't a house, thought Denton. It was an actual, honest-to-goodness mansion. Built like a box sitting on the crest of a hill, the villa seemed to look down on the surrounding neighborhood of wealthy homes, quiet and distinguished. Unlike other Roman villas, the safe house had a big garden on all sides, the plot of the property triangular, faced by three streets, surrounded by twelve-foot-high black iron gates.

As they drove up the hill and into the driveway, outside on the sidewalk two uniformed *carabinieri* stood casual guard, opening the gate for the two cars carrying the party back from the airport and closing it behind them. Getting out of the car by the front door, Denton took a quick look around. There were eyes on him, he was sure, but he didn't see anyone.

"Are those two at the gate the only ones you have here?" he asked Lorca.

Chisholm snorted without looking at Denton, though Lorca gave him a smile. "No," he said.

The drivers of the cars carried their luggage inside, helped by a couple of aged servants at least a million years old. Though it unnerved her to see them struggle with their bags, Marianne was wise enough not to humiliate them by trying to help. She walked in with Gettier and Barberi, Denton following them, preoccupied with Paula Baker. It was how Lorca caught him off guard.

"I must be going," he told Denton, offering his hand. "It was a pleasure meeting you," he said, smiling brilliantly.

"Likewise," he said as he realized Chisholm had no intention of going into the villa with the rest. Not yet anyway. He should have seen it coming, seeing how they clicked at the airport. Making the best of it, Denton shook hands with Lorca and walked into the house after the other three.

Lorca and Chisholm loitered outside by the cars, the two finally all alone.

"I am expending many men, trying to make the nun's stay here safe," Lorca started off, lighting a cigarette. "I don't like expending many men like this."

"Neither would I," said Chisholm. "That building over there," she said, pointing casually at a little bungalow almost hidden from view by the trees and plants, "it's where your men are, right? Cameras, surveillance, whatever."

"Yes, but they are not my men," said Lorca, pleased, Denton having missed it completely. "The old servants' wing. The men are Ministry of Justice men. This is their villa. They lended it to me to guard the nun."

"It's very nice. Very tasteful," she said absently, as she admired the home.

Lorca bowed smilingly. "This used to be a fascist's palazzo until the war ended. Now we use it to guard Black Hand witnesses, et cetera. No one can come here without authorization. But I am still using many men to protect your nun. Your report on what happened in America was . . . not very long," he said politely.

Chisholm smiled, then laughed. "We gave you the name and picture of the most celebrated assassin alive. 'Not very long'?"

"Agent Chisholm—"

"Margaret," she interrupted.

"Margaret," he said, letting her name linger on his lips. "You know the name is useless now, the photograph of only marginal value. You gave us the forger lead, and we are investigating. But don't you have anything else for me?"

She leaned on the rear end of the car, crossing her ankles. "Detective Lorca—"

"Frederico," he said, smiling, the two of them liking each other a whole lot.

"Freddy," she corrected, clapping her hands together and rubbing them slowly. "That's all we have."

"So what would you suggest we do?" he asked.

"I say you pay our forger friend a visit," she said.

"That would be quite . . . aggressive, no? My superiors think I should—how do you say?—back off."

Chisholm shrugged, smiling, thinking, hating that she was getting so excited as she watched Lorca dangle the possibility of hitting on the forger, but helpless to stop the rush.

"Sometimes you need to rattle some cages to flush the game out," she said, ruinously mixing her metaphors, but so what: Lorca was bringing her back into the game.

"Well, I was ordered to co-operate with my American colleagues. If you suggest . . ."

"I do so suggest," she said seriously. You pays your money and youse gets your high. Fuck it.

But Lorca was thinking of something else. "I understand that Mr. Denton has no real field experience—he is useless as a protector of the nun."

"Yes, I know, that would be my job while in Rome."

"I think tomorrow I will have a free man I can have watch the nun. And maybe, if you wanted to, if you were not too tired, you could . . . 'observe' as I contact the forger, mmh?"

A greedy little smile started playing on Chisholm's lips.

The two *carabinieri* standing casual guard outside the safe house weren't as casual as they pretended. The American tourist trundling up the hill had sharp eyes; she caught sight of their very discreet radio earpieces.

The two *carabinieri* talked, sure, and they seemed like other uniformed cops pulling guard duty, bored and resigned. But they never caught each other's eyes, always keeping a roving watch on the street and the homes around the gated entrance. It was really a perfect entryway, the lowest point of the property, at the bottommost corner of the hill; taking a few steps to cross the street, they could observe the entire property's perimeter, which is what the two guards constantly did, strolling away from the gate and casting an eye on the hill, seeing anyone approaching.

They had seen her, of course, as she walked up the hill toward the villa. Aside from it being their job, she was a good-looking woman in that sunny, all-American way that seems positively alien in Italy. But they were surprised by her camera, which she pulled out suddenly though without any self-consciousness, just like a tourist would, snapping away at the pretty homes in the neighborhood. She knew she wouldn't get to keep the film, but the film wasn't important. Just the feel of the terrain.

"Hey!" one of the guards said in Italian, waving an angry hand at her when he saw her start taking pictures. "What do you think you're doing?"

"Uh, what?" she said in English as the guard approached her. The other guard, she saw, was suddenly very stiff, very careful, not looking at her or at his partner but at the surrounding street, shrewdly calculating that her picture taking might be some kind of diversion.

"What is this, can't you read?" the approaching *carabiniere* asked her, still in Italian, waving at a discreet signpost that had a camera circled and crossed out in red on a white background.

"*Non parle italiano*," she said with the thickest American accent she could muster, looking nervous and cautious to the *carabiniere*, who relaxed. A tourist, probably.

"You can't, ah, take any peectures, lady," he said in really rotten high school English.

"Why not?" she asked, like a silly tourist would—offended, as if she'd had fundamental rights taken away.

"Eh, the rules, the rules," said the *carabiniere*, snatching her camera away and exposing the film before she had a chance to object.

"Hey! That's my film!" she exploded, reaching for the camera, far too late.

"Eh, eh, restricted, eh?" said the *carabiniere* as she retrieved her camera and the ruined film. He waved his arms around as he snapped the fingers of both hands. "Restricted, yes? You go now, go."

"What about my film, you ruined my film!"

"So sorry," he said, bowing as he took a step back and smiled. "You go now, yes? No peectures, the sign says."

She stared after the *carabiniere*, looking hurt and still offended as he retreated to stand casual guard with his partner. Both of them seemed to ignore her and to relax, but they were carefully keeping an eye on both her and the street. Real professionals, she thought, not doubting for a second that more men were a call away.

She continued on up the hill, away from the *carabiniere*, examining the perimeter of the villa as casually as the two cops kept an eye on her. Cresting the hill and wandering on through the neighborhood, paying no more attention to the equally lovely sights around, Beckwith started to wonder how she would get inside the safe house. Because Beckwith knew that she would, one way or another.

Inside, Marianne talked and talked to Cardinal Barberi and Edmund Gettier, talking for hours about the project and how happy she was to see them again. Talking to fill the house. But by early afternoon, she was yawning and really tired, so old Edmund Gettier and the even older Cardinal Barberi bid their goodbyes and left her to sleep off the jet lag.

They shared a ride back to the cardinal's apartment off the Piazza Colomo, one of the police limousines taking them there.

Piazza Colomo was a pedestrian square. The streets around it had been closed off when Rome traffic exploded in the late seventies, so the police chauffeur stopped the car at the southwest corner, by the thick iron posts barring cars from the square. He helped Gettier with the cardinal's wheelchair, picking up the feather-light old man and putting him in it.

"Would you like me to push you?" he asked, but Gettier was already behind it.

"I'll do it, thank you."

The chauffeur got back behind the wheel and drove off as the two men began crossing the piazza. It was a big square, a hundred and fifty yards to the side, rounded at the corners and ringed with the facades of old buildings all around. Gettier pushed the cardinal slowly, carefully; the piazza was charmingly cobbled, sure, but murder on wheelchairs.

They said nothing for a third of the way across as around them people walked on their separate ways, afternoon sunlight dappling softly as a shadow edge crossed the square.

"I can't wait for the renovations to begin," said the cardinal as if to himself. "Marianne looked tired—don't let her go tomorrow. She can use some rest. She can start on Monday. There's no rush."

"All right," said Gettier absently, thinking.

They went on for a while, neither speaking, Barberi listening to the silence.

"You object to her being here," the cardinal finally said.

"Yes," Gettier admitted, slowing down even more to talk. "The idea of her being in Rome just . . .'gives me the shivers,' " he said, using the American phrase.

" 'Shiver'? Ah—quaking, running hot-cold."

"Yes," Gettier said. "This murderer is in Italy—that's what the Americans are saying. If that's the case, why should she come here as if she were looking for him? Why not make her stay in America?"

"It's complicated," Barberi said vaguely.

"It isn't, and you know that. Sooner or later, Marianne might get hurt."

"You don't know that," the cardinal rebuffed, craning his neck around to look at Gettier's eyes if only for a moment. "The police, the Americans, they will protect her, and nothing will happen."

"I could do the work—I don't mind," Gettier pressed.

"Yes, I know—"

"You know I'm not looking to take what's hers. I don't need to make my professional reputation, but her being here is *dangerous*—stupid really."

"She *has* to be here to—"

"Who insisted Marianne lead the renovations?" Gettier interrupted a little pedantically.

"You did," said Barberi, humoring Edmund. "But—"

"Do you think that I *care* that this will make Marianne's reputation? That I feel threatened? I'm thrilled!"

"I know," Barberi said.

"Then send her back to America."

"Neri thinks it's best if she works."

"Neri wants what's best for Opus Dei, the most prestige—"

"Maybe," Barberi cut him off, turning serious. "But maybe it has to do with Marianne. Do you know what would happen to her if she stays in America? How dead she would become?"

Gettier said nothing to that, remembering the scene at the hangar. Barberi pressed on, growing tired, but still: "Working on the basilica will give her life—you *know* this." And Gettier had no argument to that. But he pushed on anyway.

"Marianne could stay in America advising me, still the titular head of the renovations. I could get De Plannisoles to assist me, you could advise us just as you are doing now."

"I can't go to the Vatican every day to see how you are doing," said the cardinal, ignoring what Edmund Gettier was saying. "I'm too . . . old, ill, infirm, too . . . dilapidated, like the buildings around us." He laughed, waving his hands about at the buildings surrounding them, which stood as motionless and tired as a troop of returning soldiers.

Gettier stopped pushing the wheelchair and went around it to face Cardinal Barberi. "If she comes to harm, it will be on my head. Because

I can replace her on the project—but she can't be replaced. If this . . . murderer succeeds, Marianne can't be replaced."

"Yes, I know. But I think she will die if she stays in America," Barberi said finally, decided. Gettier knew there was nothing more he could say to that.

He pushed the wheelchair on, neither man saying anything until they said their goodbyes at the cardinal's apartment, on the first floor of one of the buildings surrounding the square. Sister Aurora, Barberi's nurse and maid, invited Professor Gettier to stay for dinner, but he refused offhandedly, almost rudely, preoccupied. Barberi wanted to say more, but he was just too tired to comfort Gettier, who left with a look of real fear and awful premonitions. The fear, Barberi thought, made him look almost young. He said a silent prayer for Edmund as Sister Aurora closed the door of the apartment.

For his part, Edmund Gettier walked across the Piazza Colomo, back to the corner where the limousine had dropped him off. Casually, he saw a public phone, and on the spur of the moment decided to vent some steam.

He had no idea if he would find him, but the operator was very helpful and in a minute, he heard him, the enemy, on the line.

"This is Alberto Neri," the bastard said.

"This is Professor Edmund Gettier," he said.

"Ah, Professor—"

"I hope you burn in hell, you bastard, fooling an old man like that—"

"I'm sorry, what do you mean—"

"You know what I mean. Pretending Marianne is here for her 'spiritual well-being.' If something happens to her, I will hold you personally responsible."

"My dear Professor—"

Gettier hung up. He didn't feel much better. Actually, he felt foolish, making empty, idle threats like that. What would he do, kill the man? But he hoped it would achieve a little of what he wanted.

Gettier hailed a cab and went to his apartment.

EIGHT

Nighttown

ighttime. Sepsis was at a party of wealthy degenerates, his best cover. Throughout the big house, a nineteenth-century palazzo done up in rococo decor, people danced in the darkness, lit by blue lights and neon greens, the music hard and ruthless. The partyers—all roughly his age—moved to the beat that matched their mood as they talked and drank and smoked and eyed each other narrowly, nine-inch-nail heels impaling the parquet flooring, incautious cigarettes moving with the conversations and leaving trails of red light in the darkness. And through it all, Sepsis glided, detached, looking at the people with the same eye he cast at architecture, or at targets.

He was really unnoticeable here. The men were far handsomer than he, dressed in sleek suits and slicked hair, features aristocratic and haughty, responding only to other men of volubility and personal force. And the women, so perfect they could set a heart on fire from afar, seemed like movable statues with the same inscrutability of unliving things, unwilling to notice him if he did not deign to notice them. They only responded to the cruel men, ready to drop their panties for them right on the dance floor if need be; in fact, one breathtakingly lovely woman, dark and fiery, was fucking one of these cruel young men in a corner of one of the rooms off the main hall where people were dancing. Sepsis had stumbled in on the pair while looking for a telephone, but they didn't even bother to glance his way, preoccupied as they were.

They were cruel men and they were beautiful women, yes. But to Sepsis, they were scrims. They were just cover. Honestly, who would think to look for a shy, bookish, serious-minded assassin in a party full of Eurotrash?

As Sepsis walked through the house looking for a phone, Giancarlo bumped into him. Immediately he threw an arm around Sepsis and pointed out the sights.

"So what do you think of my soiree, my friend?"

Sepsis smiled up at Giancarlo, liking him. "*C'est bon,*" he said dead-pan.

"Is that all you've got to say?" Giancarlo exploded happily. "I bet you've never been to a party as good as this in boring old Paris."

Sepsis couldn't come up with any witty retort to this as Giancarlo let him go and was almost immediately swallowed back into the party.

Sepsis and Giancarlo went way back. In Croatia, a few years ago, Sepsis had been traveling through the war zone. There he had come across this young Italian, Giancarlo Bustamante, who along with some friends had gone to Croatia to hunt for humans.

Croats offered to take rich Europeans through the war zone and give them a chance to kill people. Usually the game was refugees, since of course refugees don't shoot back. So in some bombed-out city or town, a group of Europeans would go out one morning, find a nice spot on the top of a building, and shoot someone. The going rate was about three thousand dollars per head, but the Croats could usually be bargained down to a tenth of that price—or even better, a flat fee of a thousand U.S. dollars for all the shooting you wanted. It was best to go with Croats, who just got drunk and giggly while the hunting party waited around for a target. Serbs usually got mean when they were drunk, a couple of Frenchmen on safari getting killed by their Serb guides. Muslim Serbs, on the other hand, usually took your money and then demanded more and more as the day wore on. But with Croats, all it took was a thousand dollars and a couple of bottles of scotch and you were set for a day of safari.

Sepsis hadn't been there to shoot anyone. He'd just gone to see a war up close, maybe take a few pictures while he was at it. Giancarlo and Sepsis had struck up an immediate friendship, though of course the Italian had no idea what Sepsis did for a living. He assumed he did what Giancarlo himself did: live off his rich parents. In a way, Giancarlo was right. And so whenever Sepsis was in town, he lived with Giancarlo and his set of friends, posing as a Frenchman from a wealthy background. During the day, Sepsis would cross town and deal with the mundane details of his real work—assassination—confident that no one from his social set would run across him, since in large metropolitan cities, how often do you cross the borders of the neighborhoods of your social class? Rarely, if ever. Go to another neighborhood, you might as well be visiting another planet.

Sepsis moved about the house, going upstairs to find a phone. The second floor was as stuffed with people as the first, only here drugs were in play, men and women with roving eyes and not so expensive clothes whispering out of the sides of their mouths, pushing their wares in the hallways.

Sepsis took no drugs. Neither did he drink. But even stone-cold sober, he loved going to these parties, letting them evolve as he watched from the periphery, drifting from one little clique to the next as soon as he felt he was becoming noticeable.

But not tonight. Tonight, Sepsis was depressed and flat, simply not up for a night of partying. He wanted to curl up in some hotel room with a stack of books on his bed and read straight through the dawn, catch up on his Updike maybe, which he had been neglecting. He always thought that Updike's style and his own were very similar—elegant and precise for the most part, messy only when the situation called for it.

But Sepsis was working tonight, looking for a phone, needing to get in touch with his contact. So he trundled through the house, stepping out of the way of a woman—a girl of seventeen really, if that—who ran screaming down the hallway, tearing at her clothing hysterically as she caromed against the walls, obviously on a bad trip.

The second floor was too full, but on the third floor hardly anyone at all was about, and he quickly found a small room with a telephone. He left the door open to keep his eye on any approaching figure as he dialed and spoke into the phone in English. "Yes," he said by way of greeting. On the other end of the line, a voice answered in a whisper, also in English.

"She's in Rome, intact."

"Yes, I know that," he said arrogantly, as he scanned the titles in the bookcase by the phone. "I'm already getting the men I need to deal with her."

The voice on the other end went ballistic. "We *agreed*. No killing—"

"Don't tell me what we agreed on," Sepsis interrupted, in a voice with a streak crueler than any at this party. "I didn't agree to anything except indulging your whims *if* I could. If."

"If you don't do what I asked, I won't help you."

"Don't help me and then I blow you out of the water," he said casually, meaning it. Sepsis listened to the silence as the source debated what to say to that.

"But there's good news," the intel source offered by way of conciliation, not wanting to get into a pissing contest with Sepsis.

"Oh?" he said, a title catching his eye; it was Eco's *L'Isola del Giorno Prima*, the spine unbroken, unread. He pulled it out of the bookcase and started paging through it, pleased with himself that he could simultaneously read Italian and speak in English.

"The other target is here as well," the intel source went on.

"Ahh . . ." said Sepsis.

"You can be as 'direct' as you want with *that* target."

"I'll do what I please," he said contemptuously.

The contact exploded. "I only agreed to this craziness if it was carried out on *my* conditions—"

"This is my game," Sepsis hissed cruelly, feeling . . . feeling *wonderful*, now that he—finally—had the upper hand. "I am running things now, this is my job, like I told you from the start. If you don't follow my orders, I'll blow you away without a second's thought. Remember—you are one phone call away from being blown." Then Sepsis laughed. "No pun intended."

The intel source almost exploded again, a harsh hiss of air coming on across the phone lines, the source preparing to launch into a major tirade. But then there was the sound of something like a hiccup, almost as if the source had been strangled by someone, and then there was silence. Sepsis smiled. The source was finally catching on. Sepsis ran the show now, finally.

"This is my game, so just tell me where they are," said Sepsis, smiling as he looked up. And there he saw the most amazing sight.

In the doorway to the small room was a woman he would have gladly killed for; she had caught him by surprise, *L'Isola del Giorno Prima* and the heat of the conversation having distracted him from his lookout. Tall, thin, but owning a body, in a dress that covered it like paint, she stood there, watching Sepsis. He couldn't see her face, backlit as she was by the hallway light, but he was sure she was smiling indulgently at him. Just to see that smile, he stepped out of the light of the hallway, into the shadows, the woman turning to face him, the hallway light falling on her shiny black fuck-me pumps and gleaming dark undress-me eyes. She bobbed just slightly, almost imperceptibly, only just a little bit stoned, but that smile was still on her face, the sight alone of her smile and her eyes getting Sepsis into a sexy, catlike mood, an in-the-mood mood, as the voice on the other end droned on and on.

"She is staying at a secure, unbreachable location which I do not think you could get into with all the men in—"

With no heat, offhandedly as he stared at the beautiful woman in the doorway, Sepsis shot right back: "No. Unbreachable for a bomb, maybe. But I'm past that. There is no such thing as an invulnerable location for me. Get me the address of this place. Get me the layout. Get me their itinerary," he said as the gorgeous woman, Italian, black-haired, walked directly toward him, her walk and the sway of her body creating an endless kaleidoscope of inviting curves and pleasing contrasts of light and shadow.

"You know what you have to do?" his contact answered, still trying to work things out.

"Don't tell me my job. Just get the intelligence I need. I'll be in touch."

The voice on the other line faltered for a split second. "Understood," it said as Sepsis hung up the phone, still staring at the gorgeous woman. Then he smiled.

In the darkness of his apartment, Cardinal Barberi slept soundly, the way only the elderly and the infant can. He would soon die, he knew that. The renovations of the basilica might be keeping him alive, but sooner or later his old body would give out, as was to be expected.

He didn't begrudge death, thinking of it somewhat paganly as a separate entity. But it did anger him that he wouldn't be around to see the final result of his efforts. Terence Cardinal Park had been lucky that way. He had been Barberi's predecessor on the Arts Committee, and had had the great good fortune to die just after they had finished renovating the Sistine Chapel. Lucky bastard. Barberi hoped that he lived to see the reinforcement of the catacomb support columns and walls, Sister Marianne's job. But from that to seeing the final makeover of the basilica interiors and exteriors . . . fifteen years, minimum. Cardinal Barberi turned in his sleep.

Archbishop Neri did not sleep that well. Ever since the explosion at the convent three weeks ago, he had been pushing his contacts in America to find out what was happening, with no results. Why the convent was bombed, why Sister Marianne was shot at—no answers, and now this silence. Opus Dei had contacts with the Arabs, especially with the Sunni Muslims in Saudi Arabia, who always knew everything going on with the Shia, and they hadn't gotten back to him. Which didn't mean anything on its face, but Neri knew better: When Arabs say they don't know anything, they know something. When Arabs don't respond, it's because they're too embarrassed to admit they really are ignorant of what's going on.

Without turning on the lights, Neri got up and started doing jumping jacks to exhaust himself to sleep. The silence was what was bothering him.

"How tight is your security?" he had asked Frederico Lorca.

"She is untouchable in the safe house, and the American FBI agent will be with her most of the time."

"What about your men?" Neri pressed.

"Archbishop, understand: I cannot spare the manpower on something like this, and since the FBI agent will be with her, it seems pointless."

"What if they try to harm her again? They shot at her in an American police station."

"I am aware of that. But understand, we are looking for Sepsis as best we can. Either I have my men look for him, or I protect the nun. If the nun were in America, then we wouldn't have these problems."

"We need her here," Neri said.

And that was the fundamental chance Neri was taking. In truth, Sister Marianne *wasn't* needed in Rome for the renovations. Edmund Gettier could have done all the work equally well, which is what Cardinal Barberi had told him.

"The thought of this awful man doing something to Marianne . . . I would die sooner than I will if something horrible happens to her," Barberi told him. "So I've made up my mind that she ought to stay in America. Gettier can do the work. It will take more time, but he's a smart man—"

"Don't," Neri said, deciding to risk it. "If she stays in America, her soul will be dead."

Barberi looked up at Neri, his enormous eyebrows arching almost to the crown of his head. "What are you talking about?"

Feeling dirty, unclean, Neri gritted his teeth and used the spiritual card. "Staying in America after all her sisters have been killed, with all due respect, think what this would do. All that time on her hands and only one thing to dwell on."

"I see . . ." the cardinal said, troubled.

Archbishop Neri blessed his luck at how politically naive Cardinal Barberi was. He didn't understand what Sister Marianne represented to Opus Dei, the prestige it entailed for a mere nun to be heading a major renovation effort like this one. But Neri was not without a conscience. Like Gettier—like everyone, really—he assumed that sooner or later the assassin would have one more go at the nun, very possibly succeeding. Very likely succeeding. He quit doing his jumping jacks and began doing push-ups.

Cardinal Barberi was a great cardinal, Neri thought. Good, God-fearing, generous, humble, amazing in every way. But Neri hated him a bit, for not seeing through his machinations and putting a stop to them. He thought a little contemptuously of Gettier's idle threat, considering it nothing at all to worry about, for all practical purposes. But Neri knew he would have done something similar to the foolish call if it had been *his* pupil at risk.

Pausing in mid push-up, Neri realized it *was* his pupil at risk. He had known Sister Marianne longer than Gettier had, after all. Yet he was risking her anyway.

The doubts came, and Neri stopped doing push-ups, kneeling by his bedside to pray. But prayer did not assuage his doubts about what he was doing. In fact, it only made them sharper, and more real.

Nighttime. Sister Marianne woke up around two-thirty in the morning, her head spinning with thoughts that would not go away, which was not unusual.

Ever since the bombing, for nights on end, or whenever she wasn't working, all she could think of was the face of the anonymous man. And all she kept feeling was a bitterness that she knew would swallow her whole.

She wanted to forgive. In her mind, in her intellectual conscience, she wanted to forgive the young, anonymous man, forgive him for all the destruction he had wreaked on her life—forgive him for all the deaths he had caused, forgive him for all the pain she felt. She wanted to forgive—and harbor no cruelty.

But her heart hated him. Oh, it so hated him.

Turning over onto her back, she started to pray the Lord's Prayer, concentrating with all her might on the words and their meaning. But shot through her prayer, shards of hatred and bitterness kept cutting through. When she was done, she breathed carefully, trying to still her heart. But it was no better.

To sleep, she started counting up prime numbers, but by 61 she had run out of patience. So she got out of bed dressed only in her nightgown and stealthily made her way down to the first floor of the safe house.

She was quiet. Not much in the way of street sounds came in from the outside; no sound at all in fact. And there was a new moon tonight, making it impossible to see as she felt her way through the house, imagining the relief plan of the villa in her head. When she got to the kitchen, she felt about, trying to remember where the switch was, finally finding it. She hit the lights.

"Jesus Christ!" she said, startled. Then her hands flew to her mouth as she said, "Oh no!" between her fingers.

Sitting there in her nightgown was Agent Chisholm, staring at a half-drunk glass of milk that stood alone on the kitchen table. She looked up at Marianne, unblinking, the change of light not seeming to bother her.

"Are you okay?" she asked.

Marianne was too frustrated to answer. "Oh no," she muttered, furious with herself for taking the Lord's name in vain, again.

"Are you okay?" Agent Chisholm asked again, this time with a slight edge to her voice, still unmoving. Marianne looked up at her.

"I—I'm fine, you startled me and I . . ." She trailed off, then sighed. "I took—" Then she stopped, feeling foolish in the presence of this woman, feeling that she, Marianne, somehow lacked seriousness. "This bad habit I . . . Nothing, I— Agh!"

Agent Chisholm frowned at this weirdness, dismissing it as she drank some milk, then set the glass on the table, staring at it some more with her hands on her lap. Marianne just stood there, watching her, the silence yawning between them.

"I'm just going to get something to drink and I'll be on my way," Marianne said lamely.

Agent Chisholm didn't respond to this as Marianne went to the cupboard and took out a glass.

After she helped herself to some juice, she turned to say goodnight to Agent Chisholm; meaning to, anyway. But instead she said, "You don't like me very much, do you, Agent Chisholm?"

It was the last thing either of the two women expected Marianne to say. Margaret looked up at her and blinked. In the silence, the refrigerator's generator turned and hummed soothingly.

"I like you fine. What makes you say that?"

The penguin gave her a look, holding the glass of juice with both hands, bowing her head slightly, her eyes never leaving Chisholm's. It wasn't a harsh look, but it was knowing.

"Well, no, I . . . I don't like you very much."

"Why? Did I say or do anything offensive?"

Chisholm looked back at her. But she was too tired to put up any kind of defense, so she looked away. "No no, it's nothing, it's . . . you. Your . . . religiousness. Your fervor. Every time I look at you, you're not *you*. You're your religion. You're a walking advertisement for the Catholic Church."

Marianne smiled a little. "Every time I look at you, I see a walking advertisement for the FBI. That doesn't make me like you or dislike you more or less," she said as she sat in the chair to Agent Chisholm's right.

"I guess what I feel is that every time you look at me you're . . . judging me, judging everything I do, whether you see me do it or not. I've done a lot of things I'm not too proud of, and every time I look at you, you remind me of them. You seem so pure when I look at you that I hate that you're so pure while I'm so . . . soiled with the things I've done."

Marianne looked at her, startled, then burst out laughing, surprising Margaret into anger.

"What is so funny? What is so goddamned funny?"

Marianne stopped abruptly, a little uneasy. Very uneasy, actually. Frightened in fact.

"I'm sorry. What you said . . . it struck me funny."

Chisholm looked away like a door closing with such finality Marianne thought it would never open again.

"Really," Marianne said, putting a hand on Agent Chisholm's forearm. The gesture made her look at Marianne again, frightening her again. But she didn't let go at the look. Instead, she looked at Agent Chisholm for a second longer before removing it and folding her hands on the table. She stared at them, then glanced at Agent Chisholm, calmly.

"Agent Chisholm, do you know how I became a nun? . . . I woke up in my apartment one morning, I must have been nineteen—not quite twenty. I had a heroin hangover. My vagina had sores. Blood was flowing from my anus. There were two men in my bed. I didn't remember picking them up, but I remembered the night before. I remembered their grins and I . . . I felt like—death. Like I was a walking dead woman. Like my soul was rotting and putrid. . . . I wanted to kill myself, but I was so stoned that I didn't know how. So I decided to take a walk. . . . I went outside. It was beautiful, just, I don't know . . . beautiful. And I thought, How did I get here? My family was wealthy, I was bright, pretty. The best schools, the best upbringing. Perfect in every way. And here I was . . . It was early, and it was cold. So I walked into this church. It's pretty funny if you think about it: I'm cold, I'm stoned, I want to die—I'll figure it out in church. I wanted to be alone so I sat in a confessional. I thought it was empty, but a priest was taking confession. I wasn't even Catholic then, but I was so stoned and so confused that I confessed everything. I confessed about the men and women I'd slept with. I confessed about all the drugs I'd taken. I confessed about all the lies I'd told my family and friends, how I'd cheated and hurt them again and again. I confessed . . . everything. And after that I was . . . better, somehow. I left the church, and I never went back to that particular church again, but . . . four years after that, I became a nun. . . . I've been a nun for twelve years. And there isn't a single day when I don't think that I am the most . . . soiled person I know. That's why I laughed," she said, putting her hand on Chisholm's forearm again, staring at Chisholm to make sure she understood. "Because you think I'm pure and pristine. But you don't know me. You don't know me at all. That's why I laughed. I didn't mean to hurt your feelings. I was laughing at what you thought I was . . . but I wasn't belittling you."

Sister Marianne took her hand off Chisholm's arm and drank some more juice, looking at nothing in particular. Margaret just stared at Marianne til the nun was a little embarrassed.

"Say something," said the nun, snapping Margaret out of it like a hypnotist done with his trick.

"Yeah, uh, I, no, sure, yeah . . . yes. . . . You're right. I don't know you at all."

Marianne looked at her glass of juice, decided to drink some more, but then realized something and turned to Margaret. "I don't judge you, if that's what you're worried about. I *can't* judge you. Only God can. And even if I didn't believe in God, I'm too busy condemning myself to worry about judging you." Then she drank some of her juice.

Margaret didn't know what to say, so she asked the first thing that came to her mind. "Could you ever go back to your old life?"

Sister Marianne nearly gurgled up her juice at this question, swallowing hard as she laughed and said, "Good heavens no! And I wouldn't want to if I could!"

"No, you misunderstand," Chisholm said dismissively. "I mean, do you see yourself not being a nun anymore?"

Marianne considered the question before answering, the doubts bubbling up in her mind once again before she said firmly, "No. And I wouldn't want that either. I've given up a lot, but . . . I haven't gained anything, really, by being a nun—I took a vow of poverty. But . . . I don't know. It's hard to explain. All I know is that what I'm doing, the life I lead—it's lonely, it's very difficult, we don't just sit around and pray all day—but . . . it's God's Will. I know it's what I'm on this earth to do. I just know." This was true, at least the last part of it.

"But don't you want more?" Agent Chisholm pressed.

She knows, thought Marianne. *Somehow, she knows the truth.* To Marianne, it was always a wonder how someone could become a member of law enforcement—how someone could pretend to seek truth in this world and have the arrogance to think they'd found it. But with this question, Marianne stopped wondering. *She knows,* was all she thought.

"No," Marianne answered. "No, I don't want any more."

Margaret could feel the lie, slowly turning her head away, her eyes never leaving the nun. It was a look to tear the truth out of her, and Marianne couldn't look at Agent Chisholm anymore with the lie between them.

"Before all this," she said quickly, waving her hand at the bombing and the shooting, "I was having these urges, feelings. A desire for more excitement in my life. It worried me because it was distracting me from what I was doing. But *now* . . . not anymore, believe me. Are you happy with your life, Agent Chisholm?"

"My name is Margaret."

"Margaret."

"I don't know. I have a son—"

"You do?" she said, truly surprised by this. "How old is he?"

"Twelve. I worry that I don't have the time for him, that my work keeps me away from him."

"You're lucky," Marianne said, drinking some more juice.

Margaret looked at her. "I'm not lucky. If I'm lucky, I get to have dinner with him once or twice a week." Then she paused. "I'm not so sure about my work anymore either. I'm enjoying it too much."

Margaret stared at her lap, thinking, as Marianne looked at her, then held the look until it was a stare. "What do you mean?" she asked, her words almost a whisper.

Margaret looked at Marianne. "That other time, when I was chasing those men in Washington—I liked it. And there was an incident at a stadium. And I liked that too. I mean I *really* liked it. Maybe you've had enough excitement to last you a lifetime, but I can't get enough of it. God help me, I've developed a real taste for it, and it's scaring me silly."

"I like my work too much too. And I too think it will be the end of me," Marianne murmured to the air, but Margaret was so lost in her Talk talk that she didn't really hear her.

"Almost all the time, when something doesn't go my way, all I want to do is destroy it—or destroy *some*thing, anything. Destroy something so I can feel better about it." She looked at the nun. "When I'm alone, all I want to be is out destroying something. And I'm always alone."

"Don't you have anyone?"

"No, just my son."

"Have you talked to him about—"

"No," Margaret interrupted, staring hard at the nun, then softening. "He needs me. Not the other way around. It would be . . . obscene to make him be my crutch. Everyone else might do it. But that's no reason why I should." Margaret drank some of her milk and let the night turn the conversation.

Marianne smiled. "Something will turn up, I'm sure. You'll find a nice man who'll love you."

Margaret almost laughed at the confidence in Marianne's voice. "How would *you* know? You're a nun."

Marianne cast an eye on her. "I do have some previous experience," she said, and they laughed.

"What about Agent Denton?" Marianne wondered aloud. "He's very attractive."

Margaret nearly sputtered. "Agent Denton? Now it's *you* who don't know *me*."

"He has a very nice body, a very cute ass."

Chisholm gave a start, looking at Marianne. But the nun was giving her a droll look, and they both burst out laughing.

Right around the time Sister Marianne and Agent Chisholm were discussing the cuteness of his ass (which he would have been inordinately flattered to hear), barely a floor away Nicholas Denton was making some perplexing discoveries of his own, specifically about what his staff could and could not do when the boom came down and he really needed to find things out.

He was lying under the covers in bed with a sheaf of notes around him, propped up by three pillows and smoking a cigarette, looking a little bit like one of those mandarin matriarchs who never ventured out into the greater world beyond except in a silk-covered palanquin. He was talking on a phone that had a black plastic device covering the speaker and receiver. This device, a portable voice scrambler, was one of the perks of having a senior position in CIA—you got to use all sorts of interesting toys that were really unnecessary but made you feel really cool.

"Yes, I see. Good. . . . Yes, but before that I want you to do something for me. I want you to look into Margaret Chisholm again."

"We didn't find all that much the first time," said Amalia on the other end of the phone, finishing up the day at Langley.

"No, I'm not interested in her private life," Denton said. "I want to know what cases she's been working on, specifically the cases she's currently handling."

"Mr. Denton, sir, it's not that easy to find out what a Bureau agent is up to."

"Amalia, how hard can it be? These are not Chinese politburo minutes I want, just a list of Margaret Chisholm's cases."

"Mr. Denton, Mr. Wilson wants to talk to you."

"Put him on the speakerphone."

"Hey boss, listen. Only way to find out what she's up to is to break into her office and look through her logs. I could break into their computer and go through the financial records, but it'd give me stuff like name of operation and amount of expenditure. But we wouldn't find out what the operation was about *and* we might get caught."

"*You* might get caught."

Wilson dithered. "Well, yeah, *I* might get caught."

"Amalia, Wilson, how much are you getting paid?"

"Twenty-eight thousand seven hundred and twelve dollars above board, sir. Under the table we're receiving an additional thirty-three thousand and seventeen dollars each."

"It was a rhetorical question, Amalia. With all this money you two are getting, isn't it weird that you can't do a little thing like find out what an FBI agent is doing without having to break into her office?"

Amalia and Matthew Wilson said nothing to this.

After a while of this silence, Denton ran out of patience. "Find out what she's up to with the fewest twigs broken. I'll call you the night after tomorrow night with the encryption code Romeo. Oh, and one thing: Do not go through Lehrer's people, go through our own network."

No one said anything, the silence—and the implication—stretching out until it was a kind of torture. Wilson finally had to say something.

"Leave Mr. Lehrer in the dark?"

"Completely," Denton agreed. "No paper trail, no phone calls—this conversation is between us grown-ups, is that clear?"

"Yes sir."

"Gotcha."

"Good. Good night and I'll talk to you the night after the next."

Denton hung up the phone, took off the telephone encryption device, and tossed it into his briefcase, which was open on the bed a little ways from him. He lay back in bed and thought as he snuffed out his cigarette.

For her part, Amalia started drawing up a list of contacts on the spot, sources that might have access to the kind of information Denton wanted. Matthew Wilson, though, didn't quite go off to break into the FBI computer system just yet. Instead, he tried breaking into the much more forbidding domain of Amalia's attention.

"So Amalia, uh, how 'bout a coffee after work?" Matthew Wilson, big, brawny, foolish Matthew Wilson, for the umpteenth time turned his scary, sad smile on her.

"I can't, Mr. Wilson. I have too much to do. Thank you."

"Why don't you just call me Matt for a change?" he said, smiling insecurely. "Why don't you call Nick Nick?"

"It would be inappropriate, Mr. Wilson," she said, turning back to her work.

And that was pretty much that. Wilson slunk off to play with the FBI computers and see what he could find, for the life of him not understanding his odd fixation on Amalia. It probably was true, he sourgraped. She *must* be tight with Nicky Denton.

Amalia wasn't tight with anyone. Her apartment was an efficiency not too far from Langley, and she lived there alone, without pets or friends, still reeling after four years from her rape.

She had been raped not too far from Agency headquarters when she was a dumb little analyst in Denton's section, three rungs below him back when he was working for Roper.

Like all entry-level positions, Amalia's job was a weeding-out sweatshop gig. A couple of years of résumé padding and a hook to fake out people at parties was what most college recruits wanted from their stint at Langley. Amalia, though, wanted a career at CIA. Working at Central Intelligence was not exactly shoveling shit in a Minnesota cow farm. So, wise little kid, she worked, worked real hard, never going home before midnight and trying to get someone with some authority to notice her.

One night, a mile from Langley, a tire blew out. So she got out in the rain and tried to fix it, another car stopping, the driver offering to help her. But the man didn't help her. Instead, he dragged her down to the empty field by the side of the road and raped her. But that wasn't the bad part.

As he raped her, the man's breath in her ear, her naked belly scratched by the dead, wet brush, what started as a sickeningly ordinary violation turned much worse. Much, much worse. As he raped her, her body reacted, and she began to feel pleasure.

Amalia was a small woman, five feet four in her highest heels. And she was weak. The man had been counting on that, raping her without too much difficulty as she screamed for help from the oblivious passing cars. He had held her wrists together with a single hand, twisting them painfully into the small of her back. She couldn't escape him.

But as he raped her, her body responded in the cruelest way: It gloried in the sexual act, her buttocks and hips arched back uncontrollably to give the rapist more room. And as the rape went on and on, the scratching on her belly wasn't from the rapist's rhythm—it was from her own.

She screamed. She called for help. She cried at the unfairness. She struggled. But still, she came, twice, as she cried in the dark rain, her body feeling like a sunburst inside her, her own body betraying her, the cruelest enemy.

When it was over, seconds or eons later, she couldn't feel her arms from the lack of blood. But her legs were fine. So she kicked the rapist in the groin, sending him down, rolling farther and farther from the road. The wind knocked out of him, all he could do was cough, unable to move.

Instead of running for her car and driving away to the police, Amalia waited. She waited, thinking. Then she went to the car, her arms like lead, numbly got the tire iron, and returned to the still-coughing rapist, who rolled about, clutching his groin, trying to stand up. That was when she did it.

She still couldn't feel her arms very much but she had enough strength in them to strike him on the head with the tire iron. The rapist fell to the ground even as he tried to get up again. So Amalia hit him again. And again. And again. She hit him so many times his face was smashed beyond recognition, his teeth shattered to bits. Then she hit him in the chest, the groin, the arms, the legs, everywhere. She hit him, literally, for hours.

Around three in the morning, all tired out, Amalia went back to her car and sat there, wondering what to do next. She drove home.

In her apartment, it might have been a dream except for all the blood on her clothing and hands, shards of bone having cut her face in places. She still didn't know what to do. So she called her section head, the most likable of the recruiters who had visited her in college, Nicholas Denton.

Denton took care of it. The immediate problem was the body and the car. But that was what Arthur Atmajian was there for. Atta-boy's men made the body disappear along with the rapist's car, getting their Delaware chop shop contacts to make the whole thing vanish.

It was Denton who got Amalia reassigned to be his private gofer, the better to keep an eye on her. And it was Denton who got the Agency to pay for the best psychiatrists money could buy.

But it was Denton who made her a professional assassin.

"We have a find here, Nicky," Atta-boy finally told him a fortnight after the "incident," as they were calling it. "I've been looking at the confidential psychiatrists' notes. This kid doesn't feel regret for killing the guy. She's fucked up about something else, something she's unwilling to tell the shrinks. But she doesn't give a shit about offing the guy. Do you know how rare that is?"

And that's when Denton had the idea: his own private wet-girl.

"Train her," he told Atmajian, "but she's mine. After all, I recruited her."

And that's how Amalia, once a Minnesota cow-farm girl, got to work directly for the Assistant to the Deputy Director of the Central Intelligence Agency as his own private professional assassin.

Amalia was a very lucky woman in many ways. Lucky, and unlucky. Unlike most people—almost all people, really—she could point to a single incident in her life and say with total certainty that this, this one moment, this was it—this was the core and this was the cause. Everything else was just an aftershock of this one thing. Most other people, like Denton and Chisholm and even Marianne, had a whole grabbag of events and memories that shaded and influenced and defined their present actions, sometimes confusingly so. Lucky Amalia, she had her one big moment.

But Amalia was unlucky too. The rape so dominated her life that no love, no hatred, no other suffering or joy could ever hope to overshadow it. The one big thing flattened her life and and narrowed it to a beam, turning her into nothing more than the next best thing to a living machine.

She did other things, of course; it wasn't as if she spent her days going around killing people left and right. In Denton's employ, she'd only killed five people. But assassination was the main reason Denton considered her indispensable. By the time Amalia figured it out, she didn't much care. Because every few months, when she had to go off somebody, it wasn't a random anybody she was killing—it was her own body Amalia imagined she was killing. She was so far gone, only death could make any sort of an impression.

Her last job had been a mere three weeks ago, a contact that had played wise with Denton and started jerking both ends off the middle. So Amalia garroted him in a parking lot on Denton's orders, Blue-birding him good, which was why she was calm enough now to work into the wee hours of the night, looking for contacts who could find what Denton wanted. But as she expected, getting information out of the FBI wasn't so easy. For his part, Matthew Wilson too was finding the FBI computers tougher to crack than he had anticipated.

Lying in his bed in Rome, Denton lit his last cigarette of the day. Amalia knew what she was about, and so did Wilson. If they said the only way to find out what Chisholm was working on was to break into her office, Denton was of a mind to believe them. But it irked him that it had to be so messy; there was always the danger of getting caught. He'd looked through the Macintosh computer in the safety deposit box in Dupont Circle just before the flight to Rome, on the off chance that the shadow file cabinet had come up with something interesting on Chisholm, but her name wasn't even referenced. True, Amalia and Wilson and Paula Baker had been able to dig up a little background on Chisholm, but not as much as Denton would have liked, or had implied to Chisholm in their bathroom break.

We have got to get a pipeline into the Hoover Building, Denton thought finally, hating to be in the dark.

He finished off his cigarette, put all his papers haphazardly away in his briefcase (Denton was a secret slob), and turned off the lights. Amalia wouldn't do, he thought. Too useful to be wasted on a pipeline job. Wilson was out of the question; the FBI was actively looking for Wilson, so *he* wouldn't do at all, and anyway Denton needed him. So: someone green, someone loyal, someone not too bright or useful. Denton smiled as he drifted off to sleep, making a mental list of young

Agency people loyal to him who would be perfect for the job of long-range infiltration of the Effa-Bee-Eyuh.

Nighttime. It was black in the woman's room. The ceiling was black, the curtains were black, even the light coming in from the open window was black. But it was all shades of black. Sepsis lay with the covers around him, spooned from behind by the woman from the party. They were in her apartment, and even though a slight breeze came in from the outside, the air was heavy with the thickish, mildly pungent smell of sex that Sepsis had learned was the surest aphrodisiac in the world.

"That was good," she said dreamily, drowsy but awake.

"I'm glad," he said.

They lay there silently, Sepsis looking around him, conscious of every movement, every change in his environs. But as the seconds ticked off, he started wondering what had been so good about the sex, his ego getting the best of him.

"What was the best part?" he finally asked.

"The second time. The third time it hurt—you're as big as a house."

"Really," he said casually, secretly thrilled at the compliment.

He hadn't had any sex in six months. Not because he hadn't wanted sex—the opportunity simply hadn't presented itself. That, and a German hitcher in Vienna had turned him down, preferring to sleep instead with her traveling companion, which had seriously undermined his sexual self-confidence; Sepsis considered the rejection a personal affront, almost. But now, he was sure he would have more sex in the near future.

He'd noticed how sex begot sex, and'd become convinced that it was the smell of it that women found irresistible. Whenever he had sex, women seemed to fall all over themselves to sleep with him. But when he didn't have sex for longer than a couple of weeks, women no longer found him sexually attractive. Sepsis did not think it was because of his demeanor; his demeanor was invariably the same, whether he had had sex recently or not. So he was therefore sure it was the subliminal smell of sex on him that women must respond to, just as women find only taken men truly attractive—it was wanting what others found attractive. Sepsis thought it revealed a lack of confidence in judgment.

He turned over in the bed and looked at the woman beside him. He had forgotten her name, but he hadn't forgotten other, more essential details.

"You know, when we met, when I was on the phone . . . did you hear anything?"

The woman looked at him oddly, startled somehow. "What?" she asked.

Sepsis could take no chances. He grabbed the woman by the throat and began throttling her, using his elbows to keep her hands away from his face.

Her cheeks ballooned, as did her eyes. She started thrashing, her knees slamming into him, but Sepsis had been careful: his body was not entirely facing hers, his left leg raised slightly to protect his groin. Her knee slammed into his thigh, painfully, as her hands tried to scratch his face. But her hands were unreaching, until she finally fainted from lack of oxygen.

Unmoving, her eyes wide open, Sepsis continued throttling her for another fifteen minutes, long after her bowels had evacuated, patiently squeezing to make sure she was dead. He wasn't going to repeat the mistake he made in Ireland, where he had drowned a man and left him facedown in the gutter. The man had amazingly come to, and Sepsis had had to drown him again. So this time, he squeezed patiently, ignoring the cramp that started needling his right hand. Even though they had been having sex, Sepsis still had his wristwatch on, a Swiss Army sports watch that he couldn't fasten properly. At the notch it was fastened, it was too loose; one notch tighter and it was too tight. But since it was loose, he shook his wrist slightly without letting go and watched the fluorescent minute hand as it ticked off fifteen minutes.

Lucky that no one at the party had noticed them leaving together. But then it wasn't luck; Sepsis had made sure no one saw them leave together, already knowing as they left that he was going to have to kill her for overhearing him on the telephone. Bad luck for her that the Eco book had caught his attention. If he hadn't been paging through the book, he would have noticed her approach and not been so explicit over the phone.

When he was sure she was dead, he sat up in bed and carefully removed the condom he was wearing, always a painful process. Then, he picked up the other two used condoms that were lying on the floor by the bed and carefully tied them up, making sure that no semen was left behind by passing his hand along the carpet. He went into the bathroom, unmindful of leaving footprints since he still had his socks on, aside from his watch his only clothing. He tore off a piece of toilet paper without touching anything, then tossed the three used condoms into the bowl and used the tissue paper to flush the toilet handle. Then he peed. Then he flushed away the pee. Then he flushed again. And then, just to be on the safe side, he flushed one more time, now confident that no semen or urine traces would remain.

He wasn't sure if he could be traced through urine or semen samples; he seriously doubted it, just as he doubted that the woman had heard anything important when he was speaking on the phone. It was just the *thought* that he might be risking exposure by not being careful that bothered Sepsis. Sepsis was neat and orderly about everything in his life, unlike some other assassins. He didn't believe in blind luck.

He went back into the bedroom. Even in the throes of passion, as some are wont to call it, Sepsis had been fully aware of everything he touched or might have touched as he fucked the woman. So with the little swatch of toilet paper, he went to the three spots he might have left fingerprints on, careful to wipe hard, to eliminate any traces at all.

Done with that, he put on his clothes, making sure his naked penis touched no bedclothes; even after peeing, traces of semen might remain on his penis, and he didn't want to risk it.

Clothed, ready to go, Sepsis made one careful tour of the apartment, using the gloves in his overcoat to protect his hands. The apartment was actually quite nice, and if it hadn't been for the disturbing smell of the woman's feces, Sepsis wouldn't have noticed anything unusual, the bedroom having its own little foyer entrance, with double doors blocking it off from the rest of the apartment. The smell was sure to disturb. So Sepsis found an aerosol ambiance deodorant in the space under the kitchen sink and methodically went through all the rooms, spraying. He sprayed especially vigorously in the dead woman's bedroom before closing the doors between it and the rest of the apartment.

In the main entrance foyer, Sepsis sprayed and sprayed at about two meters' distance from the front door. Satisfied, he stepped out of the apartment and closed the door firmly behind him. He debated whether to spray in the hall, deciding against it as the elevator arrived and he got in; the smell of the aerosol might tip someone off that something was wrong. He put the aerosol can in his overcoat pocket and when he got to the first floor he casually walked out, glancing at the sleeping night porter. The porter hadn't moved from a few hours before, when he and the woman had walked into the apartment building and quietly giggled at his sleeping, hulking form. Lucky for the porter he was lazy, Sepsis thought. At this time of night, so close to morning, it would have been hell to dispose of a body.

Things to See and People to Do

Aquardiente's workdays were pretty much the same, over and over. Every morning when he opened the shop, he dusted all the counters and rearranged his stamp displays while Andolini, the retard, swept the sidewalk out front. Then, if no document customers were coming (he saw them only in the mornings, one per day), he went to his backroom and sat down to work, letting Andolini handle the legitimate customers.

Stamp collectors are all the same all over the world, indecisive as old maids but tempted by the wares like sex and the teenaged girl. They come to the shop, they see what they want, they drool over it for a while, then they leave and don't come back for a few days, only to return and go through the same rigmarole of desire deferred until they finally, fitfully succumb, much like nervous virgins.

Aquardiente paid them no mind, working in his backroom until one of the stamp customers finally decided to buy something. There in the backroom, with only the curtain and the short hallway separating him from the main room of the store, he worked on documents in the mornings and stamps in the afternoons. This routine was followed like a religion, every weekday; on weekends, he indulged himself in his one foolish hobby, forging first editions of famous books. He didn't sell the books. He didn't read them either; in fact reading bored him. But he loved forging books anyway, working on a small nineteenth-century hand press he kept at home.

But on weekdays, he forged stamps and documents. And on this morning, he was busily forging the seven documents Tonio's boss had paid for. They weren't a problem at all.

Aquardiente was a clever forger. Birth certificates were his specialty, but when he forged identity papers and passports for short-term covers, he didn't forge *valid* documents: he forged documents that had already expired.

First, aside from paying him the total sum up front, the buyer of a forged document had to provide a rough physical description; a photograph wasn't usually required. Then, Aquardiente would take a photograph of some random individual whose face matched the description and use it on the document he was forging. It didn't matter that the photograph looked nothing like the person who would be using the document, because the document Aquardiente made with such care wouldn't be the one used. The document the buyer eventually used would be the one provided by the authorities.

Once he had his forged, expired document in his hands, this is what a customer did: He would go to the authorities and say, "I need a new passport"—or identity card or whatever—"the one I have is expired, see?" The official would glance at the document and see that the photograph looked only vaguely like the man requesting a new document, but so what? Hair and eye color were the same, age matched, height matched. The person might have gained or lost some weight, quite a bit of weight maybe, but again, so what? People change, especially if a document was issued four, five, ten years ago. What was important was that the photograph in the old (forged) document looked roughly like the man currently requesting a new document, and that the computer entry gave the all clear. The authorities would then issue a new, completely legal document and the document buyer would be on his way, confident that the document he was using was legal, because in fact it *was* legal—the authorities had issued it. Forgeries like Aquardiente's were usually almost impossible to catch before the fact.

That's why Lorca and Chisholm were paying the forger a visit. Dressed in tastefully casual clothes and dark sunglasses, they slowly walked arm in arm down the sidewalk this bright and sunny morning, both of them wearing loose sports jackets over their shoulder holsters. They looked like a young-middle-aged couple, out on a morning stroll.

"This street reminds me so much of Georgetown," she said to Lorca as they passed the storefronts. She stopped at a boys' clothing store, shocked at the number of zeros on the price tags until she realized they were in lira, an inflated currency.

"I have never been to Washington. I was in New York City, at a conference—I liked it."

"Washington's nicer. Remind me to get something for my son," she said absently as the two of them resumed their midmorning stroll. "Do you have people watching this location?"

"Yes," said Lorca, "two of my men are watching the forger's shop day and night." He checked his watch. "Detective Buttazoni and Detective Cabrillo are on duty now. I will introduce you later to them."

"I'd like that," she said.

They walked on in silence, in no rush, passing the stamp shop seemingly without a glance inside. But both of them saw that a customer was haggling with Aquardiente.

"That's the forger? The man with the deformed arm?"

"Yes, he's a very good forger."

"Why haven't you picked him up before?"

"We learned of him through one of our Black Hand informers five months ago."

"I thought they all lived by *omerta*," said Chisholm, smiling at Lorca.

"No, the law of silence is broken all of the time. One of these pigeon stools—"

Chisholm laughed and hid her face in Lorca's shoulder, making him smile patiently as he waited for her to explain. "Stool pigeons," she said. "Pigeon stools is something else. Appropriate, but something else. Stool pigeons."

"Yes, one of their stool pigeons told us about him. We left him alone until we needed him for a special occasion. This is a special occasion."

"Good thinking," she said. "He isn't alone, is he?"

"No, he has a man working for him, Andolini. Very big, but he is somewhat mentally decrepit. He is more for show than for using real muscles."

"Good."

"The forger knows English. Do you want to question him while I act the bad cop? Since you are my guest, it would be my honor. I will handle Andolini."

"I think I would enjoy that. Let's go back."

They turned around and walked back to the stamp shop, casually window-gazing before going in.

Inside, it was cool and dark, both Chisholm and Lorca removing their sunglasses as they held hands and casually looked at the cases of stamps. Aquardiente was dealing with a customer, an ancient man neatly dressed in a business suit and tie, though it was doubtful the man had worked in an office for at least twenty years. Andolini was nowhere around, but from a glance down the hallway that led away from the main store area, Chisholm figured he was in a backroom. She broke away from Lorca, covering the other side of the store as she looked at another case of stamps.

Ordinarily at this time of the morning, Aquardiente would be finishing up with his document forgeries in the backroom before closing shop for lunch. But the old geezer he was waiting on, Don Constantino, actually bought what he liked on the spot, stupidly not realizing he was buying forged stamps. The idiot. Aquardiente glanced contemptuously at the married couple who'd just walked in. They looked rich, but they weren't stamp collectors, merely sightseers, he could tell. He wouldn't bother with them.

Finally the old geezer paid up and turned to go, bowing his head and smiling gallantly as he walked past Chisholm, who smiled in return—her cue to approach the forger.

"Hello Mr. Forger," she said in English as behind her, Lorca closed and locked the front door after Don Constantino and pulled down the blinds.

"*Non capisco.*" The forger smiled nervously. On the counter by the cash register, there was a bell, much like a bellhop's bell. The forger rang it exactly three times.

Immediately, Andolini rushed from the back of the shop, bursting forth and racing for Chisholm. But when he saw she was a woman and that there was another man, he suddenly changed directions, rushing toward Lorca.

Andolini didn't stand a chance. Though he was easily four inches taller and forty pounds heavier, Lorca was very strong and very fast. He stepped aside from Andolini at the last moment, raising his knee directly in the path of the imbecile's approaching stomach, knocking the wind clear out of him. Lorca almost felt sorry for him, but not so sorry he would leave him be. Without a hesitation, he took out a pocket stunner from his sports coat pocket and shocked Andolini into nighty-night unconsciousness.

"Don't move," Lorca said to the forger in English, holding a gun in his hand, produced like magic.

Chisholm looked at Aquardiente, hamming it up, trying to intimidate him. "Long day? Don't want any customers bothering you anymore? Or was that your pet gorilla?"

"Thieves!" Aquardiente bluffed in English. "Thieves! You come to rob a poor working man!" He took a step toward the counter, his belly up against it as his good hand dropped out of sight.

"Put your hand where I can see it. Put your—"

As slow as an old lady, and just as obvious, Aquardiente reached for a gun he kept under the cash register. Chisholm rewarded him with a karate chop where his neck and the shoulder of his good arm met, momentarily paralyzing his entire arm, which felt suddenly like it was doused in pins and needles. Aquardiente looked stunned at the evil-looking redheaded woman. "What are you doing?" he screeched.

Without heat, Chisholm jabbed her extended, rigid fingers forward over the counter, poking Aquardiente just above the curve of his belly and below his sternum, immediately sending him down to the floor behind the counter.

"I *told* you to put your hand where I could see it," she said calmly.

She stepped around the counter and retrieved the gun Aquardiente had been reaching for. It was actually a fairly cheap automatic, the European equivalent of a Saturday night special. Perfectly useless too; it took most of Chisholm's strength to snap a cartridge into the chamber, which she did, switching the safety off and kneeling by the splayed forger.

Chisholm tsked as she stared at the forger. "You know something, my love?" she asked Lorca without taking her eyes off Aquardiente.

"Yes, my darling?" said Lorca as he secured the rest of the store.

"I've never understood why the bad guys always have to pull out a gun instead of just shooting when they have the chance. I suppose they have to show how determined they are before they shoot, don't you agree?" Chisholm was a rotten actress; but then so was Lorca.

"I always agree with everything you say, my love," he said, with all the acting concentration of someone in an Ed Wood film, not looking at Chisholm or the forger, covering the store.

"Well now, *Mr.* Aquardiente," Chisholm went on. "I'm going to ask some questions, and you are going to give me some answers, agreed?"

Aquardiente had finally recovered his wind. "I know nothing. I sell stamps, all I do is sell stamps!"

"My love? What would happen if we told all of Mr. Aquardiente's customers that he is actually an informant for the Interpol?"

"Oh, that would be very bad, my sweet," said Lorca, never standing still, careful not to be a fixed target. "All those bad criminals would want to kill Mr. Aquardiente very badly, even if it was not true."

"A terrible thing to spread lies," she said, staring straight at Aquardiente, leveling the gun right between his eyes. For an instant, focusing on the gun's barrel, his eyes crossed comically. Margaret Chisholm's belly did a sickeningly slow forward roll. But she pressed on, putting the gun right to Aquardiente's forehead, his eyes concentrating on hers.

"Go away, go away!" he screamed in fear as he lay there, his shoulders and the back of his head against the wall, the rest of his body prone, unmoving. *"Go away, I have done nothing wrong!"*

Chisholm reached with her free left hand and slapped Aquardiente with all her strength. "Shut up!" she growled, outraged at Aquardiente's behavior, and her own.

"I know nothing, nothing," he mumbled pathetically, broken and crying. All Chisholm had done was strike him a couple of times and threaten him emptily, but he was broken already. "I know *no-o-o-thing*. . . . What do you wa-a-ant?" he whined finally.

"Information," she said. With her left hand, she reached into her pocket and produced a small picture of Sepsis, the one Sister Marianne had identified in Washington from the Italian passport records. "Do you see this man?"

"Wh—"

"Do you see this man!" she shouted, harsh and terrifying.

"Yes yes yes!" he screamed back.

"Have you seen him before? *Have you?*"

"No!"

"Then you will see him soon," she went on calmly. "And when you *do* see him, you will contact us."

The forger looked at her, so frightened no sound came out of him, his mouth flapping open emptily.

She didn't know why she did it. Maybe seeing his mouth open like that, who knows? But Chisholm took the gun off the crippled forger's forehead and slid it into his mouth, his eyes going round like O's, terrified to beat the devil. The gun tasted lightly of oil. She put the gun so far into his mouth he nearly gagged, would have gagged if his fear hadn't suppressed the reflex. She grabbed the back of his head with her free hand and then leaned her face into his, her own mouth so close to his eye that when he blinked, his eyelashes brushed her lips.

"I will blow your head off," she whispered serenely, in a voice of pure seduction. "I will blow you away. Do what I want and, maybe, you live."

She leaned back, keeping her eyes on Aquardiente, the barrel of the gun still in his mouth like a steel lollipop, or a cock. She smiled at Aquardiente without realizing it, really and truly happy and completely unconscious of her pleasure.

"When the man in the picture comes to your store," she told him softly, "pull down the blinds. Pull them all the way down. That's your signal. If you pull them down even a little bit and we come here and we don't find him, I'll hurt you. And it won't be good like it is now."

So fast he wasn't aware of it, she slid the gun out of his mouth and kissed him full on the lips, hungrily devouring him with her teeth and her tongue before standing up and stepping away. She glanced at Lorca, who looked amazed, and then she looked at the forger.

He was broken. It was . . . a vacancy in the eyes. But not only in the eyes; it seemed to come from his entire body, as if the crippled forger had somehow, imperceptibly, changed into a corpse. The man was dead, in a way; a kind of metamurder like Sepsis had in mind. Chisholm looked away as she spoke.

"Remember: the blinds pulled down when the man in the picture comes to your store."

"I have never seen such a man," the broken forger moaned.

"You *will* see him," she said, dropping the picture on his lap. "Keep this, as a souvenir."

She pocketed the cheap automatic and walked out the door on Lorca's arm without a backward glance.

They walked in silence to the street corner before either of them felt like saying anything. But finally Frederico Lorca couldn't help himself, taking Chisholm's hand and swinging it back and forth as they walked on together, looking like a happily married couple, or lovers playing hooky from work for the sake of a morning rendezvous.

"I admit, I was most impressed by your performance. The gun in the mouth, and then the kiss! Ah, you were as frightening as the Angel of Death."

"God, I hate this job," was all she said, tired and with a head that was so bad.

"Eh? Why?" he asked, amazed as they passed the other pedestrians. "I thought your performance was excellent."

"Maybe," she said unconvincingly, the two of them walking through the late-afternoon sunlight of a Roman morning.

While Chisholm was busy making new friends, Sister Marianne was seeing old ones, spending her first morning in Rome visiting the reno-vation site.

She wasn't supposed to go that Friday; everyone was expecting her on Monday morning. But her impatience got the best of her and so she convinced one of the Ministry of Justice men to drive her to the site. Denton tagged along, pretending halfheartedly that he was living up to his end of the bargain and protecting the nun.

The Vatican is a city-state surrounded by Rome. A painted line a foot and a half wide separates Vatican City from Rome, a borderline the tourists and street vendors and priests and nuns casually step over with-out even realizing it. But to get into the guts of the basilica, where Marianne and Edmund Gettier would be spending their days, was a lit-tle more complicated than just strolling across some white line and smiling happily at the colorfully dressed Swiss Guards. Getting into the basilica was a major undertaking.

The main, formal entrance to the basilica is, of course, St. Peter's Square. Sister Marianne and Denton didn't go there. Instead, the Min-istry of Justice driver, Quintilio, drove them around the left arm of the square, to a discreet corner where there was a thick, high, green-painted metal gate that was topped off with outward-projecting spikes. The green gate, which formed a small courtyard against the side of the basilica, looked incredibly flimsy; at first glance, it looked like a service entrance. A Swiss Guard dressed inconspicuously in a modern uniform sat in what looked like a white-painted wooden sentry booth. As he stepped out to meet the approaching car, Denton saw that not only did the booth guard carry an Uzi, but his "wooden" booth was actually built of thick concrete.

"Sorry about this," Marianne said to him shyly.

"Don't worry about it," Denton said, telling her how careful they were at Langley as he casually watched the booth guard.

His Uzi at the ready, the booth guard spoke to Quintilio in Italian, checking his identification as he spoke into a transmitter. Satisfied, the guard stepped away and waved them in.

There was a quiet hum and the green gate rolled open. Two Swiss Guards carrying light assault rifles, bulked up by their bulletproof vests, appeared behind the gate. They stood to either side of the car, carefully watching it as it rolled into the courtyard. As the car passed the gate, Denton looked out and realized that it was a good four inches thick, easily thick enough to stop any suicide bomber.

The car stopped in the courtyard as the green gate rolled shut behind them.

"This is very embarrassing," Sister Marianne told him again, "but please, don't get out of the car until the guards say it's okay. And when you do, don't make any sudden moves."

Denton glanced at her with an "oh-kaaay" look to him. This was way stricter than anything he'd seen at Langley, or anywhere else for that matter. He looked around.

The courtyard was small and cramped, barely big enough for two or three cars. Aside from the green gate, it was surrounded by the smooth, windowless gray-brown wall of the side of the basilica. At the end of the roughly oval-shaped courtyard, there was a thick, brown door with no outside handle. With the big green gate now closed behind them, they were effectively trapped.

Rather slowly, the two Swiss Guards walked over and stood about three yards from either side of the car, waiting for them to get out. They made no move to open the car doors, much less help them out.

"Let's go," said Sister Marianne to Denton. They got out and she handed over an identity card to one of the Swiss Guards, who checked it as the other kept his distance from Marianne, Denton, and Quintilio. Neither guard said a word.

"Do they need my identification?" Denton asked, feeling suddenly very nervous.

"No, don't worry, I'm the head of the renovation project—I can bring in two unidentified guests," she said a little too firmly, as if having to convince herself, making Denton realize that she was nervous too.

Without a word, looking at her a little suspiciously, the guard handed Marianne her identification card and motioned her toward the brown door. She and Denton walked toward it, Quintilio staying by the car. The door buzzed open before they actually reached it.

They walked into a small white antechamber, the door closing behind them and locking automatically. The antechamber was completely bare except for a single bulletproof window on one of the walls. Next to the window, there was a speaker and a numeric keypad, and beyond it, a lone guard sitting at a computer console. This guard recognized Sister Marianne from her visits the year before, and he smiled, chatting with her in Italian through the wall speaker, using the idle chitchat to cover up the embarrassment of having to check her identification again on his computer and make sure she was authorized to enter. It was embarrassing, yes, but those were the rules, absolutely no one allowed inside unless they were cleared, not even the Pope; look-alikes had tried.

"Please give your access code," the guard said in Italian. Marianne punched a series of numbers into the keypad on the wall. Denton realized that the nun wasn't just giving an access code; she probably knew a slight variation of the code that would alert the security people if she were a hostage being forced to smuggle someone inside.

When the all clear came, the guard buzzed open a latchless door almost hidden in one of the walls of the antechamber, another guard behind the door opening it and letting them in.

Once they were truly inside the basilica, Marianne gave a little inconspicuous sigh of relief that Denton caught.

"I wonder if heaven will be as hard to get into," he said.

Marianne laughed. "We take security very seriously," she said.

Denton covered his surprise at her use of pronoun. "I'm sure you do," he agreed.

"We have to," she went on. "We don't want anything to happen to him," she said as she pointed up at the roof, following her finger with a brief glance.

"To God?" asked Denton, confused.

"No!" She laughed. "To the Pope."

"Ahh . . ."

She led him through hallways and vast, limitless spaces that were all dark and quiet even though it was morning.

"Does anyone work here?" Denton finally asked, curious that no one else seemed to be around.

"Of course, but upstairs. These are just for processions and big ceremonies. You should be here on a Sunday."

As they neared the work site, Denton could feel a quiet, orderly hum of activity, which the nun felt too, making her pick up the pace.

"Come on," she told Denton, pulling him by the wrist. "You have to meet everyone."

"Don't tell them what I do," he told her quickly, making her stop and look at him, uncomprehending.

"Why on earth not?" she said, genuinely naive about what people thought.

"Us CIA types don't have a very large fan club," he said, smiling.

"Oh. Okay," she said, and Denton tugged her along.

They turned a corner and there in a wide, open space was Edmund Gettier standing over a worktable as around him workmen and engineers, indistinguishable by their clothes, moved quietly about, crawling over scaffolding that lined the walls and surrounded the thick colonnades.

Aside from Edmund, all the workers and engineers were young. In fact, Sister Marianne was the oldest one of the bunch, all these twenty-somethings and very-early-thirty-somethings patiently working away at the renovation of the Vatican. From the outside, none of the camera-toting tourists would have realized that inside, a new church was being built from the ground up, from the inside out, all these kids invisibly hammering out a new structure they could all silently call their own.

A bearded, bespectacled young engineer-type was the first to see the nun as she walked in with Denton. "Marianne!" he called. Everyone turned to her and Denton as work ground to a semihalt and people came over to greet her.

Denton stood aside, watching the scene. He felt a bit of idle envy for the nun. Not real envy, but a kind of wistfulness. The sight of the nun with her friends reminded him, a touch sadly, of when he was working in the basement at Langley.

She introduced Denton to everyone, carefully not saying what he did, as he had asked. The mere fact of his being Marianne's friend made him acceptable to everyone on the site.

"You are now in the land of King Edmund," the bearded engineer who had first noticed them told Denton, laughing.

"Come on," said Marianne, "let's go to *my* domain."

Along with Gettier and the bearded engineer, Bob Rijke, they went through the ground level to a wide, unobtrusive staircase that was hidden behind some columns. It went down for a good thirty feet, spiraling gently.

"This staircase was sealed off," Denton guessed, noticing smashed bricks and mortarwork by the staircase's entrance.

"Yes," said Rijke, a Dutchman who spoke pretty good English but with an odd little accent that made him sound like a New Yorker. "This is the section that was always put off until forever." He gestured downward. "Whenever the Church found money to fix the basilica, it was always the ground floor, the cupola, the *façade*. How do you say *façade* in English?" he asked Marianne.

" 'Facade,' " she said absently as she stared around her in wide-eyed wonder, touching the walls of the staircase.

Rijke blinked and smiled sloppily, feeling foolish. "Yes, of course, facade. Only now, when it will be incredibly expensive to repair, do they find money to repair the foundations."

When they got to the bottom of the staircase, they were in a dark catacomb lit by bright, jury-rigged fluorescent lights, the space filled with portable steel girders holding up the low ceiling.

"These are the catacombs," she said proudly, making her careful way through the girders as up ahead of them, hidden by the darkness that seemed to suck up the fluorescent light, Denton heard workmen hammering something metallic.

"Who's buried here?" he asked facetiously as they walked through the maze.

"We're not sure," said the nun seriously. "The tombs, some of them go back to the twelfth century. Records have been lost."

"No ghosts, right?" he asked as he faked nervousness, making Rijke and the nun laugh, and Gettier smile at her laugh.

Workmen were hammering together a scaffolding that surrounded the colonnades, much like the ones on the upper, ground floor. But since the catacombs had a much lower ceiling, unlike the ground floor, the scaffolding here was lower and not so intricate or sturdy.

"Is there a space between the catacombs and the ground floor?" Denton asked the nun.

"Very good," answered Gettier in a tone that couldn't help being a bit patronizing, even though he meant the compliment.

"Yes," she said. "Above us? There's a burial space. For church officials, some popes. Edmund's work is phase one of the project, strengthening the columns that support the main roof. My project, the catacombs here, this is stage two, starting on Monday. Stage three will be opening the mid level and fixing the support columns there."

"That is my project," said Bob Rijke. "But *she* is the boss," he added, impulsively hugging Marianne. He was a good four inches shorter than she was, so it was a little comical, the sight of them.

They went on through the catacombs, which seemed almost limitless, belying Denton's initial impression that they were rather small. The nun, Gettier, and Rijke explained things to him as they casually walked between the girders and scaffolding, but careful not to disturb any of the colonnades, some of which were outright crumbling. Denton absently wondered where they were headed, the dark catacombs going on and on until finally, a good two hundred and fifty yards from the staircase, they came to another staircase, identical to the first, and walked up.

"How big is it down there?" he asked, amazed, as they reached the ground floor.

"It is the size of the entire basilica," said Gettier, Marianne nodding brightly.

"And it's all mine!" she said greedily. They all laughed.

———

The next Monday, Chisholm drove the nun to work and their routine started falling into place.

Maggie Chisholm had no intention of letting something like the Washington chase make a repeat performance in Rome, so she carefully mapped out various routes to the basilica as she kept a watchful eye out for anyone tailing them. Since the villa was so far from the basilica, it was easy to go by different routes every day. But still, every day, Chisholm carefully wrote down what streets she'd taken so that she wouldn't accidentally repeat herself.

In the mornings, around eight, Chisholm and Marianne would take off for the Vatican; Gettier usually walked to work from his apartment. Denton would also leave around eight, going off on his "liaison" business, whatever *that* meant; Chisholm suspected it meant hanging out with the chargé d'affaires at the embassy.

At the Vatican, Marianne and the workmen and engineers of her team would go about their business in the catacombs while Chisholm would basically loiter, her loaded gun in her holster under the sports jacket she always wore, following Marianne around and restlessly checking out the scene.

"Why are you following me?" the nun asked on the first day, perplexed by her shadow as she went upstairs to get soft drinks for everyone.

"Marianne, that's what I'm supposed to do. I'm supposed to watch out for you."

She laughed. "What could happen here?"

She had a point. What with the security of the Vatican, Chisholm thought it was a waste of time to be keeping an eye out for Sepsis, whom she wouldn't recognize anyway. The forger hadn't signaled them, and the passive surveillance hadn't produced any results. Of the hundreds of pictures they'd taken, four separate men who'd gone into the store might have been Sepsis, but because of the light and the angle, it had been impossible to tell. The photographs the passive surveillance was taking were proving to be almost as useless as the photograph the nun had identified—the son of a bitch was so anonymous he could be practically anyone. But Chisholm's conscientiousness got the better of her and so she dutifully followed the nun everywhere she went, keeping an eye out for Sepsis.

It was toughest during the lunch breaks.

"Margaret," the nun would call as they all sat around her worktable, which served as the lunch and tea table, "this is Umberto Penola. He lived in New Jersey once."

"Really . . ." she would say, smiling at a lanky Italian engineer who smiled happily and started talking to her about New Jersey, which Chisholm hated.

The nun tried. She tried to bring Chisholm inside, but everyone knew it was impossible. While the nun and all the others worked on the catacombs, Chisholm had nothing to do except wait and watch, feeling outside them all as she looked in on a neat, orderly universe to which she did not belong. It wasn't the nun's fault, though she tried mightily, trying to bring her in. But Chisholm couldn't. And after a while, she started wondering if she even wanted to be inside.

Sepsis was running late, but he made no effort to hurry. A man who hurries is a man who's noticed. Instead, he quite casually lumbered on toward Aquardiente's shop, sure that he would be harassed by the sick bastard.

But that wasn't what was on his mind. Rather, Sepsis was troubled by the lack of equability in his targets.

Since he'd taken on the job, Sepsis was upset at the predominance of women on his target list. He had killed all the nuns in the chapel, then tried to murder Chisholm, then murdered the woman he had picked up at Giancarlo's party. All had been women, Sepsis forgetting that there had been a priest in the chapel too when the bomb went off.

The thought that some criminologist somewhere would conclude that Sepsis was a misogynist was deeply troubling to him. Of course, there was no way they would ever discover he was the one who did the woman from the party, which was good; it wouldn't add to the false impression of misogyny. But he wondered if when he finally killed Chisholm and perhaps killed the nun (he hadn't made up his mind yet), intelligence services would in future refer to this job as the "woman-killing spree" or some such horrifying epithet. Troubling.

As he walked down the street, carefully feigning Tonio's idiocy, several absolutely gorgeous women passed him by. It was all he could do to pretend he didn't notice them, shuffling on with an idiot grin. He thought he was pulling it off very well, not realizing that all the gorgeous women who passed him by wondered why he wasn't noticing them. Retards, by their very innocence, always obviously look at passing women. He must be gay, they thought, or so imbecilic and stunted he did not have any sexual desire.

He got to Aquardiente's already closed shop, going in and waving at Andolini, who stood by the cash register, carefully counting up the day's receipts.

"Hi Tonio," said Andolini, smiling hugely and giving him a big wave as if an enormous gulf separated them, even though they were standing a mere yard from each other.

"Hi Mr. Andolini," said Sepsis in that equally bright way, liking him a lot. "Where's Mr. Aquardiente?" he asked, used to having the sick bastard waiting for him, hand and cock.

"He's inside—I'll tell him you're here," Andolini said, then dithered, looking at the money and then at Sepsis, who read his mind. "Don't take the money," he said wagging a stern finger at Sepsis in a grotesque imitation of a schoolmaster. "If you do, I'll beat you."

"I won't take any money!" he said, hurt-sounding. "Honest!"

"Okay." Andolini went to the hallway, stopped and turned suddenly to make sure that Sepsis wasn't taking any money, then smiled wide. "I knew you wouldn't take any money. We've had trouble with thieves."

"I'm not a thief!" said Sepsis, playing Tonio, then thinking. "Did thieves break in?"

"Yeah, one two three four five days ago, yes, five days ago. They came in and stole money from Mr. Aquardiente. Beat me up too."

"Wow. Who were they?" he asked innocently.

"A man and a woman. They looked *nice*. But they weren't nice. They were thieves."

"Wow," said Sepsis-as-Tonio.

"They hit me in the belly, then they made me sleepy. I'll go get Mr. Aquardiente."

Andolini went to the backroom. Without a hesitation, Sepsis locked the front door and pulled the blinds all the way down before following Andolini.

Across the street, Buttazoni and Cabrillo saw the blind come down, and waited to see if it was the signal or if Aquardiente was just done for the day.

"If he doesn't come out in three minutes, he's the one," said Buttazoni. Cabrillo said nothing. He was too busy strapping on his gun holster.

Inside, Sepsis got to the backroom just as Andolini was announcing his arrival to the forger.

"Oh! Here he is!" said Andolini. The instant he stepped into the backroom, Sepsis knew there was trouble.

The forger looked nervous and preoccupied, like he had things on his mind. But he didn't seem nervous to see him, making Sepsis hesitate.

"My boss sent me, just like you said—at closing time."

"Good, Tonio—eh, how are you? Leave us, will you," he said to Andolini, who went back to counting up the receipts. "How have you been?" he asked as he got a small stack of rubber-banded documents from a cabinet in the wall.

"Good," said Sepsis, unnerved that Aquardiente wasn't harassing him. Sepsis had a gun, of course. If the sick bastard didn't try something soon, Sepsis decided, he would use it.

"Good good," said the forger, holding up the pack of documents with his good hand and counting off the number of papers with his stunted hand before giving the bundle to Sepsis. For his part, Sepsis counted them slowly, stupidly, wondering as he did what had happened.

"Did someone rob you?" he asked innocently as he counted, forgetting that light mental retardation prevents people from chewing gum and walking at the same time.

"Nothing to worry about, nothing to worry about," said Aquardiente nervously, then brightening and getting off his stool, throwing his good arm over Sepsis's shoulders. Sepsis smiled up at him a bit shyly after he finished counting, trying to imagine what "Tonio" would say now.

Aquardiente's breath smelled of booze, and his eyes were just a touch watery. But whatever was depressing him wasn't keeping him from rubbing his crotch against Sepsis's thigh as he smiled more naturally, getting drunk on his desire. "I'm glad you came, I've been looking forward to it."

He dropped his good arm and grabbed Sepsis's ass. But this time, it was actually his anus that Aquardiente tried to feel up, one of his fingers trying to get up in there, even through the fabric of his jeans. Forgetting himself, Sepsis' eyes flashed, just once—a fraction of a second. And Aquardiente liked that, the wildness of the look, but it reminded him of something else—the picture. The picture the woman had given him.

"Don't—" said Sepsis, seeing Aquardiente's reaction. That was when he knew the forger was blown.

Without hesitation, Sepsis pushed Aquardiente away, pulled out his silenced gun and plugged him on the spot, two bullets right in the head, one over each eyebrow. Sepsis was using armor-piercing .22's with a long-barreled silencer; the two shots made the sound of a minor cough. Even before Aquardiente hit the ground dead, Sepsis was looking past him, thinking ahead.

Across the street, Cabrillo and Buttazoni barely got to two minutes before deciding they had to go check things out. They hadn't heard a thing. They hadn't seen anything either. But both of them were flipping off the safety on their weapons as they bounded down the stairs of the apartment building.

In the backroom, Sepsis gritted his teeth and hollered. "Mr. Andolini?" he called in that thin, reedy Tonio voice, sounding scared and desperate. "Something's happened to Mr. Aquardiente!"

Andolini reached the hallway that led to the backroom just as Buttazoni and Cabrillo got to the street.

"What happened?" asked Andolini as he approached the backroom. He turned into it and saw Aquardiente, facedown in a pool of blood. "What happened!" the retard screamed, terrified, as Sepsis aimed his gun right to his forehead and blew his head off.

Buttazoni and Cabrillo managed to jaywalk through the traffic, cars honking at them unendingly.

Sepsis looked at the two corpses, then at his gun, the only weapon he was carrying. He had seven bullets left and only one full clip in his back pocket. He decided to move—*now.*

He pocketed the stack of documents he had come for and went into the hallway. There was a back door there, of course, and the main counter room was up ahead. Go through the back door or out the front door? Instinctively, realizing how cramped the back alley would be, Sepsis started for the front door.

Buttazoni and Cabrillo got to the front door, foolishly rattling hard on the doorknob, which was locked and unyielding.

Without a thought, seeing the shadows of the plainclothes policemen through the blinds of the front door, Sepsis shot them both twice as he turned and rushed for the back door.

Outside, Buttazoni took a slug in his shoulder and another right in the throat. The bullet drilled through his voice box, severed his spine, and came out the back of his neck. The bullet didn't stop there. It flew on and struck a passing driver, drilling through her left temple, lodging halfway through her brain. Losing control of her car, she smashed into the oncoming traffic. By this time, Buttazoni was dead.

Cabrillo took a bullet in the chest, an inch above his right nipple, and another in the belly. The force of the bullets dropped him on his ass on the ground, his right arm paralyzed. But Cabrillo was left-handed, so as the dead woman driver smashed into the oncoming traffic and her body was impaled on her own steering wheel column, Cabrillo just let go with his gun, shooting into the stamp store even though he couldn't see anything inside because of the blinds.

Sepsis got lucky. None of the bullets Cabrillo shot so much as scratched him, but they sent him in a panic out the back door. If someone had been there, that would have been the end of him. But no one was about as Sepsis burst out the door and ran down the alleyway. He ran to the corner, then stopped, hard, taking a deep breath before turning the corner. He walked on as if nothing at all were the matter, the pedestrians around him moving about like cows, cows who'd heard or seen some slaughter but didn't seem too sure what to do or how to react.

Out in front of the stamp shop, Cabrillo started coughing, then lost consciousness, collapsing on the sidewalk. His right lung started filling with blood, drowning him; he would be pronounced dead at the scene. But no one was really noticing him. Rather, the spectacular car crash was what everyone was staring at and approaching, the crash having blocked traffic in both directions.

Sepsis walked away without any trouble, a bit shaken but none the worse for wear. As he looked back, there seemed to be an awful commotion, cars stopping and idling, people getting out of their vehicles to take a look at what had happened. Sepsis walked away from the commotion, curious to see what it was about, but not *that* curious.

No one challenged him. His gun was in the small of his back, under his loose jacket, but he kept his hands in his back pockets for a quick draw. He wasn't really worried though. They hadn't been expecting him, which was good. If they knew he would be there, they would have had people in the alleyway, more people out front, probably someone waiting for him in the backroom. Good, so they hadn't been expecting him.

Sepsis caught a bus, no longer keeping up the pretense of being Tonio. No one could charge him with being a misogynist now. Though with one dead mentally challenged man and one dead handicapped homosexual, he started wondering if someone might call him a homophobe, or a Nazi. Troubling.

Goddamn," said Chisholm, staring at the corpse of Aquardiente.

Medical examiner orderlies had just left the backroom with the body of Andolini on a stretcher, leaving Lorca and Chisholm alone with the dead forger. The living stood silently, thinking things over as the dead forger, well, the dead forger too contemplated what he had on his mind.

"He didn't just kill them," she said, staring. "He executed them. He knew we'd come to visit."

"Come," said Lorca as the medical examiner came in with a couple more orderlies, the room simply too small for five people and a corpse. "We have to converse."

They walked out of the shop and strolled down the sidewalk they'd been on less than a week ago, idly looking at the windows, as incon-spicuous as any other pair of pedestrians. The area around the shop was cordoned off, but the place had the feel of returning normalcy, all the press vultures already having gotten their fill of carrion.

"We have a serious problem, Margaret. With the forger dead, we have no leads."

"I know," she said, beat. The baby-sitting of the nun was wearing on her.

"I have been thinking along the following lines: If Sepsis were I, what would I do if I wanted to kill the nun?"

"Hit her where I know she'll be," she answered, thinking out loud with Frederico.

" 'Hit her,' yes. Where is that?"

"The Vatican basilica. And . . ."

"And the villa. Margaret, I am thinking that it is possible that Sep-sis will try attacking the villa."

"Alone?"

"Possibly, though I think it is unlikely. Nothing in the forger's shop indicates Sepsis was trying to secure more than one set of documents, however."

"One person, alone, might be able to get into the villa. At night? Tough, but possible."

They stopped at a men's clothing store, looking at the window dis-play without seeing anything. "What I will tell you is confidential and only my opinion," Lorca said. "My superiors disagree. Tell me what you think. You said in your Washington report that you thought the Sister Marianne has been targeted because of her work in the Vatican, correct?"

"Yes. So?"

"Sister Marianne is in the Vatican, heavily protected by the Swiss Guards and by you. But in the villa, there are only five men, two of them sitting at the entrance, easily dispatched in a concerted effort."

"I see," said Chisholm, not liking it. "A serious hit on the villa."

"Yes. My superiors do not agree with my idea because members of the Black Hand, witnesses, were never touched while they stayed at the villa. The villa has a perfect operational record in that sense. But Sepsis is a very daring assassin with extraordinary determination. Almost psychotic determination."

"I would definitely agree," she said, thinking of the three hits in Rivercity. They turned and walked on down the sidewalk. "Can you get more men to guard the villa?"

"That is the problem—I have tried, but I can't. It belongs to the Ministry of Justice. They are unwilling to allow more men to guard the villa if it is not their operation."

"Typical."

"You have similar problems in America?"

"Yes of course," she said, surprised. "You thought we all get along?"

"Yes," said Lorca frankly. "You Americans seem so orderly, it is surprising that you have jurisdictional problems like ours."

"Goes to show you . . ." They walked on in silence, Margaret mulling over the problem but inevitably going back to the dead forger. "I hate it when that happens, when someone gets blown like that," she said, referring to Aquardiente; but Frederico Lorca misunderstood her.

"Yes, Buttazoni and Cabrillo were excellent men. Not very intelligent, but brave and dependable. I will enjoy killing the man who did this," he said with chilling calmness.

"Can you put men in the villa?"

"Yes, I can. My superiors will be unhappy, but I think I can, but only three more, at most four. Now I am asking you formally, do you agree Sepsis could possibly try attacking the villa?"

"Yes, I think it is a likely event we should prepare for," she said, giving him the ammunition he would need to deal with his superiors.

"Good, thank you. Now I am thinking: If Sepsis needed documents for himself, that is one thing. He is obviously not using the Tirso Gaglio documents."

"At least not for traveling, no."

"So he must already have documents. So why would he buy more documents?"

"For someone else," said Chisholm, catching on. "He's getting documents for other people, people he might need, men he would use to hit the villa—I see . . ." she said, hooked to his line of reasoning. "These men haven't arrived yet."

"Exactly," he said. "When these men arrive, he will move. The first possibility is that he attacks the Vatican directly. Impossible and pointless. The second possibility is that he might try attacking the Sister Marianne when you are driving to the Vatican and back. But you are using various roads?"

"Yes. I doubt he'll try something like Washington again."

"Maybe he would try it again precisely because he failed."

"Good point."

"But the third possibility is, he will try attacking the villa directly. Therefore I think we should move her."

As they walked, Margaret reached over and took Frederico Lorca's arm in a very intimate gesture, bringing her lips close to his ear, the two of them looking like any happy couple without a care in the world. But Lorca heard real fear in her voice.

"Frederico, I have to tell you something very important, just between us. This is my own private suspicion, something I've been thinking about since this started. I think we have someone who is giving information to Sepsis, someone very close. I mean, look at the forger back there—Sepsis *knew* the forger was blown, he couldn't have simply suspected it and then killed him just in case. He *knew*. Someone must've told him."

"I see," he said, blinking away his surprise. "So moving the Sister out of the villa will not help."

"No," she said, staring straight ahead, looking around restlessly.

"Who?" he finally asked.

The words caught on her lips. "I can't say yet," she said. But she'd come awfully close to naming who it was she was beginning to suspect: Denton.

TEN

Meta-murder and Plain Ol' Death

He was fucking up this operation. That, and the dwarves of uncertainty were out in full force. Fuck.

After killing the forger and his bodyguard, Sepsis had to be at the docks that night to pick up the Valladolid team. So once he crossed town on the bus he'd hopped on, Sepsis backtracked by way of three taxis, getting out a couple of blocks from the safe house he'd arranged in a working-class section of town, a house that was far from his usual milieu. There, in the alleyway behind it, he had parked a van which he drove to pick up the men he was using, cursing throughout the drive.

They were six men from Valladolid, Basque separatists with plenty of experience. Like the Québecois Libre men he'd used in Washington, the men from Valladolid had no idea what they were doing, only that their superiors had ordered them to help out Sepsis on a job he would brief them on when they got to Rome.

They were all coming over illegally of course, on a ship owned by a Basque sympathizer. Sepsis was supposed to have their documents ready for them when he picked them up at the docks—that had been part of the deal. But now, with the forger dead, he didn't dare use any of the seven sets of documents he had bought.

He picked up the men at the docks without a hitch.

"You got through okay?" he asked them in Caribbean-accented Spanish as he drove to the safe house that night.

"No problem," said Gallardo, the leader of the six, a man just a couple of years older than Sepsis, not quite twenty-seven. He had a thick Basque accent, and like the others, like the men from Québecois Libre, he had no ideas of his own, only that the Basque country had to be separate. Beyond that, the future for Gallardo and his men didn't exist.

"We have a serious problem. We can't let you out of the house while you're here."

"What!"

"This is bullshit, man."

"Fuck me, take me back."

"Quiet," said Gallardo, intimidating the other, younger five into shutting up. "What's the problem?" he asked Sepsis.

"The documents we have—they're EC documents but we don't know if they're clear."

"What happened? My boss told me you had a contact for the papers."

"The contact we had—he was blown."

"Shit," said Gallardo.

"The safe house, that's no problem. It's clean and nice and comfy."

"But we can't leave while we're here," said Gallardo.

"But you can't leave while you're here," said Sepsis.

"For how long?"

"My superior, my boss, he'll tell me and then we can move on the target," said Sepsis.

Gallardo sighed, experienced enough to know these things happened. "It looks like we wait."

But the waiting was as corrosive an affair as can be imagined. The house Sepsis had rented was owned by a widow with a fear of rent taxes, which was how Sepsis liked it. She sublet the whole house and he paid cash, allowing himself to be snookered by the old woman into paying one and a half times what the place would ordinarily go for. That way the old lady, Signora Sylvia, left him alone and didn't register the transaction, afraid of losing the good money she was making off of Sepsis. So the house was safe. The problem was, none of the six could leave it.

"Let's imagine you go out into the street—you don't know Italian, do you?" Sepsis said to them. "One cop looks at you funny, then what? You get blown. My boss won't let me run that risk."

All six of the men from Valladolid bitched and moaned, but they knew he was right, even though the knowledge still didn't make it any easier.

"Who's your boss, anyway?" Gallardo asked him.

Sepsis looked at him. "You can call him Carlos if you want."

"Yeah, right," said Gallardo.

It irritated Sepsis that Carlos would never have allowed an operation to spin out of control as he had. And it was all his fault too—he should have just given more slack time between getting the forged documents and bringing in the men from Valladolid. His damned hurry was what had caused this mess. During the day, Sepsis went about trying to get everything else he needed—the weapons, the maps, the timing, doing alone what he had hoped all six of the men from Valladolid would do for him. Fuck, it was his own damn fault.

And in the back of his head, infuriatingly, he could hear his connection, the man who had taught him how to be a killer, going on and on about how "foolproof" a bomb hit would have been. Just bomb it all away, explode it till there was nothing left. Sepsis wondered if Carlos had had some controller or handler who was forever in his head, telling him how fucked up he was managing things. Probably.

The men from Valladolid didn't have much to do except watch TV, and even that was in Italian. So Sepsis had to arrange to get cable, which showed a number of Spanish-language channels. The men might still have revolted, but fortunately there was plenty of soccer on the tube, it being the middle of the soccer season. And even better, the cable carrier had the three Spanish-language channels that ran wall-to-wall soap operas, devouring the terrorists' time. So while Sepsis was off measuring distances for the hit and timing retreats—tasks the men from Valladolid would have done for him—the Basque separatists followed Milan on their unstoppable season, then changed channels to watch the treachery of Doña Isaura in *La Madrastra—The Stepmother*.

Pretty quickly, they settled into a routine: Sepsis stopped by every morning with groceries, cigarettes, and just enough pot to last them the day. The men from Valladolid spent their time watching TV while Sepsis went off to measure distances, all six of them watching soccer and soap operas while they got stoned. Wisely, Sepsis didn't bring them any sauce—with booze, they would have been at each other's throats; with pot, they just giggled and laughed at the TV.

In the evenings, he came back with more groceries and let the men cook dinner, eating with them to gauge their morale before going back to spend the night at Giancarlo Bustamante's house.

"How much longer of this?" they always asked, every day, losing their edge with each passing day.

"Soon," he repeated. At first they were talkative and happy to be there, but by the fourth day they were restless, and by the sixth they were depressed, sick of each other's company.

Every evening after dinner, as he drove back to Giancarlo Bustamante's house across town, the same thought occurred to Sepsis: What was he doing?

Failure wasn't the issue. Failure wasn't that bad. Sepsis could live with failure, as Carlos had, remembering an incident with an El Al flight, a planned hijacking in '75 that had gone very wrong. Carlos barely escaped with his life from that mess. Sepsis too had failed, once. Early in his career, when he was nineteen, he firebombed the house of a Colombian judge who lived to tell the tale.

But Carlos's failure, like Sepsis's, had been quick: Carlos had stepped on the plane with his coterie of Palestinian terrorists and been confronted by an Israeli commando unit—boom, right there in front of him. The same with Sepsis's Colombian judge: He'd blown up the house and then—boom, right there in the front pages of the morning papers he'd found out how the judge had been asleep in his backyard hammock that hot summer night.

But examining the carcass of someone else's failure wasn't the same as being right smack-dab in the middle of a possible failure of one's own.

Failure wasn't the issue. If he failed, he failed; if he succeeded, good. It was the uncertainty that was killing him. As time passed, uncertainty came and settled on his imagination, making him question and second-guess and undermine all of his methods and plans, as if some committee meeting were in session, with a dozen conflicting, bickering committee dwarves arguing over what to do and how to go about doing it. Sepsis wondered if Carlos had ever had to deal with those dwarves. He doubted it. Sepsis didn't think Carlos had the imagination for self-reflection. After all, Carlos had been just a brainless killer.

He gritted his teeth as he drove on, trying to kill his dwarves. No sense in stopping now. Sepsis knew he was too far gone to stop.

Without any of them realizing it, like all the routines of very determined, very hardworking people, their lives quietly slid into a neat, orderly groove that was disturbed only when Margaret Chisholm got nervous and shook things up for the sake of breaking any predictable, vulnerable pattern. But with nothing happening, with the forger dead and all possible leads exhausted but Sepsis himself making no obvious move on the nun, the very idea of the danger he represented started slipping away from everyone's mind, like unpaid bills that a creditor makes an initial effort to collect and then appears to let slide.

The nun worked—a lot. It was amazing to Denton and Chisholm how hard she worked, already up and dressed by six in the morning when Chisholm went down for breakfast, working throughout the day, even working during dinner, when she and Edmund Gettier frequently went to Cardinal Barberi's house on the Piazza Colomo.

The cardinal, they could all see, was fading fast. He was sucking down the oxygen all the time now, turning his townhouse into a well-nigh fire hazard. If he got too excited about something they were discussing, at the first lull in the conversation he tended to doze off.

But it wasn't out of politeness or a cheap kind of pity that Edmund Gettier and Sister Marianne consulted him: he simply knew more about the history of the basilica's construction than anyone else alive. So most nights, they had dinner together as they talked over small, seemingly trivial details that were crucial to figuring out what had to be done and when.

And through the days, without fail, Margaret Chisholm shadowed the nun, growing to like her very much in spite of the incredible tedium of the baby-sitting detail. She was stuck in the catacombs day after day, just as she'd predicted back in Washington, without a break in the monotony but wary that a break might come that would not make her any happier.

Denton, at first, didn't go with Chisholm and Gettier and the nun. Instead, he went about his liaison job—staying in touch with the chargé d'affaires at the embassy, calling on the CIA station chief, keeping up with Lorca's progress. But after a while, since there was nothing to liaison with, as Chisholm had so memorably put it, more and more Denton found himself idly twiddling his thumbs, bored silly but controlling his desire to work the phones at a marathon pace.

No no, Denton knew that working the phones would be the surest sign that his position was slipping. People at Langley would start to wonder why he was calling them up all the time, wonder what he was doing in Rome if he had all this free time on his hands, maybe begin thinking that he'd been farmed out to Rome, out of the loop. So instead, Denton called no one except Amalia and Matthew Wilson, bugging them to death while spending his time trying to come up with ideas for a new novel. Occasionally, he went to the renovation site, to see what it was like. What it was like was boring.

In the catacombs, a workman would come up to Sister Marianne with a brick. She would look at it carefully. Then she'd make a pencil scratch on it, pointing it out to the workman. They'd blabber in Italian for half an hour, incomprehensibly. Then off to work the little guy would go, carrying the brick like a crown jewel while the nun looked after him with a pleased, Cheshire cat look to her. Very odd.

On the upper level where Gettier was working, the professor took a dim view of Denton's snooping around. The professor wasn't really an old man—he was barely in his early sixties—but he seemed to have acquired the curmudgeonly attitude of an ancient, snappish old fart with no patience for the uninitiated. He also lectured rather than conversed, making it impossible for Denton to build any kind of rapport that might be useful later. It also drove Denton crazy, having to either listen respectfully and very silently to the man, or risk saying something that would inevitably turn his face into a hard mask of disapproval.

Because Gettier disapproved of everything anyone said, no matter how small or trivial—except the nun. From the get-go, Denton realized with no great leap of insight that Sister Marianne was the only person Gettier actually liked. He lectured to her too, but he actually listened carefully to whatever she had to say.

It wasn't that the nun had maneuvered Gettier into liking her, Denton saw. It was that Gettier had chosen to like her, which Denton didn't understand at all. Denton, against his better judgment, had grown to like lots of people. He had actually thought that Roper, his old boss at North American Counter Intelligence, was a really charming guy. Of course, his liking for Roper hadn't prevented him from serving him up on the *60 Minutes* platter. But one thing had nothing to do with the other. Liking someone, for Denton, was a reflex, not a conscious decision. Not so for Gettier, apparently.

"Will you be staring at me all day?" asked Gettier one day as he worked on some papers on his table on the ground level, not bothering to look Denton's way.

"Just looking around," said Denton, drifting off, wondering how he could engage the guy so that he would like him, wondering why on earth he'd *want* to be liked by him.

He took the stairs down to the catacombs, where Marianne was working, and slid up next to Chisholm, who kept her patient vigil.

"So this is what baby-sitting is like, huh?"

"A mouthful of laughs washed down with a barrel of monkeys," said Chisholm casually, keeping an eye on Marianne as she constantly scanned the basement catacombs.

"That's good," said Denton, whipping out his little black book and writing the phrase down. "Really good. You ought to be a writer."

"Do you actually use that little black book of yours?" Chisholm asked without looking at Denton.

"Of course," he said, then demurred. "Well, no, not much as of late. I can't seem to come up with any ideas for my next novel."

"What kind of novels do you write?"

"Spy novels," he answered.

"You've got to be kidding," she said, glancing at him briefly for emphasis. Or maybe to see if he was smirking. He wasn't.

"No, really. I write spy novels. For the extra cash. You know how it is at Central Intelligence—long hours, lousy pay, piddling benefits."

"I can tell without looking that you're smirking," she said, and Denton laughed.

He looked around, badly wanting a cigarette but having been warned not to light up in the basement. Just then, Gettier appeared between the support girders, making his way to Marianne's worktable, where they started talking in rapid Italian.

"What's wrong?" Denton asked Chisholm casually, glancing at Edmund and Marianne, who did not look happy at all.

Margaret, more used to the boredom of waiting around than Denton, shook her head and shrugged. So Denton walked over to the nun and Gettier.

"Anything the matter?"

Sister Marianne looked at Denton, then at Margaret, then back again, sighing. "Mr. Denton—"

"Nicholas, please," he said, smiling.

She smiled back at Denton but spoke to Margaret. "We have to go see Cardinal Barberi," she said.

"Now?"

Marianne nodded as she looked at Edmund, who nodded unhappily.

"Yes," he said to Denton and Chisholm. "It's almost lunchtime anyway. We have a serious problem we need to talk over with the cardinal."

"Okay," said Margaret.

Gettier and Sister Marianne told everyone to break for lunch. They rolled up some of the blueprints and one of the laptop computers and trundled off to the car.

On the ride over, Sister Marianne sat up front with Margaret Chisholm while Edmund Gettier and Nicholas Denton sat in the back. Denton was smoothly trying to engage the professor in some casual conversation, none too successfully, while the two women chitchatted away.

"So what did you think?" Marianne asked Margaret.

"I don't really understand what you're doing," she confessed.

"We were analyzing the structurally weakened points, checking our model against the current state. You know, it amazes me how far a model will be off from what we find when we get to the site. That's the problem we have right now. . . . The cardinal is going to be furious."

"Why's that?" Margaret asked politely, regretting it almost as soon as she spoke.

"One of the support beams is much *much* weaker than we had originally thought . . ." said Marianne, enamored of the intricacies of what she was doing, going on and on about the minutiae.

At a pause in her monologue, Margaret, a little amused, said, "You sound like you're enjoying yourself."

"I *am*," she said excitedly, fondling her computer, which rested on her lap.

They parked the car off the Piazza Colomo and got out at the southwest corner, crossing through the posts that kept the cars out of the pedestrian square. It was full of people, all on their lunch hour like the four of them. As they crossed the cobblestone ground, up ahead of them a procession of schoolchildren, all holding each other's hands, made its delicate way across the square, a teacher on either end anchoring the chain. They were first-graders, if that, five- and six-year-olds snaking through the piazza on a school outing.

Marianne walked up a little ahead of the other three as she caught sight of the kids in the semicrowded square, waving at them as they passed, the girls giggling at her, some of the boys shy. But the last boy in the procession let go of the tail-end teacher's hand and gave Marianne a deep bow, mockingly; a little wiseacre, showing off his nerve. Marianne returned the bow, equally mockingly, a not so little wiseacre herself. She could tell he was a good boy; a clown maybe, but a good boy. He was a good boy because he laughed at her mocking him, not offended, giggling and waving at her like *she* was the clown. Marianne laughed too at the smiling boy, smiling happily in the sun. Then his brains exploded out of his skull.

It was so fast. Just so fast. There is a feel to every living, breathing human being—a feel common to them all. It's impossible to miss this feel that separates humans from objects. A stone countertop doesn't have it. Neither does a bowl of fruit. Not even an animal has it. A dead animal is lacking something, yes, something akin to this feel, but not like the feel of a human being. Only people have this feel.

No matter how dark, no matter how silent, the feel betrays the presence. Eyesight is limited. Hearing capricious. Smell faulty. Touch nonexistent. But the sense to perceive the feel of living human beings . . . this simple, single sense is the one perception which is always present, always perfect and alert.

When the boy's head exploded, the feel of the boy disappeared. The boy's face was still smiling when his brains were snatched away by the bullet from the sky, tossed high across the square like so much nothing. But before Sister Marianne's eyes, the essential, undeniable feel of the boy changed.

His soul had left him. That was what had gone so fast. The living, breathing human soul of the boy: it was what left him. She was still smiling at him as she saw his brains explode, her face not yet catching up with the speed of all that was happening.

The teacher at the tail end of the procession was struck next, through her back, falling facedown on the ground as all around the piazza people looked up at the sky, some screaming, some mystified.

Sister Marianne was standing still as all around her people started dying.

Of the four of them, Chisholm was the first to react, reaching into her purse for her gun as she ran forward, ignoring where the shooting was coming from, for now, concentrating on the nun instead.

"Run!" she screamed as she grabbed Sister Marianne and shoved her forward, already seeing where they could reach safety.

They had come in from the southwest corner of the square, walking to the east side of buildings facing the square, where Cardinal Barberi's apartment was. They were too far from either of the western corners of the piazza, closer to the eastern corners. But there, in the northeastern patch of the square, Chisholm saw people fall, struck by bullets. Some were managing to escape the shooting in the square through the corner interchange, bodies smashing against the immovable posts that kept cars from driving into the piazza. But many were getting killed, an enormous amount of blood coming out of the bodies, as if they'd been hit with shotgun blasts.

But by the southeast corner, people were getting away without harm, so Chisholm shoved the nun in that direction. She turned quickly to see Denton and Gettier, who were right behind, Denton shepherding the professor as she was the nun. Chisholm glanced at the southeast corner, thirty yards away if that, running toward it as that patch was drained of people, all racing through a narrow stone archway twelve feet high. It looked like the entrance to a building, a pseudo-Gothic kind of entrance.

The sound was incredible. It was a huge sound of firing, so loud it seemed it would be simple to find the direction of the shots. But it wasn't. As Chisholm looked up at the even rooftops surrounding the piazza, she couldn't see a single rifle muzzle, nor could she tell where the shots were coming from, the echo of the square bouncing the sound everywhere. And everywhere, the bullets fell.

The bullets were coming from the rooftops above. On the rooftops of the west side of the piazza, four of the men from Valladolid were patiently squeezing off rounds. They were lying on their bellies, rifles secure, shooting. They were the ones who had strafed the procession of schoolchildren. They had strafed the innocent pedestrians racing to the northeast corner of the square. Those people were guilty of being in the north half of the piazza. The men from Valladolid had orders to kill everyone in the north half of the square, and that was what they were doing. They had no idea why.

Chisholm saw they could reach the southeast corner archway, where no one seemed to be getting shot. She turned as she and the nun neared the archway, barely fifteen yards away. Denton and Gettier were falling behind.

"*Run!*" she screamed needlessly, knowing it but unable to help it as she ran with the nun.

Behind them, at the southwest corner of the piazza, where they had come from, the people there started getting killed, four of them in quick succession, brains and bodies bursting like squashed grapes. Denton and Gettier ran faster, to the east, away from that bloodbath.

The shooting in the southwest corner came from the north-side rooftops. Gallardo and another of his men from Valladolid were poised on top, also lying on the ground, dressed in athletic clothes, like they were going to an athletic club. They were patiently killing people in the southwest corner, shooting in a slow west-to-east arc, killing off everyone behind the nun, the redheaded woman, the blond man, and the gray-haired man, who ran—as if by command—to the southeast archway.

"Targets approaching prime firing position," said Gallardo into a small radio transmitter that was strapped to his head. All the latest technology to kill the right people.

"Clear," said Sepsis. He too was lying on a rooftop, on the south side of the square. But he wasn't aiming for the people down below in the piazza. Rather, he was aiming at where the nun and the Chisholm woman would soon appear.

The Piazza Colomo was roughly square. On three of its corners, two streets intersected. But the fourth corner, the southeast, had that high and narrow archway which led straight into a narrow pedestrian alley that ran in a northeast-southwest direction. The alley and the south side of the piazza defined a triangular-shaped building with a unique, stepped rooftop. From where he lay, Sepsis was aiming at the alleyway, down which streamed the people who were running in a panic from the shooting in the piazza. Soon, the targets—his targets—would run down the narrow alleyway, directly toward him. And Sepsis would pick and choose his kills, indulging in the ideal of meta-murder.

In the piazza, Chisholm ran, pushing the nun to run faster as Denton and Gettier followed behind them, the four of them mere yards from the opening of the archway and the safety of it beyond.

Alicia was with her friends. She was six. She was standing when everyone started moving. Her dress was a bright print of tiny flowers. She was looking around at everyone running. She was beginning to panic but she wasn't sure why. Then she looked down her dress for some reason. Her left shoe was where it should be, but her right foot was gone.

Like a towering statue of some famed Goliath, the schoolchild Alicia was looking down at her feet when she fell back, falling on her bottom, her young little body bouncing on the cobblestones. But she didn't fall on her back. She sat there, feeling dumb, like a three-year-old who hasn't quite figured out this walking thing. But she never looked away from her feet. She was frowning at them, noticing that her left foot was where it was supposed to be, sticking out right there in front of her. But her right foot was lying on its side, farther away than it ought to be. It was separated from the rest of her body. Alicia touched her thighs and ran her hands down both her legs. But when she got to her knees, her right one was gone. She leaned forward and tried to grab her amputated leg.

"They're getting into the archway," said Gallardo flatly, Sepsis counting off the seconds in his head. On his reconnoitering, he had figured it took three seconds to go through the archway and into a prime firing position.

The four of them got to the archway, the last group of pedestrians to make it there to safety as still, in the piazza, an unending barrage of gunfire pursued them. The archway was a dozen feet long, the end turning sharply to the right, diagonally, as inviting as anything Chisholm had ever seen. She would have gone through it in a second, but the nun froze halfway through the arch.

"Stop!" the nun shouted, freezing as Denton and Gettier managed to get into the archway.

"Go—go—go!" screamed Chisholm, grabbing her arm and pulling her forward.

"No," said the nun, wrenching free and turning around to look back into the square.

Sepsis finished counting, and there were still no targets. But he was patient as he began to recount the three seconds he had allowed for them to go through the blind spot.

"We can't see them, can you?"

"I know, I know, they're in the blind spot of the archway."

Sister Marianne was frozen there in the archway, looking back at the piazza where bullets were still falling, people still dying.

This must be it. This must be the moment. She had always fooled herself. She had always thought it would be a gradual, incremental accounting, the payments she would render for the joy of the life she led. The days she spent teaching, the nights doing research, sacrificing a life of children of her own, giving up a family whose members would call her by intimate, loving names—she had made those forfeitures thinking they were the real and true sacrifices of the life she led. But they hadn't been sacrifices, and she knew that. Her life as a nun, so difficult to others, was a blessing, a prize, a benediction to Marianne. It was why, always behind the scrim of her life, there had been the certainty—the fear—the *knowledge*—that one day a true accounting would come round to exact the real sacrifices of the perfect life she led.

This must be it.

"*What are you waiting for, run run RUN!*" screamed Chisholm.

Marianne decided. She ran straight into the piazza, the pit in which she would pay the price she owed for the life she had led.

Denton, Gettier, and Chisholm were so shocked they didn't think to grab hold of Marianne as she bolted from the archway, racing out into the piazza. The men from Valladolid, though, all saw her break out back into the piazza, Gallardo calling Sepsis.

"She's going back into the square," he said loudly in surprise.

"I see her," said Sepsis, already retraining his rifle from its spot over-looking the narrow alley beyond the archway, elbowing his way to the edge of the south side of the piazza to have a better view of the nun as she ran.

A few stragglers in the piazza were reaching safety, able-bodied men and women still in the cross fire, scattering away through the corner in-tersections with the adjoining streets. The braver ones, or maybe the more frightened, were huddled against the doors of the townhouses lin-ing the square. Some pounded on the doors, desperate to get into the homes of strangers to avoid the shooting. Others simply stood there in the doorways, frightened stupid, watching the death before them. None of them thought to help the wounded and the dying. None of them thought to save anyone except themselves. The only moving per-son in the entire square was Marianne.

"We have a clear shot," said Gallardo calmly.

"Do *not* fire on the nun. Repeat, do *not* fire on the nun. If you see the redheaded woman, shoot her on sight. But leave the nun to me."

Across the piazza, about twenty people lay dead on the bumpy cob-blestones. A few children from the school group were still alive, sitting and crying in the middle of the square, too frightened to move. There was only one wounded adult. He was a stockbroker, done with the day's trading. He had been going to a late luncheon meeting. He was the only living adult in the piazza. The rest were dead. And still the men from Valladolid fired down below, shots puncturing the screams of panic and fear and pain of the innocent.

Marianne ran straight across the piazza, her normal human senses confused and contradictory. Up ahead she sensed with total certainty a bright and shimmering something or other. She had no idea who or what she was running toward until she reached it, a schoolgirl, her leg a bloody, sickening mess. Sister Marianne knelt there beside her, her back to Sepsis.

She was stationary, at fifty yards, kneeling steadily. In his telescopic sight, he saw nothing but the blackness of her habit covering the back of her head. There was no way he could miss. Out of the lower right corner of the sight's viewfinder, the nun's white, long-fingered hand came up as it reached and grabbed the habit. She turned her head sideways, giving him her left profile. Pulling with her right hand, sending hairpins spinning, she tore off the black cloth covering, the starched white hair band flipping off and falling away, discarded.

Sepsis had no idea what she was doing, but he watched still, curious. He was trying to make up his mind: whether to kill her bodily or, more of a challenge, kill her soul, commit meta-murder. It was very exciting to be making such decisions.

Marianne grabbed the diagonally opposite ends of the square habit, twirling it over and over like a jump rope as she whispered to the girl.

"Shh . . . shh . . ." She felt no fear. Not even resignation.

Alicia stopped reaching for her lost leg, looking up at the nun. She had never seen a nun take off her head covering before. She reached up to touch her hair, touching the nun's face instead. The nun smiled down at her as she kept twirling her head covering, as if she wanted to skip rope.

"What are you doing?" Alicia thought she asked, her severed leg forgotten, calmed by the nun's serenity.

Marianne said nothing, smiling at the girl and then looking at the amputated leg. The leg wasn't bleeding as much as it should have, because of shock. The leg was only coughing brief and spasmodic spurts of blood. She slipped the twirled habit under the bleeding stump, two inches above where it was severed, and strapped the ends together, tying them tight in a simple square knot.

Alicia looked back at her severed leg, reaching for it again, the nun's hands getting in the way. Then the nun stopped tying the stump, and so *this* time, Alicia was sure, she would manage to reach the leg.

Marianne picked up the girl, who weighed nothing. Awkwardly, taking a whole eternity, she managed to get to her feet and start running for the blind spot.

Alicia let the nun pick her up without a struggle. But she felt a sadness that she was too young to express as she watched, over the nun's shoulder, her leg being left behind. "We're forgetting my leg," said Alicia, or thought she said. She wanted her leg back but she didn't want to go back. So, grabbing the sister's neck tight tight, she watched as her leg receded from view.

Sepsis watched this all through his telescopic sight. Aiming behind the nun, he fired a single round, watching as it struck the cobblestones behind her, leaving a puff of white smoke. Then he aimed at a point a foot ahead of the nun's head and let go of another solitary round, deliberately missing again. Both bullets whistled by so close to the nun's head Sepsis was sure she would react. Wince, trip, drop the child, or scream in fear. But she didn't. All the nun did was run across the cobbled square without hesitation and without fear.

"Ah Sister," said Sepsis, smiling as he looked at her through the telescopic sight, following the nun as she disappeared into the blind spot. He was patient. He knew she'd be back.

"Stop!" screamed Margaret as Marianne reached her and Edmund and Denton. Margaret was reaching out with her arms, reaching to grab Marianne and hold her still in the cover of the blind spot. But instead, Marianne handed her the schoolchild Alicia, who was still looking dumbly at the piazza, where she'd left her leg behind.

"Stop!" Margaret called after Marianne as she left the safety of the blind spot, running back into the piazza. Margaret put down the child and took a step out of the cover of the archway, following Marianne. Immediately, bullets struck around her, making her leap back into the safety of the archway. She checked herself quickly, knowing she wasn't hit. Then she looked out across the empty piazza, staring after Marianne.

Sepsis too watched as the nun ran out again from cover, out into the square again. But this time, something caught him by surprise. Sepsis didn't feel a condescending admiration anymore. Coursing through his legs and arms, making him dizzy for just a fraction of a second, Sepsis felt fear.

The nun would not stop. Threats, pain, torture, seemingly fateful, killingly fortunate close calls—none of these would stop her. Sepsis could kill her body, yes, without question. But there was no way he could kill her the way he wanted to kill her. There was no way he could stop her by meta-murder. As he looked at her through his telescopic sight, aiming at her head surely, clearly, his body was paralyzed.

Sepsis feared the nun.

Marianne did not know where she was going, who needed saving. She simply ran back out into the piazza. She didn't see where she was running, slipping and tripping over the hem of her clothes, falling on the cobblestones. Almost immediately she got up again, looking at the ground. The simple sense told her where to go, the sense reaching out and scanning the whole of the piazza, leading her to the living souls still left there as she felt, around her, pinpoints of blackness, bodies of souls who'd gone.

She ran to her right, away from Sepsis and toward the building where Gallardo and his second were, Sepsis following her with his sight, still paralyzed by his fear of the nun.

She didn't see the two children on the ground ahead of her. Neither did she hear them. They were screaming in a riotous panic, fear, six-year-olds brought low by human designs. But all she felt was a bright, burning sensation, a certain knowledge that they were there, crouched and hugging each other in terror. She grabbed each of them around the waist, a small boy and a small girl, one under each arm, and ran back to the blind spot.

Through the telescopic sight, Sepsis could see her hair, cut jagged and without fashion, flying behind her. Slowly, reluctantly, he moved the crosshairs across his field of vision, bringing them to bear on the target, Sister Marianne, following her as she ran. There was no way he would miss. And as the screaming faded away, the light smell of cordite vanishing as in a breeze, as everything focused on the moment of action, Sepsis made his decision not in sure confidence but in fear.

"Goodbye, Sister," he said softly.

He pulled the trigger. He saw the bullet as it drilled out of the barrel of his rifle, a single black dot that grew smaller and smaller on its downward flight, perfectly aimed for her head. And then her head vanished.

There was something wrong. There was no feel like after the Canadian politician. There was no sense of completion, no rushing vacuum that tugged and whistled like the black emptiness of space. There was a something where a nothing should have been as he saw, on the cobblestones below, a brief puff of smoke through his telescopic sight. Sepsis took his eye off the sight and looked down at the piazza.

The nun was on the ground, splayed, facedown, still holding the two children tightly round their waists, both of whom struggled, wriggling in pain and panic, moving the nun's corpse. But it was no corpse. The nun rose on one knee as she pitched forward, almost overbalancing, her forward fall giving her impetus as she ran, ran on, to the safety of the blind spot, living and breathing once again, running as if no bullet had struck her. No bullet had.

She'd slipped. That was all. She had slipped. The slick leather of her hard shoes had slipped on the cobblestones and sent her down to the ground as the bullet whistled by over her head. Her God had made some sort of minor miracle happen. Not to save her. No—to tease him.

"*Scheiss . . .*"

A black rage poured over him, filling him, a hatred as fine and silky smooth as milk doused over a burning heart, emptying his mind of thought or consciousness. It was the rage against a cruel father, mocking and derisive, who does nothing but torment and perplex for the sake of his own humor. Sepsis put his eye back to the telescopic sight, his anger and frustration and fear making his aim jittery, swiveling the lens around, taking forever to reacquire the target—just a target, yes, nothing but a lowly mushroom of a target that had never carried a weapon in its short miserable life. No serious threat or power that commanded respect.

Marianne ran. She barely saw, up ahead, the blind spot where Edmund crouched, and Margaret, and Denton. But it was Denton who broke out and ran to her, covering the ten short yards from the blind spot and grabbing one of the children Marianne was carrying.

"Run!" he screamed hysterically in her ear, himself running for the safety of the blind spot as the child in his arms, the small girl, wriggled and screamed in panic and fear.

She was gone. Sepsis couldn't see her anymore, the Sister in the blind spot.

"We can't see her," the voice in his earpiece squawked.

"Shut the fuck up," he murmured patiently, waiting for her to emerge again as the sounds of approaching sirens interfered with his attention.

In the blind spot, Marianne nearly dropped the child she held, she turned so swiftly to go back into the piazza.

"No!" shouted Chisholm, grabbing her with all her strength and shoving her against the hard stone wall.

Marianne winced in pain from the shove, awakening to her surroundings. "I have to go back, *they're dying, I have to go back!*"

"Stop! Stop—enough!"

"They're killing them!" she screamed hysterically into the patient face of Margaret.

"And running out there to die won't help them any," Chisholm said, still holding her pinned to the wall.

Gettier sputtered, as panicked as anyone, "The police are here, you've done enough."

And so they were. Three armored police vans were arriving at the northwest corner of the piazza. The metal posts wouldn't allow any of the vans to roll into the square itself, so the policemen streamed out the rear doors of the vans as the vehicles whistled and hooted with bright lights flashing.

Carrying machine guns, wearing black bulletproof vests thrown over their light blue shirts, the policemen ran into the square, aiming their guns at the rooftops, trying to spot the snipers up above. In the square itself, the only ones lying about were the dead and the single wounded man. In his expensive suit, he was crawling across the cobblestones with no direction. The teacher's corpse was unmoving, though the wind tugged at her dress.

Sepsis saw the policemen but still he waited.

"We have to go," Gallardo's voice came in his ear.

"Not yet," he murmured.

"The police are here," Gallardo insisted.

"So what," said Sepsis casually. To prove his point, he swiveled his gun around and fired five shots at five different policemen, aiming for their heads, killing them all. The police scattered, running for cover against the sides of the buildings circling the piazza, screaming at each other in fear and panic, pointing up at the rooftops around them.

"They're only policemen," he murmured, assuaged by the vacuum feeling that the deaths of the five policemen had given him; assuaged, but still not sated of the feeling. Only the nun would do that. He settled back to aiming at the opening of the blind spot, waiting for the nun to come out one more time as the desire, fueled by fear, increased so swiftly of its own accord.

She would come out. He knew she would. Her face, her very expression, promised she would come out. That very promise was why he feared her, and why she had to die, deal or no deal.

One of the policemen directly under Sepsis hysterically loaded his tear gas launcher and fired up at the rooftop on the opposite side of the piazza, ten yards away from Gallardo and his man.

"They're using tear gas," was all Gallardo said, calm and controlled, nothing like the screaming, raucous soccer fan of a day ago. A real professional, thought Sepsis, glancing at him across the piazza without moving his rifle's aim away from the opening of the blind spot. The gas was foaming from a spot to the left of the men, downwind from them, not affecting them.

"Keep in position," said Sepsis.

Another tear gas canister flew up onto the roof, this one landing almost on top of Gallardo and his man, Barahona. Calmly but without hesitation, Barahona set down his rifle, grabbed the tear gas canister, and tossed it back down into the piazza.

"Shit," said Sepsis. It had been a smart move on Barahona's part, dropping the canister like that. It chugged out smoke like a dependable little machine, killing visibility of the rooftops for the policemen below. But it cut visibility for Sepsis and the men from Valladolid as well, the wind flowing to the right, to the east, toward the blind spot, enveloping it.

"Fuck," said Barahona quietly, realizing his mistake as the square filled with smoke.

He would never know if he said it from caution or from fear of the nun. Sepsis closed his eyes for a second, then spoke into the transmitter. "Withdraw," he finally said.

"Fuck!" Barahona said again.

"Meet at the rendezvous point in exactly three hours."

Sepsis rolled away from the rooftop, careful not to rise to give a target, tearing off his headset transmitter as he dismantled his rifle and shoved the parts into the dirty, sweaty clothes of a massive gym bag he had brought. He glanced over the square, at the rooftops, but the men from Valladolid were gone already. Good.

He wanted to go to the edge of the rooftop and look down, see if he could spot the nun. But Sepsis was no fool, controlling himself as he walked across the roof toward the service door that led down into the building. He didn't glance back because he knew he wouldn't see anything down below, not from where he was. But he muttered, "Next time, Sister," as he grabbed the doorknob. He so badly wanted to destroy something—anything—maybe kill a few more cops—but instead, Sepsis carefully shut the door behind him and walked down the stairs and away.

Down in the archway, tear gas drifted in like an evil yellow cloud, surrounding Margaret and Marianne, who still stood there, Margaret holding Marianne up against the wall.

"Tear gas," said Denton, covering his face with a handkerchief as he gave another to Edmund Gettier.

"Don't move," said Chisholm to Denton and Gettier without looking away from Marianne. "They'll shoot you if you run, because of the gas."

Marianne was crying, defeated. She wasn't struggling, beaten by Margaret and the truth she was coming to realize. There had been no fear in the piazza. There had been no regret, nor had there been sorrow. This knowledge was what made her realize she had yet to pay in full all the terrible costs of her life.

By the time the police had secured the rooftops around the piazza, Sepsis and the men from Valladolid were long gone.

ELEVEN

Just Another
Bureaucrat

"There, right there," said Lorca as he pointed to the screen.

Margaret got off her chair and knelt in front of the television set, looking at the frozen image. There were four gun barrels, thickened at the ends as if they were fitted with silencers.

"What are these things?" she wondered quietly, pointing at the thickened ends.

"Silencers?" assumed Lorca, glancing at Denton.

"No, we heard them loud and clear," said Denton cautiously. "It was the *sound* of the shooting that got everyone in a panic."

"I think they're amplifiers," Margaret finally concluded. "The shells were seven-point-six-two-ers? I would bet anything these things were amplifiers; makes a seven-six-two sound like a forty-five."

Before he'd had a chance to consider what he would say, Denton asked, "What for?" He bit his lip as the question slipped out, but then the question was innocuous enough.

"Amplifiers? To scare off people, let them know they're being shot at," Chisholm said dreamily as she kept on staring at the screen. "Riot police *love* to use them. They scare the bejeezus out of everybody."

Denton didn't know that. He lit a cigarette as one of the million-year-old servants in the safe house brought sandwiches and coffee and tea, setting the big tray on the table of the study where the three of them were alone. Margaret realized, surprised, that even though it was barely early afternoon, she was starved. In silence, Margaret, Denton, and Frederico Lorca picked up their coffees and teas, thanking the lady, who smiled and scurried away.

Margaret went back to kneeling in front of the television, hypnotized by the image, the only clear shot in the tape of the shooters; but from the angle of the shot there was no way any of the four could be identified. "What kind of slugs did you recover?" asked Margaret.

"Glasers," said Lorca quietly.

Margaret's eyes went wide as she turned to look at him. "Safety slugs?"

"Yes," he said.

Margaret whistled long and low as she turned back to the screen. Glaser safety slugs are bullets that look much like pencil eraser heads. Inside, they have tiny ball bearings floating in liquid Teflon. On impact, they explode, tearing flesh much like a shotgun blast does, only much more localized. They're called safety slugs because they don't bounce or ricochet and they cannot penetrate high-quality bulletproof vests. They haven't been officially manufactured in a number of years, but on the black market they cost up to fifteen dollars per bullet. Glasers are called "mushroom killers" because they're only good for killing civilians. "No wonder," she said, still staring.

"No wonder what?" asked Denton immediately, again cussing himself out for not having considered his question before asking it.

Margaret, though, answered him without missing a beat. "No wonder the slugs caused so much damage. Only a Glaser or a twenty-gauge shotgun fired at point-blank range can amputate a limb."

She got up off the floor and sat back down at the table. "Is this tape going to be made public?" she asked casually, picking up a little turkey-and-cheese sandwich that had had the crusts sawed off.

"Not for now," said Lorca, "but already lawyers for the man are making motions to have us return the tape."

"This isn't the only copy," asked Denton like a statement, as cautiously as if he were looking for mines.

"No, the original and two other copies are under key and lock. *These* four"—Lorca motioned to the screen—"were here," he continued, swiveling around in the chair and pointing at a map of Piazza Colomo. "Help me with the tray, will you please?" he asked Margaret, the two of them moving it aside to see the entire map.

"Here"—Lorca pointed—"we recovered two hundred fifty and seven spent shells. *Here*, we recovered one hundred and nine spent shells," he said, pointing to the southwest corner of the square. "And *here*, we recovered only twelve spent shells."

"I bet the twelve belonged to Sepsis," said Margaret, munching her sandwich with an eye on the map.

"I think so too," Lorca said. "This is what I am assuming: Those four fired the two hundred fifty and seven. The video does not have a view of this point, but I think there were two men here, where they fired one hundred and nine shots. Sepsis was obviously here, we all agree?" Denton and Margaret nodded without looking away from the map.

Lorca slapped the table twice, surprising Denton and Margaret into looking up at him as he sat back down. "If these assumptions I am making are true, then I am very confused."

"Why?" asked Denton.

"This Sepsis—forgive me, I am glad you are both alive, but the truth is, he could have killed you both as well as the Sister Marianne and the Professor Gettier without trouble. Six men working with him, plus Sepsis, who is one of the best shots in the world, all using Glasers—he could have had you all killed very easily. Do not be offended, please—"

Denton almost said something, but then shut himself up.

"Ego," Margaret interrupted, teasing out the answer from the telling few things they knew.

Denton almost said something then, his reflexes wanting to spew out some What-the-fuck-kind-of-idiocy-are-you-saying-now? comment. But before that could come out, he caught himself. All that came out of him was a small "Mmm?"

"Frederico, remember two years ago? The Canadian politician?" Margaret asked.

"Moncrieff, yes of course. The one-thousand-meter shot—aaaah . . ." he said, seeing it. "Killing all of you would be too easy."

"Exactly," said Margaret, pausing as she thought this all out. "It still doesn't make much sense," she went on, munching on another sandwich. "When she . . ." said Margaret, motioning with her hand forward, like a karate chop, "she was exposed for a long long time. But he didn't take the shot. He could have, but he didn't."

The three of them mulled that over until Chisholm finished her second sandwich and then turned on, taking over.

"Okay, so far we have nothing but a face and a single name. The forger is dead. There were *no* fingerprints on the shell casings, right?"

"None," said Lorca, shaking his head, genuinely worried.

"Ballistics will be back in . . . ?"

"Two days—they are hurrying."

"Okay, two days, but I bet they won't come back with anything really useful. We know his face and we know he used the name Tirso Gaglio. Suggestions?"

Denton grinned at Chisholm. "I have a feeling you have a bunch of them," he said, then winced at the idiocy of his own comment.

Chisholm, though, just bobbed her head. "Yes I do, yes I do. If Sepsis did anything, anything at all with the Gaglio identity here in Italy, there's a good chance we can find him through it."

"We checked in the government files and databases," said Lorca.

"I'm not doubting that, but let's check private databases—credit agencies, the electric company, water, telephone, gas, what else?"

"Car rentals, bus passes . . . So all private organizations," said Lorca, seeming very low-key. "This will take time to get the authority necessary."

"What's the matter?" Margaret asked him, putting her hand on his arm.

Lorca set down his cup of coffee and lit a cigarette, staring back at Margaret. "There is a great deal of pressure to apprehend Sepsis and his confederates, political pressure. A few policemen dead is one thing. Dead schoolchildren is very, very different."

"Is Higher Authority angry?" she asked.

"Higher Authority? Yes, Higher Authority is *furious*, furious that we did not apprehend Sepsis at the forger's offices, furious with myself and with my department for not preventing something impossible to prevent. And that is only my superiors. The new organs, phew," he said. "Actually, I am relieved to be here."

"The eye of the storm," said Denton, knowing as he said it that it was inane, but unable to help himself.

"What does the press know?" Margaret went on in a kindly tone, genuinely surprising Denton.

Lorca shrugged. "Very little, fortunately. The man who made the video?" he said, hooking a thumb at the frozen image on the television. "They know about his video, and they want it. They also know there was a nun involved. But the Vatican has asked me not to release the Sister Marianne's name. I will follow their request unless you think there is a good thing to have her name publicly circulated."

"No need. Less press, less mess," she said, thinking, the three of them falling silent.

Denton's mind whirled. The phrase "less press, less mess" spun round his head in a narrow, idiot circuit, completely overtaking his attention. He wanted to reach for his little black book and his pen. He wanted to say, " 'Less press, less mess'—you're a veritable fountain of good lines, Margaret. Maybe you shoulda been a writer." He wanted to write the phrase down before he forgot it. He wanted to grin and crack a smile, maybe tease out some witticism.

Instead, Denton forced his face serious, kept quiet, and did not make a single move.

Chisholm broke the silence. "We have to go on offense," she said, staring at Lorca, worried for him.

On her cue, Lorca got his shit together. "I do not want the Sister Marianne to leave this house without an armed escort. No matter where she goes, I want her surrounded by uniformed men."

"Yes. I can protect her in the Vatican, no sweat. Here we have our guard dogs. But the in-between . . ."

"I must go," said Lorca, rising and collecting his things.

"What?" said Margaret, approaching Lorca.

"As head of Rome's antiterrorist unit, it is my responsibility to explain to the familiars of the victims what happened. I meet them in fifteen minutes.

"So!" he said, smiling, killing the heaviness in the air before taking a deep breath and turning serious. "I will assign men to escort the nun every second she is out of this house. I will also check the Gaglio name in the private databases. That will take some time, some court orders, but it can be done. Anything more?"

Margaret reached up and straightened his tie and the lapels of his suit jacket. "You look great," she said, meaning it.

"Thank you," he said quietly. "Mr. Denton," said Lorca, shaking hands with him, on guard and more in control. "Margaret," he said, kissing her on the cheek. Then he left the room.

Denton almost said, "Making new friends?" but again he caught himself. Rather than say something, he coughed into his hand.

"Hmm?" asked Chisholm.

"I have to go pack," said Denton casually, almost smiling but putting a lid on that.

"Oh? Are you leaving?" she asked, and by her tone he could tell that she wouldn't have minded it if he were.

"No. I'm flying out to Washington tonight."

"What for?"

"Just for a day. I'll be back the night after tomorrow," he said, putting out a half-smoked cigarette he didn't remember having lit. He looked at Chisholm, who was giving him a quizzical stare. "I *do* have other things to take care of besides Counterparts."

"Just wanted to be clear on that. What's it for?"

Denton smiled thinly. "Oh, this and that."

He left the room. Chisholm sat down at the table in front of the huge tray, which still had plenty of good things to eat. She shrugged and picked up another of the delicious sandwiches, this one of mashed avocado and chicken lightly sprinkled with bits of green peppers. She was going to balloon in Italy.

Denton went upstairs to his room, lighting another cigarette on the way even though he didn't want one.

With the door shut behind him, he took a deep breath, closed his eyes, and exhaled. Stepping away from himself, looking at himself from an imagined distance, Denton realized that between Paula Baker and the shooting at the piazza, he was wigged out to the moon. This had to stop.

It had been a while since he'd been shot at. Quite a while. Yes, he had ordered shootings, killings, a couple of them not too long ago as a matter of fact. But the wetwork he'd ordered had all taken place at a controlled distance. It had been over ten years since he'd been in the thick of things, hanging out at ground zero.

Nicholas Denton put out his cigarette, barely lit, and went into the bathroom.

After giving his statement *in situ* to Lorca's men and being brought back to the villa, Denton had changed into casual clothes after a quick shower. But he needed to think, so he washed his face.

First he scrubbed it, then he lathered soap over it, then he washed off the soap and stood there staring at himself, face wet, letting the water drip off his chin and into the sink. Abruptly, he started to shave.

He was feeling fear. This was the emotion that was making him crazy, he calculated as he lathered his beard. Chisholm seemed actually calm after the shoot-out; in fact, she seemed more relaxed than he had ever seen her. But then she was an experienced field agent, something he was not.

Denton took chances, lots of chances, every day. But they were a paper pusher's chances—at worst, the ombudsman's office might cut him some arrest papers and send him packing to Club Fed for a couple of decades. Getting shot? That was never seriously in the cards, nothing he ever considered, even casually.

Therefore, he was feeling fear, physical fear—fear of bodily harm. It had to be that kind of fear that was making him lose his control. And that was something he simply could not afford.

He looked up at the mirror unseeingly, dragging his safety razor across his face as he started to think his way out of this jam, beginning to outthink his own emotions. Already Denton began divining ways to win.

With Margaret Chisholm, it was more complex.

Sister Marianne was sitting in the dark kitchen, only one of the overhead lights turned on, casting a gloomy, yellow sheen. She couldn't sleep. Her nightgown was a pristine white, but with the darkness outside and the weak light above, it looked ancient and mothballed, stored away for decades. There was no sound. Through the doorway, the darkness from beyond the kitchen seemed to intrude, the darkness itself not a passive absence of light but rather a light of its own, casting its own kind of rays.

"How're you feeling?" asked Margaret Chisholm suddenly, appearing out of nowhere. But this time, Sister Marianne wasn't startled by her. She looked up at Margaret as if in slow motion, but Chisholm wasn't looking at her. She was looking through the refrigerator.

"Are you all right?" she asked in a tone that gave no comfort, an inflection that was barely a question.

"Yes, I—"

When it came, it was full blast, immediate. "What *was* that, huh?" Chisholm shouted, slamming the refrigerator door shut. "What the fuck were you doing?"

Marianne only blinked. "I couldn't—not—"

"Yes you could," said Chisholm, nodding at herself, frightened, needing the anger to bloom so it could smother the fear. "Yes you could."

"They were *dying*," Marianne whispered.

She moved quickly, rushing to the nun and grabbing her puny biceps, shaking her a little. "Listen to me. No matter what happens from now on, you save your own skin. No matter what, you *run*, understood? Because the next time, you're gonna wind up on a slab, okay?" Chisholm let go and looked away, afraid of the nun's impulses and her own failure. "From now on, you're carrying a firearm," she said without turning to Marianne.

She seemed to wake up at that, a drowsy, listless sort of consciousness coming on. "I'm not one of your subordinates you can just order—"

"Yes you are," Margaret said angrily, turning to face her and stretching out the words so they sounded like those to a backward child. "You are my charge, and anything relating to your safety is my concern. You *will* carry a firearm, understood?" She opened the refrigerator again and chugged some milk straight from the carton, furious and afraid.

Marianne said nothing, watching Margaret Chisholm, understanding her but only partially. "You didn't fail," she guessed.

Chisholm laughed silently, a little bitterly, replacing the milk carton and staring at the insides of the refrigerator, unseeing. "Yes I did," she said. She kept staring, softening as the hum of the refrigerator kicked in. "I've seen a lot. I've never seen anything . . . Tomorrow—over the weekend at the latest—I'll teach you how to use a firearm. Good night." She closed the refrigerator door and turned to go.

"Margaret?" said the nun, still sitting, unmoving.

She stopped and looked at her, frozen by her hollow eyes.

"When . . . Before, in my old life . . . I . . . I was eighteen and I was rich and I was stupid and all I cared about was my own convenience, my own . . . freedom. And . . . and I was careless. Do you understand me? That child . . . would be seventeen now. It's not seventeen now. Do you understand me? It's not. . . . If someone wants to kill me, I hope they don't. But if they want my life, and all I have is a gun to stop them . . . I won't stop them. I won't live with two— My soul . . . my soul can't. I *can't*."

Margaret didn't move, staring. And Marianne couldn't stand the pity, never having earned it. So she got up and looked away, grabbing her untouched glass of juice and pouring it down the sink, washing the glass quickly.

"I didn't know—" said Margaret finally, but Marianne didn't look at her, avoiding her eyes.

"It's late, I'm tired, I have a lot to do tomorrow. I'll see you . . . Sleep well," she mumbled as she walked at a racing sprint out of the kitchen, away from Margaret. There seemed to be nothing but failure in the night air.

Denton slept like a baby on the flight back to Washington, arriving in the morning on a regular commercial flight. Amalia Bersi picked him up at Dulles and drove him straight to Langley, where he dealt with the other issues of his job that had come up since he'd been gone. He also dropped in on Phyllis Strathmore, who was de facto Paula Baker's replacement, if not yet officially so.

"I've been looking through everything, and there was nothing that unusual," she told him over lunch, the two of them eating alone in what had been Paula Baker's office. Their meeting had been a little shocking to him; Phyllis had gained a lot of weight. "Covert Finance looks pretty clean."

"Nothing at all? Not even anything a *little* strange?"

"Some spare change floating around, but nothing *that* unusual."

"Give me an example."

"Well, for instance: I came across some small-arms expenditures— I don't know what it is yet, but it's just a couple—three hundred thousand every quarter. Then there's this money that's being siphoned off—very discreetly—from the Latin America desk to pay for something out in Alexandria."

"Oh?" asked Denton, curious to see if Strathmore had figured out what those expenditures were really for. "What's that?"

"I don't know yet. It's been a steady payment scheme, no increases for the last two years or so—"

"About seven fifty a year?" he interrupted.

Phyllis wiped her mouth with her napkin before drinking some water, carefully not looking at Denton. "Something I shouldn't know about, pardner?"

"Don't worry about the thing out in Alexandria. It's something Paula, Atta-boy, and I have been running for the last few years. I can't tell you what it is right now, but when I get back from Rome, Atta-boy and I will fill in the blanks. Fair enough?"

"Fair enough," she said, trusting Denton and Atmajian, probably the only person on earth who did.

"Anything else?"

"The Asia finances are a shambles." She pouted.

"Good luck!" he laughed.

Phyllis stopped eating and put her elbows on the table, rhythmically bumping her clasped hands to her chin. "I think you and Arthur ought to consider something: It might be that Paula's accident really was an accident."

Denton leaned back and lit a cigarette. "You know what Arthur would say to that."

"Yes, yes—'There are no accidents.' But it might be that this was one of them. Look, there's no serious embezzling going on—Paula's major embezzling investigation was the rampant use of office postage for personal use. Things are looking pretty clean of late. Aside from your little scheme out in Alexandria, there's nothing all that fishy going on."

"So what was Paula Baker doing with her time?"

"There is that tiny little issue of planning out finances when every year you're not sure how much Senate is gonna give you for your covert operations. Paula's main job was juggling the numbers to keep up a steady cash flow."

Denton didn't like what he was hearing, realizing that Atta-boy's paranoia had rubbed off on him but unable to stop indulging in it. He scratched an eyebrow, thinking.

Phyllis softened. "How do you feel?" she asked, referring to the shoot-out, something everyone had heard about. "I'm surprised you're here. I would have thought you'd take some time off, get your bearings."

"No rest for the wicked," he answered, smiling, completely in control, the Nicky of always. Every hair in place, shaved, showered, smelling good, a Calvin and Hobbes tie tied perfectly in place, a faintly amused look to his eyes—this was Nicholas Denton on an even keel, cruising along A-okay, situation absolutely, positively normal. It was a normalcy that frightened Phyllis Strathmore, a normalcy—under the circumstances—that was superhuman in its ordinariness. But she didn't get a chance to think it over then and there because, without pausing but with no hurry, Denton asked, "How's it feel being back in the game?"

"It's fun. Actually it's a lot of fun, managing secret monies for secret missions. You know, in Paula's job there are so many ways to skim off the top. Amazing. I've been very very careful, looking at Paula's personal accounts. You make money off your novels. Atta-boy off the tip I give him. Kenny has that trust fund of his. Paula didn't have any money to fall back on, just her salary. She didn't skim one cent. Not one. It's that or she was so slick about it that I can't figure it out."

"You sound kind of disappointed."

"I'm not, but hell, I can't live on less than two fifty a year. How much are *you* pulling in these days?"

"I don't know, not much," he said vaguely.

"Come on," she said casually. It was odd. With her weight gain, Phyllis looked like a trustworthy old aunt you could tell all your secrets to. But Denton smiled, not fooled.

"Are we playing one of our famed one-upmanship games from way back when?"

"A little, I guess," she said, then laughed before falling serious. "Hell, can I have one?" she asked, taking one of the cigarettes from his pack. He lit it for her. "Paula made nothing—what I spend on tips in a year in New York."

"If she'd wanted to, she could have gotten a Wall Street job in a second. Money just didn't interest her that much," he said offhandedly.

"That," said Phyllis, looking him right in the eye, "is one very very dangerous quality, Nicholas."

The rest of his day was pretty anticlimactic compared to Phyllis's observation. Amalia and Wilson had been holding down the fort, keeping everything in order for the most part and calling him with any big decisions. But still a few stray matters had piled up, so Denton spent the rest of the afternoon and early evening calling up people, getting things back on-line. But at seven-thirty, though he had people to call and things to finish up, Denton left for his dinner date in Fairfax County.

He had casually invited himself over to Keith Lehrer's before flying out to Rome in the morning. But the dinner was the real reason Denton had come back to Washington at all, so he didn't want to be late.

He took a cab out to the house; Amalia and Wilson would be picking him up later. When he got to Fairfax, Lehrer was alone.

"Where's Mrs. Lehrer?" he asked politely.

"Oh, I thought we ought to have just a nice quiet dinner, you and I," said Lehrer, the game on.

The dinner itself was bullshit, the two just talking about inconsequential office things, the conversation very carefully staying away from the Rome business and the shoot-out. They retired to Lehrer's study for drinks and smokes, Lehrer having picked up the silly fashion of smoking cigars. Denton as always stuck with cigarettes.

He had to admire him. Lehrer had all the patience in the world, willing to let the entire evening pass before getting down to what this was about. So Denton decided to be the first to serve.

"They nearly got us," he said as they both stared at the fire. "An inch and they would have killed Chisholm, for sure."

"Terrible business, just terrible," said Lehrer as smoke from his cigar wafted out from between his words. "But why did you fly out to see me? That's what you really did, isn't it?"

Denton smiled as he got up and went to the compact disc player, looking through the selections. "That shooting . . . it made me realize a few things," he said as he mentally debated, then rejected putting on the Brandenburgs; too happy or too funereal, no modulation. "I thought, why not a car bomb? Why not an antitank missile or something . . . foolproof? But no, it was a surgical hit, very discriminating. Some people, like the nun and Chisholm, got shot at. Others—meaning myself—didn't. Ah! This is what I want." He put on trusty old "Jupiter" and started it on the second movement before turning back to Lehrer.

"You control Sepsis, don't you?"

"I'm surprised it took you this long to figure it out," was all Lehrer said, giving him an amused look.

Denton *was* amused—at himself. Lehrer was right, he should have seen this more clearly.

"Sometimes I'm not as clairvoyant as I'd like to be. Since when?"

"Six months ago?" Lehrer wondered aloud.

"That's what I thought—actually it's closer to seven months now," Denton said as he sat back in the wing chair and stared at the fire.

"You suspected."

"I'm a career bureaucrat, Keith. Papers papers papers, that's all I see all day. Sooner or later I see everything. Expenditures on some counterintelligence operations that were a little too costly. Payoffs to informants that didn't quite exist. I knew company monies were going somewhere, but I wasn't sure where, or for what."

"Now you know. It took me a long time to buy Sepsis. Now that he's bought, he's doing exactly what he's been ordered to do."

"So my real assignment isn't to stop Sepsis—it's to stop Chisholm."

"Exactly. Sepsis knows about you. He won't touch you. You deal with Chisholm. Let Sepsis do his job."

"Why is he trying to expunge the nun?"

"That I don't know."

Denton arched a brow, getting a reaction out of Lehrer.

"Really. I have no idea why he's targeted her. But he's a grown-up and so am I. If he wants to expunge the nun, so be it."

"So that little scene with Chisholm—it wasn't over jurisdiction. You wanted to keep the nun out of Rome. Why?"

"For reasons of his own, Sepsis wants the nun out of the picture. If he wants that, and I'm in a position to do it for him . . ."

"But the Vatican's the real target," Denton stated.

"Y-es," said Lehrer with a hitch, things finally becoming clear.

"Okay. So why the Vatican?"

Lehrer got up from his wing chair and tossed the butt of his cigar into the fire, leaning on the mantelpiece as he turned to face Denton.

"Remember Iraq? We could have taken over the whole thing. Half a million troops sitting there, primed and ready. But that wimp in the White House decided to be a good sport about it and pull out. With a good excuse we could be back in the Middle East, sitting pretty on all that oil in a couple of weeks. Say we blow up the Vatican. Say we get lucky and kill the Pope. That's a pretty good excuse to get back in the game."

It sounded to Denton like a pretty neat idea, but with some problems to it. Mainly, control. "This sounds good, but why pick the Vatican?" he asked, ready to follow up on the issues of control and supervision, and the problem of having something so major going on so far away.

Lehrer, though, completely misunderstood him. "I didn't pick the Vatican," he said, surprising the hell out of Denton.

"Oh?" he said, as casually himself as someone curious about the weather.

"Sepsis picked the target," said Lehrer as he sat back in his chair. He lit another cigar. "I wanted to go for live targets. The G-Seven are meeting in a couple of months, some big trade summit. I thought they would have been the perfect target. But Sepsis told me flat out there was no way he could nail all seven of them. Too much movement, not enough opportunities. But a stationary target . . . He figured a hit on the Vatican would achieve the same result."

"Really," said Denton. "And you agreed?"

"When I thought about it . . . sure." He stared at his cigar, then snapped back onto Denton. "It was damned brilliant of the kid, hitting the Vatican. People would be sort of upset if the leaders of the seven industrialized countries were killed—but not *that* upset. Not the same emotional force. The Vatican on the other hand . . ."

"So Sepsis is in on this plan," Denton stated.

Lehrer laughed. "No! He knows the operational side of things— eliminate a big target outside the United States. But he has no idea about the political aspects of this thing, so that's not anything we have to worry about."

"Fair enough," said Denton. "But I still have some concerns. It's tough to control operations way out there in a foreign country, a lot tougher than something on our own front lawn. Why not hit a home target instead? Really level the Twin Towers instead of just blowing up the garage, or maybe bring down the Statue of Liberty, say."

"I thought about it."

"So?"

"The new wimp in the White House, the corrupt pussy chaser? He doesn't have the balls to go it alone. The Statue of Liberty gets blown—too bad. The Vatican gets blown—well, every God-fearing Christian nation on this earth would want Arab blood. They'd ask—no, they'd *demand* an invasion. Who better to lead the invasion than us?"

"Clever. Very clever," said Denton, nodding, liking the idea, the amplitude of it. A stunt like this was no pushover, but Lehrer seemed to be pulling it off with no worries. "It's thinking big, and I like that," he continued, amazed at Lehrer's cleverness.

"Glad you approve," said Lehrer, smiling.

"But I still think it would be easier with a home target," Denton finally admitted, not liking any operation that couldn't be monitored up close.

"Think, Nicky. A home terrorist hit and we would have twenty congressional committees auditing Counter Intelligence, all of them squawking about our 'incompetence' and sniffing around our yard at will. A little bad luck, they stumble on the right trail and *we* would be blown."

"I see . . ."

"Also, the Vatican as a symbol cuts across borders. Some countries might like it if the Statue of Liberty gets blown—'down with the American imperialists,' and all that. Not so with the Vatican."

"That's true . . . but I still don't like having this so far away. And I don't like it that we're farming it out to a hired hand."

"He won't be for long, not if we bring him into the fold on a permanent footing."

"Oh, that's good, that is *very* good!" he said, meaning it. "And who gets to run him?" he asked.

They smiled at each other, both of them knowing what the answer was going to be. Lehrer wouldn't have told him any of this unless he wanted Denton to be Sepsis's controller.

"You do, of course."

Denton smiled to show his teeth. "Nice being promoted."

"The problem with handling Sepsis is that he's too independent. He likes picking his targets, picking his own methods, doing things his way."

"That's not that good," said Denton, wondering what it would be like to control someone like Sepsis. "Tough to intimidate someone like that, a free agent who's used to doing whatever he wants."

"But he's too useful to pass up. And you think . . . ?"

Denton took a leisurely drag on his cigarette, thinking things through. "I think we ought to give him a lot of space. Give him operational targets, but don't mess around with the details. If he fucks up at some point, the only thing connecting us to him would be money. And I assume that there are no twigs on that trail."

Lehrer nodded and went back to concentrating on his cigar.

The two of them smoked in silence, thinking things over. Denton could feel Lehrer studying him and he didn't mind. Actually, he was pleased. It meant Lehrer wasn't taking any chances, not even with him. A cautious man is more predictable.

"What about Chisholm?" he said finally, thinking about how he would handle the Rome situation.

"Hinder her. Make it impossible for her to succeed. She stops Sepsis she stops the plan." Lehrer stood up and poked at the fire, trying to get one of the logs back on the center of the flame. "And while you're at it, dig up some dirt on her, will you?"

Oh, we're getting personal now. Denton liked that mighty fine too. "A done deal," he said, smiling as he took a leisurely drag on his cigarette.

We gotta talk things over," said Wilson, waiting.

"No we don't, Mr. Wilson. We do what Mr. Denton says."

Amalia and Matthew Wilson stood there in the circular gravel driveway in front of Lehrer's house, waiting for Denton. Actually, Amalia waited; Wilson sort of prowled around the black Mercedes, admiring it to get his mind off what Denton wanted them to do.

From the moment Denton told them what they'd be doing tonight, the craziness of it had been eating away at Wilson's nerves, driving him batty. He suddenly stopped and faced Amalia, towering over her little bod.

"I didn't sign up for this cloak-and-dagger bullshit. I'm just a hacker, that's all I do."

"Mr. Wilson, will you please calm down?"

Wilson went back to pacing, unnerved by Amalia's serenity and the darkness and the fucking *waiting* and the fact that what they were going to do was absolutely crazy. "What's the big deal!" he finally exploded, turning to Amalia, who ignored him as she kept one eye on the door to Lehrer's house and the other on the grounds, patiently waiting. "What's the big *deal?*" he repeated with just a touch more desperation. Amalia kept on ignoring him, so he went back to his pacing.

Presently, Denton came out of the house, shaking hands with Lehrer at the door. It was a rather cold night, so Lehrer just waved to Amalia and Wilson, both of whom waved back as Denton approached them at a quick shuffle, clapping his hands once and smiling hugely as he sang under his breath, "*It's gonna be a beautiful, it's gonna be a beautiful night . . .*"

"We're going home, right?"

"No-o-o!" said Denton, feeling up. "Idle hands are the devil's workshop. *Boy,* do I feel good!"

They all got in the car and took off.

"Boys and girls, we are really playing with the biggest boys on the block. *Damn,* this is cool."

"What's the big deal, Nicky?" was all Wilson could say as they drove to Washington on the nearly empty highways. A real monorail mind, this Wilson. "Why are we doing this?"

"Calm down, Matt, nothing's gonna happen," was all Denton replied, thinking about his meeting with Lehrer as he tapped the steering wheel in time to the tune on the radio. It was Joan Osborne's

"Right Hand Man," a bluesy rock tune he really liked; Denton loved all kinds of music. "Be like Amalia. Shut up and enjoy the drive," he said, which reminded him. "Do you have everything?" he asked her. "The ID's and the camera?"

"Right here, sir," said Amalia, tapping her purse, then opening it, handing out the fake FBI identity cards that Documents had manufactured for her this afternoon. Wilson's eyes went wide as he looked at his ID cards, and in this newfound state of heightened what-the-fuck?-ness, he leaned over Amalia's and Denton's shoulders, looking at their cards before exploding.

"These ID's are fucking *crazy!*"

"Shut *up*, Matthew, for God's sake!"

You had to admire Denton. Only he could have the nerve to do something like this. He parked the black Mercedes on Seventeenth Street itself, directly across from the J. Edgar Hoover Building. It was almost two in the morning, but he made sure that the metered parking wasn't being enforced as he opened the trunk of the car and let Wilson pull out an attaché case; he didn't want a parking ticket of all things to give him away. Then they all jaywalked across the street and stepped into the FBI headquarters.

Inside, the lobby was bright and empty, like a bank after hours. A lone uniformed FBI guard sat on a raised dais behind a desk, reading a magazine. He put it down as Denton, Amalia, and Wilson approached him, all three of them bringing out their identity cards and handing them to the guard without being asked.

"I've never seen you here before," the guard said, a little suspiciously.

Denton smiled. "That's because we don't work here usually," he said, pointing to the ID cards. "We work in the New York office."

"Oh right," the guard said, examining the cards more carefully, glancing up at the trio to confirm they were the same. Then he shrugged, a little embarrassed. "Look, I'm sorry, but I have to see your driver's licenses or something like that."

"No problem," said Denton with enough bonhomie to make a Texan proud, going through his wallet and taking out the fake driver's license Amalia had given him not ten minutes ago. He glanced at it to make sure it was the fake driver's license and not his real one, then handed it to the guard, as did Amalia and Wilson. The guard, careful and slow, looked at all the documents individually, checking the FBI credentials on his computer. They came up clean of course, Wilson having made sure of that.

"Special Agent Ewan Kerr?" he asked Denton as he handed the fake identification cards back.

"You're looking at 'im." He smiled right back.

"Agent Benjamina Dover?" he asked Amalia, who just nodded.

"Agent Philip Michael Hunt?" he asked Wilson.

"Present," he answered nervously, making the guard chuckle.

He got out from behind his desk and stepped off the dais, taking out a set of keys he had attached by a thin chain to his belt.

"Sorry for the check," he said sheepishly, as he led them to the elevators, counting off the keys. "But I got orders to check everyone after midnight."

Denton tsked and frowned good-naturedly. "Don't be sorry," he said. "We could have been anybody."

The guard slipped one of the keys into the control panel of the elevators, turning one of them on. "When you leave, tell me so I can turn off the elevators."

"Sure thing," said Denton as the four of them waited in the empty lobby.

"Kind of late, isn't it?" said the guard, bored and trying to start up a conversation. "You guys working on that DEA thing?"

An elevator arrived, Amalia and Wilson getting in without a glance back. But Denton answered the security guard as he followed the other two into the elevator. "No, we're not working on the DEA thing, it's something else."

Then he half turned and grabbed hold of the elevator door before it could close, leaning forward as he smiled at the guard. "Actually," he said in a low, husky voice, as if afraid of being overheard in the empty lobby, "we're CIA agents and we've come to break into one of the offices here, to get some information we need."

Amalia and Wilson mentally cringed, trying not to show anything, but the guard laughed hugely.

"Ohhhh, now I get it. CIA agents, huh?"

"Yep," said Denton, smiling wickedly.

"Need any help?"

"Nah, I think we can manage."

"Good luck then!" said the guard, waving as the doors began closing.

"Thanks!" said Denton just as the doors closed completely.

Once the elevator began to rise, Wilson let out a huge sigh. "This reality is *way* too intense for me. I can't *believe* you just did that," he said.

"Relax," said Denton, counting off the floors. "Nobody *ever* believes you when you tell them the truth."

Wilson couldn't relax, not while he was here at the Hoover Building. Wilson, under the hacker name Slasher, was actually *wanted* by the FBI for breaking into federal computers back when he was in college. He'd later succeeded in breaking into the CIA's computers, which is how Denton came across him. In fact, it was how Denton had recruited him—in a very friendly way, he had blackmailed him into being his own little computer genius, a bit of arm-twisting that Wilson had never even noticed. After all, now he got to hack officially, for the Central Intelligence Agency. But *physically* breaking into the FBI headquarters was not what he had agreed to when he signed on with Denton.

"In and out, right?"

"If we can, yes."

"And if we can't find what we're looking for?"

"Then we stay until we do," said Denton casually.

Wilson looked like he was ready to implode and fizzle with worry, so Denton glanced at him and smiled. "Come on! This has *got* to be the biggest rush of your life."

Wilson smiled weakly at Denton. Actually, it wasn't, but he couldn't seem to open his mouth to get the words out.

The elevator doors opened and the three of them went down the hall, finally finding the offices of Chisholm and her regular work group. It had an electronic lock, the kind that uses a magnetized strip on a plastic card, so Wilson got to work to try to get his mind off where they were. He opened his attaché case and pulled out a plastic card of his own, but with a band of wires attached to it, connected to a Newton portable computer. He stuck the card into the slot and began punching numbers, Amalia looking up and down the hallway as Denton yawned; the flying back and forth was giving him terrific jet lag.

In less than twenty seconds, the door clicked. "We're in," said Wilson, putting his equipment back in the attaché case.

"That was fast," said Denton.

"Twenty years at Fort Leavenworth is good for the motivation."

"Yes, I know." Denton smiled, letting Amalia go inside first, but not solely out of politeness. Amalia had a Polaroid camera all ready. As Denton and Wilson waited outside, Amalia snapped pictures for about three minutes. Idly, Denton counted off the bursts of light from the flash that seeped out of the office door's frame. When he got to 21, Amalia opened the door wide and let them in.

They weren't in there all night, but they spent a lot more time than they thought they would, going through Chisholm's files. Amalia provided the security, going around the floor, making sure no one else was around. Wilson sat glued to a computer screen with a PowerBook computer of his own hooked up to it, downloading any data that seemed interesting.

"Oh, check out this reality," he chattered on and on. "Phony arms purchases, phony indents, phony everything. All nickel-and-dime stuff, but it adds up. Oh Jesus, listen to this. Purchases totaling two and a half million from a company called Salavis. There is no arms manufacturer by the name of Salavis. Very inelegant."

"Don't get snooty, Matthew," said Denton as he read the documents he had found, shuffling papers as he sat at Chisholm's desk with his feet up. Wilson kept up the steady stream of chatter to calm himself down.

"Busy girl, this Chisholm. Busy busy. She's getting nowhere though. Her log says all their leads are worth jack— Hold on. Holy shit. Holy fucking shit. Nicky sir? Sir, you want to take a look at this like right now."

The "Nicky sir" was what got Denton's attention, a weird little habit of Wilson's that always meant trouble. He got up from the desk and went to stand over his shoulder, looking at the screen.

"What?"

"That," said Wilson, pointing.

" 'Robert L. Hughes, arms dealer.' So what?"

"Robert L. Hughes is a company front, sir. Ours."

"How do you know this?"

"I've broken into our own computers a time or two."

"You're sure?" he asked, hard, staring at Wilson's mass-murdering visage, which was a lot more rattled than usual.

"No question," he answered right back, nervous but sure.

They went through the log, poking around together for a good forty-five minutes but coming up with nothing clear. Finally Amalia walked in, pointing to her wristwatch as she collected her purse. "Time, sir. It's a quarter to five."

Denton clapped Wilson on the shoulder. "Outstanding, young man. Now get out."

Denton went back to the desk and began replacing the papers he had been looking through in their appropriate folders as Wilson started shutting down the computers. "Take tomorrow off, then start figuring out what we got," he said to both of them. "I'm on the morning flight back to Rome. I don't want you crazy kids having to come back here again, but if you think you need to, do it."

"Yes sir," said Amalia as she took out the Polaroids she'd taken when they'd arrived. She set them on Chisholm's desk, looking at them carefully, then looking at the room. The Polaroids were of the offices, and she started moving papers, pens, chairs, everything back to where they matched the pictures.

In his desperation to be quit of the office, Wilson was all thumbs, taking forever to shut everything down and get his gear back in his attaché case. Denton, though, was calm, unrolling his sleeves and replacing his cuff links. He grabbed his suit jacket off the back of a chair just as Amalia rolled it back to where it had originally been.

"I think this field stuff is very entertaining," said Denton, fiddling with a cigarette but not daring to light it; the smell would linger into the morning, a dead giveaway. "Maybe I ought to move to Europe and be a field agent. 'Agent Denton.' Has a nice sound to it."

"I thought you *were* an agent, Nicky," said Wilson as Amalia finished up with the office. "Or *had* been, anyway."

Denton smiled. "Oh no, Matthew. I'm just a bureaucrat."

Chisholm Makes
a Mess

The morning after their midnight talk, both Chisholm and Sister Marianne woke up early, even before first light. But it was Margaret who was ready first, waiting for the nun at the bottom of the big staircase.

The conversation of the night before—the confession really—played over in Chisholm's mind, some of the things she'd said already forgotten, other moments refracted and stretched out by her memory, coming more sharply into focus.

She could barely remember her ex-husband back when they were married. They'd been married for two years, a mistake from the get-go, a marriage consummated for reasons that were so obscure to Chisholm now that it might as well have been fate or some higher power that had ordained it. When she got pregnant, almost immediately after they both realized what a mistake they'd made with their marriage, she had spent a restless, awful week, mentally debating whether or not to have an abortion. Her husband had offered the quaint argument that it was her body, her choice—an argument which was really an admission of his wish for her to have an abortion couched in the cowardly language of allowing her the freedom to do as she pleased.

She had no idea why she had allowed her pregnancy to come to term. Margaret remembered very clearly writing up a list of pros and cons for having the child, Robert Everett. She remembered writing up a list of conveniently located abortion clinics in the greater Cleveland area, where they'd both been assigned to the bank robberies division; many of the clinics had been open until late at night, and some could even service her during her lunch hour. She even remembered doing research on the physical side effects, minor as they were, of early-term abortions on bodies as healthy as hers. But she had no memory of actually making the decision not to have an abortion. Maybe she didn't want to remember, she thought now as she waited. If she had made the wrong choice, Margaret suspected, she would be dead today.

Marianne bounded down the stairs. "Good morning!" she called happily to Margaret, snapping her out of her thoughts.

"About what you said last night—" she started.

"Isn't it a beautiful day? It's going to be a *wonderful* day. Oh don't worry, I can manage," she said as Chisholm reached for one of the two briefcases Marianne was carrying. "But thanks."

"Yes, I suppose," she said randomly.

"Have you had breakfast?" the nun asked brightly, looking at Chisholm. Sister Marianne was a terrible liar. She smiled at Chisholm and she looked happy, but her eyes were huge and shiny, sort of like soap bubbles—*exactly* like soap bubbles: a thin film barely holding back their conversation of the night before, ready to pop under any pressure.

"No, I haven't had breakfast," Chisholm said. So Marianne set down both of her briefcases and led the way to the kitchen, breezily telling Natividad, the million-year-old maid-cum-cook who was killing the morning by knitting a sweater, to stay seated, Marianne herself would make a light breakfast for the three of them.

As soon as they were done, Margaret and their usual police escort took her to the basilica, Chisholm watching over her as she worked on the columns.

So the day passed, as did the next one, both of them carefully stepping over certain topics, like they do in certain Russian novels.

Though she didn't know it, Margaret watched Sister Marianne all the time, even when she prayed. She prayed a lot. After lunch on the work site, after dinner in the villa, sometimes for no reason at all, Sister Marianne would excuse herself politely and get up to go talk to her God. Margaret wondered if that was how she had managed to survive.

On the night Denton and Lehrer were having their little conversation, Margaret took a walk around the neighborhood of the villa, thinking about things.

When the shooting started in the piazza, as she'd pushed the nun toward the archway, all she could think of was getting to the rooftop and putting an end to Sepsis. Because she *was* going to put an end to him. Denton, Gettier, the nun, they were just an obstacle to her animal drive, keeping her from going up on the rooftops and killing the shooters—all of them. She'd actually started to feel a dizzying thrill of anticipation.

But then the nun had broken her. Not the shooters. Not the death going on across the square, or the fear of what might happen—none of that, no. The nun.

When she ran out into the piazza, into some certain, awful death, it had been as if the nun had grabbed hold of Margaret and slapped her face for wanting to kill the shooters, when what she should have been doing was saving the innocent and not catering to some base, wanton addiction to violence that had no end other than its own perpetuation. The slap in the face that was the nun's example had paralyzed her more surely than all the killers of the world. And it had shamed her. It was why she'd suddenly been so angry with Marianne when she stumbled on her in the kitchen.

After her walk, she called Rivera from the private phone in her room. "Hi," she said quietly. "How's it going?"

"I read your faxed report," he said, businesslike. "Anything to add?"

"No, just wanted to call up and see, y'know, how things are going."

"Things are great, but I gotta hop—I'll talk to you tomorrow. Don't send me anything if you're in a holding pattern, just tell me new news, okay?"

"Okay," she said.

Rivera softened, concentrating on Margaret. "How's my girl, you doing good?"

"Yeah." She smiled.

"Staying out of the way of the bullets?"

"Mostly."

"That Lorca's a good man. His report on that shoot-out thing was a lot better than yours was."

"You know me . . ."

"Yeah I do. . . . Okay, I really gotta go now. You be good."

"Okay."

The receiver clicked, but Chisholm didn't hang up. She counted back the number of hours it would be in San Diego—just after three in the afternoon. Robby would have just gotten home from school, so she dialed.

"Hello?"

"Robby!" she said, excited to be talking to him.

"Hi Mom," he said with a flat, normal voice, to her relief. "How's it goin'?"

"How's it goin' with you, kiddo?"

"A'right. School here's easier than in D.C."

"I bet." She laughed at his arrogance. "I've missed you so much—whatcha been up to?"

"Ah, nothin' much, just hanging out. Oh yeah, I got thirty-five million in Imperial Dungeons, it was real cool. I got to the fourth level and everything. But then I died when I forgot about the Gorgons."

Briefly, Margaret wondered if she could get someone at the Bureau to track down the inventor of Nintendo and have him charged with corruption of minors and conspiracy.

"What?" asked Robby, realizing the mistake he'd made.

Margaret let it slide. "Nothing, nothing," she said, letting the silence hang a bit so he knew how displeased she was.

But he cut through the silence with a question of his own. "Mom? I was talking to Dad and I was wondering: Would it be okay if I spent Christmas with him this year?"

"I thought he was going to be back in Washington for Christmas," she said, unnerved by the turn in the conversation.

"Nah, he said the Bureau's gonna keep him in San Diego till next summer. Please, Mom? I always spend the Christmases with you and this time I wanna spend it with Dad."

"Spend Christmas *and* Thanksgiving?"

"No!" he said, to her relief. "I spend Thanksgiving with *you* and *Christmas* with him and Dana."

"Oh," she said, relieved. It actually sounded like a good idea. "Sure, kiddo," she said magnanimously. "How's your father? Is he saying nice things about me?"

The next night, Marianne and Margaret Chisholm arrived late, around nine in the evening, both of them incredibly tired but for vastly different reasons. Marianne was tired but still energized; just beat after a hard day's work. Margaret was tired from a long day of thinking and doubt. They were going straight for the kitchen when they were intercepted by Denton, who'd been in the study off the main hallway.

"How was your trip?" asked Marianne.

"Terrific!" he said happily. "My, you look beat."

"I am." She smiled tiredly. "I'm going to get some dinner. Would you like to join us?"

"I already ate, but I'd love to join you. Just give me a minute, I have to talk to Margaret."

Marianne nodded and turned to the kitchen. Denton steeled himself to deal with Chisholm as he motioned for her to go with him to the study, but she surprised him again.

As soon as the door was closed, she turned to face him and said,

"Look, I'm sorry about getting so upset with you the other day after the shooting. It was wrong of me. I didn't think that you'd never had any kind of field experience and so I—"

"Forget it," he said. "I was upset by the whole thing, you were upset by the whole thing. Let's just pretend it never happened, okay?"

She took a breath. "Okay."

"Now I wanted to talk to you about something."

"What?" she asked, sitting down on a sofa, Denton leaning on the back of a chair opposite her.

"I talked to Lorca this afternoon after I got back. He's still trying to get subpoenas to look through all the private databases—not good news. It might be weeks—weeks plural—before he gets them."

"Shit," said Margaret. "What about all this political pressure he was talking about?"

"It's an Italian thing. Tomorrow I'm going to talk to the chargé d'affaires at the embassy here and see if we can't put some pressure of our own. But I talked to a colleague of mine at Langley—yesterday? Today? I am so jet-lagged I don't even know what day it is."

"It's Wednesday."

"Thank God. Anyway, this colleague told me the Italian courts have been pushed around so much that now they're trying to seem tough when faced with political pressure."

"Great."

Denton lit a cigarette and leaned forward on the back of the chair. "Margaret, we have to rethink this thing a bit here. We don't have any leads at all. And I have a feeling Sepsis knows the nun's here. Sooner or later, he's gonna take a serious crack at us all, probably here at the villa."

"Yes," she said, letting her suspicions about Denton bloom as she watched him very carefully. "Or he might try to hit us on the road between here and the Vatican."

"Here, on the road to the Vatican—it doesn't matter," he said with total naturalness, and Chisholm didn't know what to think. Maybe she was just getting too paranoid for her own good. "Why don't we just send her back to the States?" he asked. "I mean, we have to ask ourselves, what do we really have? We don't have anything, not on Sepsis.

Lorca told me ballistics were useless and that he didn't have a clue where the Glasers came from. If the nun stays, sooner or later Sepsis is gonna Bluebird her."

"Be careful with your CIA-speak," she said, but she knew he was right. "It's out of our hands, Denton. The Church people want her here, and she wants to stay too. It's a free country."

"Yes I know. Pity," he said seemingly serious, then smiling at Chisholm, who laughed.

"How was your trip to Washington? What were you doing there, anyway?"

"Oh, nothing much, the usual paperwork." Denton lit a cigarette and checked his watch, glancing at the television. "I love Italy—no baseball, no basketball, no football, just soccer. Milan is playing in about ten minutes. Join me?"

"No, thanks, no, I hate sports. I'm going out for a walk."

"Suit yourself."

Margaret left the safe house and restlessly wandered the streets, as she'd done every night, thinking about Denton. She was getting too paranoid, she decided, beginning to rethink her idea of an intel source as she walked down the street. Maybe there was no intel source. Maybe she didn't know what the hell she was doing anymore.

The Wednesday of Denton's return, Chisholm walked two miles, and on Thursday she walked five. By Friday night, bored with going over the same terrain night after night, she walked down the hill toward the river, determined to walk until her legs gave out on her.

The walking calmed her. She didn't walk particularly fast, nor did she consciously pace herself. She just walked like her legs wanted to walk, not controlling it, just as she let her mind wander about in its own perverse little circuits, restlessly but without harm, now that she was alone.

Before she knew it, she was out of the neighborhood of the villa, walking through a dark street with yellow stone walls on either side, the lights of the cross street up ahead bright and colorful, a street on which she could see so many people milling about on their own peculiar destinies.

The city at night. The city at night, the Eternal City, as much like any American city, or any other in the world for that matter. The neon signs advertised stores, restaurants, bars, and shops much as in any other city, the signs all the same: Sony, American Airlines, Xerox, what have you. Even the movies that were being advertised were no different from the ones found in American cities, everything down to the images on the movie posters, only the letters shuffled around for the sake of a foreign language. When she glanced at the posters, for a second Margaret thought she had become dyslexic, only remembering she was in a foreign city when she concentrated hard on what the odd combinations of letters spelled.

Maybe the architecture was different. Maybe the local landmarks, the Coliseum, the Vatican, the little statues and piazzas, all the monolithic knickknacks, were different and unique to Rome. But everything of the *living* city—the businesses, the people's clothing, the drowning of the night stars by the bright city streetlights—they were all the same, no different from Boston or New York or Washington. In fact, wandering around Rome, Margaret was struck by how similar to Georgetown everything was, the underlying foreignness of the city hidden behind the patina of American culture that covered everything like a sheen or a scrim. She was sure the Roman ghosts didn't mind. After all, once they too had covered the rest of the world in their own film of dominance.

She got to a pedestrian mall, open-aired, full of people and businesses apparently open all night, a Friday night—lovers and couples and children and loners scattered about, some bobbing like floats, others lost in the flood of people. On the sides, against the squat buildings, realms of tables and chairs were filled with people talking and drinking and eating and smoking, each area like a country on a political map, delineated from its neighbors by the colors and styles of the chairs, tables, and parasols, all carefully wound closed to allow for the clear darkness above. At one of these nation-cafés, Margaret nearly stumbled on an empty table that was barely two feet across, if that. On the spur of the moment, she sat down, the table on the periphery: not in the middle of the other tables, but not quite bothering the flow of pedestrians. A little island off one of the coasts, an island of her own.

She ordered a Harvey Wallbanger from a harried waiter and sat there thinking, thoughts like fireflies twitching in the blood. She was halfway through her drink when a blond, athletic-looking woman, so American she might as well have been carrying a sign, made her way through the current of pedestrians and approached her table like salvation.

"Uh, *prego*—" she began in halting, thick-accented Italian.

Margaret casually cut her off. "I speak English," she said.

The woman looked incredibly relieved. "Thank God, I was hoping you were an American. I thought Italy was supposed to be full of us."

"Nope, just us two I guess. What can I do for you?"

"I'm trying to find the Ristorante San Marco," she said, glancing at a piece of paper as she stiffly read out the name. "Do you know where it is?"

"No, I have no idea. This place might be it, but I wouldn't know, I don't live here."

"Oh, sorry—you have that . . . expatriate look, so I thought you might know."

"No, I've only been here a couple of weeks."

"Are you with someone? Mind if I join you?" the blonde asked.

"Sure," said Margaret, tired but perking up a bit, letting the evening of the mind slip away and hoping instead for a real kind of conversation.

"I'm Cecilia, by the way, Cecilia Rubens," she said as she took a chair, offering her hand across the minuscule table.

"Margaret Chisholm."

"So what are you doing here in Italy?"

Margaret smiled tiredly, toying with her drink. "That's a complicated question. Working, mostly. You?"

"I had a business meeting in Paris. I had some time coming so I decided to take my vacation here. Italians are great, I guess. But the women—all they want to do is take you home and feed you pasta. These women, complete strangers, as soon as they find out I'm an American, invite me to their homes for dinner. They're so sweet. But the men—all *they* want to do is take you home and get you in bed."

The blonde laughed and Margaret smiled.

"I haven't been out much so I wouldn't know. How long are you going to be here?" she asked politely.

"Not for much longer," said Beckwith, smiling.

———

Frederico Lorca had just spent an incredibly frustrating week trying to get the subpoenas to check out all the databases he wanted.

Judge Emiliano Brück was supposed to be overseeing this case, but he wasn't being very helpful, the goddamned Kraut. He, Brück, was from northern Italy, making him practically a German so far as legality was concerned.

"Using judicial subpoenas for every little hunch a police officer has is not acceptable," he pontificated, in a tone to make Lorca scream in frustration. "I appreciate your position, but you have to appreciate mine."

"I appreciate your position, but I'm not asking for subpoenas just for my health," Lorca told the judge. "We have no leads, sir. None. This is as good a hunch as any, probably better than most."

"What about the names you recovered from this Aquardiente's shop?"

"They're useless—this assassin would never use them."

"Ah, but do you *know* that?"

"No sir, I don't know that. But it's an intelligent assumption."

"But it's not certain knowledge."

So Lorca spent Tuesday, Wednesday, and Thursday tracking anyone using any of the seven names they had come up with at Aquardiente's shop. Of course, none of the names had been used.

"See?" said Brück over the phone on Friday morning. "Now you *know*. You're not going on some blind assumption."

Lorca thought briefly and then said, "If I checked out all the private databases, I wouldn't be operating under a blind assumption."

"You have no justification for looking at them," Brück shot right back. "If you were *justified*, well, that would be a different thing."

"I have a *belief* that the Gaglio name is there."

"Belief is not enough. You need a belief *and* a justification for that belief before you can discover if it's true. You should study epistemology, being as you are a police officer, Detective Lorca."

And on it went, this bullshit. If the subpoenas had been merely the prelude to something amazingly difficult, Frederico Lorca would have been more patient, much calmer. But the fact was, the information could be gotten *right there*, right in his office.

Piero Roberto, a young computer engineer, sat in a small cubicle on the other side of the floor Lorca worked on. The kid's office was incredibly simple; all it had was a desk and chair, a single computer monitor, and a single keyboard. The thick wire taped to the floor was what was important. Piero Roberto could access any computer database in the country through that lonely wire, and quite a few in the rest of Europe. That was what he did for the police. With the right subpoena, he would dutifully go into some computer, copy the information needed, and then hand it to the detective who'd requested it. With the right subpoena, the whole thing could be done in a couple of hours. But of course Lorca didn't have the subpoenas, Judge Brück lecturing him as if he were an idiot, a mediocre man's way of asserting authority.

Tantalus, that's what I am, thought Lorca, spending most of Friday calling up other judges who might overrule Brück and eyeing Piero Roberto as he ambled about the office; eyeing the kid as if he were a goddess he had to possess *now*. If the forger were still alive, Lorca would have hired him on the spot to make the subpoena. But Aquardiente was dead, so Lorca kept pestering other judges to overrule Brück. Of course, none wanted to.

That evening, after an obscure Torino judge refused to step in on the case and overrule Brück, Lorca finally lost his patience. He got up and closed the blinds of his office, sitting back at his desk in perfect stillness, thinking. Without a subpoena, any evidence that led to Sepsis's arrest would be inadmissible. Sepsis would walk off scot-free. But then here came the real question: Did he really think Sepsis would be captured alive?

Lorca got out of his office and made his way through the maze of cubicles to Piero Roberto's, most everyone gone for the weekend already. The kid himself was getting ready to leave, but he sat right back down when he saw Lorca.

"You have to do something for me," Lorca told him without preamble.

"You got the subpoenas," he said, knowing what it was all about.

Lorca let Roberto think what he would, protecting the kid. "I need you to print up these lists tonight," he said, giving Piero Roberto a handwritten list of databases.

"Telephone, gas, electric, water, credit cards, car rentals . . ." He whistled as he looked at the list. "This is gonna take some time."

"I need it right now."

"We'll be here until midnight," Roberto whined. "My friends and I are going to see the Milan game, I'll do it—"

"Milan played Wednesday," Lorca interrupted.

"They're playing again tonight. Do you know how hard it was to get tickets—"

"Too bad. Do it now," he said, his very abruptness cowing the kid, who turned to his terminal with a resigned slump to his shoulders and started going through the list.

It was dazzling how quickly it all happened. He had all the lists printed by ten that night, but as he looked through each one, his heart sank. No telephone in the Gaglio name, no water, no power. With each list he went through, the more discouraged he became. This was, really, the last shot.

For some reason, Roberto couldn't arrange the names alphabetically. Probably too eager to catch the second period of the Milan game. So Lorca went through all the lists carefully, scanning the pages, uneasy that he might miss something, sure that it was very likely he would. He flipped the penultimate page of the list of new cable television customers and there it was, three names from the top: Tirso Gaglio. And right beside it there was an address.

"My God," he whispered, staring at the name and at the address. He tore off the page haphazardly and grabbed his suit jacket, wrestling it on as he ran out of his office to his car. Margaret was going to be thrilled.

It was a little after eleven at night, Sister Marianne already in bed with the lights out, praying.

Prayer was always an iffy thing with Marianne. Most times she took the easy way with a mantric kind of prayer, a prayer to clear the mind and approach God on the sly, slippery and cunning, the Rosary always best. Praying like this without mind or attention was like being a gate-crasher at a party God was throwing where—perhaps—with enough discretion and sufficient tact He wouldn't notice you as an individual but as just another supplicant without special distinction or particular ignominy.

But then there was the rare, difficult thing, the thoughtful prayer— the prayer of all the heart and the complete mind. It was the prayer that was something like knocking on God's front door and pleading for ad-mittance to His face. It always took courage. It always started simply. Yet it always invited doubt; the doubt, the sheer feeling of absurdity in the face of an untouchable, invisible, reluctant God Who was not sym-pathetic to human suffering merely for the fact of its being suffering, the awful doubt in prayer the test of faith. It was no surprise to Mari-anne that religions with an avowedly mantric prayer were more popu-lar with educated people than Catholicism. The sheer, obvious fact of self-consciousness was what kept people away from honest prayer, for who could beg an audience with God without losing one's nerve?

This was the prayer Sister Marianne was trying to achieve. And tonight she was failing, though she tried. She had said her evening Rosary as always, only this time as the prelude to the harder, more hon-est prayer she had in mind, but it simply did not come. The doubts of her faith, never defeated, came again. It wasn't doubt in her faith in God; it was doubt of herself and her worth to Him.

Restless, wanting to talk, Sister Marianne finally stopped trying to pray and sat up in bed, turning on her nightstand light to see the time. It was eleven-thirty, a little after that. She got out of bed, put on a robe, and walked out of her room.

Her room was at the end of the second-floor hallway, tucked at the end of the north wing of the villa. So Marianne walked down the long, wide hallway to the top of the stairs. But instead of going down to the kitchen again, she passed the staircase and went to the south wing, to Margaret's door, where light seeped out of the bottom. And she opened it.

"Margaret, I was thinking— Oh my God!" she said.

The radio was playing some big-band jazz, maybe "Cotton Tail" or something brassy and big like that, odd music for what Marianne saw. Sitting at the foot of the neatly made bed was Margaret, kissing the belly of a blond woman, her fingers in the process of unbuttoning her blouse. The woman, Beckwith, had her eyes closed, her hands clasping Margaret's head, holding her to her belly. They both turned sharply toward Marianne, frozen in the moment, and though they were still dressed, the breach in their intimacy was so shocking it seemed as cruel as a violation.

"I—I—I'm sorry, I didn't, I didn't . . ." Marianne sputtered, hurriedly closing the door and walking away.

"Shit," said Margaret softly, getting up from the bed quickly as she called, "Marianne. Marianne, wait."

Halfway between the door and the bed, Chisholm turned to Beckwith. "Cecilia, I'm sorry about this, I—"

"Cecilia Rubens"—Beckwith—was reaching for something in her big loose purse, a leather blob out of which Chisholm suddenly saw the handle of a gun.

On reflex, Chisholm took one fast step and then lunged at her, going for her arm, spinning Beckwith's whole body as the gun was knocked out of her hand. It slid easily and smoothly beneath the bed, neither of the two women thinking about it as Chisholm slammed Beckwith up against the wall by the window, lifting her a foot off the ground with her momentum.

Chisholm's gun was in her own purse, on the other side of the room on the table by the head of the bed. Chisholm dropped Cecilia or whatever her name was and lunged diagonally across the bed, trying to reach for her purse. It was barely a foot away, but Beckwith recovered fast.

She jumped on Chisholm's back, grabbing her by the waist and pulling her away from the purse, figuring there must be a gun inside it. Chisholm squirmed and twisted around, flexing her leg and kicking Beckwith square in the face with her bare foot. Stunned, Beckwith still didn't let go, pulling Chisholm still farther across the bed, away from her gun.

Neither woman made a sound. "Cotton Tail," big and brassy and frisky, slid into an easy saxophone solo as casual as a nighttime stroll. Chisholm was kicking at Beckwith, managing to free herself from her until suddenly Beckwith just let go and lunged for *her* purse on the floor, whipping out a switchblade as if the purse had a gremlin that was handing her things. She sliced the air in front of her, going for Chisholm's belly.

Chisholm couldn't afford to turn her back on Beckwith now. The assassin lunged at her with the knife again, again cutting the air horizontally, going for Chisholm's belly. She overstepped backward, avoiding the knife but getting tripped up by the bed and falling back on it to a sitting position. Beckwith jumped at her, the switchblade in her fist, now going for Chisholm's face.

Chisholm caught the knife wrist, but with the momentum she fell on her back on the bed. Beckwith used her weight to push the knife into Chisholm's face, the tip barely inches from her cheekbone. Still neither woman made a sound. They didn't grunt, they didn't yell. And the only look to either one of their eyes was determination, and an odd sort of patience.

The tip of the knife was coming closer; then it stopped, Beckwith using all her strength, which simply wasn't enough. So she let go a bit, rising off of Chisholm to get a second wind. A mistake, because Chisholm managed to get her knee up between them and hit her in the belly she had just been kissing.

Beckwith rolled over sideways from the blow, grunting in pain as Chisholm slithered out and ran around the bed to the night table. But with a huge lunge, Beckwith was at the corner, slicing the air by the night table, then rolling over, on her feet, guarding the purse as if it were hers. She sliced the air where Chisholm's belly was, and with the backward step she took to avoid the cut, Chisholm hit the wall, pinned. This time, Beckwith stabbed at her belly.

Chisholm caught the knife wrist with both hands. Beckwith slammed the heel of her left hand against the side of Chisholm's face, but Chisholm didn't let go of the knife hand. So Beckwith wrenched it back and forth, freeing it, immediately aiming for Chisholm's face again as she threw herself at her, using the wall as she had the bed before, the knife point once again moving toward Chisholm's face.

In her left hand Chisholm held Beckwith's knife wrist. And in her right hand she held Beckwith's left arm. But this time, though, Beckwith was strong enough, and the knife point began moving closer to Chisholm's face. Chisholm was losing, and they both sensed this.

It was a pivot move. It was fast and it was the end. Planting her right foot forward, without letting go of Beckwith's knife wrist or her left arm, Chisholm took a step forward as she swiveled Beckwith around much as if they were dancing, slamming her against the wall. And when she hit the wall, opening the space between their bodies, Chisholm suddenly stopped holding the knife point away from her face and instead guided it downward as she took a step back to avoid the arcing blade, guiding Beckwith's knife right into her belly, sticking it in as far as it would go.

The look on Beckwith's face was a mortal kind of surprise. Chisholm had seen it before, and looking right at Beckwith's eyes, she smiled like an evil doppelganger. *Yes,* she seemed to be saying without words. *You're dead, and I killed you.*

Still holding on to Beckwith's wrist, she cut up her belly, slicing horizontally, cutting the intestines as blood poured out. That was when Beckwith started to scream.

Chisholm, surprised, put her hand over Beckwith's mouth, but still she screamed.

"Stop screaming," she whispered futilely. "Stop screaming, you fucking bitch!"

And as "Cotton Tail" eased into a brief, unaccompanied, woodenly staccato drum solo, Chisholm took a step back to give herself some room and gave Beckwith's larynx a smooth, clean karate chop.

She stopped screaming. Her larynx broke with a sound like a two-by-four snapping, harsh and sudden, visibly swelling beneath the unbroken skin of her throat. Chisholm let go of her, letting her drop to the floor, and there she lay, agonizing.

"Don't die, oh you fucking bitch, don't die!" she whispered at the dying Beckwith, kneeling beside her as she realized how little she knew.

Beckwith's hands moved from her belly to her throat, indecisive, as her face, so lovely, contorted in pain and panic, the blood turning her face red in hysteria, then blue from lack of oxygen. Still she thrashed, without a sound.

"Who sent you? Who sent you? How did you know me? How did you know me, you fucking bitch?" she went on whispering, with no reply.

Beckwith's fingernails were clipped short, but she managed to scar deep gouges in the side of her neck, trying to breathe. In time, she might have torn out her own throat, but finally she lost consciousness, and shortly, the smell of her feces flooded the room like a single steady wave, death.

"Oh fuck oh fuck oh fuck! Fuck!" Chisholm whispered, terrified of what had happened as the consequences of it all became clear in her mind.

She stood and looked around her, the blood pooling everywhere, rolling implacably, and then she looked down at herself. Her hands were covered in blood like gloves of glistening rubber. She rubbed them on the thighs of her jeans without thinking, turning to stare at the body of Beckwith. Then she looked away as the DJ on the radio babbled on and on in incomprehensible Italian.

She was unhurt, not a scratch on her. But where she was now was perhaps worse than if she'd died.

Abruptly, without thinking, she opened her door and stepped out into the long hallway, walking down to Denton's door and knocking.

"Who is it?" Denton asked pleasantly, muffled behind the door.

"It's me," she said.

"Ah Margaret, you missed a great game, Milan was in awesome— What happened to you?" he asked as he opened the door and saw all the blood.

"What do you think? You're—you're the only one who can help me. Can I trust you?" she asked.

Denton, for once, didn't smile. "I guess you're just going to have to."

At the moment Denton stepped out of his door to help Chisholm with the body, Detective Frederico Lorca was coming across the name Tirso Gaglio.

―――――――

This is manna from heaven. So thought Denton as he examined Beck-with's dead body.

He was kneeling beside it, looking at it carefully, unwilling to touch it but drawn to it anyway. Chisholm was in the bathroom, washing up and getting herself together as Beckwith's blood stopped rolling about the floor of the room and settled down to some serious coagulating.

Still kneeling, staring at her wide-open, dead eyes, Denton whispered to her, like he had done once before: "Well well well. Beckwith is back."

Denton was carefully holding the hem of his bathrobe away from the blood, and now he picked it up slightly as he stood up and took a step back from the body. He lit a cigarette.

Major manna from heaven, he thought, holding his hand to his mouth, covering it as he stared at the corpse. But it would only be manna if he could solve this problem: getting rid of the body.

It was just so ironic to Denton that the FBI was so famously parochial when it came to homosexuality, considering that the man who built the Bureau into what it was had been ravingly gay, openly living with his lover, Clyde Tolson was it? Denton had forgotten, and anyway it was beside the point. The point was, he had to make the body disappear, or else Chisholm would be exposed and therefore fired. If she was exposed, if everyone knew about her, he wouldn't have anything to control her with, now would he? He started thinking harder.

In the bathroom, Chisholm knew this was the end. All that was left was for her to pull herself together enough to call Rivera and Lorca. She probably wouldn't be arrested. After all, it *was* self-defense. But she would be taken off Counterparts for breaching security. She would be shunted to some minor post, probably in some field office far from Washington. And in a year or so, if that, she would be maneuvered into resigning, or fired for some reason. Probably for the phone-shooting incident.

She dried her hands after washing them again, took a deep, shaky breath, and stared at herself. Splotches of blood soiled the thighs of her jeans and her blouse. Her mascara had washed off when she scrubbed her face, her eyelashes now almost invisible. So this was what it was like, the end. She stared at herself in the mirror long enough to memorize what she saw, then stepped out of the bathroom to face Denton.

Almost as soon as she stepped back into the room, she knew she couldn't handle it. Denton turned to her and she looked away at the corpse. But then she couldn't handle that either, so she looked away from it as well, finding nothing she could lock eyes on in the entire room. She felt horribly vulnerable and weak, but to Denton she looked a bit like a trapped, caged animal of terrible ferocity.

"I'm fucked," she said to no one in particular.

"I would say that was an accurate assessment of the situation, Margaret," he said, nodding as he spoke to the corpse. He took a long drag on his cigarette, thinking at a blinding pace, going through every possibility. He saw no way out. "I can't make a body disappear," he said without looking at her. "That's not what I do for Central Intelligence." Then he smiled bittersweetly, catching Chisholm's eye. "Our Mafia contacts handle that end of things."

Chisholm let go a bitter laugh of her own as she looked back at the face of the corpse. Denton grew serious, his smile fading as he too looked back at Beckwith's corpse. It gave no answers.

"Someone is going to have to stand still and take this," he said finally, looking at Chisholm.

She looked scared, to him. But she also looked relieved, as if in a way this was all for the best, her exposure and her eventual, inevitable dismissal. He started thinking out loud, trying to find an answer, Chisholm not hearing a thing he said.

"She was sent here to assassinate the nun, that seems pretty clear. Sepsis tried doing the major hit at the piazza, failed, so now he's being subtle about it, or sort of subtle anyway. Get to the nun by using you. You were the conduit and the obstacle. It could have just as easily . . ."

He had it. It was so easy, he should have realized it the moment she called. He had it. He turned to Chisholm, elated, grinning like a shark and feeling like a million. "Pack your things," he said suddenly, merry sunshine–happy.

"What?" she asked, startled by his elation.

He had it, he had it right smart and good. "We're going to switch rooms. I went out looking for sex. To hell with security and precautions—I'm just a bureaucrat. I let my little head think for my big one. I picked up this woman who turned out to be an assassin. I got lucky and managed to kill her. Pack your things."

Chisholm started shaking her head, doubting him even as the idea began to win her over. "Denton, you're crazy—"

"Think, Margaret," he said, grinning like a schoolkid. "You are an experienced field agent who got careless, mortally careless. I'm just a dumb bureaucrat who got lucky. You, a Bureau agent, were having homosexual sex. I'm just a horny Agency man who wanted a quick lay. I'll get a reprimand, a wink and a nod, and gain a reputation within the Agency of being an assassin killer, which—I won't lie to you—I won't mind having. But you'll get fired from the FBI and maybe even lose custody of your son. Think, Margaret. I'll get my things, you start packing. When we're done, I'll call Lorca and have this mess cleaned up."

"There's no way any of this will fly!" she said, half convinced but still not trusting that it could be so easily done, twisting the truth like this. "I doubt anyone will believe even *half* this cockamamie—"

"Doubt is for pussies, Margaret," said Denton, looking her right in the eye. "Start packing." He turned to the door.

"Don't tell Marianne," Margaret blurted out before she could stop herself.

Denton stopped and turned back. "I won't," he said, but he didn't go, realizing Chisholm wanted to say something else; he didn't have a clue as to what it might be.

Chisholm squirmed, relieved, ashamed, scared. She screwed up her courage and looked him in the eye. "Thanks," she said.

Denton smiled. "I don't do favors, Margaret. I collect debts."

By the time Frederico Lorca walked into the villa to tell them about the good news, Denton had everything under control.

Part 3

POWER WINDOWS

THIRTEEN

Defenestration/
Truth

It was early afternoon on the next day, a Saturday, when the raid finally went down. It happened in a quiet, working-class section of the city. Lorca, Denton, Sepsis, they would all be there. And so would Special Agent Margaret Chisholm. It would be a raid like none she'd ever seen before, and when it was over, she would never want another.

The streets were empty but for a few stray children and some random pedestrians, which was why Lorca had parked the car around the corner from the house: far enough not to arouse curiosity from anyone inside the target house, but at such an angle that they had a clear view of its front door. He and Chisholm sat tight in the car, waiting and watching.

The target house was no different from any of the others—single-storied, whitewashed, with a small front garden through which a waxed and polished red brick path led from the sidewalk to the front door proper. There was a belly-high gate between the sidewalk and the target house's property, as much for decoration as for keeping the neighborhood dogs from pissing and shitting in the front garden, which was well groomed, fecund, and green. There were no side entrances, but rather, all the houses shared side walls and a single roof stretching from side to side of the block. Nothing much seemed to be happening inside as the two of them watched and waited with their eyes steady on the target house.

"What do they call this waiting in English?"

"Stakeout."

"Steak out."

"No. Stakeout. One word."

"Steak out. Like steak, eh, meat from cows?"

"No, stakeout. S-T-A-K-E. It's a different word, same sound."

"Ah, so when we finish the stakeout, we go out to eat a steak."

Lorca laughed and Chisholm mock-scowled at him.

"Oh! That was stupid, Frederico, you are so stupid, just like an Italian. That's what I hate about Italy—full of stupid Italian men."

"Stupid Italians? I'll tell you about a stupid American, Margaret. How did anyone in the CIA hire an agent as stupid as Denton? The man who hired Denton must be an idiot."

"Denton's not that stupid."

"To bring to a safe house an assassin is the height of stupidity."

"Maybe he was lonely."

"Lonely? If he was lonely I could introduced him to my wife's sister. She is ugly, yes, but well, beggars can't be electors."

" 'Choosers.' "

"Call it what have you."

"I don't know . . . What about her, anything?"

"Nothing. I told you, I checked this morning. The assassin was probably Sepsis's agent, no photographic or fingerprint records anywhere, I checked with Interpol."

"No, *stupido*, your wife's sister."

"Ah! She's a cow. But stupid, like Denton. Maybe they would be happy together. . . . I hate stake outing."

"Staking out. No. You hate stake out. No, no, you hate stakeouts."

"What have you."

"How much longer?"

Lorca checked his watch. "Two minutes. Four men will run into the back entrance while we go with the garbagemen. Two men are covering the roofs, so no chases. Remember, you and Agent Denton are only observing, correct?"

Chisholm took out her revolver, checked to make sure it was loaded and the safety off, then replaced it in the holster under her jacket. "Correct."

"Why don't you move to Italy? Work with me."

"Why don't you move to America?"

"Too many stupid American women."

They laughed, but their eyes never veered from the left, where they could see the house.

Presently, from their right, two garbagemen appeared. They were dressed in orange coveralls, reminding Chisholm of convicts back home, and they were pushing an oil barrel welded to a bruised and battered handtruck which appeared to have several brooms sticking out of it. They were walking alongside the curb, casually approaching the target house, looking for all the world as if they were bullshitting away a tired afternoon of garbage collecting.

"Heads up," Chisholm said, watching as the garbagemen crossed the street directly in front of their car. Lorca's radio transmitter squawked static, then burst out in muted Italian. Lorca answered in a quick, brief burst of Italian of his own. Without turning their way, one of the garbagemen in front of them nodded slowly, as if he'd heard something he concurred with.

"The men are in position," said Lorca. "Let's go."

Lorca and Chisholm stepped out of the car with no hurry and crossed the street to the sidewalk opposite the target house, walking parallel to and slightly behind the two garbagemen.

At the house next to the target house, the garbagemen went into the front garden with their rolling garbage can and dumped the neatly stacked bags of trash into the oil barrel. Then they turned around and walked out of the garden, the man who was pushing the garbage dolly rearranging the broom handles sticking out of it. They seemed oddly bent. They were automatic assault rifles.

On the same sidewalk as Lorca and Chisholm, approaching them at about forty yards, Denton was walking along, alone, about thirty yards from the target house. They ignored each other as Lorca and Chisholm, arm in arm, crossed the street diagonally, approaching the target house as the garbagemen pretended to ring the bell at the outside gate to the target house and then go into the garden to pick up the trash. They rolled the garbage can right up to the front door, and that's when they pulled out their assault rifles. Behind them, Lorca and Chisholm pulled out their guns too, ready to back up the garbagemen.

Inside the house, the six men from Valladolid were sitting around the kitchen table, making an early-evening dinner. Their weapons were around, of course, strewn about the house in the rooms and in the kitchen there, all within easy reach. But violence wasn't on their minds. Dinner was. So they talked and argued about dinner and whether what they were making (grilled steaks with sautéed mushrooms) was going to turn out any good or not. Sepsis wasn't around. He wasn't around because he was taking a shit.

His pants around his ankles, he was sitting on the toilet, reading the *International Herald-Tribune* as he squinted the smoke from his cigarette out of his eyes. He'd pinched his loaf already, but he didn't dare come out, unwilling to interfere with the dinner plans of the men from Valladolid.

Ever since the piazza shoot-out, they'd been fighting over dinner. Gallardo on the one hand seemed to know what he was doing, cooking-wise. Barahona, however, constantly undercut his judgment, arguing with Gallardo over every little thing—too much or too little of this or that, too hot, too cold, the two of them bitching and bickering like a couple of old women. It would have been a weird sight, the two Basque terrorists shouting at each other over how to go about making dinner, but of course it had little to do with how dinner was made and everything to do with who was the leader and who knew what was what as far as their real work was concerned.

So in the last few days, as they waited while he prepared everything for the strike on the villa, Sepsis had fallen into the habit of going to the bathroom for a nice quiet dump while the two men argued about how to cook dinner. When the arguing was over and the food done, they'd come looking for him and Sepsis would enjoy a nice meal. Gallardo was an excellent cook.

Now, he sat reading calmly while listening with one ear to the bitching over dinner.

The kitchen, at the back of the house, had a door that led outside, to the narrow alleyway behind all the houses of the block. But some years ago, the old widow who owned the house had been robbed, so she had changed it from a windowed door to a thick, solidly wooden door. Bad news for the men from Valladolid; they couldn't see the four cops from Lorca's section waiting outside for the signal.

The two garbagemen out front had their weapons out, ready. They gave the signal on the transmitters strapped to their sleeves and politely rang the doorbell.

Inside, it was Barahona who walked from the kitchen to the front door, calling out over his shoulder as he went. He was the one who went to the door because he was losing the argument with Gallardo, and so—sloppily—he didn't look through the peephole. If he had, he wouldn't have seen anything, since the garbagemen had thrown some tape over it. That would have been enough to clue him in. But he didn't look through the peephole, opening the door as he kept on calling over his shoulder at Gallardo.

"What?" he said before turning around to face the two garbagemen. "*Chucha!*" he said in Spanish as, simultaneously, the four cops burst in through the back door.

Barahona at the front door didn't even need to go for his gun—he was holding it right in his hand. He raised it and shot one of the garbagemen in the face, killing him just as the garbageman squeezed the trigger on his automatic assault rifle, killing Barahona as his last act on this earth.

In the back, the four uniformed policemen burst into the kitchen, assault rifles at the ready. Gallardo, holding a huge pan of sautéing garlic and mushrooms, threw it and its contents at the four cops as he reached for his Uzi. The other four men from Valladolid reached across the table for their guns too as the four cops, keyed up to the moon and frightened by the flying garlic, opened up on them, spraying them with machine gun fire right where they sat, killing them.

It was weird that the cops paid so much attention to the four sitting at the kitchen table. The sight of all those weapons there, lying so nearby, was what probably drew their attention to the men at the table. Pity. They should have been paying a little more attention to Gallardo there by the stove. From their point of view, they didn't see him drop his hand onto the kitchen counter next to him and pull out the Uzi, spraying them all even before he had properly aimed, instantly killing three of them.

But the fourth cop, as green and pissing-in-his-pants scared as his three now-dead friends, in pure panic at getting shot in the thigh (mildly serious) and chest (minor, wearing bulletproof vest) turned his assault rifle on Gallardo and shot him through the chest and neck, killing him instantly. He died so suddenly and was thrown with such force by the bullets that he didn't fall to the ground. Instead, he slumped over the lit gas stove.

All of this, from the moment the cops burst in on Barahona until Gallardo pitched forward dead, took three and one quarter seconds— less time than it takes to sneeze. It was in fact so fast that Lorca and Chisholm hadn't even stepped into the house before it was all over.

"*Help me, I'm dying!*" screamed the sole survivor of the kitchen de-bacle, far from dying but so terrified by what he saw and felt that in a way he *was* dying.

The lone surviving garbageman stood there in the living room, aware of the screaming cop but making no move to go into the house without cover, which was what Lorca and Chisholm did, the three of them covering the living room, making sure no one else was around.

In the kitchen, there was blood everywhere, sprayed and splattered by the shooting; so much, in fact, it was tough to realize the kitchen was painted canary yellow. Bits of lung tissue and feces, grayish dark red and liquidy light brown respectively—property of the four men from

Valladolid who'd been sitting at the table—were sprayed all over one half of the kitchen's walls and cabinet doors, as if someone had taken a couple of buckets of goo and thrown them all over the place. Gallardo, on the stove, was literally cooking, the stove itself impeccably clean but the area to the left of it covered in gore from Gallardo's throat, which was seeping blood onto the gas range underneath him, the blood instantly boiling when it touched the range and hissing as it burned away. The dead cops, all shot in the head, where their vests had given them no protection, lay slumped on the floor, gaping wounds where their faces and skulls had been, their bodies still pumping blood, pump pump pumping like oil wells drilled straight into a planet with a core of blood. The screaming cop, the only living being in this mess, kept on screaming hysterically as he lay there on the ground, half sitting, staring at all that was around him, completely broken by all the death around him. In an area fifteen feet square, there were eight men dead and one wounded, the entire kitchen slowly but steadily flooding under a rising tide of blood. So steady was the tide's rise, one wondered when it would be before small little waves started to lap against the cabinets and ripple across this sea.

Outside, Denton had heard the incredible commotion, but he stayed put on the sidewalk in front of the house, not at all wanting to get in the way of any bullets, especially since he was unarmed. The only sound he heard coming from inside as he stared after Lorca, Chisholm, and the garbageman was a woman screaming hysterically.

The hysterical woman was the wounded, screaming cop, who kept on screaming for help, ignored. The carnage had so shattered him that his career as a policeman was over, though he didn't know it yet.

In the bathroom, Sepsis kept his shirt on. When the shooting started, he carefully pulled up his pants, pocketed his smokes, which had been lying there by his feet, and checked that his gun, his silenced .32 with armor-piercing bullets, was loaded and the safety off. He waited patiently, not daring to open the door without knowing what was out there.

In the living room, Lorca, Chisholm, and the surviving garbageman decided to secure the house before making their careful way into the kitchen, deciding without any formal discussion. Since he was carrying an assault rifle, the garbageman led the other two.

At the end of the rectangular living room, crossing it like a T, there was a distribution hallway. To the left, it led off to the kitchen, where the solitary screaming was coming from. To the right, the hallway led off to three bedrooms, their doors open or ajar. Between these two ends, there was the bathroom door and two closet doors, all closed. In no rush, very cautiously, the garbageman checked that the three bedrooms were empty as Chisholm and Lorca backed him up.

"Clear," said the garbageman, Sepsis assuming from the sound that they had been checking the bedrooms.

Abruptly, he put down the toilet seat cover, unlocked the handle to the bathroom door beside it, and leaned against the wall that faced the toilet. Looking at the mirror above the sink and a small shaving mirror in the shower stall, Sepsis could not see the reflection of the bathroom door. Therefore, if anyone opened it, no mirror would give him away. Sepsis settled down to wait for them to come to him.

With Lorca and Chisholm covering him, the garbageman turned from the three bedrooms and made his way down the hall toward the kitchen. At the closed bathroom door, he turned the handle and swung the door open, sticking his assault rifle inside, Chisholm and Lorca right behind him, also aiming into the bathroom.

Sepsis, against the wall, softly caught the back of the opening bathroom door with his free hand, slowing and stopping it as he watched the muzzle of the assault rifle peek in. He was about to shoot his gun through the flimsy bathroom door and kill the man with the assault rifle, but he stopped himself, realizing he didn't know who else was out there. Controlling himself, he waited, holding his breath.

Smoothly, the assault rifle pulled out of the bathroom. The screaming of the sole surviving cop made it hard to hear, but Sepsis caught the sounds of footsteps walking away from the bathroom, his cue to slowly push the door closed, leaving it open just a crack so he could see out into the hallway.

Through the slit, he saw part of the back of a man in an orange garbageman's uniform and heard some talking under the screaming.

"Shut up," Lorca was saying to the wounded cop as they walked into the bloodbath, Lorca not looking at him as he covered the kitchen, horrified by the killings. The garbageman and Chisholm made sure everyone was dead, unavoidably stepping on the blood that by now completely covered the floor of the kitchen like black molten rubber. The wounded cop just kept on screaming and pleading for help.

"Jesus Christ, what a mess," said Chisholm, her gun in both hands as she toed all the bodies in the kitchen. "Get the two on the roof down here."

Lorca called on a transmitter as he kept his gun trained on the corpses, speaking to the officers on the roof in Italian. "They're coming down and getting an ambulance," he told Margaret in English. "Also some extra policemen are coming to help."

The three of them—Lorca, Chisholm, and the surviving garbageman—looked around until they were sure everyone was dead. Then the garbageman knelt and tried to stop the screaming cop's bleeding, talking to him in Italian.

Sepsis moved when he heard Lorca call the rooftop cops. Quietly, he slipped out of the bathroom, training his gun in the direction of the kitchen, no one in there seeing him as he went down the hallway, into one of the empty bedrooms. He shut the door carefully behind him, keeping it open just a crack, enough to see outside.

Chisholm turned around and looked down the hallway to the living room, seeing the three doors that were closed. Remembering the floor plans they'd been looking at just before the raid, she knew the two next to the bathroom were small closets. She decided to check them out.

"Lorca," she said, pointing with her gun into the hallway. Lorca covered her as she opened the doors to the closets and to the bathroom once again, just in case, but there was nothing. Both of them finally relaxed, bringing their guns down for the first time since they'd stepped into the house.

"What a fuckup," she said, walking back to the kitchen.

Out there, the two rooftop policemen, wearing bulky bulletproof vests like the kitchen cops, walked through the back door into the kitchen, shocked by the carnage, stepping over the bodies and leaving footprints on the coagulating blood.

"Too crowded, there's too many people here," Lorca said in Italian. "You two," he said to the new arrivals. "The rest of the house is secure. Go to the living room, make sure the two dead men out there are really dead."

The two cops followed orders, squeezing through the hallway past Chisholm and Lorca, going toward the living room as Denton came through the hallway as well. On their way to the living room to check that the other two were dead, the two rooftop cops ignored the bedroom doors. Sepsis, though, saw them good.

Denton was supposed to stay outside until Chisholm or Lorca gave him the all clear, but he hadn't been able to resist anymore. He had walked into the house and stood at the threshold, looking at the two dead men, Barahona and the other garbageman, and then walked into the kitchen, completely oblivious of any danger.

"What the fuck are you doing here?" asked Chisholm without looking at him, freaked by all the dead bodies and how quickly they'd mounted.

"Did we get him?" Denton asked, staring at all the corpses in the kitchen, not noticing as Lorca and Chisholm gave each other a look. Denton had asked precisely what was on both their minds.

"I don't know, they're all shot too bad. What the hell are you doing here, anyway? You were supposed to wait outside, like a good little boy."

"Skippy wants to see," he said with no humor, incredulous at the bloodshed in the living room and what he now saw of the kitchen.

"Well, go back to the living room," she said, and Denton didn't argue with her, shocked that so much violence had happened so quickly.

Lorca shook his head. "This was costly. Four of my men dead for six terrorists. At least we have Sepsis."

"Show me which one is him, then I'll believe it," said Chisholm.

"I see your point." None of the terrorists were recognizable at first blush.

"What is that smell?" asked Lorca, stepping forward toward Gallardo, for the first time realizing he was being cooked. He pulled the body off the stove and turned off the gas range. "My God," was all he managed to say, looking at the cooked chest and face of Gallardo, the neck wound already partially cauterized by the gas range. Lorca looked around the kitchen, staring at everything as he bent his head in Chisholm's direction.

"Margaret," he asked, unbelieving of all that had happened, "honestly, have you ever seen anything like this?"

She shook her head, which right now was a steady, pulsating pain, even though none of this had been her fault, or anybody's fault really. The screaming cop was still screaming, making her head worse. "Frederico, tell your man to shut the fuck up."

Denton had walked back into the living room toward the two rooftop cops, who were kneeling beside the dead men. Not wanting to see them up close but unable to stop himself, Denton went around the two rooftop cops and knelt by Barahona's body, looking at it up close.

That was when Sepsis made his move. He stepped out of the bedroom, aiming his gun in the direction of the kitchen as he walked into the living room, Denton and the two rooftop cops still kneeling around the bodies and unaware of what was about to happen. Denton especially should have seen him, since of the three of them he was the only one who was looking inside, in the direction Sepsis was coming from. But Denton didn't notice Sepsis until he was barely two yards away, far too late.

Sepsis shot the cops with his silenced gun, catching both of them at the base of the skull before they even knew what happened. Denton jumped, recoiling from the blood squirting all over the place as the rooftop cops' arteries were severed by the shots and began pumping blood all over the carpeting.

He looked up and saw Sepsis, aiming his gun right at him.

"The lion of the ages, face-to-face at last," he whispered, staring at the gun muzzle mere inches from his face, a cold, black look to Sepsis. Because of the wounded cop's screaming and shouting, no one else realized Sepsis was alive. Denton was about to say something else when Sepsis held a finger to his lips without moving the gun away from Denton's face.

For Denton, the gesture, somehow, made things worse. When he saw the gun, he'd decided that he would probably die now. But with the silencing finger, Denton was unsure, giving him a glimpse of hope, which made everything more frightening.

Perfectly calm, Sepsis checked that Denton didn't have a gun and was nowhere near one. He gestured to him with his own gun, motioning with a flick of his wrist for him to get up against the wall, away from the door. Denton didn't hesitate, moving out of the way of Sepsis as he in turn circled around the bodies lying there, in the process of stepping over the bodies to get out the front door, Denton still unsure if Sepsis was going to kill him. Abruptly, he decided he didn't want to wait around to find out.

"He's here he's here he's got a gun he's HERE!" he shouted, squeezing himself against the wall as hard as he could, as if it would make him invisible.

Lorca was the first on the move, followed by Chisholm down the narrow hallway, running too fast and passing the corner of the hall, coming into plain sight of Sepsis, who shot him right through the face and chest, killing him instantly.

Chisholm didn't make the same mistake, sticking out only her left hand holding the gun, shooting without looking around the corner, missing both Sepsis and Denton by inches, if that.

"Don't shoot for God's sake don't shoot me!" Denton screamed as he tried to turn micron-thin up against the wall. Sepsis debated whether to go into the kitchen and kill the Chisholm bitch, but he heard sirens, sirens.

He stepped out of the house and into the street just as two police cars rounded the corner where Lorca and Chisholm had parked their car. Four policemen got out of the two cop cars and Sepsis didn't hesitate—he fired at the first cop with the presence of mind to pull out a gun, catching him in the chest just above the frame of the window of the open car door, the other three cops ducking as Sepsis ran.

"He's getting away!" shouted Denton as Chisholm ran out the door, chasing Sepsis down the street, the three cops ditching their cars and racing after Sepsis on foot, sure he wouldn't get away. Denton went to

Lorca, turning him over and realizing at a glance that he was dead, a gaping bloody mess where his nose used to be. He picked up Lorca's gun and ran out of the house.

Sepsis turned left at the corner and raced up to the next block where, to the right, there was a park of some kind, edged on all sides by trees and bushes. The three cops and Chisholm ran after him, none of the Italians knowing who Chisholm was but figuring she must be a friend if she was running after their friend's killer with such a big gun.

Sepsis sprayed cover fire behind him as he ran, firing over his shoulder without looking, though none of the cops dared shoot back, the neighborhood crammed with homes where a single stray round could cause far too much damage—something Sepsis was counting on.

When he broke through the trees and bushes of the park, Sepsis realized he was in a playground, the place green and full of benches. Rectangular patches of grass were cut by packed tan dirt paths, everything a little shabby as around the park children, families, people were looking at him. Some realized he was running with a gun, more realizing something was wrong when three *carabinieri* and a redheaded woman burst into the park and raced after the man.

"*Get out get out get out!*" the three cops screamed at the people in the park, two of them slowing down to aim at Sepsis, who was running flat out and straight. But they couldn't shoot—a woman with a baby stroller ambled into their line of sight, directly in Sepsis's path.

The oblivious woman was Carmela, a youngish, fat working-class mother who was debating this Saturday afternoon whether or not she wanted to separate from her husband. She was thinking about it, worrying about money and what she would do to support herself and her sixteen-month-old daughter, how she would make ends meet if she went ahead and divorced her husband. He wasn't a bad man, but she hadn't felt happy in their married life for a long time, thinking it her right to have a happy life, thinking a divorce might be necessary to secure such a life. This was what she was thinking when a thin but strong young man grabbed her around the throat and held a gun under her cheek.

It was the only thing Sepsis could think of, unbelievably surprised by the arrival of the four backup cops, and he needed the time to sort things out. Holding the screaming woman with his left forearm around her throat, he aimed his gun at her head, kicking his knee into the base of her spine to keep her from struggling.

"Step back or I blow the bitch away!" he shouted in a bizarre hodge-podge of French and German, screaming at the three Italian cops and Chisholm, none of whom moved, standing three yards from him with their guns aimed at his head, all four of them knowing they might hit the woman, all four of them wondering if they could tackle Sepsis with-out getting themselves or the woman killed. And while they stood with their guns at the ready, they all screamed furious obscenities and rage at each other.

None of the people in this terrible standoff understood what they themselves were screaming, much less what the others were shouting. The policemen screamed at Sepsis in Italian, Sepsis himself unknow-ingly switching back and forth between his native French and his na-tive German as Chisholm threatened to send him to his grave in English. The innocent woman screamed too as she struggled mightily, terrified as she watched her baby's stroller slowly roll away from her. She was terrified for herself, yes, but the more seconds went by, the more she was terrified the stroller would tip over and her baby fall.

And as the seconds threatened to turn into a minute, Chisholm felt a wave coming on, a wave that had been coming since she'd heard the brief, violent burst of killing fire in the house, a wave of violence and murder to mask the dreadful exhilaration, an exhilaration that added more tide to the wave. For the first time, Sepsis stood there, right there in front of her. Something very bad was going to happen right now.

It was done for . . . convenience? Maybe for the sake of convenience, yes, as the screaming whore-bitch was struggling so violently in Sepsis's grasp she threatened to break free and leave him exposed. So he shot her through the head with one of the armor-piercing bullets, killing her instantly.

It happened before any of the three policemen or Chisholm was aware of it, this empty killing of the woman, but she immediately stopped thrashing, Sepsis holding her up with his left forearm like a shield while with his right hand he brought the gun to bear on each of the three policemen, squeezing off a single round to the head, killing each of them in turn before bringing the weapon to bear on Chisholm—*cüff cüff cüff*—

He was aiming at her before she was even aware that his hostage was dead, the gun aimed right for her face when he pulled the trigger. It just clicked.

The wave finally rose when he extended his arm to shoot the three cops. It rose swiftly but it didn't crest when the gun was aimed at her. Chisholm was just coming to grips with it, still processing the fact of the death of the young mother when Sepsis pointed his gun at her. With each bullet he fired, with each policeman he killed, the wave rose some more, a thicker, stronger undertow adding to the wave that was coming, coming, cresting as she saw him kill the cops. And even when he clicked the empty gun at her face, even then, Chisholm's wave still hadn't crested but took a second, a second more before it broke.

During that second, Sepsis clicked and clicked the empty gun, pulling the trigger as his mind counted, hoping for a jammed weapon even as he knew it was no jam, the gun's wide ejection spring tossing out the last shell casings as he fired on the last of the cops. He was out of bullets, and he stared at Chisholm, clicking the weapon as he watched the wave in her finally crest and begin to break all over him.

Because it did come, finally, the breaking wave of red red rage and fury pouring out across the tan, packed dirt of the little park like the cruelest red tide to ever wash ashore, Chisholm still holding her gun with both hands, the extended barrel less than two yards from Sepsis, Chisholm knowing she had four bullets in the gun and two speed-loaders in her pockets, but not thinking of that, not at all, not thinking of anything as finally she lost consciousness of what she was doing as easily and pleasingly as in a seduction, the wave breaking all around her, inside her, drowning her, crashing just as she took in one last gulp of air, huge and final, and let go with the gun straight at Sepsis.

He saw it coming and covered himself as best he could with the corpse of the dead mother just as the huge sound of Chisholm's gun filled the universe.

BLAM-BLAM-BLAM-BLAM!

The corpse took all the bullets in the chest, all of them reaching for Sepsis, he could feel it, needles reaching for him beyond the young mother's flesh but blocked by her body until finally Chisholm was emptily clicking her gun at him. He dropped the corpse and looked down at himself.

He was untouched. No bullets, no wounds, not even grazes as he touched his body all over, feeling himself as he looked down, then up at Chisholm.

They looked at each other, startled, both holding their empty guns, both very much alive and unhurt.

Chisholm was the first to react, digging in the right pocket of her sports jacket, the pocket flap getting in the way as she felt for one of the speedloaders that were banging against her hip, right there for the taking, flipping open her revolver as she dug around for more bullets.

Sepsis unthinkingly realized what Chisholm was doing, rushing toward her with his arms outstretched and giving her a terrific shove, neatly catching each of her breasts in his hands as he pushed her back so hard and so fast she tripped back and fell, scrambling around back to her feet even before she hit the ground. Through the trees in the distance, Sepsis saw Denton coming, which decided him to run.

He turned and ran flat out of the park, bursting through the row of trees and bushes that lined the edges of the park and racing right into the middle of traffic. Few cars were around, and those few that were accustomed to people crossing the street anywhere—one of the bad habits of Italian pedestrians—so they braked without thought as Sepsis ran across the middle of the street toward an intersection, turning there.

In the distance, Chisholm saw him as he turned the corner just as she too burst through the trees and bushes at the edge of the park, running across the street as she tried to reload her gun. The effort to concentrate on running and reloading was slowing her down, so she forgot about reloading and ran flat out, racing to the corner where Sepsis had turned, Denton right behind but so out of shape he was losing ground.

Down the sidewalk they ran, Sepsis and Chisholm, right through the thick of pedestrians which on this street was much thicker for some obscure reason. Why they were there Sepsis had no clue, but he used them anyway, pulling at the pedestrians, making them lose their balance and fall in Chisholm's path, hopefully tripping her up. But Chisholm was wise to his strategies, crashing into the wobbling pedestrians herself, sending them flying and out of her way.

The sun was orange, the light like late-afternoon sunlight once again as they ran on the sidewalk, unable to run in the middle of the street for the passing cars that would have run them down. Sepsis suddenly turned hard to the right, disappearing into a building, Chisholm close enough that she didn't stop to think he might try to ambush her. She turned right and followed him an instant later.

The building was one of those old, narrow slot buildings, with a dark wood-paneled lobby that led deep into a narrow cul-de-sac, the stairs leading up to the left, two elevators leading up to the right. Sepsis was about to take the stairs up when Chisholm took a leaping dive, smashing him against the far wall like her brothers had taught her, endlessly long ago.

"Fucking bitch!" Sepsis raged, grabbing Chisholm by the arm and throwing her against one of the elevators, denting the door. He was pulling back to hit her in the face when Chisholm kicked out with her booted foot, square-toed and fashionable, catching his shin right on the money.

Sepsis screamed and nearly toppled over from the pain of the kick, grabbing his shin, which he thought must surely be broken, as Chisholm took two steps away from him to give herself the room and the time to reload her gun.

She had to get distance, Chisholm realized as she hysterically tried to get her hand into her jacket pocket. He was stronger than she was. She had to gain some distance, some time to load her gun again and blow this motherfucker straight to hell or she would be the one dead:

"C'mon fucker C'MON!" she screamed without realizing it. She finally grabbed hold of one of the speedloaders and pulled it out of her pocket.

Again without thought, Sepsis ran forward and shoved Chisholm away, this time not so firmly but strong enough that Chisholm dropped her speedloader. She grabbed her gun by the pipe in her right hand and clobbered Sepsis with it on the forehead, hard, but she overswung, giving him the space to smash a left fist against the side of her face, sending her to her knees on the ground.

"Now I'm going to kill you, you bitch," he said in German she did not understand, just before Chisholm, lying prone on the ground at his feet, recovered enough to swing the butt of her gun against the same shin she'd kicked, making Sepsis scream and hop away from her as she recovered enough to stand and try to tackle him again.

But he was strong. He grabbed her cleanly by the throat and started throttling her, pulling her face closer to his as he flexed out his elbows, making it impossible for Chisholm to scratch his eyes out. She kneed him, going for his groin as she scratched, but Sepsis had been prepared, his body twisted so that the thick meat of his thigh protected his groin, Chisholm smashing his thigh again and again as she quit trying for his face and pulled at his arms, not yet losing it but growing weaker as he squeezed.

For the first time, they stared straight at each other, inches away. Pouring out of her eyes, red red tendrils reached for Sepsis's very mind, her eyes reaching for his brains, those evil tendrils trying to suck them out through his skull. And all Chisholm felt was a black vacuum at the core of this man, a perfect black emptiness that would only be satisfied when her body was torn and disintegrated to shreds.

"*Hey!*" Denton screamed at the opening of the building, pointing a gun at them both. Without a thought, Sepsis threw Chisholm aside and ran up the stairs, his shin killing him, probably broken, but Sepsis biting the pain away as he took two steps at a time up the staircase.

Denton ran into the lobby, wheezing like a broken-down machine as he knelt by Chisholm, who lay there, recovering. "Are you okay?" he gasped.

"*Get him!*" she screamed, getting up herself and running after Sepsis up the flight of stairs. She couldn't slow down to reach for her speed-loader and put an end to him, but she could follow, which she did, running and running.

Denton was too winded from his cigarettes, grabbing his knees as he stood there in the lobby, wanting to follow them but too beat to move. And then the elevator door, the one Sepsis had dented with Chisholm's body? It opened, an elderly, unconcerned gentleman stepping out and giving Denton a detached glance before walking out of the building. Denton got in the elevator and hit the button for the top floor.

Chisholm and Sepsis ran up the stairs, always a half-floor separating them, zigzagging up the stairs, racing across the floor, then taking the next landing up, always up, tearing through the dark wood-paneled stairs as around them the apartment residents came out to see what the commotion was all about. They could hear shouts, screams, grunts from them both as the woman chased the man. But neither Sepsis nor Chisholm realized the sounds they were making. Neither of them had any conscious thoughts anymore. They didn't think of themselves with thoughts, with pain. There was, once again, between them only a space which they each filled with their own peculiar colors.

On the seventh-floor landing, as he ran for the next flight of stairs up, Sepsis stepped wrong and winced at the pain in his shin, missing a stride. It was enough of a break for Chisholm. With a fast burst of long strides and a final leap, she jumped for Sepsis's legs, tackling them cleanly and bringing him down.

With the force of her fall, Chisholm lost her grip on her gun and on Sepsis's legs. The gun slid down the long, dark hallway of the seventh floor as Sepsis rolled away and stood up faster than Chisholm did, kicking out at her midriff just as she was trying to stand up, sending her to the ground again.

He should have turned. He should have turned and run, run away. But he didn't. He took a couple of steps forward and kicked her again.

This time, she caught his leg and gave it a fast twist, sending him to the ground and leaving him be as she went for her gun, which lay a bare two yards away, simultaneously reaching for the other speedloader in her pocket.

But Sepsis stood up and kicked her again before she could get the gun, sending her sprawling down toward the window at the end of the dark and narrow hallway, Chisholm looking to Sepsis like a sack of shit he was gonna fuck up, fuck her up like he wanted to. He kicked her again before she could get up, Chisholm falling on her back right by the end of the hallway, trapped as dull sunlight came in through the lone window behind her.

He knelt beside her, the wind knocked out of her, and grabbed her head by the ears, slamming it against the ledge of the window, slamming it as hard as he could, Chisholm fighting, resisting, holding the back of her head with her right hand as with her left she tried and failed to hit his face, it was too late, fuck you it's too fucking late, I'm gonna fuck you up and throw you—

Out of nowhere, Denton shouted: *"Stop! I have a gun!"*

Sepsis hesitated, turning to Denton, who was coming down the staircase and into the dark hallway, holding a gun like he said he was. And in that moment of hesitation, Chisholm got her second wind.

Wrenching her right hand out from under her head, she grabbed Sepsis's crotch, her left hand neatly catching his throat. And with all she had in her, with that strength that enables mothers to overturn burning cars when their babies are trapped inside, Margaret Chisholm picked up Sepsis and flipped him over her shoulder, throwing him through the shattering glass window, letting him fall out into empty space that might as well have been black for all the salvation it would provide.

Sepsis looked back at the window as he fell, not realizing he was screaming, his entire field of vision captured by Chisholm's inverted, smirking, hateful stare, receding, pulling away, as if it were she who was rising, not he descending, falling, going down, his last conscious thought not of himself or his life or his death but of her red red hair that seemed to wave little strands at him as the wind blew through it.

Chisholm stared after him all the way down, watching as Sepsis, staring at her, fell the seven stories, the moment stretching, stretching like a scrim that someone was trying to tear through. His hands were outstretched toward her. His face was all O's, eyes, mouth. His head was falling faster than the rest of him. His eyes never left her face, the scrim stretching so far that any moment now it would tear for good.

He hit the ground. His head, when it hit, sounded like a bowling ball or a watermelon, hollow. It burst on impact, blood and brains gushing out of his ears and eye sockets. Shards of bone fragment tore through his face, disfiguring it, his jawbone snapping off and flapping loosely. The rest of his body, when it landed, didn't burst. Rather, it bounced, bounced high, about a foot up off the ground, his burst head anchoring the body and keeping it from moving very far as bits of shattered glass rained down all over him. His screaming, though, didn't stop when he landed but went on for a fraction of a second more before not cutting out but fading.

Margaret Chisholm saw the whole thing. All she did was stare at the body down below, leaning on the window ledge as she held her breath, fear and hatred and relief and shame held back but beginning to pour in and create a consciousness for her one more time, a consciousness that meant that it was not Sepsis but she who was still alive.

Oh that mean consciousness, such a tricky devil. Margaret tried to prepare for it as she stared at Sepsis's dead body down below, ushering in pictures of the shoot-out at the square, of the dead mushrooms at the metro station, of Frederico Lorca and how his family would suffer when they learned he was dead. She brought in all these pictures, all these weapons against her consciousness, her needle and thread to sew up the tear in the scrim, but it wouldn't be enough, she could see. It would never, ever be enough, because it was death.

Denton ran to Chisholm, sticking his head out the window and staring after the body down below, wheezing and pissed. "Oh that's right, the Chisholm Method: Kill them all, let God sort them out," he said, furious.

Chisholm didn't hear him. She was too busy getting the shakes, bad, her entire body reacting like to a poison as it started convulsing—first in her chest, her heart wanting to explode—then her belly—her arms—her entire body, shaking, horrified. She slowly shuffled backward, away from the shattered window, her first conscious, logical thought since she'd thrown Sepsis out of it that she herself might "accidentally" fall in after him.

"Help," she said, a bare hiccup of a sound, snapping Denton away from the sight of Sepsis's corpse.

Her back was to him as she walked away. "Margaret?" he said, approaching her as she began to twirl around, trying to keep her balance but losing it. He took two fast steps and caught her before she collapsed, holding her up and pulling her toward him as she shook spasmodically, as if she were colder than any human being had ever been in all of time. The scrim was finally torn for Margaret Chisholm, and with it came the end of all doubt.

First Prayer

In her room at the villa, alone, Sister Marianne knelt on the floor. She took her rosary and braided it through her fingers, tying her hands together. Then she bowed her head and prayed for the soul of the man who had wanted to murder her.

Her work was all forgotten. She had spent the day with Edmund in the study, the two of them absorbed in their notes and calculations. Some insignificant problem had been so worrying them that they almost didn't hear the telephone ring.

"The man is dead," Margaret told her. When she asked what had happened, Margaret said, "Just know that you're safe now." And then she'd hung up.

Even as Marianne had excused herself and gone up to her room to pray, even then, a sadness she could not understand swept through her. She did not understand where it came from, or what it meant. As she knelt to pray, she thought it was relief that made her cry: relief that no more harm would be done to the innocent, relief that she herself had nothing to fear anymore.

But it wasn't relief. As she began to pray, she realized what it was: it was sorrow. The man was dead—he was past salvation. All the cruel and evil things he had done could no longer be forgiven. There was nothing he could do now, because now, he was at God's mercy.

So she prayed. She prayed to God, marshaling all of her courage and asking Him to His face to forgive the man who had done so much evil. Without hesitation, she took back all the sorrowful, angry accusations she had brought against him, calling back all the nights spent damning him for the deaths of her sisters, disowning all her pleas for justice in the face of all the innocent deaths he had caused, denying and rejecting and repudiating all her reproaches and recriminations. She took it back, took it all back, praying—pleading—begging God to forgive, please, only forgiveness, yes, forgive him all he has done, as You forgive us for not saving the living all around us—

Marianne slumped on the floor, crying into her hands, her courage broken. It wasn't the dead she prayed for, she finally understood: the dead were past all prayers. It was for the damning unforgivingness of the living toward the living that she prayed.

She sat there for a long long time.

Marianne?" Edmund knocked on her door, leaning into her room.

"Yes?" she said, turning to him, realizing for the first time that it was pitch-black in her room.

"Come," he said.

FOURTEEN

The Contrary Wills
of Man and
God / Belief

Margaret Chisholm lay on her bed, fully clothed, staring at the ceiling as she waited for the phone.

It was dark, around nine or so, the sole light in her room coming from her nightstand lamp. The ceiling had been recently painted, and as she looked, she could make out the lines of the brushstrokes, the angle of the lamplight casting subtle, tiny shadows like cat scratches. She waited and waited, and so far, this was the worst part of her day. She didn't mind giving her statement to the Italian cops, nor did she mind the tedium of writing her Bureau report. But the waiting that made space for the thinking and the dwelling—this was the worst part. The second-worst part.

The telephone rang and Maggie picked it up on the first ring.

"Chisholm," she said.

"How's my girl?" Mario Rivera asked through a smile.

"It's over."

He sighed. "I know, I read your report," he said. "How are you hold-ing up?"

"Okay I guess."

"So what was the deal with this guy?" he asked, all business, hoping it would take Maggie's mind off this last job. "Why'd he want to off the nun?"

"He took the answer with him," she said, Rivera surprised she wasn't even curious.

"Too bad," he recovered. "Any ideas?"

"None whatsoever."

And that was all she said, letting the silence hang.

"You okay?" he finally asked, really worried.

"Yeah. Yeah. Mario, I think this was the last time I'll be going out in the field. I don't think I can take this anymore."

Rivera controlled a little tug of rising panic. "Don't worry about it, anything you want. You wanna work at Quantico maybe? Hang out with the little brats some?"

"Mario . . . I didn't need to do him. But I did him anyway. And I *liked* it. I liked it a lot."

"Shh, shhh, shh, I know, I know, it can happen sometimes. You get so wound up, it can happen. You'll get back home, you need a month, you need two months, you need as much as you want, you got it. You're a hero, Maggie!"

"I'm a murderer," she answered quietly. "Nothing but a stone-cold killer."

"Maggie, Maggie, listen. You're not," said Rivera, his growing des-peration making him angry. "You're no killer. You're a good agent, the best. You get on a plane *tonight*. You get back here immediately, this is an order. You did *great*, okay? And nothing is gonna change and we'll just sit down and talk this over. You did your job. Where's Denton? I want to talk to Denton."

Denton was downstairs in the study, talking on the phone with his feet up on an ottoman as he flipped the television remote control between CNN and a Napolitano game; Napolitano was up two zip.

"We're going to be heading out in a couple of days, can you meet me at the airport? The red-eye, probably," he said, turning as he heard Chisholm walk in.

"Hold on, hold on, baby, I can't talk right now, something's come up. I'll talk to you later, buh-bye," he said, hanging up and turning off the television without looking. "What?" he asked.

"Mario Rivera wants to talk to you—on the phone upstairs," said Chisholm tiredly.

She sighed. This is the end, she thought. This is how it happens. You surrender your weapon and pretty soon you're talking to shrinks, and after that you're out. Maggie didn't know if she was terrified, humiliated, or finally relieved that it was over. "Where's Marianne?" she asked, looking up at Denton.

Denton hadn't moved. "She and Gettier went out. Look, are you all right? You look like someone died—what happened?"

"Everything's just peachy-keen. Where'd they go?"

"I don't know, the Vatican I think. So what does Rivera want?" he asked, walking to the door but still keeping an eye on Chisholm anyway.

"What's she doing at the Vatican at this hour?"

"Some architecture stuff, I don't know—"

"What?" she interrupted, frowning.

Denton looked at her. "What's the matter?" he asked as her face sagged.

"Oh my God," she said. "The nun is the intel source."

Marianne was at the wheel as she and Gettier reached the basilica gates. The Swiss Guards shined their flashlights on them and scrupulously checked their identification cards even though they knew Marianne and Gettier well. The night security cameras were on, monitoring the guards.

"It's kind of late, isn't it?" one of the guards asked in Italian.

"I have a surprise for Sister Marianne," Gettier said. "Actually, could a couple of you help me with it? It's in the trunk and I don't think Sister Marianne and I can manage it by ourselves."

"Sure, Professor Gettier." The guard smiled. "I'll help you myself."

He waved to the gatekeeper, who let their car in, the guard, a barrel-chested older man by the name of Sommers, walking behind the car into the parking area beside the gate.

"What is it?" Marianne asked wanly, trying to work up some enthusiasm. Maybe it would be good to work, she thought. Nighttime was almost always the best time to work.

"You'll see," Gettier teased, trying to cheer her up as he opened the trunk for Sommers and another, junior guard. "Can you handle it? It's heavy," he cautioned, motioning to a crate in the trunk, a wooden crate about three feet long and nailed shut, with a couple of handles on the sides.

"No problem," said Sommers. He and the younger man, Johansen, easily lifted it out of the trunk. Johansen was about to close the trunk when Gettier stopped him.

"Wait, I have to get something," he said, lifting up the flooring of the trunk and getting the tire iron. He slammed the trunk closed.

"What *is* it?" Marianne said, amused that Gettier liked teasing her this way.

"Be patient," he said, smiling. The four of them trundled off with the crate.

Chisholm was driving like crazy, not bothering to stop at the red lights, which in a city like Rome is as close to insanity as you want to get.

"Slow down for Chrissake!" Denton hollered, loading the gun he carried with him whenever he was on CIA business, per the rules. He loaded it with more ease and dexterity than Chisholm would have given him credit for, a little unnervingly so.

"Be careful with that thing," she said absently.

"So you're saying that the intel source is the nun, huh?" Denton cracked, sarcastic.

"Yes!" Margaret nearly shouted, but not exhilarated, no—in a panic. "Marianne was the source."

"Gre-ea-at." Denton nodded sagely. "So she tipped Sepsis off so he could kill her."

"You're not listening, Denton," she said heatedly. "Sepsis was always one step ahead of us. He knew where Marianne would be in America. He knew where she'd be in Rome. He knew we were all going to be in plain sight when we crossed the plaza to get to Barberi's place. That means he had an intel source. The nun was the source. She knew every-thing. But *she* didn't contact Sepsis—Gettier did."

"Oh, so now Gettier is the source, mm-hmm," he said sarcastically before he exploded. "That's crazy! Why would Gettier *do* that! We checked him out, he and the nun are buddy-buddy. And what about today? If Gettier was the source, Sepsis would have known about our raid."

"That's what tipped me off to Gettier. Gettier didn't tell Sepsis about the raid because *Marianne* didn't know about it. You knew, I knew, Lorca knew. But Marianne didn't know, which is why Gettier didn't know. That's why we caught Sepsis with his pants down."

Against his better judgment, Denton started half believing this cock-and-bull scenario. "Okay okay okay, assuming Gettier passed information to Sepsis, why would he want to deal with Marianne now?"

"Hey, I don't know! I just know it," she said, without looking at Denton.

"You sound like a raving lunatic," he said as he stared at her.

"Yeah, well, whatever the reason Gettier wants the nun out of the picture, it's the same reason Sepsis wanted her dead in the first place. Call up Vatican security and tell them what's going down. Do you know how to fire that gun?"

Denton didn't even bother to answer that, looking at Chisholm cool and detached as she drove on.

"I think you ought to stop the car," he said calmly. "I think you ought to think carefully about what you're saying, and about what you're doing."

Chisholm glanced at him quickly, the first time she'd looked at him during the entire drive. "We had a *deal*, Denton. You do intelligence, I do the fieldwork. That was the deal. Honor it."

Denton didn't move, still staring at Chisholm, still cool, still detached. Abruptly, he pulled out his cellular phone and started dialing, mumbling as he called, "Give you a hand and you take the whole deck."

Gettier and Marianne stood over Gettier's worktable on the ground level, poring over blueprints as Sommers and Johansen manhandled the big crate. At this hour of the night, there was none of the usual activity, just the four of them under the work lights of the table.

"Do you need any help?" Gettier asked solicitously, but the guards smiled.

"No, my Professor," Sommers grunted. "We need the exercise." The two guards picked up the crate and heaved it onto the table.

"Gently," Gettier admonished a little patronizingly, as was his way, though not really worried that the guards might damage its contents. They put it on the table without a hitch, right on the edge for easy access.

"Will that be all, my Professor?" huffed Sommers.

"Just one moment, please stay," he said, turning to Marianne and smiling. He pointed at the blueprints. "So these are the most structurally weakened?" he asked her, pointing to some of the columns.

"Yes, especially here." She indicated the columns under the Sistine Chapel. "It wouldn't do for the chapel to collapse after all that work. If we don't strengthen these over here," she said, pointing to a different set of columns, "with one bad earthquake the whole basilica will come crashing down on our heads."

"So that's one, two, three . . ." Gettier counted the worst of the columns. "Nine columns. If these aren't strengthened first, then the entire structure collapses?"

"Yes," answered Marianne.

"Yes." Gettier turned and smiled at the guards. "Don't go," he repeated. "I need your help with something." He approached the crate, twirling the tire iron in his hand.

"So what couldn't wait till the morning?"

"I can't believe you are so impatient." Gettier smiled indulgently, trying to open the crate with the tire iron. Johansen made a move to do it for him, but Gettier waved him off. "I can do it."

Gettier pried the crate open and stuck his hand inside, rummaging through it with all the patience in the world.

"What *is* it?" Marianne asked, laughing, enjoying herself.

Gettier smiled at her again, his back to the guards. He winked at Marianne. "Watch," he said.

He turned on the guards, pulling his right hand from inside the crate. He held an automatic pistol with a silencer, and he shot both guards square in the face. One bullet went through the right cheekbone of Johansen, the other through the left eyebrow arch of Sommers, both of them instantly falling to the ground, dead before they hit it.

Marianne's face melted, her lips still smiling as her eyes turned horrified, staring as the bodies of the two guards fell motionless to the ground. She ran to them, trying to save them.

Gettier ignored her efforts. Instead, he opened the crate and began unpacking small canister-shaped devices with little boxes attached to the ends, each canister barely nine inches long and four inches in diameter. He set them neatly on the table as Marianne fruitlessly tried saving the two dead guards.

Finally she turned to Gettier. "What have you done!" she screamed.

"I killed them," he said, still ignoring Marianne as he pulled a satchel out of the crate. Quickly, he counted up the canisters he had extracted, nine of them, his lips moving silently.

"Why!" she whispered like a scream.

Gettier held up a finger at her without looking up, as if ordering her not to break his concentration. Then he put the canisters in the satchel and zipped it up before turning to Marianne.

"They were in my way, Marianne." He approached the still-kneeling Marianne, whose eyes never left Gettier, grabbing her by the upper arm and getting her to her feet, dragging her along.

"Now come along, Sister. There is much work to be done. Opus Demoni: The Work of the Devil."

The lieutenant in charge of the night detail of the Swiss Guards, Hess, thankfully not only understood English, he remembered Chisholm.

"Frederico Lorca introduced us," he told her as he was rounding up his squad, a platoon of twenty.

"I forgot. . . . Lorca's dead."

"Yes, I know," he said, turning to his men and giving them their orders.

Like their American counterparts, the Swiss Guards were dressed in black, helmeted, and carrying the latest in equipment, though they were outfitted with Uzis, which Denton found ironic—the Israelis arming the Vatican.

Once Hess had given them their orders, they scattered, Hess and another guard staying with Denton and Chisholm.

"Come, we go," he told the Americans, walking quickly up through some passageways and emerging into an obscure corner of what turned out to be a huge chapel, easily seating a thousand people.

"Hauptmann," Hess whispered at the other guard, pointing twice at the main entrance to the chapel. Hauptmann ran to secure the doors.

"Jesus Christ, this place is huge," Denton whispered, but Chisholm had eyes only for Hess as the two conferred.

"My men are securing the perimeter and requesting assistance," the lieutenant said, calm as could be. "They know we are looking for a man in his early sixties and a nun—they've been ordered not to touch either of them. They know you are with me, so they won't fire on you. You and I will begin searching until this assistance arrives. Agreed?"

"Agreed," she said, trying to overcome her misgivings and succeeding. "Denton," she called.

The four of them started covering the ground floor.

But Gettier and Marianne weren't on the ground floor anymore. Gettier was strapping one of the canisters to a support column in the catacombs, using generous lengths of plumber's tape, wrapping the bomb twice around before tearing the tape with his teeth.

"I admire you greatly, Marianne. I hope you know that," Gettier said. "I've always *liked* you, of course, yes, but more than that I've learned to admire you."

He gave the canister bomb a final shake to make sure it was secured, then turned to Marianne, smiling. "You've been most troublesome. Three times we warned you to stay away, but you never tired, you never relented. I thought the bombing of the chapel would be enough, but you know how the young are. He thought you needed an extra bit of warning. So he shot at you at the police station. But *still* you came. So we had to warn you at Piazza Colomo. But you still went on, as if nothing. That determination is rare."

"*You* tried to kill me?" she asked.

"No!" he said, genuinely shocked. "And don't worry, I won't kill you now."

"What is this, Edmund, what have you done?" she said as Gettier took her by the elbow and guided her to another column, carefully counting the other columns so that he reached the right one. "You've murdered two men, you've killed in cold blood before God—"

"Don't give me your religious pieties, please," he said tiredly, his eyes glued to the columns, counting them. "Today has been a difficult day—ah, this is the one!"

He let go of Marianne, dropped the satchel, and pulled out another canister and the tape, strapping the canister to the weakened column.

As he worked, rolling the plumber's tape around the bomb and column, he smiled without looking at Marianne.

"You know what happened today? I had the most remarkable conversation of my life. After you, my favorite pupil, went off to talk to your God, I spoke to the murderer of my other favorite pupil."

Marianne stared at Gettier, speechless, as he turned his attention back to securing the bomb to the column. He tore off the tape again with his teeth and shook the bomb to make sure it stayed. Then he turned to face Marianne.

"Do you know what it is like to listen to the murderer of your student tell you about the 'good news'? Do you? All right, listen: Imagine if I told you that your favorite student—Dugan, was he? Imagine if I told you that Dugan had been killed. Imagine how you would feel. I wish I could explain it to you, explain it to you so you would *know*. But I can't explain it, it is indescribable."

He put the tape back in the satchel, ignoring Marianne, but she made no move to run.

"Stop. Stop, please," she pleaded.

Gettier picked up the satchel. "I can't . . . and I don't want to."

Forty yards away, at the top of the stairs leading to the catacombs, Hess, Hauptmann, Denton, and Chisholm stopped at the door leading down. Hess made some hand gestures to Hauptmann, who left them; then he turned to Chisholm.

"One of you stays, the other goes with me. Who has more experience?"

"I do," said Chisholm.

Hess pulled out a small pocket transmitter with a floppy antenna, turning it on and handing it to Denton. "Stay here. If you see anything, call us."

With that, Chisholm and Hess started down the stairs into the catacombs. Denton didn't like this at all.

"Hey," he whispered to Chisholm, but she turned savage eyes on him.

"We had a deal," she snarled as she went down the stairs after Hess.

But it wasn't the snarl that frightened Denton—it was the fear. For the first time, Denton saw Chisholm truly afraid.

Chisholm and Hess went down the curving steps, lit by fluorescent lights that made the darkness eerie and hellish. Hess was at the point, leading them, his Uzi close to his body so neither the muzzle nor its shadow would give him away.

Yᵒu see these bombs?" Gettier asked rhetorically, holding up the satchel for emphasis as he lightly pulled Sister Marianne along. "With nine of these, I will bring down the monument of Catholic belief. I wish I could snap my fingers to show you how quick it will be."

"Don't do this, Edmund, please," she begged, terrified . . . but not about the basilica. "Think of yourself, of your s—"

"Enough of this," Gettier said, stopping, looking straight at Marianne almost with contempt. "You, you are the will of God. And I am the will of man. You plead and ask and offer to barter. You *pray*, as if that will make some kind of difference. I, on the other hand—I act. Who is most effective? Eh?" He resumed walking and pulling Marianne along as he counted columns, trying to find the right one.

"Please. Please, I'm begging you. Stop this," she said, horrified that she had nothing else she could say to stop him, horrified that perhaps he was right—she really *did* have nothing more than pleadings and prayer.

Gettier paid no attention to her, stopping at another column and strapping another bomb to it. He glanced at the frustration in Marianne's eyes . . . and felt pity for her, remembering that she had once been his student.

"When I saw you break out of cover to save those schoolchildren, I was very impressed. But now, you, this—you demean yourself." He tsked as he had back in Cambridge. "All this pleading, 'please please please please,' " he mimicked cruelly, tsking again. "Don't. You were in better form at the piazza."

Marianne stared at him, hating him for the first time in her life, furious to be so humiliated. Abruptly, she turned and walked away, surprising Gettier into dropping his bomb, which bounced thickly but harmlessly on the ground. He made a quick dash and easily caught hold of Marianne again.

"Let me go!" she shouted, letting her anger show.

"I said I would not kill you, but that does not make you free to go as you like. You are my passport out of here."

Seventy-five yards away, amid the twists and turns of the catacombs, Hess and Chisholm heard the nun and looked at each other. They couldn't make out the words, but they knew it was Marianne. Hess gestured forward and Chisholm nodded, the two of them making their way through the vast, constricted corridors.

Gettier and Marianne hadn't moved, the two of them frozen, staring at each other.

"Why did he kill all of my sisters?" she said, weeping, angry for the first time in so long she couldn't remember.

Gettier stared back, but relented. "I'm sorry he killed them, it wasn't my idea. It was just some message that he was sending me—"

"A *message!*" she screamed uncontrollably.

He looked her in the eye. "Yes," he said. Then he turned away, dragging Marianne with him as he went through the catacombs to the northeast staircase, talking as he walked. "I never wanted you to be hurt—that was the bargain I struck with him. No matter what happened, you would not be harmed, and he agreed."

"Not be harmed? He killed all my sisters, friends I had known for years. And then at the police station? At the piazza?"

"He didn't try to kill you—if he had wanted to kill you, you would be dead." Gettier stopped and turned to face Marianne. "It was simple. It was all about access to the Vatican catacombs. As you yourself pointed out, one good push would be enough to bring the entire basilica down. Or a few well-placed bombs. If you couldn't come to Rome, I would lead the entire basilica restoration project. I would have unlimited access to the basilica, especially to the catacombs. I could have some 'consultant'—namely, my other pupil—come in and place all the bombs in broad daylight, without arousing suspicion. We could have destroyed the basilica in peace. But with you running around the Vat-ican, I could never have gotten close without arousing suspicion. That's why he targeted you—he had to make the authorities so afraid for your safety that they wouldn't allow you to come to Rome."

"He should have killed me instead, instead of all my sisters," Mari-anne said bitterly, looking away.

Gettier stroked her face, making her look at him. "I would never have allowed that. I love you as much as I loved him."

Then he pulled Marianne up the stairs to the doorway.

Denton was bored and frightened, a state he found decidedly annoying. So he wandered about the basilica, poking his head at random through different doors. Some were locked, but most were open, and he found himself slipping about, hoping above all to run across some Swiss Guard with a big Uzi.

He came to one such door, small and unpretentious, and opened it, literally flabbergasted. Inside was the Sistine Chapel.

It was quite small, so small in fact that a medium-sized New En-gland parish would not have fit. A riot of color showered down on him, colors so vivid and powerful that he couldn't make head or tail of the images for several seconds.

The famed picture of God touching Adam's outstretched hand was there, but not as Denton remembered it. It was not a brownish gray but a powerful, almost violent blue sky against which strong dark colors made up the image of God, the eyes so real they might as well have been God's own.

Without a thought, Denton left the door open as he walked inside, the chapel surrounding him.

This was God. It was so powerful, so monumental, yet so simple it had to be God. Not the work of God, no—God Himself. Who but God could have done such a thing, or given any mere man the ability to do such a thing?

That's what Denton thought. He was so enraptured that he didn't hear the voices until they were almost upon him.

Everything I am, everything I knew, everything I had learned, I passed on to him, like any teacher should. There was nothing I did not teach him, as there was nothing I did not teach you."

"*You* taught him?" she asked, horrified as they walked down a hallway, passing one open door after another, Marianne surprised that the night crew had not closed all the doors as they were supposed to.

"Everything, but not architecture—he hated architecture," Gettier said wistfully, a little hurt.

"You're a tea— You're a— He was a *killer!*" she shouted. "How could you teach such—"

"How do you think I taught *you?*" he said as he dragged her along.

"Don't move!" Denton shouted, holding his gun on Gettier.

Gettier moved like a cat, or like an amazing dancer. Without hesitation, he whirled Marianne around and held her against him, his arm across her belly, holding her like a shield. And without hesitation, he put his gun right to her head, most of her body protecting him.

"Put your weapon on the ground, Mr. Denton. I have no quarrel with you, but I will kill the nun if you do not put your weapon down."

And with that, he began walking forward.

"Margaret, I have him!" Denton shouted over his shoulder, never taking his eyes off Gettier, forgetting all about the transmitter in his pocket as he retreated back into the chapel. "Chisholm!"

"Ah, so the famous Agent Chisholm is here as well, eh?" said Gettier, still walking forward, crossing the threshold into the chapel. "That is good. Put your weapon on the ground, Mr. Denton. Put your weapon—"

Denton never saw it coming. He was, after all, just a bureaucrat.

As if still dancing, Gettier twirled Marianne away, releasing her, the left hand that had held her grabbing Denton's outstretched hand, the hand that held the gun. In one fluid movement, Gettier twisted Denton's wrist so hard and so fast that not only did his arm but his entire body twist around. When the move was over, Gettier had Denton's wrist pinned to his back, his gun dropped on the floor, Gettier's gun right at Denton's temple.

"You shouldn't have," said Gettier right into his ear.

He kicked away Denton's discarded gun just as rapid footfalls approached. Gettier turned Denton around, holding him as a shield facing the door of the chapel as Hess came in first, aiming the Uzi right at Gettier—

But Gettier was faster. So Hess was dead.

"No—!" screamed Marianne, her scream cut off by the cough of Gettier's gun.

"I have you," said Margaret Chisholm.

She was at the door of the chapel, only her face and her gun visible, aiming right for Gettier as he began moving about with Denton in a perverse dance, retreating into the chapel, putting distance between them, his bobbing and weaving making it impossible for Chisholm to aim.

"Come now, Agent Chisholm, I know how much you dislike the Central Intelligence Agency, but do you dislike it enough to risk one of its men?"

"Shoot him!" Denton shouted.

"Shut up." Gettier sighed pedantically. "If she shoots, you will be dead. Isn't that right, Agent Chisholm? So why don't you put your weapon on the ground and kick it over to me."

Chisholm blinked. And then something happened.

Slowly, without taking her aim off Gettier, Chisholm got out from behind her cover and began approaching him. She was completely exposed, with nothing to hide behind as she walked into the chapel toward Gettier. All he had to do was take his gun off Denton and aim it at Chisholm and she would be dead. Chisholm knew this. She knew what she was doing. She knew *exactly* what she was doing.

"Put the weapon down and you'll live," she said with no real venom.

"Put *your* weapon down or Denton here dies."

"Shoot him, Margaret, he's bluffing," was Denton's unwise contribution.

"Am I?" said Gettier.

In a single fluid motion, he brought his gun down and shot Denton in the calf, audibly breaking the bones. Denton screamed in agony, his legs automatically giving out under him, but Gettier, with amazing strength, held him up with one hand, using his grip on Denton's wrist to give him an incentive to stay on his feet.

"The next time I shoot him, his brains will see sunlight," Gettier said casually, still bobbing and weaving, ruining Chisholm's aim. "Put your weapon on the ground and kick it over to me," he repeated.

Still training her gun on him, she said, "I drop my gun and then you kill me."

"Of course," he said, as if it were the most obvious thing in the world. "Do you have any doubt?"

Abruptly, Chisholm dropped her gun arm.

"Drop the gun and kick it over to me," he said patiently.

So that's what Margaret did, placing the gun on the ground to prevent it from going off accidentally, then shoving it across the floor with her foot. It was too far away for her to lunge for it, so Gettier knew he was safe. He dropped Denton, who promptly rolled into a ball and tried to stop the bleeding in his leg.

"I saw you, Agent Chisholm. In my mind, I saw you kill my pupil," he said as he aimed his gun right for Chisholm's face, coming closer and closer. "Put your hands behind your head and kneel on the ground."

"He deserved it," she said as she knelt. Horribly, with an evil, disgusting look in her eye, she went on: "You know, when I killed him? I was looking at him straight in the eye. I watched him fall all the way down. Too bad you weren't there to see it live."

But Gettier smiled, not sucked in. "Go on, rave all you want."

She lunged suddenly, faster than she would have ever believed possible—but Gettier was faster, leaping back and bringing his gun hand down on her temple, smashing the side of her head and sending her sprawling, stunned.

"Good try! I would have expected nothing less from you," he said. "Now, again, put your hands behind your head and kneel before me."

Chisholm shook her head clear before slowly kneeling again, sitting on her heels. Then, equally slowly, she began raising her hands, trying hard to work up some hope for another chance. But Gettier was wise to her, keeping his distance and almost laughing at her efforts.

"I can see through you, Agent Chisholm," he said as he walked around Chisholm's kneeling figure, standing behind her, his gun never veering from her head. "Every effort you are making now, I did years ago, when you were still just a child."

And then that pedantic edge crept into his voice, the lecturer's voice that is somehow, by definition, cruel. "Don't you know who I am, Agent Chisholm? I was the quote 'unidentified terrorist' you have always been looking for. I put the bombs in the cars and at the airports, at the hotels and in the cafés. I am that screen you barely see, but suspect is there all along. You had your try. Now it is my turn. Goodbye, Agent Chisholm."

"Stop," said the nun.

They all turned to look at her. Denton was lying on the floor, five yards from the kneeling Chisholm, holding his calf, still trying to stop the bleeding. Standing behind Chisholm was Gettier, the gun aimed right at her head. And Chisholm herself was kneeling with her hands at the nape of her neck, unmoving. But all of them looked up and stared.

The nun, the once passive figure, the human reflection of the static beliefs she professed—it was she who held the weapon, Chisholm's gun, aiming it directly at Gettier.

"Please. Stop," the nun asked again.

"*Shoot him!*" Denton screamed. "What are you waiting for, shoot him!"

"No," said Chisholm.

"Yes, shoot me," said Gettier, looking straight at Sister Marianne. He stepped away from Chisholm, who partially blocked Sister Marianne's aim, and gave her a clear target. "Come now. I won't kill you, I promise. I won't even raise my weapon at you. And you know that I've always kept my word. Shoot me."

But Sister Marianne didn't move, holding the gun with both hands, aiming right for his heart. She stood there, weeping, as suddenly it all became very clear—the real cost of the life she had led.

"Please, Edmund, please. As my friend," she asked in a voice that did not dare rise beyond a whisper. "Please. Stop."

But Gettier only smiled sadly. "You can't shoot me, can you? No, it would be a sin to shoot me if it isn't in self-defense."

He motioned with the gun toward Chisholm's head. "If you shoot me, you will be committing a mortal sin. And if I shoot her and then beg for forgiveness, you must forgive me, isn't that right? It's your job, after all. If you shoot me now, you commit a mortal sin. If you shoot me after I beg for forgiveness for killing Chisholm, that is also a mortal sin. You can't shoot me, no matter what I do."

Sister Marianne held the weapon, the thing seemingly ready to slip from her hands at any moment. But Margaret Chisholm knew it wouldn't slip. It would never slip.

"Don't shoot him," she said to Marianne, knowing what she was saying. "You'll destroy everything you believe in."

And there it was, finally—the choice laid naked before her. Always in Marianne's mind it shadowed her, always loitering a moment away from her path, a truth as hard as belief itself. Now, it finally faced her: What price her belief?

For the first time, Marianne's eyes left Gettier's to glance to Margaret. As she always knew, there was only truth in those flat, brown eyes, like the truth in the Pythia's eyes. The truth was not comforting. It was, at its core . . . indifferent. The truth could be sacrificed for the sake of her beliefs. That's what the indifference in Margaret's eyes told her: The truth would remain whether Marianne believed in it or not. And when she glanced back at Edmund, her mentor, her friend and her father, she saw what he was—doubt, the screen behind which she had never dared look. Until now. Because behind the screen was the simple, awful question: Did she believe the truth? Or would she believe the lies and equivocations bought by an easy doubt? She did not know which was more painful: looking at the screen of the tempting lie or the face of the hard, mean truth. But it was what her belief would cost her. It would be the one or the other. But not both.

"Stop," she whispered so softly no sound was heard. But the word was spoken.

Gettier watched her sadly, pitying her as he said, "You are truly the will of God—impotent. And I am the will of man."

"No," she whispered.

"I act," he said as he cocked the gun.

"*No!*"

She fired three times, in quick succession, her eyes never blinking, not even once. Gettier was struck by all three bullets, all in the chest, his body flying backward and away. The gun in his hand discharged, but harmlessly, slipping out of his grasp as it flew through the air, away from his body, which crumpled in a heap.

But even before his body had fallen to rest, Sister Marianne ran to him. She ran and knelt beside him, taking his head in her arms and cradling him to her. His eyes were open, unseeing, not a mark on his face as the blood from his chest drenched them both—his body, her arms, the floor around them, red red blood seeming to bleed from the very earth.

"No," she said to him. And as she brought his head to her breast, she looked up to heaven and begged—demanded—pleaded—for a reason for such awful decisions, screaming forever the one word:

No.

Not once did she let go of the gun.

SECOND PRAYER

They were praying, all of them. As far as the eye could see, dominating this enclosed universe, the nuns were all on their knees, their heads all bowed, their hands clutched before them in prayer as their faces concentrated on Jesus Christ, Our Savior and the Son of the Lord, Our Father. The nuns were all praying to Him.

The enormous chapel, light and airy and bright, counterpointing the black-robed nuns, seemed to reach and stretch out and up, limitlessly. Yet it was somehow filled to the brim with them, with human beings, these Sisters all so deeply fixed and founded in their prayers. And amid that multitude of appeal was Sister Marianne, struggling as always in asking for permission to His face, permission to be . . . a part of things.

Now, a favored supplicant, innocent in confession and graced by the Sacrament, Marianne prayed amid and alongside all her sisters, where she belonged, all the accounts finally settled. There could never be true grace, nor true innocence now. Those were the real costs her life had accrued.

Margaret Chisholm stood in the back of the vast chapel, behind all the nuns, as she watched them, waiting patiently. She was waiting to say goodbye.

As she watched, she smiled a little at all the nuns so neatly, evenly spaced, all identically dressed, all bowed and praying without motion and with perfect concentration. What God wouldn't be impressed, she thought, at the terrifying seriousness of these supplications? But fast on the heels of that, Margaret wondered how much God would need to be impressed, to forgive so much. And with that, her smile flickered and faded, coming up against such a hard, mean truth. She turned and retreated to the threshold of the chapel, unwilling to leave, knowing she would.

She looked at the praying nuns one last time, her mind reaching out to Marianne, who was there, somewhere, lost amid all the other supplicants whose prayers for forgiveness and grace might be just as desperate as the calls of one looking to save a life, or one hoping to cheat a death. Margaret looked at the nuns, murmuring as her heart faded like her smile, a last goodbye before she turned away.

"The killer in me is now the killer in you."

She hesitated to say more, to run into the chapel screaming for forgiveness, or to silently whisper her small, terrible supplication. But she didn't.

She turned and walked away.

Isn't she coming out to say goodbye?" asked Denton, leaning forward in the back of the car, the cast on his leg looking like a thick, knee-high sock.

"No," she said as she sat down beside him, closing the car door without a hesitation. "She was busy. Let's go."

". . . the Greater the Unknown" / Justification

Nicholas Denton and Margaret Chisholm woke up together as early-morning sunlight streamed through the window—that is, the airplane's jolt on landing at Dulles Airport made them wake up with a start, Margaret getting her bearings as she planned out what she had to do now that she was back in D.C., Denton still sleepily wondering where the hell he was. To him, the steel-hued sunlight pouring in through the plane's windows felt like hot needles jabbing his brain, a decidedly unpleasant feeling.

"It was nice working with you, Denton," Margaret said as she pulled her carry-on bag from the overhead compartment.

"It was nice— Oh damn!" Denton said, awake finally and looking up at Chisholm. "What time is it?"

"It's five-thirty," Chisholm said. "Why?"

"Is someone picking you up?"

"No. Sanders left a car for me at the airport parking lot last night. Don't tell me you didn't make arrangements."

Denton shrugged, smiling. "Mind giving me a lift?"

"Where do you live?" asked Chisholm, none too happy.

"Fairfax. Please?"

Chisholm thought a bit, then realized it was early, the whole day ahead of her. "Okay," she said. "But *you* pay for the skycap."

They were on their way in less than fifteen minutes, bypassing the customs inspection because they were federal employees out on business.

The drive to Denton's house was pretty quiet, Margaret planning out what she had to do to restart Archangel, Denton seemingly still not fully awake, yawning hugely as they drove.

"You're not a morning person," Chisholm observed.

"Absolutely not. Ten-thirty at the office is the crack of dawn for me."

Chisholm smiled. "How you get away with the stuff you pull I'll never know."

Denton smiled at that before closing his eyes and napping some more. Then Chisholm was shaking him awake.

"Denton. Is this it?"

They were on a deserted road in Fairfax County, at the entrance to a large estate. In the distance, about a hundred yards away, was an English Tudor–style home, boxlike and vast.

"Home sweet home." Denton yawned as Chisholm turned into the entrance road and drove up to the house. She parked, got out, and went around to the passenger side to help Denton, but he was managing well enough.

"Don't worry—a lot easier to get out than in," he said as he straightened up and picked up his walking stick. "So what do you think?" he asked, pointing at the house with the stick. He started putting on his gloves.

Chisholm turned around to look at the place. It was huge, but it felt empty. "I find it hard to believe you live here, Denton," she said, admiring the house. "I imagined some bachelor pad, not an English country house. How much money did you embezzle from CIA to buy this?" She was smiling as she turned to Denton.

Denton was holding an automatic pistol with a silencer, trained directly at her.

"Funny you should say that, Margaret," he said, looking right at her, awake and alert and, somehow, *amused.* "Embezzling is why we're here—Archangel."

"What?" was all she could say, not quite understanding what was happening.

"I'm talking about embezzlement, Margaret. You never should have touched Archangel. Not if you knew what's good for you."

And then it was all so clear. Margaret Chisholm took a step forward. "You bastard. You fucking bastard!"

"Don't come near me, Agent Chisholm, I have no intention of repeating the mistake I made with Gettier—keep your distance. I hate to have to use a gun on you, but I'm afraid I must, in my condition. Be forewarned, I *will* use this gun if I have to."

Chisholm stopped, unsure. She was sure she could tackle Denton. But behind the amused smile he wore, there was something very serious and very deadly—a certainty in his eyes that he *would* shoot her, if need be. And it was a risk Chisholm was no longer sure she could take. Not anymore.

Denton read her mind and smiled a little wider. Without taking his eyes off her he hung his walking stick in the crook of his right arm, his gun arm, and pulled something from his overcoat pocket. It was a pair of handcuffs.

"Put these on please," he said as he tossed the handcuffs at her.

She didn't move to catch them. They struck her chest and fell at her feet, her eyes never leaving Denton's. "Just what do you think you're doing," she said. Her gun was in her luggage; even if she could get to it, it was disassembled. So she would have to go for Denton's gun. She could bend to pick up the cuffs, then lunge. Half his leg was in a cast after all.

Again as if reading her mind, Denton took a step back as he said,

"Stay where you are and put the cuffs on please." But Chisholm made no move.

Denton tsked. "Margaret, you're making this very difficult for me. I don't want to have to shoot you or hurt you. But you are putting on those handcuffs. *Now.* For your own safety," he said bizarrely.

Chisholm knelt slowly and picked up the cuffs, still looking straight at Denton, who was too far away to be tackled but close enough that he could shoot her without missing. " 'For my own safety'—for your own fucking convenience is what it is. Bastard. I thought—I thought you were someone I could trust. Behind all the slick smiles and all the smooth operating, I thought you were decent. But you're nothing, *nothing!*"

Denton glanced at Chisholm with an empty look that belied no emotion or feeling. "Put on the handcuffs, Margaret. Please. And put these on too." He tossed her a pair of gloves from the same pocket the cuffs came from, and they too fell to the ground at Margaret's feet. Neither of them made a move.

Denton sighed. "We could stand here all morning debating whether or not you put on the cuffs and the gloves, but frankly both of us have better things to do. Put them both on please. I want to show you something."

He shook his gun casually, motioning for her to obey with an ironically diffident look. Reluctantly, she snapped on the cuffs.

"Tighter, please."

She tightened them a notch.

"Tighter. I can see you could slip them off if you wanted to. Tighter."

She tightened them one more notch, but then realized that now they were too tight to slip off, her eyes betraying her. Denton smiled, nodding his head happily as he kept the gun trained on Chisholm.

"Good, that's better. Now please, put on the gloves."

Chisholm picked up the gloves and put them on as she said, "I'm going to kill you, Denton. I swear it."

"You won't kill me, Margaret. You don't have it in you anymore." He motioned with the gun. "Knock on the front door please."

Chisholm, handcuffed and gloved, went to the front door as Denton carefully hobbled away to stay out of her reach. Still staring at each other, Chisholm knocked on the front door. She had her back to the door as she stared at Denton, so she didn't see who answered until he was right in front of her.

"Ah, Nicky. And Agent Chisholm in tow," Keith Lehrer said, smiling happily in pajamas and a bathrobe. "Come in, come in," he said as he opened the door wide.

The three of them were in Lehrer's study.

"A cold morning today," Lehrer said as he tossed a log into the fire, careful not to come between Denton and Chisholm.

She was sitting in one of the wing chairs, staring unblinkingly at Denton with a look that was all rage, a rage so fine and narrow Denton didn't dare move his gun away from her. So he sat across from her in the other wing chair, watching her as he spoke to Lehrer. "I couldn't get rid of her, but then I thought it would be nice to bring her gift-wrapped. She killed Sepsis. I couldn't stop her."

"Yes, I know," said Lehrer as he finished up with the fire and made his way around Denton to his desk. "Rivera forwarded a copy of her report. Pity. A real shame." He sat down in the desk chair. "We could have gotten a lot of mileage out of Sepsis."

Denton took a cigarette from his jacket pocket and lit it. "Yes," he said between puffs, careful not to be blinded by the smoke. "But I have enough information to discredit her completely. You know she was actually stupid enough to bring a whore to the safe house in Rome?" he said, smiling with an arched brow, not for a second letting on that he knew who Beckwith had been.

"Silly bitch," said Lehrer, looking at Chisholm as if she were an object; not because she was a woman, or because she worked for the FBI, but simply because she'd gotten in his way.

Denton took a deep drag on his cigarette, scissoring it with his free hand. "The whore alone is enough to ruin her," he said to Lehrer as he continued to stare at Chisholm. Then he frowned as he smiled, wondering. "About the whore—she was yours, wasn't she, Keith?"

Lehrer hesitated, surprised by Denton. "Why do you think that?" he asked casually.

"Because if she wasn't yours, she would have tried for me instead of Chisholm. I was, how should I put it?—a surer lay."

Lehrer laughed but said nothing, waiting out Denton.

Denton took a page from Chisholm as he stared at her, talking to Lehrer. "Now, with Chisholm out of the picture, there will be no more Archangel investigation," he said, finally starting to lay his hand out on the table.

Chisholm stared right back at Denton. "It was always about Archangel, wasn't it? You fucking pigs—"

"How did you know about Archangel?" Lehrer interrupted.

Denton smiled at that, thinking of the shadow file cabinet in Alexandria. "I told you, Keith, I'm a career bureaucrat. Papers papers papers, always crossing my desk. I kept running across references to something called Lamplight. Then I found out Agent Chisholm was investigating a strange embezzlement scheme that she was calling Archangel. Lamplight and Archangel were mirror images of each other, but I still couldn't piece it together until you specifically ordered me to dig up some dirt on Agent Chisholm. Then I knew they were one and the same thing."

"You're welcome to come aboard," Lehrer said quietly.

Denton smiled a smile of pure happiness, the air in the study turning viscous and oily. He was still staring straight at Margaret Chisholm, but he didn't really see her.

"How much money are we talking about?" he asked.

"Fifty-seven million and counting. Enough to go around," Lehrer answered, staring at Denton, gauging him, thinking he would join them. Hoping he would. But still, somehow, unsure.

"How many members in the party?"

"I don't think we should have her around, listening to this," Lehrer said, finally noticing Chisholm's sentient presence. But Denton disagreed.

"Oh I think we should," he said dreamily through a smile. "In a way, I think we owe her. She nearly caught you. Two or three more weeks and

Lamplight or Archangel or whatever you want to call this little party would have been blown wide open. How many in the party?"

Lehrer hesitated, then said, "Just myself, Director Farnham, and Deputy Director Michaelus. And now you."

"Farnham, Michaelus, you, and me. A nice cozy little party of four. I like that."

"I'm glad." Lehrer smiled.

"Tell me something though. What if I'd failed to get something on her? What trump were you holding?"

"Pictures."

"Pictures?"

Lehrer unlocked a desk drawer and pulled out a manila folder, removing a sheaf of photographs and laying them on the table beside Denton. He glanced at them fleetingly, seeing enough, his eyes going North in a heavy way. He whistled, poorly.

"I see. Interesting. Hair's different, but that's her. Who's that with her?" he asked, staring again at Chisholm.

"After her divorce, Agent Chisholm was . . . indiscreet with a swinging couple. One of them supplied us with the pictures. The FBI puritans will fire her on the spot." Lehrer retrieved the photographs and shuffled through them casually, leaning back in his chair.

Denton put out his cigarette and immediately lit another, always keeping his eyes on Chisholm's. Chisholm was crying. She was staring at Denton, unbowed, unbeaten, but finally, terrifically opposed—an invincible force that had been finally stopped. So she cried, tears rolling down the flesh of her cheeks, with no silent pleas. And Denton stared right back at her with the dead eyes of a shark. He said, "Funny that an organization started by a homosexual should hate homosexuals so much."

"Rivera will shut down their Archangel investigation," Lehrer said with a snap, looking up at Chisholm as he felt sure that this was his game now. "An investigation that produces no results is no investigation worth running, especially an investigation run by a discredited agent. We'll seal up the leaks. And all will be back to normal."

"You fuckers," Chisholm said to Denton. "You fuckers, I'll kill you, I swear I'll kill you all."

In her fury and anger and humiliation, Chisholm made a move to get up and do something to Denton. And she would have, if he had misspoken.

"Think of your child, Margaret," he said, for the first time talking to her, looking her right in the eye. "If you get up from that chair, I'll be forced to shoot you. What do you prefer—a discredited exit from the FBI or a motherless child? Think. A dead mother is a lot worse than an unemployed one."

"I'll kill you, Denton, I swear I'll kill you."

The red red tendrils came again, and this time Denton didn't smile indulgently. "We'll see . . ." he said darkly. He spoke to Lehrer then, his voice brighter but his eyes still on Chisholm. "These are just prints though, they can be manufactured. Do you have the negatives?"

Lehrer went through the manila folder again and came up with an unmarked letter-sized envelope, bright white and unsealed. He opened it, peered inside, then handed it to Denton, who did not take it.

"Could you hold this please?" he said to Lehrer, motioning with the gun.

"Of course," Lehrer said, and Chisholm pulled herself together. Lehrer wasn't a young man, and he might not be that good a shot. So, still staring at Denton, she watched from the corner of her eye as Lehrer rose from behind the desk and went around to take the gun and hold it against her.

"Don't try it," Denton said to her, knowing full well what she was thinking. He handed the gun to Lehrer, and it was too quick and they were too far. Lehrer had the gun trained on her now.

"Why don't you cuff her so she won't move?" asked Lehrer sensibly enough.

"Don't have any more handcuffs," said Denton casually, as he thumbed through the photographic negatives. He did have another pair of handcuffs, right there in the pocket of his overcoat, but it was much more exciting having Chisholm on the loose and imminently threatening. His brain bubbling with fear and the challenge, Denton casually held the negatives up to the light of the fireplace. He gave another poor excuse for a whistle.

"My my, these *are* incendiary. No way to deny them, that's for sure." He looked at Chisholm and then at Lehrer, and the bastard had the nerve to smile.

Without taking his eyes off Chisholm, Lehrer said, "So even if she had lived and even if you hadn't been able to discredit her, I still had something to control her with."

"Yes, you certainly did. Clever. Here, I'll take that," Denton said, looking at Chisholm as he retook the gun so swiftly and smoothly she didn't get a chance to move. And with a sense of finality, Chisholm knew she would never get the chance.

"I should have let Gettier kill you," she said to Denton.

He made a sad face. "That's a mean thought, Margaret."

The two men stood side by side, looking down at her, seeming to lord it over Chisholm, Denton smiling once again.

"You didn't have anything else?" Denton finally asked Lehrer without looking at him. "A backup, so to speak?"

"Just the pictures," he said, satisfied. "But they were more than enough. . . . A good agent."

"A *very* good agent—she nearly caught you," Denton said, smiling sardonically at Chisholm.

But just like that, his eyes lost fixed focus and looked beyond her. His face still wore that cruel smiling mask, but his voice was completely flat.

"I'll join you, Keith," he said dreamily. "I'll join you in Lamplight. But only if you tell me one thing: What do you want in return?"

Lehrer didn't miss a beat. "Nothing that I—"

"Keith." Denton cut him off, brittle and metallic. "Nothing's for free. What's it going to cost for me to join your party," he asked like a statement. "I want to know, now."

Lehrer hesitated, thinking, staring at Denton as he leaned back against the edge of the desk. He glanced at Chisholm and decided to use her. "We can deal with that after she's gone—"

"No," Denton interrupted him again, still smiling like the dead. "Tell me what you want *now*. Tell me now or we can forget about everything."

Lehrer stared at Denton's profile, then looked away at the carpet, thinking. Then, finally, leaning forward but without looking at Denton, he spoke softly, almost whispering in Denton's ear.

"I want to know what's inside the building in Alexandria," he confessed.

Denton smiled like the newborn. He was being blackmailed, he realized. That was the game Lehrer was playing. It was a very friendly kind of blackmail—more arm-twisting than out-and-out blackmailing. But it was blackmail nonetheless.

If he didn't join the party, Lehrer would blow the shadow file cabinet wide open. That was what Lehrer had. Denton and Atta-boy would probably be arrested, and there was a good chance the shadow file cabinet would be putatively "blown" only to reappear somewhere else, this time under Lehrer's control. Here he was, pushing Lehrer around with the implied threat of blowing Lamplight to the moon, only to discover that Lehrer had *his* balls on the chopping block. Denton for one found it incredibly ironic: *he* was supposed to be king of the blackmailers. Very smooth on Lehrer's part. *Very* smooth. "So . . . I get to join you and Farnham and Michaelus. And in return, you get to go inside the office building in Alexandria. Is that it?"

"Yes."

"Just you, or Farnham and Michaelus too?"

"Just me," he confessed.

"So they don't know about the office building in Alexandria."

Lehrer said nothing to that, and he didn't need to. No one else knew squat. If they did, *they'd* be approaching him instead of Lehrer.

Denton smiled. Life was more than good—it was damn near perfect. He knew what the offer was and he knew what it would cost and he knew where the pressure was coming from. He smiled wide and free, all his decisions suddenly made as Lehrer waited for his reply, Denton lost in his total happiness.

The wait, the silent seconds ticking off, finally started to get on

Lehrer's nerves. He looked away from Denton, around the study, his eyes inevitably falling on the broken Chisholm.

She was staring at Denton, looking like she hadn't heard a thing, still silently crying through wide-open eyes. But she wasn't broken, Lehrer saw. She was just a caged, dangerous animal, an animal that would leap at the first opportunity. Lehrer glanced at the handcuffs keeping her still, and for the first time noticed the gloves she was wearing. He turned to Denton, letting his casual puzzlement soothe his worries as he waited for Denton's reply.

"Nicholas," he asked, "why is she wearing gloves?"

The question snapped him out of his reverie. Denton smiled to show his teeth, looking straight at Chisholm. And it was a look to scare the devil himself.

"The gloves? They're so she won't leave any fingerprints when they come to clean up."

With that, Denton turned the gun on Lehrer, putting it right to his eye before Chisholm or Lehrer himself knew what was going on, far too late for Lehrer. Denton pulled the trigger, the sound barely a cough, the bullet going directly through Lehrer's eyeball and through his brain, lodging in the back of his skull hard enough to puncture the skin, a puncture through which blood and bits of brain matter squirted out. For a brief instant, Lehrer stood there, dead already, the rest of his body not knowing it was dead, and then finally the information was received and his legs gave out from under him, Keith Lehrer falling against the desk to a sitting position on the carpeted floor, dead as Teddy Roosevelt.

"Jesus!" Chisholm gasped, standing up in reflex and staring at the dead man. She turned and stared at his killer.

Denton contemplated Lehrer's body, for the first time ignoring Margaret Chisholm. Though it was awkward, what with his broken leg, he bent down and put the gun in Lehrer's hand. Then he stood and looked at his arrangements.

"A very neat way to die. Not messy at all," Denton said to no one in particular. He glanced at Chisholm, dug into his pocket, and tossed her a set of keys.

"What did you do?" Chisholm asked, stunned. Denton looked at her, genuinely perplexed.

"What do you think I did? I shot Lehrer and now I have to make it look like a suicide. Don't take off the gloves," Denton remonstrated. "It wouldn't do for you to leave fingerprints all over the house."

He turned to Lehrer's body and arranged the gun again, his cast making it difficult to kneel. But he managed, setting Lehrer's fingers firmly on the gun. Gingerly, he set the gun safety back on, then jabbed Lehrer's index finger up against the trigger. When it stayed put, he switched the safety back to the off position and stood up.

"What do you think?" he asked Chisholm, looking at Lehrer's body.

Chisholm didn't know what to think. She just stared at Denton as he fussed over the body and took a couple of steps back to view his handiwork in perspective. He must have been satisfied, because he picked up the manila folder and turned to the fire.

"Sorry about the theatrics," he said as he started tossing the pictures into the fire one at a time. "I just had to let him have his moment in the sun."

Chisholm just stared at Denton, absently uncuffing herself. The sound made him turn around.

"Don't go taking off your gloves now. Like I told you, they're for your own protection."

Chisholm stood up and carefully approached Denton. "What—what was this?"

He turned to her and smiled, tossing the last of the photographs into the fire. He lit a cigarette and leaned on the mantelpiece.

"I knew you could handle Sepsis. Lehrer ran him. The Vatican bombing was part of some insane plan to get us into a war in the Middle East, just crazy. Actually though, it was a *neat* plan, very ambitious—but it was crazy. Too crazy for me. So I let you stop Sepsis. But there was no way you could get close to Archangel. I had to take out Archangel myself."

It was the calmness and casualness to Denton that was sending her into a tailspin. There was nothing to him like any adrenaline, or excitement or fear, only a gauzy sheen of amusement.

"But I had no idea Lehrer was in on it. I didn't even know someone in CIA was involved. All I had was phony purchases and phony payments, nothing more. Rivera was going to shut me down in a matter of weeks."

Denton laughed as he looked down at the fire, toeing in the last remains of the photographs. "You were so close you didn't even know it. When Sepsis took a crack at you in your minivan? That was over Archangel, not the nun. You were about to turn your investigation to the phony dealers. All of those covers . . . none of them could have stood up to any kind of serious scrutiny. Lehrer knew it. If you'd kept pushing, as you're wont to do, he would have had you killed. Another week or two and there would have been another shoot-out or an accident of some sort, or maybe some very tragic wreck on a highway. The convent bombing was just luck. Just luck that Rivera pulled you off Archangel to run Counterparts. I still don't know why he did it," he finished, turning his eyes back to the fire.

Chisholm's eyes too drifted dreamily toward the flames. "Rivera thought I was burned out, thought I needed a vacation."

Denton laughed, hugely amused. "Oh my goodness. Not quite irony, no, but—delicious. The possibilities!"

"Denton," Chisholm asked, looking at him carefully, "why this? Why this . . . humiliation?"

He stopped smiling and gave her back the stare. "I am truly sorry, Margaret. I mean that. But I had to find out what he was holding against you. Lehrer always kept things close and tight. He had to think he'd won. He wouldn't have told me what he had on you otherwise. I'm sorry," he said. And then he smiled again. "And I do hope you won't kill me."

Chisholm couldn't help smiling back.

Outside, it was still early in the morning, not quite seven. The two of them were leaning against Chisholm's car, talking as Denton finished his cigarette and toyed with his walking stick.

"I think I'm going to use a walking stick on a regular basis. Don't you think it gives me an air of . . . *je ne sais quoi?* Then again, it might seem a bit pretentious, at my age."

"About Archangel," Chisholm non-sequitured.

Denton sighed. "Yes, about Archangel. Let's make a deal: Drop Archangel and let me close it up. It won't affect me one way or another if this comes to public light, but it will certainly make things easier for the Agency. You could make a lot of friends . . ."

"Why didn't you join him?" Chisholm pressed.

Denton kept looking at the walking stick, wondering what he would tell this strange, fascinating woman. "In Archangel?" he stalled, trying to figure out what his answer would be.

But Chisholm was patient. "Yes," she answered, looking at him as he made up his mind what to say.

"I had my reasons," he said, smiling darkly as he stared at nothing.

"What were they?" she pressed gently, needing to know.

He turned his dark smile on her. "You don't know me at all, do you?"

Chisholm couldn't help but smile at that. "No, I don't."

"Margaret, I have a family to care for."

Chisholm frowned. "I thought you said you weren't married."

"I lied." Denton smiled back, as if it were the most obvious thing in the world. "You probably won't believe this, but my wife was my high school sweetheart. She's perfectly ordinary. She's a schoolteacher. We have three children, all very average. Our house, believe it or not, has a white picket fence. They know I work for CIA, but they don't know what I do. I know what I do. I have people killed. I ruin people's lives. But I know why I do these things—to protect my family, and people like them. Not for gain, certainly not for profit. Archangel was . . . outside of what I would do, what I *could* do."

She looked at him shrewdly for a moment. "Never can stop lying, now can you?" she said, on guard against his bullshit but not bitter about it; just patiently waiting him out. "That isn't it. Maybe it's part of it, but it isn't it."

Denton smiled wryly, knowing she was right and knowing he wouldn't tell her, at least not completely. "I suggest you go," he said, but he didn't move.

"Are you going to keep the negatives?" Chisholm finally asked, but Denton didn't seem to understand.

"What negatives," he said flatly. He lit another cigarette, then took out the envelope with the negatives. Carefully, he set the negatives on fire with his cigarette lighter, burning them all before dropping the slight remains to the ground. Chisholm bent down to pick up those remains.

Denton frowned at her, completely confused. "What are you *doing?*"

"They'll find these, when they look into the death."

Denton laughed. "Afraid of leaving clues, are we? Margaret, *I'm* going to be controlling the inquiry into Lehrer's death. And they won't find anything I don't want them to find."

Chisholm straightened, feeling foolish. Then she looked at Denton with dawning realization. "With Lehrer dead, you'll become Deputy Director of CIA. Isn't that right?"

Denton smiled and walked away, politely opening the driver-side door of the car for her.

"You'll pretend you came here to confront him about Archangel, you'll say he pulled a gun on you, that you argued, that he shot himself. You'll hem and haw and in the end you'll 'reluctantly' accept Lehrer's job. And whether it gets shut down or not, you'll use Lamplight or Archangel or whatever you call it to control Director Farnham and the other deputy director, what's his name—"

"Michaelus, Deputy Director for Covert Operations, what's called the Special Directorate."

"Michaelus, right. You're going to run CIA from the safety of your career bureaucrat's office." Chisholm had one foot in the car, but she was still unwilling to leave. "You're going to run CIA for as long as you like."

Denton smiled at her, liking her. "Drive carefully, Margaret. It was a pleasure working with you."

With that, he turned and walked back to the house.

"Denton?" she called, and he turned to face her.

"Yes?"

"Thanks. Thanks for . . . Thanks."

He smiled that shark smile. "I told you once, Margaret: I don't do favors. I collect debts. In the future, it would be wise of you to keep that in mind, Agent Chisholm."

He turned and hobbled back into the house. Chisholm got in her car and drove away.

FINAL PRAYERS

But it did not end there. It did not end that simply.

Chisholm drove home that early morning, rush hour already making the beltway an impossible drive. So it was eight by the time she pulled up to her house.

She got out of the car and stared at her home, a small, neat house, just like many others up and down the street. Leaving her baggage in the trunk—and Denton's too, she realized—she walked into the house, alone.

Inside, nothing had changed. No little gremlins had come in to make things neater or cleaner, or messier or uglier for that matter. It was the same house, almost a stranger's. She opened windows and let in a breeze, airing out the stuffiness of the place as she brought in her baggage.

She unpacked and put everything away in its place. Then she showered as the washing machine did the clothes from her trip. By nine o'clock, she was washed up, all neat and ready, looking for things to do around the house.

But there was nothing to do. There were no more trapdoors she could poke her head into. And so Margaret Chisholm stood there in the kitchen, looking around the cold and empty house, waiting to be needed.

For his part, just after she left, Denton too realized he'd left his luggage in Margaret Chisholm's car, but it didn't matter. He would get someone from the office to fetch it. What he *was* concerned about was getting to a phone.

Inside Lehrer's house, Denton debated making the call as he dialed up Amalia's number and had her get everyone at Langley freaking over Lehrer's "suicide." He wanted the building to shake to its very foundations, and he knew Amalia wouldn't disappoint.

As he waited for CIA's in-house forensic team to show up, Denton wondered whether he should risk making the call, finally deciding to do it. He could get Matthew Wilson or Atta-boy to edit the phone records, if need be.

It took a while for the connection to get through, and as he waited, he looked at the body lying there on the floor beside him, thinking of the reasons for what he had done, the reasons he'd kept from Margaret Chisholm. "Looking good, Keith," he said happily to the corpse. "Looking better than Paula Baker did, you low-life son of a bitch."

"Hello?" said a voice in Italian.

"Hello?" said Denton in English. "It's me. It's done. Like we suspected, it was Lehrer from the start—all of it. He will no longer be a factor. . . . You really don't want to know. . . . Yes, I will. . . . I see. Good. I will talk to you soon. Do take care now. . . . Thank you, and you too. Goodbye, Archbishop Neri."

Denton hung up the phone. He smiled at Lehrer's corpse and lit a cigarette. It really was a shame no one believed him when he told the truth: Sister Alice *did* give him a taste of hell with all those weekend detentions, rapping his knuckles over and over as she shouted, "Smoking? *Smoking!* Is this what a *good* Catholic boy would do?" God, he missed the old bird. Even though that was a lifetime ago, and even though he was a grown man, Nicholas Denton still thought of himself as a good Catholic boy. A good Catholic boy who knows that revenge is always the best of reasons.

She prays. She has reasons for believing the truths she holds—she has knowledge. And yet, still, she prays.

She prays for the soul of the child she once could have held. She prays for the soul of her mentor, the man she murdered. She prays for all her sisters, for the policemen and for the detective, for the innocent and for the gone, for their murderer, for Cardinal Barberi—God rest his soul. She prays for all the dead.

But it's hard. She tries, but the dead are fading. Now, her prayers turn to the living. She can't help herself. She has the certain knowledge of salvation, of others' if not her own. She knows that God knows their souls and will let them be a part of Him. But still she prays.

She was praying as she walked across the cobbled square, trying hard to pray for the dead. But in the middle of the square, she came across six students, very young men and women. They were playing African drums for handouts, and before she could help it, she had forgotten all about the dead as she stood there, watching the living.

They smiled at her, their only spectator, beating on their drums. She had to go, but she lingered, watching them, feeling surrounded by them as they played as steady as a beating heart. She wanted to close her eyes and stay there forever, but she couldn't. So she gave them some money, wished them well, and walked on her way.

But the beat of the drums would not disappear. It receded, yes, but it never did quite fade away, the sound of their bellowing drums still with her, still playing over and over in her mind: a complex yet steady rhythm; a mystic rhythm. A dark and luxuriant sound.

And with the morn those angel faces smile
Which I have loved long since and lost awhile.